For The
Price
of a
Hat

GEOFF NEWMAN

ISBN: 978-1-4834-0268-0 (sc)
ISBN: 978-1-4834-0267-3 (e)

Because of the dynamic nature of the Internet, any web addresses or links contained in this book may have changed since publication and may no longer be valid. The views expressed in this work are solely those of the author and do not necessarily reflect the views of the publisher, and the publisher hereby disclaims any responsibility for them.

Any people depicted in stock imagery provided by Thinkstock are models, and such images are being used for illustrative purposes only. Certain stock imagery © Thinkstock.

Lulu Publishing Services rev. date: 5/23/2017

ANCIENT PROVERB _
FOR WANT OF A NAIL

For want of a nail the shoe was lost.
For want of a shoe the horse was lost.
For want of a horse the rider was lost.
For want of a rider the message was lost.
For want of a message the battle was lost.
For want of a battle the kingdom was lost.
And all for the want of a horseshoe nail.

DEDICATION

THIS BOOK IS DEDICATED to the memory of Sergeant Malcolm Herd of Strathclyde Police Air Support Unit and to all the professionals who provide us with their skill and care in the fields of medicine, rescue and civil protection outside the warm and comforting environment of the hospital where adaptability and resourcefulness are key qualities in challenging and sometimes dangerous environments.

ACKNOWLEDGEMENTS

A WRITER CANNOT DELIVER his creation without support and help from others so I would like to record my thanks to my wife Lesley, my daughters Milly and Tabetha and other family members who have helped me with this project. A special thanks to John Knight for his original cover design and Milly for the current cover design. I am also indebted to Rob, Bob, Diana, Gloria, Jean, Paul K, Paul N. Jacques, Simon, Sean C and Sean B. Chris, Nigel P.T, Hannah (my editor) Darren King (my mentor) and the Helston Lizard Inner Wheel Book Club who also helped me to make a rough and ready novel into something worthy of the name.

CHAPTER 1

22nd February 1999
The A30 Highway, Goss Moor, Cornwall

THE RHYTHMIC SWISH, SWISH, swish of the wipers made the car radio impossible to hear, but that didn't seem to matter. Jack was having to concentrate on driving in trying conditions. 'Mizzle', they call it in Cornwall, a tortuous mix of fine rain and mist that visits the west country on a regular basis winter and summer alike. The wipers seemed to make little progress for after each stroke the screen was instantly covered with another sheet of pearls that turned the scene ahead into a mini Regent's Street of Christmas lights.

Jack cursed the driver in front who insisted on using his rear fog lights and was constantly dabbing his brakes so that the brake lights added to the plethora of distractions and made him squint each time they appeared. It did nothing for his temper. Every now and again the line of cars would plough through a stream of water running across the road, and a great dollop would land on the windscreen making it impossible to focus for two or three agonising seconds.

His day was coming to a close, the journey home to Cornwall had deteriorated in line with the weather. The rush-hour traffic made it even worse. It wasn't what he needed at the end of a long, tedious day at police HQ in Exeter.

His mind was whirring away trying to deal with the vagaries of internal police politics. 'What a bunch of self-serving arseholes,' was his contribution to the conversation he was having with the empty seat beside him. He had driven all the way from Truro to Exeter only to experience a tedious lecture by the Assistant Chief Constable about the need to foster good relations with the press. Apparently, his continuing battles with journalists in general and one or two hacks, in particular, were not appreciated by management. His abrasive style in the presence of the media had once more brought him nothing but pain. Maybe he should lighten up after all, give them a break... yeah, right! Like that's ever going to happen.

The impact between the Land Rover and the family saloon took place in slow motion right before his eyes. There was a huge cloud of spray and debris, so he jumped on the brakes in an attempt to stop before he ran into what remained of the two cars that had collided in such spectacular fashion.

He left his headlights on to illuminate the scene and headed for the tangle of wrecks. The mizzle cooled his face and soaked his jacket, but he didn't seem to notice. The Land Rover driver had tried to take a turn across the oncoming traffic through a gap that wasn't there. The saloon car hit the front corner of the Land Rover with tremendous force and appeared to disintegrate. Both cars were sent spinning ending up across both carriageways.

The hissing of steam from a broken radiator partially drowned the screams coming from the remains of the family saloon. Bystanders had gathered around, seemingly unable to decide what to do. He came across the Land Rover and helped the driver hobble clear then leant him against the rear of his car. He appeared to be walking wounded, his bloodied face vaguely familiar. Jack put his finger under the man's chin and lifted his head to get a clear view of his injuries in the glare the headlights.

"Jesus, is that you Neil?" Jack could smell whisky and quickly understood the picture. The current Truro Police Station drunk, there was always at least one, was this chump, Detective Sergeant Neil Jenkins.

"You've bloody well done it now mate. Have you broken anything?" Jack looked him up and down, but a blank stare was his only response; Neil was out of it. It looked like he had escaped with barely a scratch although his face was bloody and his right thumb dislocated. Jack left him in disgust and turned to the wreckage of the other car.

A long, stifled scream from the direction of the family saloon drew Jack's attention. He left Neil and walked across to the wreck, pushing gently through the onlookers gaping at the carnage. He could hear someone on their mobile phone giving out details of the incident, so help should soon be on the way.

The airbags had done their job and covered the driver and front seat passenger in white powder in the process. The female front seat passenger appeared to be conscious and was screaming in pain, but the driver was not moving. Jack tried the driver's door, but it was jammed solid. He tried the rear door, it opened. He was horrified to find that there was a rear seat passenger, a young girl in a crumpled heap on the floor. She made no sound at all; he thought she was dead. He pulled at her shoulder and she gave a sudden, heaving breath and a gurgle. He carefully rolled her onto the rear seat and tried to arrange her in the recovery position. His first aid skills were limited, but he knew that her airway needed protection.

The horrid rattling gurgle from the girl was a sign her breathing was anything but secure. Her face was a bloody mess and it was clear from the blood on the back of the driver's head that the girl had smashed her face on the back of his skull causing serious injuries to both of them.

He began to stress about helping her breathing but her face was a mangle of teeth and jawbone. He couldn't work out what to do and for the first time in his life felt the creeping weight of panic descend upon him. The inability to move any part of his body was the classic sign that the situation had overloaded his ability to think rationally, he was freezing up, his breathing stopped. It was a classic 'panic attack'.

At that critical moment, the cavalry arrived, and the first ambulance crew began to get to work assessing the injured. A face peered through the back door and greeted him in a calm and seemingly casual way.

"Hello there, what do we have here?" Jack clicked out of his trance.

"Jack Mawgan, Detective Inspector. I was passing by and tried to help, she's struggling to breathe, but I don't know how to help her." He slid over to the passenger side allowing the paramedic a better view of the girl.

"Paul Harris, Jack, nice to meet you," he said in a curiously matter-of-fact way while at the same time taking a closer look at the girl's facial injuries." Now, this young lass doesn't appear to be very well," He took another look then disappeared out of the door, returning moments later with a red and green rucksack. He took a small pack from the bag and looked Jack in the eye.

"I'm going to put a tube down her trachea to protect her airway, but I'll need your help to keep her head at the right angle. It's going to be a bit tricky because she's got a lot of facial damage,"

"Just tell me what to do," Jack watched closely as Paul assembled his tools and then carefully chose a tube from a selection of different sizes arranged on one side of the pack.

"I'll set her head at the right angle and you keep it steady,"

"Okay," Jack put his hands on either side of her head and held her tight. At that moment, something happened, something bad. The gurgling stopped, he could tell she had stopped breathing. The panic returned and Jack felt ready to burst. His anguish was obvious from the terrified look on his face as he watched Paul busying himself for the task ahead.

"She's stopped breathing,"

"Yes Jack, so we had better move things along," His calm voice and gentle Cornish lilt did nothing to ease Jack's concern. He watched as Paul assembled the necessary equipment. The device he had chosen to gain access to the back of her mouth had a curved lever and a light to illuminate the target area. It took him what seemed to be an age of probing into the flesh, bone and teeth that were once her lower jaw before he slid the tube down her airway and her chest heaved with an intake of breath. That simple sign of life burst the bubble of fear that had been building inside Jack. He felt a huge surge of relief course through him like a gigantic slug of adrenalin. He almost burst into tears.

"Well, Jack, looks like we've given this young lass a chance of living to tell the tale but she's not out of the woods yet. We need to get her to A&E - smartish,"

Paul was soon on his way to Treliske Hospital with the girl while his colleagues dealt with the seriously injured driver and front seat passenger. Both were trapped and were the subject of frenzied efforts by the Fire Service team.

Jack could see Neil Jenkins, now swathed in a head bandage and arm in a sling, smoking a cigarette and sitting on the step at the back of an ambulance. He was busy on his mobile phone, no doubt, thought Jack, up to his wheeling and dealing. 'That will be the end of him,' he thought to himself. Drunk driving was not something the police tolerated so Neil would probably find himself counting paperclips at best or looking for another job at worst.

He finally returned to his car and sat staring at the remains of the collision. He began to shake uncontrollably as the delayed shock hit him. The tears came easily. It surprised him just how easily. It was relief, pure unadulterated relief.

The traffic police had arrived and were busy trying to clear the road. As he sat watching the emergency services go about their duties in a calm and efficient way he saw what he recognised as an unmarked police car pull up beside Neil on the far side of the wrecks. Without hesitating, Neil climbed in the back seat, and the car took off at a rate of knots.

It took half an hour before the road was a cleared by which time Jack had regained some composure and was able to continue his journey home. It wasn't long before the cold, hard Detective Inspector persona was back in command. Those that knew him would recognise the old Jack but after the night's traumas he was, deep inside, a changed man. A very different kind of person. Holding the life of another human being in his hands had brought out a compassionate side of him, a side that was normally well hidden from public view. It had been a truly sobering experience.

That Evening
Lower Spargo Cottage, Perranarworthal, Cornwall

Doctor Pamela Mawgan was a very able woman, hardened by years working as a hospital doctor. Nowadays she enjoyed the less arduous task of working part time as a GP at the local surgery in Devoran. As a mother of two sons, Nathan and Josh, she had been through the usual emotional mill that parenthood delivers. She had a well-developed understanding of the human condition and used her skill and compassion to manage a relatively harmonious home for two boisterous boys and a police detective husband who worked all the hours that God sent.

Pam made a pot of tea, and they sat at the kitchen table facing each other. Pam had her auburn hair up revealing her long neck and neat little ears. Her hair colour was natural and her makeup was, as always, applied sparingly. She had a good complexion and a pretty and interesting face, but it was her radiant smile that transformed her into the beautiful woman that so enthralled Jack.

She was no wallflower and nobody's fool so as Jack sat at the dinner table idly prodding at the spaghetti left on his plate, she pushed a cup of tea in his direction and stepped into the pregnant silence.

"Penny for them," Jack smiled and put the fork down but did not know where to start. Eventually, he found the words he needed to begin unloading what had been an emotional day.

"All those years you were in A&E did you ever experience total panic? You know, completely freeze-up,"

"Frequently, well, during the early years anyway,"

"How did you cope?"

"Luckily most of the time there was someone else to lean on but, yes, when you were on your own it was tough, but we had been trained to take a deep breath and to use the skills we had been given to make a diagnosis. Use our powers of observation and the technology we had available and then get stuck in. Keeping someone alive does, in the end, come down to some pretty basic principles,"

"What if they die while you are doing your best?"

"That's the downside of being any clinician, doctor, nurse or ambulance tech. You take it on the chin and move on,"

"What, you mean it doesn't affect you?"

"Of course it does. Now come on, open up what happened out there today?

"Today I found myself trying to save a life, but I didn't have the wherewithal to do it, not the skill, not the knowledge and certainly not the equipment,"

"And?"

"I panicked, well, nearly panicked. I froze,"

"Then what,"

"Then this bloody hero called Paul appeared out of nowhere, watched her die then calmly stuck a tube down her throat and brought her back to life again,"

"Wow, you mean they have ambulance technicians who can intubate now, that's good news,"

"Anyway, when that girl drew breath through that tube thing I went from the edge of oblivion to the happiest chap in the world. I cried like a baby. I've never done that before. I put it down to the adrenalin factor,"

"Maybe, but more likely your brain flooded your body with endorphins, they're a natural form of opiates, and they make you feel woooonnndddderfulll. They are the body's natural 'feel-happy' drug,"

"Jeepers, it certainly gave me a high. Anyway, that didn't last long because I saw the bloke who caused the accident, one of our own, picked up on the sly by someone in one of our unmarked cars,"

"Do I know him?"

"Neil Jenkins, Detective Sergeant, bit of drunk, had a fling with his partner, Alex Sullivan. You remember that good looking blonde you were chatting to at the Christmas party. Apparently, she was separated from her husband for quite a while and started seeing Neil not long after her divorce came through. Caused a bit of a stir when it hit the local gossip-mongers and nearly wrecked his own marriage,"

"If he's hitting the bottle maybe that's a tell-tale sign that he needs help,"

"Bugger Jenkins, he can take care of himself. He's probably done for anyway. They'll get him for drunk driving and not trouble us anymore." He checked his watch, "Do you think you can call your mates at Treliske and find out about the girl? It would help me sleep tonight if I knew how she got on,"

"Drama queen!" she replied with just enough humour to let him know she was teasing, "You're never usually interested in the broken bodies you keep turning up,"

"That's not fair; they're usually dead. We are talking about a young lass who passed away right in front of me and was brought her back to life by a man with more skill in his little finger than I have in my whole body,"

"Don't exaggerate, I've seen you with the Elastoplast, you're a dab hand with a sticking plaster. Anyway, she didn't die, she stopped breathing, there is a difference,"

"So, you say, it didn't feel like that at the time. I was sure she was a goner. It was just amazing to see Paul so calm. He just got on with the job. The man just oozed confidence. We so underestimate those guys,"

"That confidence comes from training and experience - and not so much of the 'guys', don't forget the girls, we're in the mix too these days," Jack picked up his plate and scraped the remains of his spaghetti Bolognese into the bin then put the plate in the dishwasher.

"Okay, I'll give the supervisor a call," Pam was now putting things away in the cupboard. Jack put his hands on her shoulder and gently massaged the back of her neck, turned her around and kissed her on the forehead.

"Thank you, can you also find out what station Paul works at only I would like to thank him personally,"

"Surname?"

"Can't remember," She pulled a face, put her arms around his neck and kissed him on the lips.

"I'll see what I can do,"

Ten minutes later she came back into the kitchen only to find that Jack had disappeared. She found him sitting in his armchair in the lounge reading the daily paper and sipping malt whisky from a glass tumbler. She sat down on the sofa. He put the paper down and waited for the news.

"She is in intensive care at Derriford and will need a lot of work on her face if she pulls through. The driver was her father, and he didn't make it, fractured skull,"

"Hell! She hit him face-on in the back of his head, she wasn't wearing her seatbelt,"

"That will be a toughie to live with. The mother's at Treliske and has some chest injuries related to the seat belt, some facial bruising from the airbag and two broken ankles, one of which is going to give the surgeons a bit of a problem. It must have been some impact. I'm amazed that your chum was just walking wounded,"

"He's not my chum. He was lucky to be surrounded by a Land Rover. The other car hit him right on the front corner. No airbags in those old Land Rovers so he must have had his seat belt on or he would have been beaten up pretty badly,"

"Well, I asked after him, but he didn't turn up in A&E, so heaven knows who's treating his injuries,"

"He's a bad penny, so he'll turn up somewhere. What about Paul? Did you find out what station he is working at?"

"Only one 'Paul' on shift over that side of the county on that day apparently and that was a 'Paul Harris' and works out of the Camelford Station,"

"Paul Harris, yes I remember now. I must try to get over there sometime,"

Sunday 4th July 1999,
Penvale Farm, Bodmin Moor, Cornwall

'He'll turn up somewhere'. Those words had come back to haunt him. Less than six months after the accident Neil Jenkins had 'turned up' alright, smack in the middle of his latest murder investigation.

Jack stood on a small rise just outside Penvale Farm and took in the magnificence that was Bodmin Moor on a beautiful July day. He was fuming inside, however, struggling to contain his fury. Neil's four months on 'sick leave' after his crash may have cured his physical injuries, but Jack was at a loss as to how Neil had avoided the drunk-driving charge. Clearly, this reprobate had connections.

Having people like Neil around did nothing to appease his paranoia. Things had not been going well since the Chief Constable handed him a commendation for solving the 'Appledore murders'. The North Devon CID had taken umbrage because an outsider from Truro had been brought in over their heads. Jack's performance as a detective had brought more than accolades for he knew the grapevine carried rumours of retribution. He had better watch his back.

Inhaling the fresh moorland air somehow reminded him of holidays and filled him with longing for a break from the pressures of running not two but now three murder enquiries. The caressing breeze carried with it the grassy aromas laced with hints of heather and peat. It was a beautifully raw and natural place, but he knew only too well that this wild moorland chunk of Cornwall could be entirely different and most uninviting, even dangerous when the swirling winter mists and horizontal rain, sleet and snow enveloped the treeless hills. He shuddered involuntarily at the thought, turned and walked back to the crime scene.

Every police officer that has ever set foot on Bodmin Moor knows the story that made the name Penvale Farm famous. The brutal murder of Charlotte Dymond, a servant at the farm, took place at Roughtor in April 1844. The killer cut her throat and the spot where she was found marked by a granite pillar. They say her ghost will forever roam the Moor. Whatever dark secrets surrounded that particular moorland farm it was apparently destined to feature in the crime statistics one more time.

Jack walked back into the farmyard and nodded to the uniformed constable guarding the entrance. He headed for the barn where the SOCOs were dealing with the bodies of what they believed to be those of the elderly farmer and his wife. The constable made a note on his Scenes of Crime Record Sheet and peered after the figure striding purposefully and confidently towards the knot of figures clad in white SOCO suits.

"Look at this gov'," it was Jenkins. He carried a supermarket bag and offered it to Jack, with the top wide open so he could inspect the contents.

"What is it?" the interior of the bag was in shadow; he couldn't see inside.

"It was found in a freezer in the outhouse. It means that theft was not the motive," Jenkins added. Jack reached inside and pulled out a cash box. He tested the lock, but it was open. Inside it was stuffed with fifty and twenty-pound notes.

"Have you counted it?' he asked.

"Over five thousand quid,"

"Damn," said Jack, "I should have had my gloves on. Make sure the SOCO's log that I have touched it without protection will you,"

"Right'o gov', I'll put it in an evidence bag straight away," He felt a fool for making such an elementary mistake. It was that bastard Jenkins, his very presence distracted him. He was beginning to wish that he could dispense with his help, but with so much going on he needed every able body available make matters worse, the head SOCO was an officious little jobs-worth who had made a career of winding up the senior detectives at every opportunity. Jack had crossed swords with this guy before, and the air of hostility between the two was palpable.

Coming to grief at any time is an unwelcome punctuation mark in any career, but for Jack, whose will to hold the line on diplomacy was at an all-time low, it rapidly became impossible. Being told that all Scenes of Crime activity would cease due to the late arrival of the mobile refreshment facilities sent him into a rage. He prevailed, in not too gentle a fashion, upon the two young operatives to keep working by the promise of some sandwiches he ordered from the local pub. Regular refreshments would arrive later Jack promised them. Before long the senior SOCO intervened and ordered 'down tools'.

The loud altercation drew the attention of Rachel Balls, a local journalist well known for her anti-police activities and author of many an editorial attacking the racist, misogynistic and overbearing actions of most of the

Devon and Cornwall Constabulary. She enjoyed many highly descriptive epithets thanks to her surname. Policemen were none too shy when it came to a good sexist moniker. She, on the other hand, particularly enjoyed sticking it to local hero, Jack Mawgan, who, she felt, was too big for his boots and not worthy of the accolades heaped upon him in recent years.

Rachel had somehow evaded the perimeter and turned up alongside the ongoing argument between Jack and the head SOCO.

"Mr Mawgan," she yelled, "are you always this rude to your hard-working support staff?"

"What? How the fuck did you get here?" He turned to find a uniformed officer. "Constable, yes you, over here. Kindly escort this 'lady' out of my crime scene,"

"Your crime scene?" she yelled back as the constable grasped her by the elbow, "you own Cornwall now do you? What about freedom of the press Inspector? We have rights you know,"

"Rights? Don't talk to me about rights. You misuse your rights to write absolute bollocks about what we do. We keep you safe at night,"

"You'll read about this Inspector you can be sure of that," she said as they frog marched her out of the barn.

"Write all you want then roll up that rag of yours and shove it up your pretty little arse,"

"You can't intimidate my staff like you intimidate the press you know," said the head SOCO. Jack spun around to address the diminutive figure standing right behind him and immediately found himself the victim of a jabbing index finger. "You're a bloody disgrace," The jabbing finger struck Jack like a bullet in the chest. It served only to push him over the top. He shoved his aggressor so hard that he stumbled backwards and landed on his backside on a pile of stinking manure.

"You'll pay for that," the whimpering SOCO said as he scrambled to his feet. Jack ignored him and walked back to his car.

The day was rapidly falling apart, but the arrival of a mobile catering van hijacked from a layby on the A30 by Detective Constable Alex Sullivan brought about a welcome change. She had used her considerable charms on the uncertain owner who eventually succumbed and followed her back to Penvale Farm. It wasn't long before the cook had a stack of bacon butties ready to go. You can't beat the smell of frying bacon when it comes to lifting spirits.

The evening brought a change in the weather and more besides. Jack was enjoying some peace and quiet at home with son Josh. Josh was turning out to have inherited his father's enthusiasm for computers and now knew more about PCs than Jack could imagine possible in one so young.

If Jack's career had taken its intended path when he was at Bristol University, he might have become a computer specialist and not a policeman like his father. Unfortunately, he got the best introduction possible to life as a policeman… and thrown out of university all at the same time. He had carried out a citizen's arrest on a notorious intruder in one of the lady's halls. The university had an automatic punishment for illegal entry of the female quarters so, despite his protestations and support from the victim of the assault and the young lady that had invited him to share her bed, they sent him down. Life can deliver some cruel twists, but it didn't seem to have a lasting effect on his life. In fact, that day, as events were to prove, fate had delivered him new career path. He didn't look back.

Josh had learnt skills that frightened the pants off his father. There were things Jack dare not share with Pam for fear of being accused of leading their youngest son astray. Hacking other people's computers was just a game to Josh. One he played with more curiosity than malice. Jack tried to discourage it but found himself just as curious as his son.

The warble of Jack's work mobile broke into their fun. It was Detective Chief Inspector Sidney Patterson, his boss.

"Hello sir, how can I help?"

"Jack, I need you to come to my office right away,"

"What, now? What's so important?"

"Your career, so get your arse down here now," The click left no room for debate. Sidney was on the warpath.

Truro Police Station

"What's on Sir, what's the panic?"

"Come in Jack, shut the door, take a seat," He pointed to the chair on the other side of his desk. Jack duly obeyed, somewhat dismayed by Sidney's tone. The desk was a clutter of papers and the computer monitor plastered with yellow and pink PostIt notes. Sidney wasn't the most sophisticated man when it came to admin.

"I have received a complaint from Rachel Balls of the Cornish Morning News. It seems you were extremely rude to her in front of the SOCO team and ordered your men to manhandle her away from the crime scene,"

"Ah!" Jack waved his hand in a dismissive gesture, "Rachel Bollocks, she's a bloody nuisance windbag and somehow got inside the crime scene without, I might add, any authority,"

"Nonetheless Jack this is an official complaint from her editor, so I've got to look into it,"

"What a load of horseshit. I need this like a hole in the head,"

"There's worse to come Jack,"

"Go on,"

"Herbie Johansson has also put in a formal complaint only he's alleging that you hit him,"

"What! He poked me in the chest, and I just pushed him away,"

"That's not what the witnesses are saying,"

"What bloody witnesses,"

"His staff, he says you bullied them to work without a break so you could finish the scene today,"

"Load of tosh sir, a load of tosh. We were short of the on-scene support stuff, no mobile canteen, so I arranged for an alternative, it just took a couple of hours to arrive. They're not bloody pussycats, are they?"

"I don't know Jack, I wasn't there. There's more I'm afraid. The evidence log shows that they found the cash box at Penvale Farm with £5,400 in it but when the SOCOs checked it later at the store it only contained £4,500. Herbie says that the only fingerprints on the box, other than the victim's, were yours,"

"More bollocks,"

"You didn't touch it?"

"Yes, I did, but I told Jenkins to log that on SOCO's 'scene-log',"

"Well, here's a copy of the scene log and there's no entry signed by you,"

"Of course not, I was up to my ears. Jenkins handed me the box, and he could see I wasn't wearing any gloves,"

"But you took it from him anyway?"

"Yes, I admit that, but I asked Jenkins to put it in the log for God's sake,"

"Even so you were supposed to sign the entry, but there was no entry, and so there was no signature to argue about,"

"Jesus Christ this feels like I'm being stitched up,"

"I'm sorry to have to do this to you Jack but I need your locker key, and I need you to witness me opening it," Jack lowered his head and shook it slowly from side to side in despair.

"Come on then, let's take a look but if there is anything there, then some bastard's planted it," Sidney's expression became very sullen. He wasn't happy that any of this was going on during his watch. It could only spell trouble with a capital 'T' and paperwork with capital 'P'. Sidney hated doing disciplinaries, they screwed up his plans and put a big hole in his manpower.

Jack took the padlock from his locker and Sidney began to go through the contents. In a draw at the bottom, he found a brown envelope full of twenty-pound notes.

"Yours?" he asked. Jack was speechless and just stared at the money.

"Right Jack, I'll have to put you on suspension until we can get to the bottom of all of this crap,"

The CPS prepared a charge of 'theft against Jack, and the preliminary evidence gathered. Had they proceeded then Jack would have been facing a trial for committing a criminal offence and everything that went with it but Neil Jenkins, of all people, saved the day. He provided a written statement backing up Jack's version of events and putting Herbie Johansson in the frame for stealing the cash and handing it to Neil to plant in Jack's locker. Neil insisted he was under the impression it was just a harmless jape. Herbie, on the other hand, wanted revenge but he had not counted on Neil's sudden 'Damascene conversion' to truth and righteousness. The whole affair resulted in Neil's admonishment, Jack's suspension and ultimately, some months later, Herbie losing his job. Exactly what had brought about Neil's conversion from the dark side remained a mystery, but Jack suspected that there were still people up the chain of command who didn't want to see his future damaged by stupid and ill-considered in-fighting.

CHAPTER 2

Friday, 26th November 1999, 10.30 Devon & Cornwall Police HQ, Exeter, Devon

THE HEAVY OAK DOOR to the Assistant Chief Constable's office slammed shut behind him with a resounding bang. Jack knew that a door had just closed on an important part of his life. Nothing would ever be the same again.

The Disciplinary Board convened to decide the case against Detective Inspector Jack Mawgan would now deliberate over the evidence.

Jack was fortunate that the cross-examination of those involved in setting him up had, from his point of view, gone well and lent credibility to his assertion that his enemies within Devon and Cornwall Constabulary had intended to pin a charge of 'misconduct' on him. Had they succeeded then it would have put a serious dent his career.

He guessed that with a bit of help from Herbie Johansson and Neil Jenkins the Barnstable boys were behind the rather clumsy attempt to stitch him up and take him down a peg or two. If the intention was just to embarrass then their plot had gone badly wrong for they had failed to make allowances for Herbie's desire for revenge. The full-blown disciplinary hearing had resulted in trapping them into backing their attempted frame-up with more lies. Jack would face dismissal and an ignominious end to his otherwise distinguished career if the Board were taken in by those lies.

The bad news for Jack was the make-up of the Disciplinary Board. The senior officers gathered to examine Jack's case were all HQ types. None had previously served in CID. They had been raised and nurtured in the kind of culture that often seems to develop in large organisations, like the police force, where the process of 'administration' takes over and becomes the focus of everyone's day-to-day life. Management becomes self-absorbed and totally involved with the competition for high office. At the Exeter HQ, the actual substance of policing had become buried with the political baggage that drags on the world of modern policing... committees, evaluations, data analysis, initiatives, consultations and worst of all, 'targets'. The grubby, smelly, gut-churning work of poking through the dross of humanity's unsavoury activities was for others. Jack was one of them, one of the 'others'.

Finally, the moment came where he was ushered in to hear the verdict. The head of the board was a female officer with a reputation as a 'hard case', and a chip on her shoulder about the way detectives behaved. Their apparent lack of regard for the rules and regulations had often been a pet hate, and she never missed an opportunity to give them a hard time. She was in her fifties and held the rank of Assistant Chief Constable. She was a thin-faced woman with short grey hair and a pale complexion. Her pallor gave Jack the impression that her angular features were carved from marble. She had coal black eyes that were like arrows seeking out eye contact. They stared right through him leaving him with a feeling of nakedness and inadequacy.

Her demeanour was that of a medieval executioner, leaning on the axe while waiting to dispatch the malevolent miscreant on a journey to a finer place. She read out the Board's verdict while the other two members sat in silence and stared at the back of their hands, unable to look Jack in the eye.

Afterwards, sitting in the staff canteen, Jack's Federation rep., Tony Bell, explained the situation. A waitress delivered their order for two cups of tea. Jack was in a state of shock and not quite able to comprehend the details of his new situation.

"Cheer up, Jack, you've still got a job,"

"But the bastards found me guilty," he replied bitterly.

"Unfortunately, yes," He picked up the papers detailing the Disciplinary Board's findings and read them to Jack who sat with elbows on the table, chin resting in his hands and an expression of inconsolable disgust.

"The following constitutes the findings of this Board. We find him guilty of the following five offences as specified in the Constabulary Disciplinary Code:

1. Conduct to the prejudice of good order and discipline. That was for telling the SOCO to 'fuck off out of it' in front of four colleagues

and a female member of the press," Tony added his commentary as if there was a need to remind Jack of each of his 'crimes'.

2. Contravention of police regulations, or any police orders, whether written or verbal; because you failed to follow the correct procedure at the crime scene.

3. Neglect of duty; for failing to report the inappropriate handling of evidence to the Senior Scenes of Crime Officer.

4. The unlawful or unnecessary exercise of authority resulting in loss or injury to any other person or the Government; for thumping the Senior Scenes of Crime Officer when he remonstrated with you about bullying his subordinates.

5. Conduct calculated to bring the public service into disrepute. Specifically, for telling a member of the press to take her 'rag', roll it up and shove it where the sun doesn't shine,"

Jack closed his eyes and shook his head. "So, what about my demotion?"

"Ah, yes, you have been put down to Detective Sergeant with immediate effect,"

"What, right now, today?"

"Yes, as of now, you are back to DS,"

"Bastards! Fucking inconsiderate, ignorant fucking bastards,"

"Jack, it could have been a lot worse. If you had been charged with theft, like Herbie Johansson, and then found guilty, then you would have been out on your ear and no pension,"

"Yes, sure. I feel fucking blessed. Twenty-two years' service and what do I have to show for it? A drinking habit, hypertension and a George Medal in a fancy box,"

Tony looked perplexed. What George Medal? There was nothing in Jack's records about a George Medal. He must have been kidding. "What are you on about Jack?"

"Never mind Tony, water under the bloody bridge. It was a long time ago. Doesn't seem to matter now anyway," He sat staring at the steaming cup of tea for a moment.

"By the way, I'm fucked if I'm going to write a letter of apology to that bitch of a journalist. She can whistle for it. She deserved all she got."

"It's not that simple. If you choose not to comply with the instructions of the Disciplinary Hearing they could kick you out on your ear,"

"Well, we'll have to see about that. Anyway, maybe the time has come to review my options?"

"What do you mean by that,"

"Ah, forget it. That's the other me talking, the one that could cheerfully say goodbye to this dysfunctional heap of crap,"

"Well don't do anything stupid, we need you, just remember that," Jack couldn't help smiling at the curious accolade.

"I can't understand why Neil didn't come forward and explain his part in this damn nonsense in person. Did he think I would fill him in, right there in the court for all to see?"

"Neil gave his written statement, and in the end, it supported your version of events. I reckon he had a change of heart somewhere along the way. That's what got you off the hook on the possible theft charge. The other evidence was pretty thin and despite what you may think the ACC seemed to have a good idea what was going on,"

"Yes, Neil came up with the goods, but his change of heart leaves so many questions unanswered. In a way, I was surprised he spoke up. We had a major falling out after his road accident. We haven't exactly been on speaking terms since then,"

"I heard about that, you were involved too weren't you?"

"I was there. I saw it happen. The driver of the car he hit was killed, and the young girl in the back seat almost died in my arms,"

"A sad story by all accounts,"

"You don't know the half of it. Neil was pissed as a newt, but as we have come to realise, our Neil has connections, and somehow he got away with it,"

"It hasn't gone unnoticed Jack. I've had the nod from Internal Affairs, and I'm going to have to talk to him about his drinking,"

"More than that, Tony, you need to find out who, upstairs, is in Neil's pocket. It's obvious from what went on in there that Mr Jenkins is doing the bidding of someone here at HQ and they must have seen the way things were going when Herbie lost his sense of reason. That set the cat amongst the pigeons, and their little game threatened to blow up in their face. Getting me off a possible theft charge suddenly became more important than getting me in the shit for handling the box without my gloves on and making me look a right plonker,"

"But you only have yourself to blame for treating the press like that,"

"Like what? Bloody hacks are not interested in telling the truth only telling a good story to sell papers. Show me a journalist without an agenda and then we can discuss telling the truth,"

"You think so?"

"I know so. Somebody helped that bloody woman to get on to my crime scene, I know it,"

"Jenkins?"

"He could be in the frame for any of the shit going on that day. Still, can't sit around here whinging all day. I have a life to sort out and I'm buggered if I will give the bastards the pleasure of seeing me grovelling around as a bag-man to some young upstart DI,"

Jack stood up and was surprised to find his legs a bit wobbly. The nervous tension and subsequent relief that it was over had left him weak, exhausted. He needed air. Leaving his tea untouched on the table he muttered his thanks and farewells to Tony who yelled after him.

"I'll send the formal stuff through in the internal mail. Don't forget the letter," The only sign that Jack had heard what he said was a middle finger salute as he disappeared out the door.

The car park was a short walk away past the red brick buildings of Police HQ. He stood beside his car under the leafless oak trees he looked around at the quiet and tranquil scene. He breathed in deeply, purging his lungs of the stale canteen air.

The smell of winter replaced the fug of fried food. With his head now clear the emotions of the day subsided enough for him to consider driving back home to Cornwall. He opened the door of the car and allowed the soft leather seat to envelop his weary body.

His home was a cottage tucked away in the small Cornish village of Perranarworthal. By the time he pulled his Jag into the driveway, his mind had been made up. He was not going to write that damn letter, and he wasn't going back to being a DS. If he did it would mean working for a new DI, probably in another division, moving house again and uprooting Josh from his new school. That would be too much for him to swallow and he couldn't do that to Pam. She was very happy in their little cottage, and she had just sorted the garden and looking just how she wanted. Instead, he decided, he would take advantage of the latest redundancy programme, draw his pension and try to find another career that would deliver as much job satisfaction as the time he had spent as a detective. Maybe he could find a different outlet for those skills that had made him a valued member of society. Fighting crime is one thing, but he didn't join up to fight the people who were supposed to be colleagues.

Dr Pamela Mawgan was at work in the surgery at Devoran when her mobile phone bleeped to signal the arrival of an SMS. She apologised to the elderly patient she was dealing with and checked the message. Jack was back home. She was worried about him. He had left home that morning with the black cloud of depression harassing him and the stale smell of last night's whisky on his breath. He hadn't been looking forward to his 'day in court' and had had a sleepless night that showed in his face. His suspension had so far lasted more than two months and every day had been hell.

She had a feeling that this would be a turning point in their lives and her instincts told her that the news would not be good. There were moments when she resented the way his commitment to his job had dominated their lives. She was upset that they had repaid his unwavering loyalty with an unrelenting workload delivered by an apparently ungrateful management.

When her three o'clock appointment failed to show up she took it as a sign and rushed out to her car telling the receptionist that she would be back at four.

Arriving home, she found Jack sitting at the breakfast table drinking a cup of tea and reading the daily paper. He seemed relaxed and smiled as she came through the door. She could tell that things had not gone well for while his lips smiled his eyes betrayed his true feelings. She came close and kissed him lightly on the mouth then hugged him tightly.

They sat in the kitchen sipping tea while Jack explained what had happened. She didn't object when he told her he planned to leave the police and was going to send in his notice right away. By the end of the year he would be free of all that stress and worry.

Their financial situation was reasonably secure as Pam's salary as a part-time GP was quite good and Jack would be able to count on his pension.

With one son at university and the other at a private school, however, the loss of Jack's salary would certainly mean that there would have to be changes.

"Have you thought about what you said last year, after the accident? You were inspired by the skill and dedication of the paramedics and even said that it was a 'cool' job. Why don't you give it a try?"

"What, me, a paramedic?"

"Why not?"

"Well it's a thought I suppose, but I'm not sure that a very second-hand detective in his forties is going to be accepted for that kind of training. Do they even take recruits my age?"

"I'm sure they do for goodness sake, it's not as if you are past it. You've got another twenty years in you. Give it some thought; I'll back you. You're and adrenalin junkie, made for life with sirens and blue lights, go for it," Jack smiled at that jibe.

"I was reading the local paper a week or so back, and the Ambulance Service down here were advertising for trainee ATs, Ambulance Technicians. It's the first step to being a paramedic,"

"Well, there you are then, give them a call,"

As it turned out, they did indeed take recruits in their forties, and Jack was offered a training placement with the local Ambulance Service. The road to realising his new ambition to be a paramedic like Paul Harris would prove longer and more tortuous than he imagined but every journey begins with the first step so with a certain amount of trepidation he took it.

He was owed more leave than the one-month notice he was obliged to give, so his rapid departure eased the pain. There were aspects of the job he loved, but when he reminded himself of the crap that went with it, he felt relief that he wouldn't have to endure it anymore. A little over two weeks after handing in his notice he was able to join a small group of Trainee Ambulance Technicians at the Ambulance Service Training Centre in Chippenham, Wiltshire for a six-week residential course.

The first week of January 2000 saw Jack beginning to move his life in an entirely different direction. After many years spent following the trail left by the dead, he would now be using his skills to help sick and injured people to stay alive. To say that it felt surreal was an understatement. The first six months' probation was to prove a remarkable experience. Up to that point,

Jack's perspective on the world was one viewed through a policeman's eyes. It was not one that changes very easily. A detective questions everything and is suspicious of anything or anyone unusual, and these habits are difficult if not impossible to change.

The fact that ex-copper, Jack, would now wear a green uniform meant that the Cornish community had gained a trainee paramedic, but they would not, as events were to prove, be entirely losing one of their finest policemen.

Saturday, 15ᵗʰ April 2000, 09.55
Boskenna Farm Estate, Cornwall

It sounded like a muted 'crack', like a boot treading on a rotten twig. It came from the edge of the nearby woods, partially masked by the sound of the wind in the trees. A .22 calibre bullet, fired from a silenced rifle, hit Desmond just above the right ear; nobody in and around Boskenna Farm Estate was any the wiser, not even the birds stirred.

The lightweight, hollow-point, subsonic bullet killed him instantly, fragmenting and churning the contents of his skull with brutal efficiency.

That type of ammunition is designed to wreak havoc on the body without necessarily exiting the target. There was little sign, apart from a tiny entry wound, that the small but deadly missile had delivered a significant amount of energy that with devastating and fatal consequences.

Desmond's subsequent collapse caused him to fall against the breakfast table, knocking over a glass of chilled tomato juice and scattering his papers over the patio. They were blown away by a gust of the light spring airs on what had begun, at least, as a pleasant April morning.

Margaret, Desmond's wife, was startled by the sound of breaking glass as the upturned tumbler of tomato juice finally made it to the edge of the teak table and smashed onto the beautiful and expensive slabs of Delabole slate. The stream of juice moved slowly towards the still and silent figure joining a pool of blood seeping from the small hole left by the fatal bullet.

Margaret looked out onto the patio. "Desmond," she screamed, seeing her husband lying motionless. She wailed uncontrollably as she ran from the lounge calling for Mary, the housemaid.

Ever since Desmond's heart attack last autumn she had feared that this day would come. She was a woman who had suffered at Desmond's hands in more ways than one, but the prospect of life without him was one she did not want to contemplate. 'Would he survive this one?' She thought as she arrived by his side. Knowing nothing about first aid, she simply draped herself over Desmond's lifeless figure and sobbed and sobbed.

"I've called the ambulance," said Mary to an unhearing Margaret. Mary too was in a tearful state and equally ignorant about any life-saving measures that might give Desmond the slightest glimmer of hope. Not that anyone or anything could bring Desmond back from his present state. This collapse was no heart attack. He was stone dead and beyond the skills of any medic.

An emergency ambulance, complete with paramedic and assistant, was just a few minutes away, parked up in one of their regular waiting spots at the Victoria Services on the main A30. It easily arrived within the target response time of nineteen minutes and the crew set about walking quickly but calmly to the spot where Desmond lay with a still sobbing Margaret clinging to his lifeless body. An earnest Mary guided them in.

"He's gone and had another of they heart attacks she reckons," she said, her voice quivering with emotion, "Mrs Duffy do say that if he didn't stop workin' so 'ard it were only matter a time afore he 'ad another,"

Paramedic Edwin O'Connor and Trainee Ambulance Technician Jack Mawgan set down their equipment and carefully pulled Margaret away. Tears and mascara stained her cheeks. She was pale with fright. She was still wailing "no, no, don't leave me like this," as Mary came to her aid.

"All right Mrs Duffy let's have a look at what we have here, what's Mr Duffy's name?"

"Des," she said with trembling voice. "Desmond," she added as if there was a need for extra clarity.

Jack was busy opening the intubation pack and setting up the defibrillator while Edwin knelt down, checked skin temperature and colouration and felt for a pulse. He looked at his watch and realised it had probably been ten minutes since the collapse without any intervention. He shook his head, 'not good' he thought.

"Hello Desmond, can you hear me?" no response. "Mrs Duffy, has Desmond got a history of heart problems?" asked Edwin.

"Yes," she said, "he had a heart attack last September, and they put one of those 'stent' things inside him. But they said he would need a bypass sometime, or he may have another one," Edwin looked at Jack. The exchange said it all. No pulse. "Defib?" said Jack quizzically.

Edwin leant forward to check the head wound Des had apparently acquired in the fall. "Looks like he cracked his head on the table on the way down or maybe smacked it on the patio when he landed. There's blood on the right temple. Look at his eyes," said Edwin now on all fours and peering into Desmond's face. "Both pupils are blown. There's cranial damage somewhere, but it's odd that both should go like that,"

Jack looked carefully and put his finger on the bullet entry site. "Hang on," said Jack quietly, "if I'm not mistaken that's a bloody bullet wound," Edwin moved the matted hair to one side and got a good look at the ooze of blood coming from the neat little hole above Desmond's ear.

"Hell," said Edwin, "you're right,"

"No point in doing CPR, this bloke's as dead as a post," whispered Jack, anxious not to let Margaret hear his comments. They both knelt there, stunned, and not quite sure what to do or say next. "I've seen a few of those in my time," said Jack at last.

"I suppose so," replied Edwin, noticing the peculiar look on Jack's face. The patio was now a murder scene and Jack, an ex-homicide detective, was scanning it with an expert eye, soaking up the detail. He had unconsciously switched into detective mode.

He noticed a piece of paper in Desmond's hand. It was tightly held and damp from the mixture of tomato juice and blood.

Jack succumbed to an irresistible urge to see what it said on the paper that Des held so tightly. Without the burden of responsibility for dealing with this crime, Jack convinced himself that the rules did not need such close attention. He leant forward to uncurl the crumpled page with a latex-gloved hand. The portable radio clipped to the technician's pack burst into life, "CornAmb seven-two HeliMed is on the way over," Edwin picked up the radio.

"CornAmb Control this is CornAmb seven-two over,"

"CornAmb seven-two reading you loud and clear. HeliMed is en route ETA six minutes,"

"Roger. You can cancel HeliMed; the patient is 'purple' over," There was a pause while Dave Nicol in Ambulance Control digested this information.

"Roger, break-break, HeliMed did you copy over,"

"This is HeliMed we copied your last, returning to base,"

"Control from seven-two can you let the Police know that we would like their attendance at the scene. This incident is going to be one for them. We will remain on scene until they arrive. Show us off watch at minute two-three," Edwin was one of Cornwall's senior paramedics and a highly respected long-serving member of the Service, so Dave did as he was asked and adjusted his state-board to show the seven-two-crew off-watch at Boskenna Farm Estate.

"That's a roger seven-two," Edwin turned to see Jack holding open the page, still gripped by Desmond's lifeless hand. "I don't think we should touch anything Jack," said Edwin.

"Just looking," said Jack taking care not to stain his latex-gloved hand with the red cocktail that now lay in pools in the cracks and crevices of the slate patio. Jack's trained eyes saw a half page of A4, torn from the bottom of what had once been a full page. It had a message printed on it, just a few words...

SILENCE IS GOLDEN = £££££
ANOTHER FIVE WOULD DO NICELY

Beneath this in the right-hand corner and slightly obscured by the stain left by the blood and juice was what appeared to be an office stamp with what looked like the words 'FOR GLORY'. Odd, thought Jack, very odd. Whatever message had been on the upper part of the page was now nowhere to be seen. He had seen office stamps with 'PAID' or 'URGENT' on them but never one that said 'FOR GLORY'. He carefully replaced the paper under Desmond's hand to ensure it did not blow away in the fitful breeze.

The sound of multiple sirens grew louder as Jack mulled over the morning's events. Murder had been his speciality as a detective and solving murder cases had always given him the greatest satisfaction. His juices were flowing, and his brain was working overtime.

CHAPTER 3

Thursday 20th January 1966, 15.00 – Army HQ, Aden. The Office of General Sir Gordon Sanders KCB, Commanding Officer Land Forces

THE BRITISH PRIME MINISTER, The Right Honourable Harold Wilson, was a man of great humanity and considerable intellect. He was also a man with a mission, and there were many like-minded politicians determined to modernise the British ideas of morality.

Life was tough for the Government on the home front, but they were even tougher abroad, and it was a testing time in the history of the British Empire. They were facing a destructive insurgency in Southern Arabia, and their vital military base in Aden was under immense pressure. The Chief of the Defence Staff in London had sent a signal to the local military commander in Aden informing him that there were significant changes ahead and he was sending a briefing team to bring him up to date with the Government's plans.

Events in Aden were coming to a head, and the emissaries from London were carrying an awkward message for the Military Command. General Sanders, The Commander of Land Forces in Aden, was, however, about to discover that the messengers had more on their minds than the politics of Empire. A series of curious incidents in Aden threatened those at the very heart of Government who were toiling day and night to turn around the laws on sexual orientation.

The military situation had deteriorated and certain members of the Army had been up to mischief in their off-duty time and were stirring up trouble with the locals. The rebels in South Yemen were nonetheless gaining ground, and the future for the British military garrison was bleak.

General Sanders was sorting through the afternoon mail when his adjutant, Captain Mattocks, appeared in the office doorway.

"Sir, Captain Allcock and Mr Conway to see you,"

"Thank you, Mattocks, do come in gentlemen, take a seat," Two armless chairs were arranged in front of the General's large leather-topped mahogany desk on which rested the General's blotter, notepad, pen-stand, ashtray and a hand-carved name tally announcing 'General G.T.A Sanders'. The 'Sir' and the suffix 'KCB' had yet to be added. His elevation to 'Knight Commander of the Most Honourable Order of the Bath' had only been announced a few weeks earlier, in the New Year Honours.

The MI6 visitor was looking suitably enigmatic wearing a grey Burberry raincoat and carrying an umbrella. Fashion icon he was not, but he could blend into any crowd in any town in Britain unnoticed. His choice of topcoat was entirely appropriate for a cooler than average winter's day in this outpost of a dwindling Empire. The umbrella was also a sign that he had just stepped off the flight from RAF Brize Norton, which was the General guessed, enjoying a typically wet and miserable spell of January weather. Mr Conway accepted Mattocks' offer to take his coat and took a seat.

"Well, gentlemen," the General began, pen-poised, notepad at the ready, "to what do I owe this pleasure? We don't often see you chaps on our patch," His tone wasn't quite welcoming and the strained smile he wore betrayed his inner lack of joy.

Captain Allcock spoke first, "General, Mr Conway has some interesting information that has found its way to MI6 in London, and he needs to discuss the implications with you. He's looking for some help and cooperation to make sure we don't create any...er...difficulties for the future,"

The General's response was immediate and brusque. "Difficulties for the bloody future! It's help with the difficulties I've got right now that would be really useful," There was a hint of sarcasm in his tone as he laid into his visitors, "We've lost over fifty men in the last two years alone, and we are not winning the battle with the insurgents. Our 'unseen enemy' as the British press would have it. They are not so bloody invisible when you're on the wrong end of an anti-tank mine, believe me. Every day they blow up something or somebody, and I need a lot more than fine words if I am to keep the lid on a situation that is rapidly getting out of control,"

The visitors seemed unmoved. Eyeing the General's pen, Conway said, "There will be no notes of this conversation General. This is one of those meetings that never happened,"

The General theatrically replaced his pen in the pen rack, slowly opened the top drawer of his desk and took out a packet of cigars; an indulgence his doctor said was 'ill-advised'. It was, however, one he decided he needed to get him through the sixteen-hour days he worked during these difficult times. He removed one from the pack and peeled away the paper sleeve. He wasn't going to let a little problem with his blood pressure get in the way of this vital nicotine fix. He flipped the top from his Zippo lighter and let the flame embrace the end of his cigar. He drew slowly, inspected the glowing tip to make sure that it was well alight, blew a plume of smoke in Conway's direction, sat back in his chair and said, "Do go on,"

Conway remained silent. The General eyed him up and down. He was, he thought, a perfect choice for a spook. A grey man in a grey suit who would pass unnoticed almost anywhere.

Allcock turned to Conway who shuffled awkwardly in his chair and began to speak. "We have intelligence from inside the Front for the Liberation of South Yemen, FLOSY. During the last six months, there have been four assassinations of key personnel within FLOSY and their former associates the NLF, National Liberation Front.

"Nobody knows who or how they are targeting the dead men but each has been found in an alley or a backstreet in the Crater District with his throat cut. Before you ask these assassinations are nothing to do with our people," The subtle emphasis on the word 'our' was meant to identify other spooks.

"Christ Almighty," said the General, "if it's not your people do we have a secret ally working behind the scenes? If so, then I suggest you bloody well find out who they are – smartish,"

"No General," said Conway, "It's more complicated than that," It was his turn to pull his briefcase onto his lap, open the flap and take out a file. "This man," he placed two photographs on the desk so that the General could see clearly, "is Sergeant Hamish McGovern, of the Argyll & Sutherland Highlanders. He's an Arab speaker, and we believe he's our killer,"

The General looked at the two photographs. One showed a clean-shaven Sergeant in regimental uniform, and the other showed McGovern as a dirty-faced scruff in Arab clothing.

"McGovern was stopped by a patrol in the Crater district and subsequently could not explain his situation adequately. He was detained and placed in the capable hands of Captain Allcock who was, unfortunately, unable to obtain any additional information about McGovern's activities. However, his clothing was blood stained, and a knife found close to where he was detained. The Patrol Leader believes it was his and he had tried to get rid of it when he saw them and realised he could not escape. The knife was also blood-stained,"

General Sanders drew on his cigar and blew another plume in Conway's direction. He sat forward, placing his cigar in the brass ashtray fashioned from the base of a 105mm shell casing. He put his hands flat on the desk, chewed over in his mind what he had just heard and realised that this was not going to be the end of the tale.

The silence was contrived, but Conway was a man whose mental toughness was more than equal to the task at hand. He remained impassive; his expression could mean anything and nothing. The dark arts of spookdom thought the General.

After a minute of silence, he resumed his cigar-smoking posture, sat back in his chair, looked at each of them in turn and said, "So are you now going to tell me what this is all about? I imagine you are. A few dead locals, a Jock who's gone native and you come all the way from London to bother me with a load of nonsense. I know you chaps too well to think that, so please, let's cut to the chase and tell me what this is all about," His raised voice conveyed a growing sense of frustration.

Conway opened his file again and took out another photograph. "This is Lieutenant David Lucas, 17th/21st Lancers. On the 17th May 1965, he was killed by a road-side bomb on Airport Road,"

He waited for the General to finish studying the picture of a young army officer in the dress uniform of the Lancers. The confident, smiling face of untroubled and arrogant youth beamed from the photograph. The General looked up. Conway placed the second photograph on the desk. The image was almost identical to the first with a young cavalry officer in an identical pose and also wearing a confident smile although something about his bearing told the General that it was closer to a smirk of superiority than a manifestation of inner happiness.

Without mincing his words, Conway said, "This is Lieutenant William Chaloner. Lieutenants Chaloner and Lucas were lovers, homosexuals. They have been under 'review' since November 1964 when we first became aware of their relationship,"

"Review!" burst in the General, "what the hell do you mean, review? Correct me if I am wrong but isn't homosexuality illegal? Why were they not arrested and thrown in jail as soon as you knew what they were up to?"

"Well General, it's more complex than that, and in any case, such decisions are taken at a higher level. It was apparently decided to monitor the situation and delay any action. As I am sure you are aware our Prime Minister believes that homosexuality should be decriminalised and is working towards changing the law as we speak. Let's say that some influential members of the Administration who are of that persuasion would be very unhappy if we made a fuss and bother at what they see as a critical moment in the development of the necessary white papers,"

"What, pray, have these two," he paused for effect, "gentlemen, got to do with these murders on my patch and how come this is the first I get to know about them?"

"Well sir," it was Allcock speaking, "we cannot tie McGovern to Chaloner directly here in Aden, but we have identified a series of financial links. Money moves from Chaloner's account to McGovern's account, and the payments coincide with each assassination. Putting two and two together we can assume that Chaloner is paying McGovern to kill the people he thinks were responsible for Lucas's death,"

"But you can't expect me to believe that a British soldier pops his Arab fancy-dress kit on and takes a ride into the most dangerous parts of Aden, to find people he does not know, and kill them," said the General. "Anyway, what put you chaps onto this link between McGovern and Chaloner? How much was he paying him?"

Allcock took a deep breath and read from his notes, "McGovern is an Arab speaker. He was born in Libya, the son of an Engineer working for BP before the Second World War. He was educated at the local International School until the age of twelve.

"When he returned to Edinburgh at the beginning of the war he went badly off the rails and ended up doing time at a young offenders' institution for drugs related offences. He was a 'runner', not a 'user'.

"He enlisted in the Army at nineteen and kept a clean sheet until his first tour of duty here when he was put under surveillance by the MPs after they suspected he was visiting areas of the City that were 'off-limits'.

"He is divorced and has a history of drunkenness and violence. He was busted to corporal in fifty-nine after breaking the jaw of a colleague in a fight and subsequently threatening the arresting officer with a knife.

"McGovern was promoted back to Sergeant last year here in Aden after saving the life of his Troop Commander when he fell into the hands of a group of NLF. He had been seconded to the 17th/21st as an interpreter and was on patrol on Airport Road when an explosion disabled the TC's Ferret and the enemy took him captive. The rest of the Ferret crew were left to burn.

"It seems that his Arab-speaking skills came in handy when he somehow convinced the NLF chaps that he was the real Commander and offered himself in return for his TC. We are not sure what happened after that because he has never told the full story. However, he emerged a little while later, after the rest of the patrol heard the sound of exploding grenades. He was all in one piece and completely unharmed.

"The activities of the last six months may shed some light on that particular little piece of regimental history, but we have yet to get our teeth into that. Whatever McGovern was doing we have good reason to believe he is up to his neck in the local drugs trade and maybe some other mischief as well.

"We found the link because Chaloner is always short of cash and on this occasion, he tried to cover his expenses by stealing his brother's chequebook and making out cheques to his creditors, forging his brother's signature. He managed to get away with it for over a year, but in the end, the auditors couldn't reconcile the expenditures, and the scam was uncovered. Needless to say, we got to hear about it; any financial irregularities involving serving officers must be notified to his CO by the bank in question. In the end, his brother elected not to press charges. He probably won't be on his brother's Christmas card list anymore, but that's his concern. Cheques were traced to various banks and four, each for five thousand pounds, were paid into

McGovern's UK account via the Standard Chartered Bank in Aden. Not very bright really, either of them,"

"If McGovern was put under surveillance by the MPs how come we were not aware of this curious activity?" asked the General.

"Not sure sir, we are looking into that. The MPs were told to keep tabs on McGovern not a shabbily dressed local. That may be the answer,"

"So how did you come by all this other information about the assassinations? One dead Arab these days is neither here nor there," said the General.

Conway stepped in. "We have a man inside the FLOSY, with whom we had exchanged a coded signal and then a note left at one of our regular 'dead-letter drops',"

"And this nonsense about the Death or Glory Boys?"

"Let's just say we have our sources and leave it at that,"

"This is an odd turn of affairs, very odd. Not to say queer, eh, Allcock?" The General laughed at his own joke, but the others remained stony-faced. "I suppose I'm going to have to handle his Court Martial and you are here to tell me how you want it done quietly?"

General Sanders stubbed the remains of his cigar in the ashtray, got up from his seat and walked over to the cocktail cabinet hidden behind the false drawers of a mahogany filing cabinet. He inspected his stock of malt whiskies, poured himself a glass of Lagavulin and sipped it before returning to stand behind his desk. He was above average height and once cut a fine figure, but these days he spent too much time sat at that desk and his tunic was a little too tight for comfort. The pressures of the job were taking their toll and his rosy complexion was another sign that his health was beginning to wane. Whisky was one more indulgence his doctor objected to but the General had a contrary opinion and apparently thought the 'water-of-life' was another necessary evil.

He held the glass up to the light and for a moment admired the amber fluid. His mind was trying to take it all in. What were these two really up to? He looked into the glass as if searching for answers then gave the remaining dram a swirl before polishing it off in one gulp. Placing the empty glass on the desk, he looked Conway in the eye.

"You have come to me with this tale of woe for a reason, so cut the crap get to the point,"

Conway cleared his throat and began to explain. "This is top secret, General and it must go no further. Given the prevailing situation here in Aden the government has decided that it would be best all round if we were to leave within the next few months and hand Aden its independence. When the time is right, there will be an announcement to that effect. In the meantime, the Chiefs of Staff have decided that a small reduction of manpower in the region would be appropriate and the Reconnaissance Units will be withdrawn along with various Air Force and Naval units. This will take place beginning next week and be complete before the announcement of a full withdrawal. As soon as the insurgents get wind of our departure, they will no doubt harry our forces all the way to the exit, so Command wants it done quietly. There will be no Court Martial,"

"What then of Chaloner?" asked the General, knowing that reconnaissance units meant the Ferret Scout Cars of the 17th/21stLancers.

"That is not your concern General. I have been sent here to brief you and to be sure you…understand…the situation," said Conway. General Sanders viewed 'Spooks' as a necessary evil but he didn't like them when they were in London, and he especially didn't like them sniffing around his command. The meaning insinuated into the word 'understand' by its very deliberate delivery was meant to ensure that nothing related to the Chaloner story would ever leave that room. He knew very well that Chaloner's family were well connected in Government circles and he could smell the whiff of privilege working its way through upper echelons of the MoD.

Sanders shrugged his shoulders in a mixture of resignation and disbelief at what the modern army had become. He was depressed at the thought that the year ahead, his final year of service was going to be dominated by a miserable withdrawal. It would no doubt be a nightmare with many more lives lost as they fought off the inevitable insurgent attacks. At least the end was in sight, and then it would be a quiet retirement to his Gloucestershire farm where his wife would bully him and the grandchildren test his patience.

CHAPTER 4

Saturday, 20ᵗʰ May 2000 – Milngavie, Glasgow

DESMOND ARCHIBALD DUFFY, AT the comparatively young age of just fifty-five, was buried with all the usual ceremony and paraphernalia of his native Glasgow. A horse-drawn hearse was bathed in floral tributes pronouncing 'DES' and one huge one from Margaret that spelled-out her undying love – 'GOODBYE DARLING'. At least that was the message that was intended for the many onlookers. The florist had baulked at the notion of a second line that said '& GOOD RIDDANCE' and felt that Margaret was probably joking when she muttered this to herself during their negotiations.

Margaret thought that she had inherited a fortune but had found to her sorrow, and her anger, that she was the proud owner of a large stack of unpaid bills and no ready cash with which to pay them. It had become apparent that Desmond had mortgaged everything to the hilt. His secret pile of offshore cash was unfortunately so secret that Margaret had no idea where it was. She had to borrow money from her brother to pay for the funeral. The only person, other than Des, who knew how to unlock his wealth was his solicitor, Isaac Goldsworthy. Unfortunately for Margaret he now lay in a coma in a private hospital in Torquay. He suffered a severe stroke upon hearing of Desmond's demise. Unpicking the threads of Desmond's fortune would take a very long time.

The service was held at St Paul's Church of Scotland in Milngavie but only after a not insignificant bribe had been paid to the Moderator of St Pauls. At first, he was not too keen on Desmond's return to his birthplace. The Moderator had been active in the East End of Glasgow in the '60s and

'70s. He had first-hand experience of Desmond's 'other' activities including those that had made Strathclyde Police a frequent visitor to his door and had eventually caused the 'serious Neds', the Glasgow 'Mafia', to blackball him from the City and force him to leave the country.

Such were Desmond's dabbling in the field of 'legal highs' and various other methods of chemical entertainment that he had gathered a big enough stash to be able to leave quietly with both kneecaps intact, all his fingernails, a bride-to-be who was young enough to be his daughter and a burning desire to survive.

In fact, he did more than just survive when in 1980, at the age of thirty-five, he found solace and security by crossing the border and settling in faraway Cornwall. He bought the Boskenna Farm Estate from the impoverished Petherick tin mining family and 'fixed-up' their primary residence, Tremayne House, in what could only be described as Pseudo-Modern Mock Elizabethan. A ghastly mess that summed up Desmond's excess wealth and complete lack of taste.

At one stage Des was persuaded by a trusted associate to invest in the aviation business by setting up a helicopter charter company. He hoped to tap into the growing demand for this form of luxury travel. After a year of wheeler dealing he became the proud owner of the first and only executive helicopter charter company in the South West.

His big break came when Western Hydro took over the South-Western Dynamo Company in April 1998 and placed the Helicopter Power Line Inspection contract out to tender. The task of inspecting the region's thousands of miles of overhead electricity supply cables had been carried out using helicopters for many years, and the steady revenue from such a contract can be vital to the survival of every struggling small helicopter company where a regular income stream paid the bills.

Once the contract award was announced, and Dragon Helicopters was declared the winner Desmond set about finding every way he could to cut the overheads and squeeze every penny of profit out of it.

Despite this pressure on costs, Desmond insisted that his pilots were issued with the now standard Flight Crew Helmet because the kind of low-level flying required for the task was far more dangerous than the routine transportation of personnel from A to B.

The unfortunate fatal crash of the Dragon Helicopters' Bell JetRanger eighteen months later brought home the need for such protection for while the pilot survived, the Line Inspector on board, a Western Hydro employee, had died of severe head injuries. His employer had denied him access to this expensive but vital protective equipment.

Relationships were strained by the issue of helmet availability and the fact that poor maintenance of the helicopter was being cited as the possible cause of the accident.

The consequences of the man's death were beginning to multiply now that the best lawyers in the land were chewing over the bones of what may become a case of 'corporate manslaughter'. Who was at fault? Dragon or Western Hydro? Much would depend on how that question was resolved.

While Des was doing his best to rip off Western Hydro, their CEO was doing pretty much the same thing and was busy asset stripping what remained of the newly acquired SWDC.

The CEO was none other than The Honourable Sir William Arthur Chaloner, retired cavalry officer and a businessman with some strange ideas when it came to ethics in the world of commerce.

He was born in 1942 and educated at Eton. He had joined the Army after leaving Eton in 1960. He was born the second son of the late Viscount Barberry, the carpet magnate and founder of Chaloner Carpets the largest carpet maker in Kidderminster and second largest in the country.

Sir William's brother, George Alexander Chaloner had inherited the family fortune and was now the 5th Viscount Barberry, Baron Barberry of Stone, a little village outside Kidderminster and the site of the family mansion and estate.

The brothers did not get on, however, and William had spent his Army years struggling to make ends meet. The lack of funds had not stopped him having a riotous time.

In fact, Sir William was always better at spending money than making it and his survival on the Board of Directors owed more to his ruthless cunning and barefaced cheek than any business skills.

Although his sexual orientation had nearly led to a court martial and an ignominious end to his army career, he was fortunate to have had friends of similar persuasion in the Government at the time and had managed to survive despite a few minor scandals. Having spent many years as a closet 'gay', he now lived openly with a male partner about whom very little was known beyond the fact that he was also an ex-military man and much younger than his patron.

Sir William's relationship with the head of Dragon Helicopters was fractious, to say the least. He thought that the uncouth Glaswegian was 'nothing more than a grubby crook with the management skills of a haggis and the subtlety of a house-brick'.

Sir William Chaloner's management skills relied on a feudal arrogance that would even have scared the pants off the average medieval overlord. His ideas about justice were based on the traditions of 'trial by ordeal'. One would not pick a fight with William Chaloner if you knew what he was capable of. Many who did are no longer alive to tell the tale.

CHAPTER 5

- -

Saturday, 3rd June – Lower Spargo Cottage, Perranarworthal

JACK MAWGAN SAT IN his favourite armchair reading his daily paper and resting his tired legs after a busy early shift. He was a stocky six-footer with the physique of a Rugby player but would be the first to admit that his fitness was now a long way from the athlete he once was. He had spent almost the entire eight-hour shift on his feet and had to carry a patient a long way across a crowded beach and up the cliff path at Kynance Cove.

Pam appeared in the doorway.

"Cup of tea?" she said, "and what are you smiling at?"

"Oh, I just thought, what would my old Dad have said if he could see me now," replied Jack. He followed Pam into the kitchen as she filled the kettle from the tap and turned to find the teapot.

"I had a very strange thing happen today and can't quite work out what to do about it.'

"Go on, try me,"

"I met Sidney; you remember Sidney Patterson, the DCI at Truro?"

"Sidney, let me think. Sidney with the mother who's just had her hip done. He has diabetes?"

"It's always the same with you medicos you only ever remember people by their ailments. Yes, Sidney with the diabetes thing. You remember the murder I went to last month? The one out at Withiel, the businessman shot on his patio,"

"I certainly do. You came back from work that day with that 'policeman' look on your face," she playfully scowled at him, "that was the first time I'd seen you that animated since the accident," Jack paused for a moment as if the DVD had stuck and the movie had frozen. He clicked back into reality a few seconds later and picked up the thread of the conversation as though it were normal. They both knew, however, that mention of 'the accident' had given Jack another 'flash-back'. He had to struggle to get his mind out of the past and back to the here and now.

"Sidney is the DCI on the case, so I asked him how things were going,"

"What did he say?"

"He told me that they have some suspects but can't say much at this stage,"

"Isn't that what you would expect him to say?"

"Sure, but then I asked how he got on with deciphering the cryptic note on the piece of paper in the victim's hand. What took me back was his reply, he said he didn't know what I was talking about. There was no piece of paper in the victim's hand,"

"Isn't that a bit odd?" said Pam, "I remember you telling me about it. You said it was like a riddle,"

"Yes, a strange kind of riddle, but the paper was there, and I read it; Edwin saw me and scolded me for tampering with the crime scene. I made a sketch of what I had seen when I got back to HQ. It's still upstairs in the office I think,"

"What are you going to do? If vital evidence is missing, then you have to tell someone,"

"Yes, you are right of course, but I'm not sure who to speak to. I smell a rat. That reprobate Neil Jenkins is involved. I'll have to think about it,"

Jack wasn't entirely honest with Pam. If there is one thing a straight copper hates most, it's a bent copper. If Jenkins was somehow involved, then he needed to tread carefully if his aim was to see justice done and for Jenkins to get the punishment he deserved.

Jack retired to his office and switched on his computer. Playing around with Josh they had studied the work of hackers and had experimented with some of the software used by the top guys to gain access to other computers. Just out of professional curiosity of course. Until now he had never seriously considered hacking into somebody's system to cause mischief. They had been satisfied with simply being nosey. Faced with the need for information he exercised the possibility of hacking into the police computers in his mind.

First, he had to get his head around that missing piece of paper with his sketch of the 'riddle'. He searched the office moving and sifted through piles of papers until he eventually found it. How on earth had it disappeared from the crime-scene? If Sidney didn't get to see it what had happened to it? He thought carefully about that day and re-ran, minute by minute, his time at the scene in his head.

The note was still there when Edwin covered Desmond's body with a blanket. The last he saw if it the breeze had folded it over and no part of the message was visible. He was sure that the blanket would have prevented the note from blowing away. If someone had taken it, then there was a very short list of possible culprits. It had to be either Mary the housemaid, Mrs Duffy or whoever was the first to uncover Des and spot the note. That was likely to have been Neil Jenkins; he was acting as Sidney Patterson's number two that day.

Jack bristled at the memory. It had taken all his willpower not to thump Jenkins on the nose when they had met. The thought of the accident and the disciplinary hearing wound him up every time it came to mind. He knew that Jenkins had somehow got away without any charges. But seeing him there, in the flesh…he had boiled inside. Somehow Neil Jenkins' connections had kept him from facing justice. Was he 'on the square' or was that an old wives' tale? Was being a member of a Masonic Lodge the invisible cloak that protected him? Did he deliberately stitch Jack up when he handed him the cash-box that day at Penvale Farm? Was it a cunning trick by Jenkins on behalf of others? Or were his motives more devious than that? Too many unanswered questions for Jack's liking.

He recalled that after the shooting at Tremayne House the first wave of Police had been ordered to secure the perimeter of the estate in an attempt to corral the shooter. The next to arrive were the armed response team and the detectives from Truro CID, Patterson and Jenkins. Since Jack's departure from the Truro CID team they were short of a DI and the 'office-bound' Sidney was forced to get involved with day-to-day operations.

Jack had met Sidney and Neil at the edge of the Patio where they had surveyed the scene before accepting Mary's offer of a cup of tea in the kitchen. Jack gave them a summary of events and explained what they had seen and heard. The two detectives had started to take notes, but after about five minutes of chat Neil took one look at Jack, sensed the air of hostility and hurriedly left saying he would check the body. The two women came in the French windows as Neil went out. While Edwin loaded the equipment back into the ambulance, Jack passed the time of day with Sidney.

As Jack and Edwin left Tremayne House, there had been an invasion of SOCOs and Bobbies sent to support the investigation so it is likely that any opportunity to remove the note would have disappeared once two or more officers were at the scene. To contemplate the possibility that more than one officer was involved would mean a conspiracy and Jack felt that unlikely. His detective's nose told him that this one didn't smell of a conspiracy between a couple of regular 'bobbies'. Rather it had the whiff of some of Desmond's less likeable acquaintances.

Jack's instincts focused on the hidden meaning of that note. Who wrote it, who delivered it and by what means. What did its cryptic message mean and finally, who took it and why?

He decided the situation called for a little homework, so he fired up his PC and began to search the Internet. Within the hour, he was in possession of some interesting information. It wasn't difficult to locate articles, and stories about Desmond's various confrontations with authority and Jack began to print and collate a file of his antics. While the details turned out to be fascinating, there was no obvious 'smoking gun' to give him direction. There was a need to tap into information that he knew already existed, knew was accessible but also knew that it would be illegal even to try to get at it.

Hacking was NOT to be practised by a serving police officer unless he had the necessary authority. The question in his mind was could he justify doing it now that he was no longer a policeman? His instincts guided him along the lines that Justice would need to be seen to be done. He resolved to think on it a little longer.

It took Jack 24 hours and another shift with Edwin to clear his head and to convince himself that his role in society had changed. Reassured by this analysis, Jack felt he was able to push the bounds of legal activity provided it was, indeed, in the interests of justice. If Neil Jenkins had avoided justice after the accident, then maybe the corruption that had saved him went further than he thought. The difficult question was how could Jenkins be connected with Desmond Duffy's underworld?

Getting access to the files of most public organisations was a simple matter provided the right software was to hand, and the 'hacker' had a good understanding of the firewalls he would have to deal with. He decided to collect as much information as he could about those who he had decided were 'in the frame' for stealing the note. That little piece of paper might be a clue, or it might be a red herring. He needed to know more about the progress made by Sidney and his team before trying to draw too many conclusions.

Equally important would be the need to remain an unseen and unnoticed enquirer. It meant that everything he was planning to do required the protection of his identity and to leave the files inspected or copied in such a state that nobody would be aware that someone outside the police was making enquiries. And if by chance there was a trail left behind then it should be one that did not lead to Perranarworthal.

He, therefore, decided that he should enlist the help of the Argentinian Police – not with their knowledge of course but with a trick Josh had shown him. Jack set up a series of interconnected servers in Russia, South Africa, Hong Kong and the USA using commercially available facilities. To these, he added software that created 'diverters'. Attempts to backtrack his activity would be diverted to a server in Argentina operated by the Argentinian Police. Jack knew that the Argentinians were quite vulnerable. Ever since the Falklands War, the British authorities had been accessing their internal networks and monitoring their activity for signs of another military build-up.

He had made this discovery during a drunken encounter with a member of the security services while rock climbing in Wales with a collection of guys from the United Services Mountain Climbing Club. The informant had not spelt out the situation in detail but while gently boasting about the military's grip on future events 'down south', he'd let slip that their 'gateway' had been through the Police HQ in Buenos Aires.

Believing that he had exhausted Josh's hacking skills and not wishing to provide him with some that he shouldn't acquire he leant on some contacts to help. Sure enough, after a couple of days' hard graft at the keyboard and some discrete calls from the local call box to a variety of contacts, ex-colleagues and old student friends, he had created his private 'hackers network'. It was complete with a link into and out of the Departamento Central de Policía, Moreno Street, Buenos Aires. Now anyone backtracking his research would find that the Argentinian Police had a mysterious interest in the Desmond Duffy affair.

An old chum from university days had introduced him to a piece of software that allowed him to run a large number of multiplexed VPN gateways simultaneously and together with his 'diverter' protection he was confident that he could work from his home PC without fear of detection. The software hopped at random between each VPN in the same way that modern military 'frequency-hopping' high-security radios did. It was impossible to crack the system without the right 'log-on' codes.

Beginning his research in earnest, he first targeted what was likely to be the easiest and most productive source, Sidney. He knew the password for DCI Patterson's computer and also knew that it was unlikely to have changed. Sidney was one of those non-believers in technology. If Jack was a computer whiz, then Sidney was a computer dunce – with a memory like a sieve. He had his password written on a Post-It note stuck to his computer monitor and hadn't changed it once in all the time that Jack had been at Truro CID. Jack was betting that it was still valid.

Sure enough, the software designed to defeat the police firewall was up to the job, and Jack was soon sifting through Sidney's files. He found his preliminary report on the Duffy case and copies of witness statements. Clicking on an application icon that looked like a vacuum cleaner he then blocked and copied the files. This 'hoover' software was so smart that it left no record of this activity thus Sidney would be unaware that someone had been snooping.

Saving these files was potentially dangerous, but Jack had designed his system so that the data would reside on one of the remote servers. If anyone were to access his computer, there would, therefore, be nothing untoward to compromise him. Also, if the correct protocol were not followed during the 'boot-up', then the secondary hard drive would overwrite the primary drive with enough garbage to ensure that no known data-recovery system could get back his personal records.

Jack was acutely aware that the critical data on the Duffy case would be held on the specialist 'HOLMES' computer system. The Home Office Large Major Enquiry System was a stand-alone computer network with its dedicated firewalls – a step up from the kind of protection he had to deal with at the Truro 'nick'. Jack hoped that Sidney made his usual notes before moving the detail across to HOLMES. He was in luck. Sidney was paranoid about keeping personal records, and there were plenty for Jack to sift through.

The problem with acquiring so much data is that to make sense of it has to be read and understood. Wading through Sidney's stuff took the rest of Jack's spare time. The files revealed that the police were following the line that Desmond was the subject of a professional 'hit' and that this was in some way connected with his past in the Glasgow underworld. Sidney had been to Glasgow and had spent a considerable amount of time at the Pitt Street HQ of Strathclyde Police reviewing the possible links with the drug gangs in that part of the world.

Indications were that there were two strong possibilities. The most significant player in Desmond's previous 'career' and the man most likely to have issued the 'go or die' order back in 1980 was Bernie 'The Hammer' Gordon, who had subsequently died of a stroke in 1992. His lieutenants were his son, Davy Gordon, and his right-hand man, Ronnie 'Magnum' Morrison.

Ronnie was Bernie's hard man, his 'executioner', but he was getting on a bit now and wasn't thought to be personally involved in any action in Cornwall. However, Strathclyde Police couldn't rule out that he may have acted as a 'facilitator' given his murderous 'trade' and his possible connections within it.

Davy Gordon was described as an 'enigma'. He was part of a new breed of heavyweight criminal and the head of arguably the most influential gang in the south and east of Glasgow controlling about 45% of the city's drug trade. Their 'expertise' included protection rackets, prostitution, tobacco smuggling, illegal betting activities and the manufacture and distribution of illegal vodka.

Davy Gordon apparently had no obvious connection with any criminal activities but, like his father before him was under almost constant police surveillance. He lived in a gated compound in a smart new house surrounded by a six-foot wall just outside Paisley, off the Ferguslie Road. Despite having no visible means of support Gordon was the registered keeper of two black Audi A6 cars and one black Audi 4x4 all with specially darkened windows. He shopped at the best stores and supported a wife with expensive tastes in jewellery and clothes. He also had a couple of mistresses who had expensive apartments off Buchanan Street in the city centre, but he did not appear to have any offspring.

This breed of criminal devoted an enormous amount of time and resources to protecting their privacy and hiding their activities. They used lawyers and 'cut-outs' to handle their day-to-day businesses and never went within a mile of anything that could in any way compromise their situation.

Strathclyde Police had no indication that there was any link with Cornwall. Their observations, phone-taps and other evidence showed links within Scotland and Northern Ireland but nothing at all south of the border. Sidney was apparently convinced that despite the lack of proof to support his theory there was, somewhere, a connection with the crooks in Scotland.

Jack shut down his PC, read through his notes a second time then went downstairs to the lounge and put them in the log-burner. Although he was confident in the strength of his computer defences his paranoia came to the fore. He struck a match then made sure the papers were destroyed completely by raking the ashes with a poker. He thought that Glasgow somehow didn't have the right smell to it. He thought Sidney was chasing shadows.

With all these possibilities churning around in his head he changed and set off for work.

CHAPTER 6

Saturday, 10th June, 05.30 – Carland Cross

JACK AND EDWIN BOTH eyed the clock with nervous apprehension. It was half an hour before the last of three night shifts was due to end, and they were keeping their fingers crossed that the tedious night would end quietly. It was not to be.

"CornAmb 72 from Control, over,"

"This is 72," said Jack. He was still under probation so had yet to take his Emergency Response Driving course up at Bodmin. He was taking care of the radio instead.

"72 proceed on red to Trelassick Farm, Kestle Mill. Farm vehicle overturned query driver trapped," Edwin already had the vehicle moving by the time the dispatcher had said those magic words "proceed on red," That was the all clear to use Edwin's driving skills to the limit and get to Trelassick Farm as soon as possible.

"72 mobile from Carland Cross to Trelassick Farm, Kestle Mill," Jack and Edwin's combined local knowledge would get them to Kestle Mill but locating the exact farm would need the OS map. They hurtled down the A30 in the Mercedes emergency ambulance, and soon Edwin was indicating left for the A3076 for Kestle Mill when just in time Jack said, "Straight on Edwin, there's a better route down the next turn off. I've found the farm, and it's best we take the 3058," Edwin cancelled the indicators and pushed on down the A30. Arriving at the turn-off on the A3058 Edwin double de-clutched and with engine roaring expertly swung the vehicle around the loop that took them off the dual carriageway and onto the side-road.

"Second right and then first left," said Jack and with Edwin working the gearbox hard they accelerated up the hill and around the twisting corners hoping to goodness that there was nothing larger than a small car coming the other way. Edwin had kept a clean accident-free record for more years than he cared to remember and seemed at times to have a sixth sense about what lay around the next corner.

They took a sharp turn and came to an abrupt halt behind a couple of cars parked carelessly in the middle of the road. On the far side of the mini traffic jam Jack could see the curious sight of a tractor with all four wheels pointing skywards. The huddle around the tractor parted as they approached the familiar sound of moaning and wailing.

The farmer had somehow managed to hit the Cornish hedge. The scars on the roadside gave an inkling of how he had managed to flip his tractor upside-down.

Edwin knelt beside the semi-conscious driver. A passer-by was cradling his head. The stranger must have been as stunned as Jack by the gory sight before them. The tractor was equipped with two steel plates beside the driving position. They formed the attachment points for the front-loader, and one of these had brutally ripped open the farmer's right thigh. It was laid open to the bone and with the weight of the tractor on top of him the driver was firmly pinned to the road.

Edwin was quickly into his usual routine and asked the victim his name. There was no response. The man cradling him said with a trembling voice,

"'tis Bert, Bert Thompson, from Trelassick," in a voice breaking with emotion. Bert's terrible wound was covered in the black oil draining from an engine and gearbox that was never designed to be upside down.

The stench was toxic and added to the discomfort of those gathered around the scene. The sound of Fire Brigade sirens slowly increased in intensity as Edwin made a risk assessment and decided that, despite the extent of his injuries, possible fractures to femur and pelvis, Bert's vital signs were holding up. There was no indication of damage to the femoral artery although it must have been very close.

Blood loss was apparently minimal, but it is hard to assess a patient covered in sump oil. Bert's luck, if you can in any way describe his situation as 'lucky', appeared to be 'in', but in his semi-conscious state he wasn't in a position to realise just how lucky he had been. Edwin was busy completing his assessment. No head injury to speak off, just a graze. No apparent spinal injuries and by carefully feeling each neck vertebra Edwin made sure there was no damage to this critical area.

With a hissing of air brakes and scattering of onlookers, the Fire Brigade pulled their massive fire truck into the small space beside the upturned tractor. Shortly afterwards the Watch Chief arrived next to Edwin, they exchanged professional niceties before discussing the strategy for moving the tractor. With no lifting gear beyond that used in mine-shaft rescues, it was decided to position the tender so that its winch could be used to roll the tractor away from Bert. He would then be gently moved to safety, placed on the 'scoop' stretcher and his wound assessed in more detail. Edwin looked at his watch, six-thirty. Edwin knew that HeliMed, the Cornwall Air Ambulance, did not come on duty until seven a.m. by which time he hoped to be well on the way to A&E.

"Give Control a sitrep on the radio please Jack, I'll put a line in and give him some Nubain. I'll need the scoop, O2 and the extra-large GP dressing from the Main Pack. It will be a wrap and pack and on the road as quickly as possible. A&E will need our general assessment plus we need an orthopaedic surgeon at the ready as soon as possible," Jack did as he was asked, sending the message and bringing the equipment to Edwin's side. Bert's wife was sobbing quietly with a neighbour's arm around her shoulder. Jack went over to her.

"Mrs Thompson?" she nodded. "Bert's had a bit of a nasty knock I'm afraid, but from what we can see it looks worse than it is and he's holding up well. We'll soon have him back at Treliske Hospital, and he'll get the best treatment possible from the surgeons up there,"

"'t was that bloody ol' tractor of 'is," she said between sobs, "tis a wreck. Steering's all wobbly an' 'e drives it too fast,"

At that very moment, PC Tom Henderson arrived in a patrol car with a colleague that Jack didn't recognise.

"Hello Inspector," said Henderson momentarily confused by the familiar face in an unfamiliar uniform.

"It's just 'Jack' these days, Tom," said Jack with mild embarrassment and slapped him on the shoulder.

"Okay sir, what's going on here?" Jack explained the situation and asked if Tom could clear away the vehicles that were preventing the Ambulance getting out of the lane and then take care of the mess they would leave behind.

With blue lights flashing, headlights blazing and the sirens wailing they left the scene. The body language of Edwin's Mercedes was dynamic and purposeful. Somehow it was as if the ambulance had a functioning vascular system and the adrenalin was now flowing through its veins giving Edwin the 'oomph' to turn the three-tonne vehicle into a sports car.

The extra-long night shift took its toll, and Jack arrived home exhausted at ten o'clock. Without ceremony, he rolled into bed, curtains drawn and alarm clock set for five p.m. He knew that he would wake before then as the unnatural sleep-cycle that comes with three days of night-shift was a real killer. Recovery to something like normal would take all of his three days off.

Sure enough, at four in the afternoon Jack's consciousness crawled slowly back into what remained of the day. He sat on the edge of the bed and struggled to wake up completely. Pam made him a cup of tea.

"Can we pencil in lunch with Mum and Dad tomorrow?" she asked, handing him one of his favourite chocolate digestives, "they quite fancy a carvery down at the Norway Inn. It's usually good food down there,"

"Sure," said Jack, the word spoken as enthusiastically as he could muster in his semi-comatose state. He always liked visiting their local pubs. The Norway Inn was named for the many ships from the Norwegian ports that had brought in timber for pit props and exported the highly-prized tin ingots to Europe and beyond. Back in those days, Perranarworthal was close to the heart of the tin mining and iron works industries. The nearby village of Devoran had been a thriving harbour but had now silted up. It was now just a resting place for those yachts and small boats that could live in amongst the shallow waters and mud banks and cope with the fluctuation of the tides.

The remains of the massive ironworks complex at Perran Foundry sat darkly on the western side of the Estuary, looking damp and mysterious and covered in lichen. Back in the 1700's, it was the largest foundry in the UK, but by the end of the 19th Century it was no longer viable, and iron working ceased.

Lunch with the in-laws would mean that he would need to finish working on the case earlier than he had hoped but as Sundays were deemed by Pam to be 'family days', they got together with her parents whenever this was possible.

Saturdays were, whenever possible, Pam's baking days and he now sat at his desk with a cup of coffee and the remains of a large slice of her lemon drizzle cake. Fuel for a mind that faced a challenging task ahead. He was busy at the PC, downloading the copies he made of Sidney's files. He sat, staring at page after page, making notes as he went.

It appeared that forensics had all but finished their work. Some of the tests involved growing cultures from swabs that were used to check samples for DNA. This experimental procedure would take another week or so according to the memos in Sidney's file. He wished that the originals were available for him to analyse but unless and until he could find a way into 'HOLMES' he would have to rely on Sidney's copious notes.

The SOCOs examination of the area close to the edge of the woods overlooking the patio at Tremayne House had revealed a sapling with marks that indicated it was used as a rest by the shooter. The sapling was three metres in from the boundary, 100mm thick and had scarring that would suggest that the shooter was average height and had used a strap to bind the weapon to the tree in military sniper fashion. Minute samples of DNA were found on the tree, and it was these that were undergoing further tests.

There were no signs of entry or passage through the woods despite weeks of searching. The outer boundary fence had no scars or tell-tale marks so how he, or she, climbed over the fence was a mystery. The shooter may have arrived at night but must have left in daylight. There was one sighting, about the right time of day, of a man cycling near Ruthernbridge. He was described as having an olive complexion and 'athletic' physique and had a rucksack on his back.

Jack came across Sidney's notes on the ballistic report. The bullet, or more accurately the fragments of the bullet, had been retrieved from Desmond during the autopsy and tests revealed that it was an Eley Subsonic, Hollow Point .22 calibre. The fragments were not going to help to identify the weapon that fired it for they were damaged extensively and nothing useful could be determined from them save the make and calibre.

The comments made by a firearms expert proposed the American Ruger or Russian made SV-99 Sniper Rifle developed from the BI-7 competition version popular with cross-country biathlon skiers. The shot was fired from 110 yards on a day when there was a light, gusty breeze and probably hit exactly what the assassin was aiming at, Duffy's skull. It had to be a 'head-shot for the lethality of the weapon and bullet at that range was at the limits of kill probability. The shooter was either very lucky or very good.

The use of the silencer and a subsonic bullet indicated that the attacker put a higher priority on stealth than he did on making sure his shot was fatal. The use of a hypersonic ammunition would have pretty well guaranteed a kill at that range, but the noise would have given the game away big time, silencer or no silencer. Whoever fired the shot must have been supremely confident in his ability to kill with a single shot but nervous about making a clean getaway.

There were precious few clues and even less in the way of leads. No wonder Sidney had set off for Glasgow, probably more in hope than expectation. There were a couple of photos of the body, and these confirmed that the note had been removed by the time the SOCOs had started work.

Jack pondered the curious note once more. It had, for him, assumed the special status as the one decent clue in the whole case. However, now that it had disappeared, he was the only one to have seen it and therefore the only one able to understand its significance. He would be able to comprehend it a lot better if he could work out the answer to the question of how it had got there and what it had meant? Perhaps equally significant would be the answer to the question 'where was it now,'?

It seemed to him that 'SILENCE IS GOLDEN = £££££' would be a reference to payment for keeping quiet about something that someone knew about Des, but what? It didn't make sense to send Des that note if the blackmailer then had him assassinated. Why shoot the golden goose? Was there a third party involved? Was there a 'Gloria' somewhere related to the assassin? If so, who could that be? Jack had never seen or heard anything like it before in his entire career. It was a riddle to end all riddles but the more puzzled he became, the more his detective's mind fed on the challenge.

'ANOTHER FIVE WOULD DO NICELY.' What was that all about? Another £5, £500 or maybe £5,000. No, those small sums didn't fit in with murder. Another £500,000 would certainly put it in the big league, and another £5 million pounds would definitely get someone's attention, but whose? Okay so maybe it was blackmail. Was Des having an affair? Jack sifted through the notes on the witness statements until he found Sidney's comments on what Mary had said. Her morning routine was detailed, and there was nothing out of the ordinary. She was as clean as a whistle, but something caught his eye.

He scribbled the word GLORIA on his pad. The police had apparently carried out a family profile on Mary and turned up the fact that her niece, Gloria Curnow, was a twenty-five-year-old Solicitor's Clerk. She lived in St Columb Major and worked in Newquay. Jack knew that Des must have a 'thing' for younger women. Margaret was, after all, 18 years his junior. Could the FOR GLORY stamp refer to this Gloria?

Margaret's witness statement apparently revealed that she had asked Mary to lay the table on the patio because Des had told her that he wanted to have breakfast outside again. Margaret had collected the newspapers from the hall table; Mary had taken them out of the box at the main gate on her way in at eight o'clock together with any mail that had arrived in the morning post or had been left from the previous day if the post had been late. She routinely placed the papers on the hall table and the mail in the rack. That day there had been the usual Saturday Telegraph and Friday's Glasgow Herald. It appeared that Des had a soft spot for his home town. There had been no mail on that day. Mary had laid the table at about nine o'clock, but Des had not appeared until about half past nine.

He had been seen to be carrying some work papers and what seemed like an unopened plain white envelope with only the name 'Mr D. Duffy' and no address upon it. What on earth was Sidney playing at? It was there in black and white – Mary had seen the envelope and mentioned it in her statement. Sidney was definitely losing it, probably with a little 'help' from Jenkins. The witness statement by the newsagent revealed that they organised the postal subscription for the Glasgow Herald and that each day they would remove the address wrapper and place it with Desmond's Telegraph.

There was no mention of an envelope being found at the scene. That was strange. If the note had been delivered in an envelope, where was the envelope now, why no forensics on it? It could only mean one thing; both the envelope and the note had been taken. He desperately wanted to see the detailed forensic reports, but again he came up against the difficulties of getting into HOLMES.

That anomaly pointed the finger at Neil Jenkins for the witness statements were clear, the envelope's existence had been recorded, but there was nothing in Sidney's notes to indicate that it had been found at the scene of the crime. Dear old Sidney had missed that vital clue. Now he had a few ideas to go on. The envelope was one to think about. Mary's niece was another. If there was evidence that implicated Gloria Curnow in an affair with Des, then maybe Margaret found out. That put her in the frame too. 'Damn', he thought to himself, all that work and he still ended up with the same three possibilities.

That was enough research for the day. Pam would nag him about this studying and remind him that he should have his head in his medical textbooks and work towards his Ambulance Tech's qualification. The all-important assessment at the end of his probationary period was on the horizon.

After supper, Jack sat in his armchair sipping a cup of coffee and thinking about the meaning of the note. He decided that the rubber stamp could not refer to a person for who would go to all the trouble of making a rubber stamp that used the abbreviated form of a lady's name? But in his opinion, it did have to be blackmail. It was the only thing that made any sense. He was convinced that Neil Jenkins was involved up to his neck. What he needed was more proof.

CHAPTER 7

Sunday, 11th June, 08.00
Lower Spargo Cottage, Perranarworthal

JACK WAS ON A high when he woke up. Pam and Josh were still fast asleep, so he decided to grab a bowl of cereal and went back upstairs to the office, switched on the PC and set about sifting Sidney's files for information about the security at Tremayne House. It had been bugging Jack all night that there should be a log of any CCTV recordings, provided, of course, that Desmond had been sensible enough to keep his system serviceable. If there were coverage of the patio, then it would show who tampered with the note.

His luck was in for the original logs were filed along with Sidney's notes. He found sections labelled 'House 1', 'House 2', 'Service Entrance' and 'Main Entrance'. A quick perusal of the logs revealed a big fat zero. Jack noticed however that the logs all stopped at the same time –10.08 a.m. That was thirteen minutes after the shot was fired and just before Jack and Edwin arrived. That meant that the period when the note disappeared was not recorded and the moment when Jack examined it had also been cut. At the top of the page containing the log of entries was a space for the officer carrying out the analysis to put his name and describe the camera location. Jack's eye fell on the box marked 'Name'. It was signed by 'DS Jenkins'.

Now Jack was pretty sure that it was Neil who had taken the note and the envelope.

Pam was up and about and busy tidying up in readiness for her parents' visit. Jack would not describe his wife as particularly 'house-proud' but his mother-in-law, a retired nursing sister of the old school, certainly was.

Lunch at the Norway Inn was, as usual, excellent. Suitably replete the family walked back to the cottage where Larry and Jack would chat for a while before falling asleep in the armchairs. Pam and her mum would wander around the garden admiring the bluebells and analysing the success or otherwise of the large assortment of flowers and shrubs. Pam would dutifully hang on every word of advice that would inevitably flow from this gardening oracle.

Josh amused himself on his computer and caught up on the homework he was supposed to have ready for the morning.

Teatime was homemade cake, and endless cups of tea poured from the 'best' teapot and served in the 'best' teacups.

When the in-laws finally took their leave, there was an overwhelming feeling of togetherness that brought home the meaning of 'family'.

Waking from a sound sleep, Jack sat up in bed, took in the time on his alarm clock, and marvelled at how his body clock seemed, at last, to be in perfect time with the real one. It was seven fifty-five. He leant across and cancelled the alarm just moments before it went off. Last night he had had time to think about the 'case' and had been pre-occupied with working out what to do about Jenkins. If it was Neil, what on earth could the motive be for taking the note? Was he involved with blackmailing Des?

After attending to some chores that Pam had lined up, he waited for her to come in from work and they had dinner together. Jack then made a lame excuse about checking his e-mail and went upstairs to the office, fired up his PC and contemplated his next move.

He checked his mail. There was a message from his eldest son Nathan who was away on a wildlife expedition in Canada. He printed it out for Pam to read. He wondered if there were any hidden treasures in Neil's e-mails and decided to take a look. After half an hour of sifting through Neil's office e-mail, he found what he had been looking for, his personal e-mail address.

With that information, Jack was able to put some of his intelligent software to good use and hack into Neil's personal e-mail account.

Very soon he was pouring over the contents of Neil's inbox. Bingo! There at the top of the list was a mail with the cryptic message, 'time to collect my goods. Usual place 10.00 tomorrow, bring them with you'. Jack checked the timestamp on the message. It was sent today so the rendezvous would indeed be tomorrow. He went to Neil's 'sent' mailbox and found mail addressed to the unknown sender and received the day after Desmond's murder. It said 'have kept them safe. Do you want them destroyed?' There was a reply from the same address the next day saying, 'keep them safe, I want them back. I'll be in touch.'

It looked like Neil's contact had kept his word, and Jack had found them out just in the nick of time. After a few minutes contemplation, he knew what he needed to do. He had no idea where the 'usual place' was so the only way he could establish who had sent the message would be to find out where Neil lived, what kind of car he drove and to follow him to the rendezvous.

He went back to the Truro CID folder, downloaded the contents of Neil's files. There should be a 'Next of Kin' form filed somewhere. Sure enough, it was in his personal folder. Jack noted the address: 22, Trevails Crescent, Newquay. He hoped that Neil had not separated from his wife, Patricia. She was the person named on the form.

Jack looked it up using the latest version of the 'AutoRoute' software and sketched out a game plan for the following day. He would take the Thunderbird because the bike would be more flexible than Pam's car and he certainly couldn't use his Jag for fear of being recognised.

He had no idea what car Neil Jenkins drove and had no practical way of finding out. The DVLA and National Police Computers were a 'no-no' unless necessary as they had some new firewalls that Jack's hacking advisor was not confident could be circumvented without sending their surveillance systems into an apoplectic fit. At this stage of the game, it was an unnecessary risk. He was more than happy to keep a very low profile for the time being. Suppressing his natural 'gung-ho' urges was never easy, but after years of learning the hard way, he now knew how to let his head rule his heart.

Cadhay Manor, Ottery St Mary

Sir William paced up and down while Gerard de Beaumont stood passively by and watched as the man who was both his boss and his lover struggled with the difficulties posed by the recent and unfortunate turn of events.

"Yes Gerry, I know that the letter was a mistake but don't fret so, Jenkins has taken care of that,"

"Exactement! So now we 'ave to take care of Jenkins," It was a statement of fact rather than a question. "Are you sure that 'e knows where the Tank Museum is?"

"Yes, it was the place he chose for our very first meet. Where the bastard took five thousand pounds from me. He thought it rather amusing apparently,"

"Yes, very droll, your regimental alma mater, funny ha ha. I wish you had told me about that at the time. It would have given me great pleasure to stick my pistol in 'is mouth and blow 'is brains out,"

"If you had we would not have him in our pocket now, would we? It's never a bad thing to have a policeman on our side,"

"On our side? Don't forget that bastard 'as got something on you, 'e found you in the toilets with a rent boy, so we have that hanging over us so long as he is around.

"Look, Gerry, it was a moment of madness, and you know how it is. One gets sudden urges, sudden needs and, well, I couldn't help myself,"

"That is in the past, forget it, move on, we 'ave important things to do. You must get that damn letter and its envelope back. I simply don't understand why you even sent 'im that note in the first place,"

"I sent the note to his office by messenger. I never thought for one minute that he wouldn't open it as soon as he got it. How was I supposed to know that he would take the blessed thing home instead of opening it right away? When I got that damn blackmail note I just had to reply immediately, I was furious,"

"Oui, alors, you replied by signing the note and licking your DNA all over the fucking envelope, Merde! Stupide!"

"At least I had the foresight to tear off the original letter, and I didn't exactly sign it,"

"As good as,"

"Let's not fight; it upsets me,"

"Ok, but you sort this mess out yourself. I'll muddy-up the plates on your car, and you go down to Bovington and get the bloody note and envelope back then take a match to them as soon as you can,"

"Leave it to me, Gerry. I'll get them back, and then I do hope we can put this behind us?"

"I'm not so sure we can do that. Not sure at all. I know you like 'aving the tame policeman to play your games with, but I think 'e 'as outlived 'is usefulness. 'e knows too much. 'e certainly knows that you and I were involved in getting rid of that Glaswegian piece of shit,"

"Jenkins doesn't know it was you who shot him. Believe me, Gerry I have never even mentioned you to him. I've kept your name out of this completely,"

"Don't be naïve. You don't think 'e believes that you did it, do you? 'e's a policeman. It's 'is job to know about us and I'm sure 'e does. Non, we 'ave to work out 'ow and when to remove 'im from the picture altogether,"

"Let's talk about this when you are in a better mood, Gerry. We can go to 'Oliver's' for lunch and I'll treat you to your favourite, 'fruits de mer'. You know you love it there. We need to sort out the guest list for our Summer Garden Party. Last year's was such a success," Gerard let his shoulders fall, a sign of resignation. He smiled a crooked smile and nodded agreement. This man he loved and cared for could be such a stupid, selfish bastard one minute and generous to a fault the next.

"You always win in the end,"

"That's why you love me, Gerry?" Sir William took him by the elbow and directed him towards the stairway. Gerard was a ruggedly handsome man, a little taller than Sir William, olive skinned, dark haired and with an oriental influence to his otherwise European features. Many of their friends and acquaintances found their unusual and enigmatic relationship difficult to comprehend. They each seemed able to take on the role of dominant personality as the situation demanded, always, apparently, without offending the other.

CHAPTER 8

Tuesday, 13th June, 06.00 – Newquay

TREVAILS CRESCENT WAS OPPOSITE the cemetery on Rialton Road. It was a dead-end and this made Jack's task a lot easier for he could find a spot nearby to observe the entrance to the Crescent and wait until Neil departed.

At six a.m. Jack parked his bike out of sight inside the entrance to the cemetery and found a vantage point behind the perimeter hedge that provided cover yet allowed a good view of cars emerging from the Crescent. It was just as well Jack had made an early start for after no more than ten minutes Neil Jenkins appeared at the wheel of a silver Ford Focus. Jack put on his helmet and set off, keeping far enough back to minimise the chance of being spotted.

Three and a half hours later, and much to Jack's surprise and relief the journey came to an end. They had arrived at Bovington Tank Museum, in Dorset. The trip had been uneventful save for the roadworks outside Dorchester where he was caught by a set of temporary traffic lights and considered himself lucky to catch up with Neil as he had very nearly set off in pursuit of another silver Focus that had appeared on that road. He was very glad he had chosen the Thunderbird and not Pam's car. In such circumstances, it was a relatively straightforward task to move through the remains of the rush-hour traffic. The day was brightening as the Ford Focus approached the Museum complex. Jack paused opposite the entrance to the car park. It was almost empty. It was a quarter to ten and the Museum had yet to open its doors. Jack watched Neil park on the far side, turn off his engine and wind down the driver's window. He felt very exposed but thought the best tactic was to act casually, lean the bike on its side stand and to sit nonchalantly on it. He could not take his helmet off for fear of recognition but lifted the visor to make the wait more comfortable.

At two minutes past ten a black, late model Range Rover, splattered in mud, cruised passed him and into the car park. The mud had all the hallmarks of having been 'applied' rather than 'acquired' as it had almost entirely obscured the registration.

Jack's police instincts suddenly had the hairs on the back of his neck standing up. Sure enough, the Range Rover pulled alongside Neil's car, facing the opposite direction. The deeply tinted window descended and a figure wearing dark glasses collected the envelope handed across by Neil's unseen hand. The Range Rover window closed and it immediately eased away out of the car park.

It disappeared behind the Museum buildings and Jack started the Thunderbird and set off in pursuit. The Range Rover eventually found its way to the A352 and headed north. The journey was quite straight forward, following the A35 then the A354 towards Salisbury. Everything went well until Jack, feeling the need to try to get something from the mud-splattered rear number-plate, closed the gap.

All he could make out were the first two letters, 'WA' but the position of the letters on the plate told him it was a personalised registration.

No sooner had Jack made this discovery than the target spun around a roundabout twice. That manoeuvre caught Jack out. The driver was no fool after all and was carrying out a cunning plan straight from the villain's handbook, designed to reveal anyone who might be following. Jack rode straight on but was suddenly surprised to find the Range Rover large in his rear-view mirrors and approaching him rapidly from behind. With the roar of its V8 it kept coming and nearly made contact but a swift twist of the throttle meant that he could accelerate safely away.

He had a sudden burst of adrenalin as he realised that the hunter had become the hunted. His seventy-horse power T-Bird quickly allowed him to pull away and at the next roundabout he tried the same trick and was able to get back on the tail of the Range Rover once more. That was the signal for the driver of the Range Rover to freak out and accelerate away. The driver was behaving like a madman and using some crazy overtaking manoeuvres to try and shake Jack from his tail.

The target set off westwards towards Wilton and approached the traffic lights at the 'T' junction with the A3094 close to Quidhampton. At first, the driver slowed in response to the red light but with two vehicles ahead of him he accelerated around the outside of the queue and crossed the junction, surprising a driver emerging onto the main road.

The Range Rover clipped the front of the innocent pick-up who tried to take late evasive action but lost control in the process, spun around and headed straight for the pavement. Audrey Hampton was, at that moment guiding her pushchair with baby Michael sound asleep inside and holding the hand of her nine-year-old daughter Virginia. She looked up to see the blur of a bright red pickup hurtling towards her.

11.00 – Wiltshire Police HQ, Devizes

Sergeant Andy Roberts was the Police Helicopter coordinator for the day and was listening keenly to the exchange that was going on between the ground units and the force helicopter. The officers in charge of the mission that day intended to take out a drugs gang. They had been planning the operation for two years and that morning it was close to the critical conclusion of an enormous amount of work.

The Wiltshire Air Support Unit was unique in the UK. It was a Police helicopter that doubled as an Air Ambulance and generally carried a paramedic as a member of the crew. The theory was that 50% of something is a better option than 100% of nothing so for both the Wiltshire Police and the Wiltshire Ambulance Service a compromise was the only solution for neither had funds to support their helicopter. The problem with this solution was always the danger of conflicting priorities. The Air Support helicopter was currently the only unit with 'eyeball' on the drug-dealer's Mercedes 4x4.

Paramedic 'Dusty' Miller was back at Wiltshire Ambulance HQ. He should have been on board the helicopter but had been told 'not today'. He would be on ground duties instead due to a prior Police commitment. It wasn't the first time and until the Ambulance Service could afford a helicopter, it wouldn't be the last.

11.50 – Junction of the A36 and the A3094

The minute Jack saw the Range Rover take off through the red light his instincts were those of the 'thief-taker' policeman but after a moment's reflection he was back to being an ambulance technician. He went back to the accident parked his bike beside the pavement, took out the first aid kit he carried in the side-box and hurried to join the group of onlookers gathering beside the tangled mess of pick-up, pushchair, broken brick wall and mangled bodies.

The pungent odours of oil and coolant on hot metal and the stench of burning rubber added to a cocktail of aromas and wafted across the site with a timely gust of wind. Jack picked his way through the debris to the side of the woman.

A pale and shaking man in carpenter's overalls declared that he was the driver of the pick-up and started nervously and tearfully confessing his sorrow at not being able to avoid the innocent trio of passers-by. The pushchair was smashed beyond recognition and Jack took a quick look at the contents. He quickly realised that with his skull distorted that way, baby Michael was obviously beyond help. He had taken the full force of the pick-up and been crushed against the brick wall. He looked up at the faces that had gathered around and saw a man with a mobile phone against his ear."999, Ambulance?" Jack asked questioningly. The man nodded and responded by asking, "where exactly are we?"

"A36," said another member of the group, "Wilton Road,"

Jack moved his attention to the two remaining members of the Hampton family both of whom were still in the land of the living, if only just. A quick look at the woman told Jack he was dealing with a compound fractured left tibia and fibula, possible fractured left femur and possible pelvic damage as well. She had taken a bang on the head but was beginning to regain consciousness. Her face was swollen, and she was partially trapped under the front of the pick-up. She was lying on top of daughter Virginia and had protected her from the direct impact, but a close look at the young girl revealed the tell-tale signs of severe head injury. She was bleeding from the ears and nose, and one pupil was wide-open.

The wailing of sirens preceded the arrival of the Police, and the Fire

Brigade and a PC in white cap and high-visibility jacket soon joined them. Jack looked up at the Traffic Cop and introduced himself, "Jack Mawgan, off-duty ambulance-tech,"

"That's a bit of luck," replied the policeman, "the ambulance is on the way, but it will be a while yet, it's got to come from the other side of Salisbury. Been one of those days. What have we got?" Jack opened up his first aid kit. It was evident to the watching policeman that he was well prepared. Like many of his colleagues, he always carried this cut-down version of their first response equipment with him. It's not often that you find yourself at the scene of an accident or incident but when you do, it's no good having the skills if you don't have the equipment. Jack kept one in the Jag and one in the side-box of the bike. He looked up to see the white helmeted figure of the Fire Chief.

"This one's trapped by the bricks and the front of the truck," he gestured towards Audrey, "severe leg fractures on the left side, can't see the right yet, semi-conscious, breathing okay but losing blood. We need to haul the pick up out of the way so we can gain access fast. The girl has a serious head injury; do you have an Air Ambulance in these parts?"

"Yes, but it's off-line today," the policeman replied.

"Bloody typical," said Jack, "look, give me a hand here," He pulled a cervical collar from his bag and began to place it around Audrey's neck. Jack had only six months of training, and he was frantically trying to recall what Edwin would have done in similar situations. First, check the patient is in a safe place. Can't do much about that until we get the truck moved. Then A, B, C was the mnemonic... Airway – clear, Breathing – check, use mouth-to-mouth if necessary, Circulation – check pulse stop any bleeding.

He took a look at Virginia. Her breathing was slow and steady with a slight gurgling. He knew he needed to get to her quickly; her airway sounded like it was compromised. It's easy for unconscious people to swallow their tongue.

The Fire Chief was busy organising the removal of the pick-up from Audrey's right leg. "Chief," yelled Jack, "what medical kit have you got on board?"

"Usual stuff," he replied, "I'll get the bag,"

"Bless him," Jack said to himself, "let's hope there's some useful equipment carried by the Wiltshire Fire and Rescue Service,"

Jack was now desperate to put a line into each of the two survivors for their venous systems would be closing down and every passing minute would make it harder to find a good vein. Jack had only been taught the protocol a few weeks before and had very little practice at what was a tricky procedure.

He took a grey Venflon from his pouch and inspected the back of Audrey's hands. The left one had veins that he could just discern; the right one was flat as a pancake. The left it would be. He cleaned the area with a sterile wipe and as carefully as he could manage, crouched awkwardly in the wreckage and slipped the needle into the vein. 'Beginner's luck', thought Jack as a small flush of blood in the cannula signalled his success. He taped it securely in place and gratefully received a large bag of 'stuff' from the Fire Chief.

Inspecting the contents, he found two infusion bags of saline and a pack of cervical collars in amongst the dressings and assorted first aid equipment.

"Excellent," said Jack and set about checking the use-by date on the saline bag before hooking it up to Audrey's cannula. He looked up at the people watching him work. "Hold that," he said to the person nearest and handed a middle-aged man in a suit the saline bag. "Hold that waist high until I get back to you,"

His attention then turned to Virginia. He had already registered that with such a bad head injury he was not going to be able to do anything much to help beyond protecting her spine and airway.

He was worried about the mother; she would bleed out if he didn't do something to restore her volume quickly. Where was the ambulance? He needed some help.

The nine-year-old girl reminded him of that dreadful day last year when he wasn't able to do anything to help. There were times when the horrific detail of that day would haunt him. He began to shake as he recalled staring disbelievingly into the sightless eyes of that young girl at Goss Moor, her nose no longer recognisable as a nose, her mouth no longer identifiable as a mouth and her jaw hanging loosely down. The hole where her mouth should be was just a gurgling mass of blood, teeth and torn flesh. He knew she was choking but did not know what to do about it. His blood boiled when he thought once more about Neil Jenkins. He had escaped scot-free despite very nearly causing that girls death. He was snapped out of his daze by the sound of distant sirens wailing. "The ambulance, thank God," He went to daughter Virginia as at last the Rescue Crew began to move the pick-up. He moved her neck carefully backwards a little. The gurgling was replaced by the sound of low but steady breathing. He almost burst into tears with relief. This time it would be different, he would not panic, this time he was ready.

Two ambulance men in green uniforms stepped purposefully through the chaos and arrived next to him. He introduced himself and briefed them on the casualties. The paramedic was John Farnell and his colleague Peter Rowland. Together they started to work to stabilise Audrey. He checked with John that it was okay to put a cannula into Virginia. He took a quick look and said, "You'll be lucky to get a line into her hand, and the veins are too small and barely visible. Try the arm," he pointed to the vein in the inside of the elbow-joint. Jack's first attempt was a failure. "No luck," said Jack in John's direction, "I think I've compromised this site now. Will you have a go? We've only got one place left?" he said, pointing to Virginia's other arm.

He felt he had let the youngster down by his failure and watched carefully as John put a strap around the upper arm just above the elbow, smacked the vein area with the back of his hand a couple of times, wiped it clean with an antiseptic pad and tried a smaller blue Venflon... it worked. John then took the saline drip from the mother and connected it to Virginia's cannula. Jack looked quizzically, and John fished around in his pack and brought out a bag of the 3.5% colloid solution Haemaccel. Seeing Jack's expression, he said, "the girl doesn't need fluids right now, but the saline will keep the line open for any drug therapy needed when she gets to the hospital. The mother needs a bit more than saline at the moment Jack; she's lost a lot of blood. This Haemaccel will boost her blood volume. Her right leg is a query double fracture but not open, her vital signs aren't too good, and she's almost certainly bleeding internally. When we've got her packaged, and in the wagon, we'll come back for the young'un and take her too,"

"Where to?"

"Salisbury A&E," replied John.

"Have you got neuro there?"

"No, it's at Frenchay, Bristol," said John "the girl will be assessed and repacked for Bristol once the consultant gives the OK,"

"But look, she needs neuro NOW," said Jack beginning to get agitated at the prospect of unnecessary delays. Like most districts in the UK, the

Ambulance Service personnel are not allowed to select the destination hospital. They have to go directly to the nearest A&E even if the patient will then be sent on to a specialist unit. Ambulance personnel were not deemed qualified to fully assess the patient's needs.

"Yes Jack, I agree, but that, unfortunately, is not our call," Unhappy with the prospect of another nine-year-old girl dying Jack turned to look for the Traffic Policeman who was busy sorting out the flow of vehicles around the accident site.

"Officer," yelled Jack. The policeman came over and bent to hear Jack's message. "What sort of car have you got?"

"Volvo V70-T5 Estate, why?" he said.

"John, how about I take the daughter straight to Frenchay in the police car, and you take the mother to Salisbury?"

"As the senior guy on scene Jack I am telling you it's against the rules but of course you're not a Wiltshire Ambulance Service employee. Feel free to ignore me, but if you do so, in front of these witnesses, it will be on your own head. I'm certainly not going to stop you because I think you are right, but it won't do your career much good when it gets back to your HQ," John was entirely reasonable, and he needed Jack to appreciate that he could not sanction something that would clearly break the rules and land them both in hot water.

"Officer," Jack turned to the policeman, "clear out the back of your car, we're taking this girl to Bristol for vital neuro-surgery. If we don't get there in time, she may well be a goner,"

The Police service has a primary duty to preserve life and limb so without hesitation the officer and his colleague set off to turn their Volvo into an impromptu ambulance. "Can we use your 'scoop'?" asked Jack, referring to the lightweight stretcher-like device that was used to move injured people off the floor and onto the gurney.

"Sure," said John, "we'll make do with a carry-sheet,"

Jack went to the back of the ambulance and found the 'scoop'. Returning to the scene, he watched as John and Peter carefully lifted a splinted and collared Audrey onto the gurney trolley and wheeled her away. Jack then had full access to Virginia for the first time. With the help of a policeman, he placed the two halves of the scoop around the small frame of the little girl and clicked them together so that now she could be lifted and carried to the waiting Police car.

When they arrived beside the Volvo, there was a mound of equipment left beside it, traffic cones and 'POLICE-ACCIDENT' signs and boxes of kit were temporarily abandoned. They placed the girl inside, and the fireman who had been holding the bag of saline handed it to Jack who was now crouched in his motorcycle leathers and trying to find a comfortable seat where no seat existed. John came rushing over clutching a 'D' size oxygen cylinder and a mask.

"Give her this," he said, "there should be enough to see you to Frenchay... I've set the flow. We'll take care of the little one," nodding towards the pushchair. "Off you go and good luck," Jack placed the mask on Virginia's mouth and nose put the elastic strap around the back of her head.

"Is that your bike?" asked a newly arrived Police Inspector who stuck his head into the driver's window.

"Yes," said Jack.

"Then I guess this is your helmet," he said holding up Jack's crash hat.

"Don't worry we'll take care of both. I'll be swapping them for a statement in due course,"

The Volvo driver climbed into his seat, flicked on the switches for the sirens and flashing lights on and set off. Under normal circumstances, the journey would take one and a half hours. It was now going to be completed in 40 minutes. It turned out to be a memorable 40 minutes in which the driving skills of the police driver, honed by years of high-speed pursuit driving, impressed the hell out of Jack. The Volvo turned out to be amazingly quick and handled like a sports car.

With the acrid smell of hot brakes filling their nostrils they arrived in dramatic fashion at the doors of A&E. The hospital team had received the details over the police radio and were ready and waiting. They unloaded Virginia onto a trolley and wheeled her into the receiving area with Jack briefing them as they went.

An hour later, sipping a cup of tea with his 'hijacked' Police crew in A&E reception, Jack called Pam and gave her an outline of events and promised a fuller account when he got back home. He checked his watch. It was two-thirty and it had already been a long day. There was more to come. Before he could tackle the long ride home he would have to return to Wilton, then a visit to Salisbury Police Station to make a statement and maybe a bite to eat in their canteen.

Jack was unable to give the Police any details about the Range Rover beyond the possibility that the first two letters of the registration were 'WA' and explained his presence in the area by telling a story about visiting a non-existent relative.

At ten o'clock that evening an exhausted Jack pulled off his leathers and told his tale to Pam and Josh who had both waited up to hear about his adventures. A sanitised version in front of Josh was later expanded upon when Jack was lying in bed with Pam. "I hope you're not going to let that murdering bastard get away with it," she said with feeling.

"Let's sleep on it and work out what to do next,"

When Pam arrived home after work, Jack was in the garage. He was tinkering with his motorbike. She made them a cup of tea and prepared her little speech. As Jack dried his hands, she began.

"Are you planning to leave the murder of this child in Wilton to the police?" Jack pulled a face.

"That depends,"

"On what? Don't try and kid me. I know you Jack Mawgan. Right now, you have placed the blame for that crash on your shoulders and you are going to be a bloody misery to live with as long as this is unresolved,"

"Well, I'm not saying that I'm entirely to blame,"

"No, but you will still fuss and fret until this is sorted and your bloody friends in the police force will take forever to sort it even if they care,"

"I'm sure they care, but." His voice faded as he realised where Pam was going.

"You can't leave it like this; I won't let you. You have to use your contacts to track this monster down and hand him over. You're a better detective than any of those bumpkins. Find him; you are no fun when you are strung out like this.

She finally came to him and held him close. He picked her up and walked slowly up the stairs and laid her on the bed, kissing passionately, long and hard while she took off his shirt.

Afterwards, they lay staring at the ceiling for a long time before Pam said, "so what now?"

"I have to see this through then, that bastard killed a young baby yesterday and I have to find out who it was and what this is all about. First things first, have you got any contacts in Frenchay who can check on how the little girl is doing? Maybe Salisbury General as well, we can see if the mother survived?"

"Of course," said Pam. She went to her handbag and took out her little address book. After calling a few friends, she finally had a phone number that would get her through the usual brick wall that halts telephone enquiries in their tracks. The duty Consultant in the ICU told Pam that little Virginia had died of a seizure as soon as they left the CT scanner but the crash team had got her back. The neuro-surgeon had carried out an emergency operation on the area with the blood clot, removed a portion of the skull to relieve the pressure and stopped the internal bleeding around the brain. She was now sedated and looking good for a recovery. No broken bones.

The Frenchay team are liaising with Salisbury to keep mother informed but she is in a bad way and not yet compos-mentis. Jack's assessment was correct. She had fractured all the bones in both legs, cracked the pelvis and was bleeding internally. She was very poorly on arrival at A&E but she was young and strong and so was hanging on in there.

Jack digested the information and smiled quietly to himself. He didn't lose her. It had been close but he hadn't lost her.

"What will you do now?" asked Pam

"If I didn't know before then, I now know for sure that Jenkins is bent but I have no idea what he is up to. I need to keep a careful eye on him and see if there were any previous communications with the mysterious Hotmail guy. I also need to talk to one of my old college chums. He's a top IT man in Bristol and will help me unlock some valuable information. I must find out who owns that Range Rover and then try and put the pieces of the jigsaw together. I want to get into the DVLA computer to track him or her down but we have to make sure I can do it safely,"

"Do everything you need to do but do it safely, please,"

"I promise,"

He wasn't one hundred percent sure he could deliver on that promise but he would give it his best shot. That evening he was in a dark place and having to live with the fact that his attempt to solve the puzzle had resulted in yet another death. He would have to live with the fact that he had played a part in the accident that killed the baby. He was rattled; his usual buoyant self-confidence had taken a big knock. He was lucky Pam was so positive, she had always been there for him, especially when the chips were down.

18.00 – Cadhay Manor, Ottery St Mary

The early evening bulletins carried the news about the death of a young baby in a collision involving a hit and run. Police circulated the description of the car involved. The world at large now knew that the police were hot on the trail of a black Range Rover.

Sir William had to get rid of the evidence of his involvement. He thought up a scheme that would serve his purpose well and called his Logistics Manager to set the ball rolling. "Is that you Wilson?" asked Sir William…

"Yes, well I apologise for calling you at home but I have an urgent task for you. I've done a deal with an old school chum from Nigeria and he's agreed to buy my Range Rover provided I ship it to him right away,"

19.00 – Lower Spargo Cottage, Perranarworthal

Jack spent the evening in the office and went out to the local phone box a couple of times to make calls that could not be traced back to him. By bedtime he had a list of all the black, post '96 Range Rovers with bespoke registrations beginning with WA. There were eight of them. The registered keepers made an interesting collection:

WAB 2 – Wallace Bullen, Harrogate.
WAC 4 – Western Hydro Corporation, Exeter.
WAP 34 – Wallasey Air Pumps Ltd, The Wirral.
WAR 1 – Bristol Ordnance Company Ltd.
WAS 2 – Jimmy Dandy, Birmingham.
WAT 15 – Walter Arthur Thomas, Kensington, London.
WAV 22 – Newquay Surf Supplies Ltd, Newquay.
WAX 66 – Nottingham Beauty Salons Ltd.

Jack sat up in bed and looked long and hard at the list and began crossing them out one by one. It had taken just a few minutes' contemplation before he had a shortlist of three that were worthy of further examination. Western Hydro Corporation, Bristol Ordnance Company and Newquay Surf Supplies Ltd. These were all within a three-hour ride and could be checked without the need for more than half a day's travel. It would be relatively easy to check if they had any fresh damage or visible repairs but the darkly tinted windows were also a good marker. That degree of tinting was illegal in the UK so it would have been an aftermarket addition rather than a factory-fit.

Pam was quietly snuffling in a deep sleep with her back to him as he rolled on his side and turned off the bedside light.

Thursday, 15th June, 05.45 – Ambulance HQ, Truro

At a quarter to six, Jack drove through the rusting gates of Ambulance HQ at Truro in time to see Edwin leaving his brand-new Rover 75. It was his pride and joy. Jack and Edwin shared an interest in cars and motorbikes, although Edwin was a BMW fan and scorned Jack's obsession with Triumphs. Edwin rode a five-year-old tourer that he and his wife, Heather, used for trips around the continent.

"Get your skates on," said Edwin, waving a tasking sheet, "we've got a burns patient to take to Derriford Hospital,"

'Must be serious,' thought Jack, 'only the bad ones go up to Plymouth.'

"We've got a right one 'ere," said Edwin; glancing down at the task sheet. "He's been involved in a petrol explosion. He's got 80 percent second-degree burns; he's been treated with Flamazine, prepped by A&E and packaged ready for us to collect direct from the main door,"

"Blimey!" said Jack, grabbing his lunchbox and following Edwin out of the door. En route to Plymouth Jack took the patient's notes from their envelope and began to study them.

"Listen to this: arrived at A&E at eight p.m. as a 'walk-in', sat in the queue until the triage nurse noticed that he not only had a beetroot face but beetroot hands and was beginning to shiver violently. It turns out that last night he was working in the pit in his garage doing a repair on the rear suspension of his car because it had failed the MOT. He planned to weld a plate over a hole in the bodywork but the fuel tank was in the way so he syphoned out as much as he could but spilt a 'bit' of petrol in the pit while doing so," He looked up from the paper, "you know what I am going to say next don't you?" Jack carried on without waiting for a reply. "When he struck the first spark with the arc-welder the petrol vapour exploded leaving him standing in the pit completely naked save for his charred underpants," Reading on, he found the tale of woe continued.

"It gets worse. He went back indoors to find a new pair of overalls but, feeling unwell, he went to bed instead. His wife returned from her work at five-thirty and found her husband in bed complaining that he was unwell because he'd had a bit of an accident. It took his wife all night to persuade him to come down to A&E. Quite a story eh!"

"It's unbelievable how stupid some people can be," replied Edwin.

CHAPTER 9

13.00, Ambulance HQ, Truro

SEVEN HOURS AFTER THEY left Jack and Edwin eventually arrived back at the HQ in Truro. They concluded it had been a satisfactory day with only minor incidents to bother them on the way back from Plymouth. The shift finished on schedule, so Jack took the opportunity to top-up his personal first aid kit.

He headed for the stores and presented his pouch to Harry the storeman. Harry disappeared into his 'Aladdin's Cave', replaced the missing items from his stock and returned five minutes later. As he handed the bag to Jack, he beckoned him closer, and in a stage whisper said, "Word around HQ is that you've been in the wars up in Wiltshire and the Chief has pencilled you in for an interview, without coffee mind, come your next shift," Harry tapped the side of his nose in conspiratorial fashion as if he had just passed on the secrets of the nuclear bomb. Jack nodded acknowledgement and thanked him before walking thoughtfully back to his bike. Well, if he were in for a bollocking he would take it on the chin. He would do it all over again now he knew that mother and daughter were still alive.

Back beside his T-Bird, he consulted his map and notes. He had the addresses given for each of the three Range Rover 'keepers' and had tracked down other key addresses associated with each vehicle courtesy of the computer records held at DVLA.

He mapped out a route that would take him through Newquay and up the A30 to addresses around Exeter, then on up to various parts of Bristol.

He went straight to the address for the registered keeper of WAV 22,

Newquay Surf Supplies. He found the Range Rover, but it didn't have tinted windows or have any signs of damage or newly repaired paintwork. One down two to go.

By six p.m. he was approaching Exeter and headed for the offices of Western Hydro. The Range Rover appeared to belong to their CEO, but there in the CEO's parking lot was very new and shiny Seven Series BMW. Jack saw that the registration was WH1. Nothing doing here, it was time to head for Ottery St Mary where this chap Chaloner had a residence called Cadhay Manor, just south of the village.

Arriving at the tree-lined entrance to the Manor, Jack could see a sizeable mansion house about half a mile away. He set off up the driveway, the wheels of the Triumph crunching on the gravel, the purr of the motor invading the tranquillity of the Georgian splendour. There was a parking area in front of the main building. Surrounding the rear of the beautiful mansion house was what looked like garages, stables and other farm buildings. There was not a soul to be seen although there were several parked cars, two tractors and a small van visible as he approached.

The red brick buildings on the South side looked like garages, so he slowly rode around to the side windows and peered inside. It was packed with farm machinery. The next building was an old stone barn that looked more like a stable, but when he peered through the small window he could see the wing mirror and driver's door of a black Range Rover. The nearside headlamp was smashed, and the windows were deeply tinted. He had found it.

"Hey you," said a distant voice, "you over there, what are you up to?" Jack looked up to see a figure in a tweed cap and plus fours gesticulating wildly with a stick. Time to go thought Jack, slipping the T-Bird into first gear and setting off up the driveway at top speed.

The steady hum of the twin cylinder Triumph provided a melodic background to his thinking as he made his way back to the south-west. As he left the Manor, his instinct was to head straight to the nearest nick and send in the heavies to turn the place over, but there was a problem. Every time he worked his way through the conversation he would have with the desk sergeant he stumbled at the part of the story where he described the dead baby. The guilt sat upon his shoulders like a ton weight.

He never did get to finish that conversation but found a good excuse to keep heading home. Anyway, he guessed the car would already be doing a disappearing act. Anyone with enough sense to hide the damn thing wouldn't take the chance of it being found a second time. Not with the scars of yesterday on it anyway. Jack wanted to see Neil Jenkins behind bars, and for that he needed evidence. If he could, he would get Chaloner too. He had stirred the pot, and the dross at the bottom had begun to appear from the murky depths.

Arriving home, too late for dinner, he enjoyed a reheated bowl of Pam's Risotto Porcini. She was an excellent chef, and Jack loved her cooking, perhaps a little too much. Pam told Jack how Josh had pushed it around his plate in feigned disgust. He was a burger and chips man and didn't trust 'foreign muck'. Things changed once he had tasted it and his protestations didn't prevent him from polishing off his plate. Jack smiled as Pam told the story. "So how did it go?" she asked as she cleared away the dishes while Jack made them some coffee.

Pam joined him at the kitchen table, Jack pushed down on the cafetière's filter rod and poured them each a mug of steaming coffee. "Come on then, don't keep me in suspense. I can tell by the grin on your face that you've had a good day,"

"I've found the Range Rover,"

"Where?" said Pam, bursting to hear more.

"Up in Devon, just outside Ottery St Mary, there's an estate there with a big house. The car was inside a shed, one of the farm outbuildings,"

"So, call the cops, slap the chains on him,"

"Yes, well, it's not going to be that simple. I was chased away by some old boy in his golfing kit. He saw me looking in the shed window so when I legged it 'tout suite' he would have put two and two together. Pound to a pinch of salt the car's long gone now,"

"We have to find it. Who owns the big house?"

"Not so much of the 'we'. What it needs is some detective work and guess who is the detective around here,"

"I bow to your superior powers of detection but remember, we're a team so if I can help just yell,"

"OK you're on, you can spell me on the PC and do some searching on the internet when I'm on shift,"

"How about you let me into the secret world of the hacker and show me how you find all this stuff. I bet you've found every porn site going,"

"Not me my darling," he leant across the table and kissed her on the lips, "if there's one thing I don't need it's porn," He winked at her, and she blushed.

"Can I invite you to my office for a little introduction to some naughtiness?"

"Ooh Mr Smithers, you are a one," she said playfully in a mock Dickensian Cockney accent.

Pam was computer literate and understood everything Jack said but with no experience of computer snooping it came as a surprise that national and international assets were so vulnerable. He explained that much of the expertise lay in the software he had acquired from college friends who were now in privileged positions.

"I'm going to take a look at Jenkins' mail again," He showed her how he could get into Neil's personal e-mail account and was about to organise a search for incriminating texts when he saw that Neil had a new mail that he had not yet opened. It was from the same mysterious sender who summoned Neil to the meeting at the Tank Museum. Jack opened it. The text read: 'Rundlestone Pumping station nine p.m. tomorrow.'

"Rundlestone?" said Pam, "where's that?" Jack made the new mail 'unread' before exiting.

"No idea, but I hope Neil checks his mail tonight or he'll be in trouble,"

"How can whoever sent that expect someone like Neil to just drop everything and come running? He's a serving policeman for God's sake," asked Pam innocently.

"Well he's either on the early shift and has given our Hotmail chap that information, or he's pulling the old 'on enquiries' trick," She looked on as Jack did a Google search for 'Rundlestone'. "Let's assume we are not talking about Rundlestone Lodge in Banff, Canada but maybe we are talking about this one, Rundlestone, Dartmoor. That will be it,"

"But what is a pumping station doing up on the Moor?" she asked.

"It's a part of the water distribution system," replied Jack, "sometimes they are for fresh water and sometimes sewerage. There is one marked on this map, at the road junction by Rundlestone Tor,"

Jack returned to searching the Internet and turned up a walker's guide with a recommended Dartmoor walk in the Rundlestone area and there, as plain as day, was a mark showing the 'Pumping Station'.

16.30 – Western Hydro Offices, Exeter

Herbert Wilson sat at his desk at Western Hydro, not amused by the task his CEO had dumped in his lap. He could not imagine what in hell's name his boss was up to. For some reason, he had decided to dispose of his Range Rover despite the fact that it was only six months old and anyway, it wasn't his to sell; it was a lease car. Company policy was to change executive cars every three years, and they were sourced through contract hire agreements with one of the major leasing companies.

Herbert's important position in the global corporation was Head of Logistics. The subsidiary companies, located all over the developing world, included South America, Africa and Asia. Wherever electrical generation was needed, and that was, in effect, everywhere, then there was a Western Hydro Office, and from that office, the Company's engineers and salesmen would oversee the installation and management of generating equipment. Having spent the day making a few enquiries, Herbert called Sir William to give him the news.

"Good afternoon Sir William some bad news I'm afraid. I doubt that we can do as you ask with your particular vehicle because we don't actually own it, it's provided under a lease agreement." That was the signal for Sir William to lose his cool.

"Look, Wilson, don't give me a hard time about this. I want you to make it happen. Remember, I sign off your annual bonus, and I always show my gratitude when people go the extra mile on my behalf. Fix it!" The conversation abruptly ended with a click. Wilson was an imaginative sort and had pondered at times the limitations of the phone system. It seems that no matter how hard you threw down the handset it still resulted in a desultory 'click'. What was needed was a system that fully conveyed your anger and frustration. It would need to translate a furious slamming into an ear-splitting 'BOOM'.

Herbert was uncertain what to do next. He called his contact at CoLease, the leasing company that had financed Sir William's Range Rover. He was luckily able to persuade the broker to allow him to pay off the book value of the car in one lump sum and then replace it immediately with a brand new and otherwise identical vehicle. In return for a quick turn-around on the paperwork, Herbert promised that he would pass some extra business in the direction of CoLease.

Herbert's next task was to arrange for the delivery of a suitable shipping container to Cadhay Manor.

Sir William had moved the car to a lock-up half a mile from The Manor as soon as he realised it had been discovered. His plan now would be to load it into the shipping container as soon as it arrived and then tell Herbert it was ready for collection. He would forward the address of his Nigerian contact, and it should be sent to Lagos at the first opportunity. Herbert called his deputy and asked him when the next container to Nigeria was likely to be shipped. He would check and get back to him.

19.30 – Michael Crain's Restaurant, Exeter

It was a challenging and turbulent time for the top management at the Devon & Cornwall Constabulary. The new Chief Constable, Merrick Winstanley, was the kind of unsavoury individual that makes it to the top by standing on the shoulders of others. As he was about to find out, you cannot use that approach to a career without making enemies. Merrick had certainly done that, and life at the top was about to become a little uncomfortable as a result. Some of the people who bore his footprint on their backs had vowed to bring him down.

They were not about to petition for a new Chief, no, they were policemen, and their mindset had been honed by years of rubbing up against the nation's toughest criminals.

A cabal of disenchanted senior officers thought that, short of assassination, they had found the best way to affect a change of Chief Constable. In their view, Merrick Winstanley neither deserved the post nor was he the best man for the job. In the ordinary way of things, it pays to make friends on the way up the greasy pole, in order, they say, to be sure people are kind to you should you ever find yourself sliding down it. Merrick

Winstanley was the kind of personality that had no intention of sliding down the greasy pole. Being nice to people wasn't on the menu.

Everyone has skeletons in the cupboard and Winstanley was no exception. Some of his 'skeletons' had been dusted off and were about to make an unwelcome reappearance. It was his good fortune, however, that one of his protégés had decided to speak up when this little 'difficulty' hove into view across the Devon horizon. The region's police force was headquartered in the far east of Devon, in Exeter, leaving those in the west of Devon and faraway Cornwall and the Isles of Scilly with a chip on their shoulders and the feeling that maybe they were insignificant and unimportant.

Those in Plymouth were of the opinion that as they were located in the centre of the region, the Constabulary HQ should, by rights, be based there. It was therefore doubly ironic that the Roman tradition of 'patronage' was alive and well at Police HQ in Exeter as that area of Devon was the only part of the peninsular totally 'Romanised' during their occupation of Britain. Roman habits it seems are very durable for the modern-day Brutus, and his henchmen were plotting the downfall of their new Caesar. But Caesar had a friend.

The beneficiary of the new Chief Constable's patronage was Chief Superintendent 'Norrie' Norris, and at that very moment, Norrie was approaching the venue in Exeter where he was due to meet his boss for a quiet evening to discuss his 'concerns'.

He couldn't quite put his finger on why, but he had a very uneasy feeling about the direction this particular meeting was headed. Generally, these intimate discussions would take place at the Middlemoor HQ in the Chief Constable's private office. That was what he expected when a few days before he had mentioned to Winstanley that he wanted to have a confidential meeting and that it was important. A meeting in a restaurant well known for the small, discrete dining booths it offered its clientele, was ringing alarm bells. Norris had a potentially embarrassing agenda to discuss, and he was uncomfortable about airing the Force's dirty linen outside the comfortable confines of the Chief Constable's inner sanctum.

Arriving at the appointed hour, a waiter showed him upstairs. Norrie found the Chief Constable sipping a glass of chilled dry sherry and already ensconced in an oak-panelled room just big enough to hold a stout round mahogany dining table surrounded by period chairs in buttoned red leather.

The table was laid for two. He was ushered into a seat adjacent to his boss thus permitting the sotto voce conversation that was to be a feature of the evening along with a stream of dishes from the 'tasting menu' that Michael Crain was famous for.

By the time they had disposed of the desserts and finished the small talk the Chief Constable's tone, and demeanour changed, just a little.

"Norrie, if I understand you correctly there are members of my staff who are actively working against me, is that right?"

"Well sir, I would go so far as to say that there are members of your staff who will stop at nothing to bring you down,"

"Good God, do they think that in this day and age they would get away with such a thing?"

"I don't believe they doubt themselves in any way. They honestly believe that they have the dirt on you and you will either go quietly, or they will get you unceremoniously kicked out,"

"How do you know all this?"

"I have a friend who is effectively a 'mole' within the group. He, like me, believes that what is happening would amount to unconstitutional anarchy and that whatever the rights and wrongs of your appointment it is not up to a handful of malcontents to undo it,"

"What on earth do they think they have that would cause me to resign. I spent my career watching my back. I don't deny that by striving to make modern policing work, I have made enemies. The Force is full of Luddites, and the working environment has more Spanish practices than you would find on a warm day on the Costa Brava. I've made it my life's work to render today's police forces fit for purpose, and in doing so I have, I know, ruffled a few feathers,"

"When you were promoted to Deputy Chief Constable in the Surrey Force you said at the time that your goal was to come back here as the Chief. From that moment, Chief Superintendent, now Assistant Chief Constable, Graham Donahue began recruiting like-minded officers and collecting muck from any corner he could find it. I don't know what you did to upset him, but he was determined to stop you coming back to Middlemoor. It seems their breakthrough came last month when Ken Morrison, the outgoing Chief Ambulance Officer for Cornwall, told them a story that led to some serious issues being uncovered,"

"Outgoing? Is Ken leaving? Last time I spoke to him he said he wouldn't take his pension for another five years,"

"The Ambulance Service is having some sort of restructuring and his services will no longer be required,"

"How do you know all this? I've heard nothing at all about a 'restructuring',"

"Ken was at the recent Emergency Services Management Conference,"

"Yes, I was there too,"

"But you didn't get an invite to the piss-up at Brian Robertson's Club after the conference finished,"

"Brian Robertson? The Chief Fire Officer? What club? A night club?"

"No, not a night club sir. There's a new 'Gentleman's Club' just off Cathedral Square, but you will only get to know about it if you are invited to know. You, it would seem, were not invited!

"The story goes that they hung one on that night and dear old Ken was out of his skull. He chose to tell a compelling tale apparently. A tale that you already know, or at least one version of it," Merrick felt uneasy; this wasn't at all what he had expected. "Ken said that in January '87 he was with Peter Livermore, the Finance Manager at the Cornwall National Health Foundation Trust at a meeting in Livermore's office. You flew down to Truro in the Force helicopter to proposition Mr Livermore, who, the previous week, had announced that the Cornwall Ambulance Service would be launching the UK's first Helicopter Emergency Medical Service. It was scheduled to start on April the first of that year.

"Ken also said that you were terrified that this unexpected turn of events would put a crimp in your plans to expand the Force Helicopter Unit. You planned on a second helicopter it seems. The new one to serve Cornwall. So you told Livermore that if he arranged for those plans to be scrapped, you would ensure that the Force's second machine would be stationed in Truro and would be available to the Ambulance Service whenever they needed it. What Livermore perhaps didn't realise was that you had spent the previous year lobbying the Police Authority about keeping the Aviation Base at Exeter and buying a second helicopter for the west of the region. Their plan was not to spend all that cash on another aviation asset but instead to move the existing helicopter to Plymouth. This, they anticipated, would pacify those councillors in Plymouth and in Cornwall who saw a helicopter in Exeter as nothing more than the Chief Constable's toy.

"Then, like a bomb landing in your backyard, the air ambulance project appeared from nowhere and stole your thunder. What you failed to appreciate, apparently, was that Livermore had visions of being a local hero and being the recipient of accolades galore and even, if he was lucky, a 'gong'. He could use the Cornwall unit as the stepping-stone to a national system of police helicopters that also provided an air ambulance service. How are we doing so far?"

Merrick was sitting in stunned silence. Norrie took an envelope from his jacket pocket and put it on the table. The whole story is in here. It's part of the evidence that your enemies have trawled up. There was a long pause, the waiter magically appeared and took their orders for coffee. Alone again Merrick took up the challenge that Norrie had delivered so eloquently.

"Yes, that happened, pretty much as you say but where's the problem, I was trying to do my best for the Force. I don't believe I was involved in any impropriety. Where's the mileage in telling that story?" His voice was lowered, and he was clearly deeply affected by this turn of events.

"That's not the problem sir,"

"Well, what is?"

"The problem, sir, is that Donahue has the files on a surveillance operation that you ran without proper authority, a surveillance operation focussed on Peter Livermore. You briefed the four DCs involved that you had intelligence about Livermore's involvement in the distribution of drugs stolen from the supplies to the Ambulance Service and sold on to criminal elements in the South West.

"You knew, as did most of your team, that that wasn't true. You also knew, apparently, that Livermore had a history of adulterous relationships and you were trying to catch him out so that you could blackmail him into accepting your proposition and cancelling the Air Ambulance project. The irony was your boys did, in fact, catch him 'at it' but he couldn't respond to your attempted blackmail and cancel the project because the CEO of the Trust had already signed a contract with the helicopter company.

"Unfortunately, it seems that you were so busy trying to manage the loss of your second force helicopter that you forgot to cover your tracks. Such was your unpopularity with the junior ranks that they made sure there was enough evidence left in the records to show what you were up to. Now Donahue has that evidence. He has you bang to rights for setting up an unauthorised surveillance operation designed to further your own, private, ends,"

Merrick sat peering into his empty coffee cup and racking his brains for a way out of this mess. He could not believe, like so many arrogant men who make it to the top that he was, after all, fallible. "So, what do you suggest I do now?"

Norris took a small Dictaphone out of his pocket and put it on the table. "This is a recording of a telephone conversation I had earlier this week with a Detective Sergeant Neil Jenkins of Truro CID. Jenkins has been with us for more than fifteen years, but he is at best a mediocre officer whose rise to Sergeant was only possible because he spent much of his time collecting and making use of evidence of misconduct by his colleagues. Whether it was trivial or otherwise, he logged it all.

"This assisted his career development as well as ensuring he was able to avoid paying the price of his own shortcomings. He went out of his way to target senior officers when he was stationed here in Exeter as a Traffic Officer and has accumulated dirt on many of our colleagues and a few local luminaries. At one stage I was his inspector so he knows me and he has thus far never given me cause for criticism. I have never managed to catch him doing anything inappropriate, and he has nothing on me. Everything I knew up until this call was 'hearsay'. By the way, Jenkins had obviously had a few bevvies inside him when I called. You can just make out some slurring of the speech so I guess he was a little more forthcoming than he might have been if he was stone-cold sober," Norris checked that they were alone and pushed the 'play' button.

"Hi Neil, this is Norrie Norris, long time no see,"

"Hi Norrie, what can I do for you?"

"Neil I'm calling because I think you may be able to help me with a little problem we have at Middlemoor right now. Can you talk?"

"Sure, only one problem you say? They must have solved the shitload of other problems that infected the place when I worked there. Anyway, it's interesting that you should call, do go on,"

"Do you know of ACC Donahue?"

"I remember a Chief Superintendent Graham Donahue,"

"That would be him a few years back, what do you remember of him?"

"Bit of an arse-wipe I seem to remember,"

"Neil, don't take this the wrong way but have you got anything on Donahue? Anything that might be useful if he, say, steps out of line and needs reigning in?"

"Well now that depends on what's in it for me?"

"What did you have in mind?"

"Let's see...the summer relief job on St Mary's is coming up soon. I reckon the wife and kids would fancy a four-week hike in the Scillies,"

"OK, I can't promise four weeks but I'm sure I can swing a couple,"

"Hmm, Donahue, let me see what we have here, Donahue, Donahue, 'D' for Donahue. Oh yes, naughty Mr Donahue, I remember him now, silly bugger, I even have some evidence in my 'Naughty Boys Box',"

"Oh really, what sort of evidence would that be?"

"November 18th, 1995, Saturday night stopped in his BMW and found to be under the influence, but I also found an 'eightball' of 'coke'. That's a shitload for one guy to have ready-use like that. Either he has a bad habit or had friends that he supplied. It has his fingerprints all over it, very useful that. It's good 'plantable' stuff. Let's see, where could you put it? In his desk, briefcase, locker, car? Lots of possibilities with that you know,"

"Was he reported?"

"What? Of course not, no profit in that is there?"

"I don't get it, supposing he just denies ever having met you that night?"

"Ah, you forget the wonders of video technology. In '93 our traffic cars were fitted with video recording systems. The tapes can be 'borrowed' and copied. Once you know that, then you don't know for sure that I didn't record your erratic driving, dangerous manoeuvre or speeding and capture your 'stop' on tape,"

"And did you?"

"Let's have a look here...yes, I've put little 'V' against the entry. Can't remember exactly what we have though. Would have to check but I don't keep the CDs handy, I'll have to make copies. I keep all the video clips on disc these days. They're a lot easier to manage,"

"Neil if you have all this stuff written down I hope you keep it safe,"

"I may be stupid Norrie, but I'm not that stupid. Anything happens to me, and a lot of shit will fall from heaven onto to those who have crossed my path. They deserve it after all,"

"Understood, I'll pull a few strings to get you over to St Mary's, and you get me the stuff I need,"

"How do I get in touch with you, I'm sure you don't want me calling the office,"

"You can use my mobile number, 0430 346246,"

"Got it, I'll wait for your call," Norrie clicked the 'STOP' button, and the two of them sat thinking about what they had just heard. "How do we use this stuff, Norrie? If you go to Donahue with it, you'll show your hand,"

"I had in mind an anonymous package that suggested it was time he took his pension or he might lose it altogether,"

"Do you think that will work?"

"Worth a try. We'll make copies, and if necessary we can send one to each of his co-conspirators. I'm sure they would not want to be seen associating with a man who uses cocaine or maybe supplies it to friends and family,"

"OK, do it, and keep me informed. You are a loyal supporter, and I am very grateful. I'll make sure your promising career continues to develop in a positive way,"

Norris knew that such promises might well be empty, but if he had to back a horse in this particular race, then he was going to back the one with the best chance of winning. Anyway, anarchy of this sort could not be allowed to happen in one of the nation's Police Forces. If it succeeded, it wouldn't be long before the inmates were running the lunatic asylum. After paying the bill, the Chief Constable said his goodbyes and left. Norris made his way back to his car. He wondered how this situation was going to pan out. It was no whim that he had chosen to involve himself in this mess. Norrie would not be fulfilling his role in this drama if he merely reported back to his handlers in London. As an MI5 'sleeper' he had to do his bit to ensure that there was genuine 'order' in the nation's Law and order programme.

CHAPTER 10

- -

Friday, 16th June, 08.00 – Ambulance HQ, Truro

JACK REPORTED FOR WORK as usual, but Edwin told him they were to remain on call and stay at HQ because the boss wanted to see him at nine a.m. sharp.

There followed a very one-sided conversation with Ken Morrison, the Chief Ambulance Officer. He was left standing while his boss continued to make notes and read from various papers on his desk. Eventually, he put his pen down and looked Jack in the eye. Ken was an elderly, time-served, old school ambulance man who had single handed transformed his rural outpost into a modern and clinically advanced unit. He had overseen the introduction of the country's first air ambulance helicopter, ran his fleet of Mercedes Emergency Ambulances on low emission LPG fuel and proudly defended his men and women whenever this was necessary.

Ken had spent a difficult morning dealing with the consequences of Jack's actions in Wiltshire. Fresh information had just arrived by fax. It was a welcome relief for the bitter pill he was about to deliver would be sweetened with some good news that would please all concerned.

He engaged Jack with his version of an inscrutable expression. Ken knew how to soften people up with a mixture of measured silence and withering glances. By the time he was ready to speak Jack's mind was beginning to whir with apprehension.

"I've spent my valuable time these last few days taking flak from the Chief Medical Officer at Salisbury General on your behalf," His pause was designed to solicit a response, Jack duly obliged.

"I'm sorry about that, sir," More silence.

"We may not be a disciplined service in the formal sense Jack, but nonetheless we do have rules, and I expect my men and women to obey them," Another expectant pause.

"Yes sir," said Jack, preparing himself for the punch-line.

"There are some who welcome the use of initiative in our world, and I count myself as one that believes that initiative does have a time and a place," Jack was about to deliver another appropriate reply but as he began Ken rudely jumped on him.

"But those that are wet behind the ears need to understand Jack; they need to recognise that too much initiative at the wrong time will cause ructions, and you have caused ructions aplenty.

"I'm sorry about that, I was trying to." His voice tailed off as the look on Ken's face turned to thunder,"

"We have rules for a reason Jack, tread carefully, very carefully," Feeling free to contribute Jack replied,

"Yes, sir," Ken picked up one of the papers.

"I have received a formal complaint from the A&E Consultant at Salisbury General Hospital via their Chief Medical Officer to the effect that you had ignored instructions from the paramedic at the scene of the Wilton accident and refused to follow the standard protocol. You had failed to bring a patient to the nearest A&E in accordance with Standing Orders," Ken looked up, but somehow he knew that it was not his turn to speak.

"However, there was another message from the same Consultant arrived this morning but this one apparently originated in Bristol Frenchay where the neurosurgeons had written a very complimentary note to Wiltshire Ambulance Service believing that you belonged to them. A copy had been forwarded to the A&E consultant at Salisbury who had felt it necessary to call me personally and explain that despite his earlier complaint he did not wish to take the matter further as the patient had in fact benefited from your attention. But for your prompt action, the young girl would have probably died during the delayed journey from Salisbury to Bristol," Jack's inner tension eased as Ken's tone changed. He sensed that he was no longer about to be given a verbal kicking, and thrown, unceremoniously, out of the Ambulance Service. Ken laid both hands flat on his desk, put his inscrutable face back on and quietly spoke to his subordinate.

"I have to say, Jack, that this is the first time in my forty years in the service that I have dished out a bollocking and commendation at the same time," There was a long pause before a faint smile appeared on Ken's face.

"Watch your step in future," he nodded towards the exit, "close the door on your way out,"

09.00 – Middlemoor Police HQ

Chief Superintendent Norris was sat in his office reading a report about community policing when his mobile alert for an SMS beeped at him. It was from Jenkins: 'coming your way tomorrow. Can we meet for handover?' Norris checked his diary and replied: '11.00 a.m. Diggers Rest Car Park, Woodbury Salterton.' Jenkins came back: 'See you there, I've told the wife to pack her bikini, don't let me down.' Norris responded: 'I'm on the case. Bye.'

Norris called the Chief and told him he was expecting a delivery from Truro in the morning.

20.00 - Rundlestone, Dartmoor

The fag end of the day saw the clouds disperse and the air up on the Moor began to chill as the heat evaporated into a clear blue sky. Conditions for motorbiking were ideal. The open roads of the Moor quickly rolled by, the sweeping bends and open terrain providing an intoxicating and thrilling ride.

Ahead Jack could see the pumping station, and he slowed to take in the detail. On the right was a junction with an old red phone box sat beside it. The side road on the right had a 'No Through Road' sign and appeared to service an abandoned farm. The Pumping Station was on the left, with a small block-built shed-type building. There was an aerial mast attached to one corner. A dense clump of pine trees overlooked the junction from one corner. Open fields otherwise dominated the area and dry-stone walls formed unbroken boundaries along the roadsides. A few isolated farms and distant bungalows made up the local habitation. Jack pulled into an open area beside the junction, opposite the pumping station, and looked for a place to hide the bike. There was nowhere suitable. He began to realise that the place had been chosen for a very good reason. It was going to be difficult to observe proceedings and remain hidden.

Finding a small layby two hundred yards up the B3357 he switched the engine off then heaved the bike onto the centre stand. He was sat facing the junction and close to the dry-stone wall so that he could not easily be seen from the Pumping Station. He checked his watch; it was eight o'clock, one hour to go and the night beckoned. Sunset would be less than half an hour after the rendezvous and an eerie silence settled over the area. He figured that with neither sight nor sound of anybody or any vehicles he was the first to arrive and took his helmet off.

He was carrying a small knapsack on his back with a flask of coffee and some sandwiches and took the opportunity to take some refreshments. With the evening gloom approaching he was confident that his presence, so far from the Pump House, would go unnoticed.

As the time for the rendezvous approached, he put the flask away and put on his helmet. He prepared himself mentally for another pursuit, vowing to make a better job of it this time.

The tension mounted as nine o'clock drew near. Neil arrived with two minutes to spare and parked in the open space opposite the Pumping Station. He got out of his car, ambled aimlessly around the parking area taking in the clean moorland air. Returning to the car, he leant against the driver's door and lit a cigarette. The smoke he exhaled blew away in the steady breeze that had sprung up to accompany the day's progress into night.

There was a sudden almighty bang, and like a sack of potatoes, Neil crumpled to the floor. Jack froze and had time to register the fact that he had just heard the unmistakeable sound of a rifle shot. Before he could move there was a second crack and he was suddenly thrown from his bike by a huge blow on the side of his head. As he lay there dazed, he realised he was still alive and sat up. He was about to haul himself upright when the rifle crack sounded twice more. Whoever was firing was using hypersonic ammunition. The sound was unmistakeable. There was a 'bang-ting', 'bang-ting', as two shots hit the bike, which fortunately hid most of him from direct view.

His assailant, he guessed, must be hiding in the dense clump of pines on the corner of the junction. There was a horrid smell of petrol leaking from his damaged fuel tank, and his vision was beginning to blur as blood dripped from his forehead.

Another motorbike started up nearby, the unmistakable sound of a high-revving Japanese four-stroke. The noise decreased in volume. The bike disappeared towards Princetown. From the direction of travel the assassin was apparently taking the cross-country route.

Jack had to think and act quickly, but his brain was scrambled by the unexpected turn of events. He had to make himself scarce.

He stood up, but his knees almost gave way as he struggled to cope with the confusion and shock. Blood trickled down his face from a crease in his forehead above his right eye. He took off the crash-hat and examined the two holes. The bullet had entered above the left eyebrow leaving a small hole and exited over the right temple. Small bore, he thought, just like Desmond Duffy.

He shivered with the effects of the shock that was now taking a grip of his whole body. He certainly wasn't in a fit state to give chase, but he did need to make himself scarce 'tout-suite'. So far there had been no sign of traffic or a single living soul. He was about to set off then stopped, took a deep breath and despite his common sense screaming 'GO' he decided he couldn't leave Neil without checking to see if he was by some miracle still alive. He took a chance and rode down the lane to Neil's car, parked the bike on the prop-stand and knelt down beside Neil's lifeless form. He felt for a pulse... nothing. It wasn't surprising for from the state of Neil's skull he could tell that the bullet had passed clean through his head and left one hell of a mess behind. It was a cruel reminder of the ballistic properties of hypersonic ammunition. He looked around... still no sign of any passers-by... he had to go.

The journey back home was problematic. The T-Bird had taken two rounds right through the petrol tank, and the fuel leak had left precious little to get home. He had stopped at a service station on the A30, as far away from Dartmoor as he could manage and bought some chewing gum. A few minutes of chewing seemed to calm his frazzled nerves and then provided a quick fix for the holes. He topped up the tank with just enough fuel to get home. There was ample time during the journey to contemplate what had just happened. He must have been sat in clear view of the assassin with his helmet off, so there were now two issues to think about. The first was that the assassin might have been able to a good enough view of his face to identify him. He hoped that the distance made this difficult, and maybe, with luck, impossible.

The second was that he could have been targeted earlier, before Neil's arrival, so why not? If he had been removed from the scene, then there would have been no witnesses left to tell the tale. His paranoia was beginning to boil over. Did the assassin want him to observe the killing and then try to frighten him off, or was it a genuine attempt to kill him? A moment's reflection brought back the trauma of the bullet striking his head. He shook involuntarily, and his blood ran cold. No, he thought, a headshot was not a warning. The shot was meant to be fatal.

The assassin was trying to add one more to his list of victims. It was likely that he survived because at almost two hundred yards, the range was too much for a .22 rifle. Plus, he thought, a huge slice of luck. The shooter was obviously a pro. He had weighed up the priorities and figured that unlike the Desmond Duffy killing he was more confident about his escape and more concerned to make a clean kill. The lack of a silencer on the rifle would have given the bullet added impetus and the hypersonic ammunition, loud as it may be, would have made doubly sure that it killed the intended victim. Right now, he was drained and desperately needed his bed and a warm and comforting Pam. It was as if all the strength in his body had evaporated.

He was as weak as a kitten. The ride home was a blur, and when he finally pulled up at Lower Spargo, he was exhausted. He washed the wound on his forehead and found a bandage in the bathroom cabinet and wound it around his head. In the morning, Pam would want to know how he had acquired the wound. A story would be required.

CHAPTER 11

Saturday, 17ᵗʰ June, 06.00 – Ambulance HQ, Truro

JACK ARRIVED AT WORK sporting a fresh bandage covering a wound apparently caused by a low beam in an old pub on Dartmoor where he had stopped for refreshments during an evening's recreational bike ride. At least that was the story he had told Pam and now a sceptical Edwin.

Edwin insisted on taking a look at the wound in the back of the ambulance and Jack reluctantly allowed him to unwind the bandage and check it out.

"Interesting pubs you frequent young Jack," said Edwin, "and they must have an unusual type of roof beam. Tell me, how did you really come by this wound? It certainly wasn't in any pub," Edwin had put Jack on the spot, and he thought carefully before answering.

"Edwin," he said, "I gave you my word that I was dedicating my career to saving lives and no longer chasing villains. Unfortunately, it's not so easy to get rid of villains when they are chasing you. You'll have to cut me a bit of slack for a while. There's some unfinished business on the go," Edwin gave Jack a tight-lipped expression before giving a response.

"Well, Jack, the incident up in Wiltshire proved to me that you have what it takes to be one of us, but you have a policeman's blood running through your veins. I know enough to understand that you cannot switch one lifestyle off and another on quite as easily as you may like,"

"Someone tried to kill me last night Edwin, but I cannot tell you why without compromising you dreadfully. You don't deserve that. You have been good to me, and I have the utmost respect for you,"

There was a tense silence for a while before Edwin, nodding to himself slowly, said, "alright Jack, I respect you too, so I'll just say this. I trust you to honour what we do here and if you ever need my help or advice that will help you stay on the straight and narrow you only have to ask,"

"Thank you. Please don't tell a soul what I have said," Edwin smiled and said, "Your secret is safe with me lad, but we need to find a better way to hide your scar. You won't be much of an advertisement for the Ambulance Service if you go around with a bandage like this one on your head,"

He found some one-inch surgical tape and cut a thin piece of lint and put some antiseptic cream on it. He then carefully attached the lint to the sticky side of the tape and laid it over the wound. The pink tape made it almost invisible. Edwin stepped back to admire his handiwork. He looked at his watch. It was seven o'clock, and they were late getting on the road. They headed off to their assigned parking position by the Shell Service Station at Carland Cross on the A30.

Edwin pulled up at the Petrol Station, parked on the road and went in for a paper and two cups of coffee. Arriving with the paper under his arm and two cappuccinos in cardboard cups he placed them on the dash. Jack helped himself to the closest and sipped it through the plastic lid. Good old Edwin had already put in the sugar. As Edwin shook open his Western Morning News, Jack caught sight of the headlines and momentarily froze.

OFF DUTY POLICEMAN DIES
IN HUNTING ACCIDENT

At that very moment, five miles away, at a campsite near Newquay, the Robinson family from Chichester were preparing for their family breakfast.

Dad was lighting the two Camping Gaz stoves that stood just inside the entrance to their substantial family tent. The stoves were out of the wind, each with its small gas bottle. Sharon put baby Anne in the high chair. Dad began to cook breakfast but before the eggs were cooked the gas bottle ran out. He went to the rear of the family car to fetch the spare.

He had never before had any difficulties when changing these bottles, but today, for some reason, the connector just would not click home on the new bottle. He tried to force it, and there was a sudden spurt of liquid propane from the nozzle. The spray of gas, half liquid, half vapour, hit baby Anne and she yelled in shock.

A split second later the invisible cloud of volatile gas reached the flame on the remaining stove. The explosion and the fireball erupted in the confines of the tent. Father and baby daughter were both enveloped in the flames. A stunned and terrified Dad emerged from flames carrying baby Anne. He had the presence of mind to run outside to the water standpipe and turn it on. He held her under the stream of cold water, cooling her skin. What a sight. Dad, with most of the exposed hairs on his body now carbon and a pink and a screaming naked Anne in his hands.

A witness to the explosion had called the ambulance, and CornAmb 72 was en route, ETA four minutes.

On the way to the campsite, Jack had time to pick up Edwin's paper and read the detail on the front page.

OFF-DUTY POLICEMAN DIES
IN HUNTING ACCIDENT

An off-duty policeman died last night in a bizarre accident on Dartmoor. This morning Devon and Cornwall Police were interviewing two local brothers caught 'lamping' for rabbits with high power hunting rifles in the vicinity of the place where the policeman's body was discovered by walkers, just after sunset.

Jack was stunned and confused. What was happening? Was Neil's murder being 'sanitised' by those with a vested interest or was this a genuine mistake? His blood ran cold. He knew what really occurred last night and it was beginning to eat away at his insides. They pulled into the campsite and immediately came upon Andrew, still holding Anne under the cold-water tap. Neighbouring campers had taken care of Sharon and her other daughter, Melissa, who were shocked but otherwise unhurt. The campsite manager briefed Edwin as he was selecting the equipment to take with him. He took in the scene, looked at his watch and turned to Jack. "Get HeliMed here now," and went off to take care of the injured.

Jack returned to the cab of their Mercedes and picked up the mike, "CornAmb this is CornAmb 72."

"72 go ahead,"

"72 requesting HeliMed assistance. An infant with burns and one adult with burns," Patients with burns would mean Plymouth Burns Unit and HeliMed could fly that trip in no time. Edwin was obviously ahead of the game.

Six minutes later HeliMed arrived and landed in the middle of the campsite. The HeliMed paramedic trotted across to Edwin and exchanged a few words then turned to the pilot and gestured to keep the engines running and the rotors turning.

Edwin wrapped the baby in a white sheet, cradled her in his arms and carried her to the helicopter. The second HeliMed crewman reversed the front passenger seat so that the paramedic would be facing backwards.

The HeliMed paramedic climbed into his seat, fastened his seat belts and gestured to Edwin to pass him the baby. In that configuration, with babe in arms, the helicopter lifted off. Edwin returned to Andrew and said to Jack, "this one will have to come with us to Treliske. We may as well take the rest of the family too and get casualty to check them over. Edwin was treating Andrew on the gurney trolley in the back of the ambulance and had covered his hands and arms with Flamazine. "The rest of you seems to be okay Mr Robinson, so we'll get you sorted and then run you back to the hospital in Truro,"

Fifteen minutes after it left the campsite Jack heard the HeliMed report landing in Plymouth. Edwin turned to Jack,

"Thought I would take a leaf out of your book Jacko-me-boy. I sent him to Plymouth direct. I may get it in the neck for that, but Doc Bytree seems to be a lot more flexible on that particular subject than his predecessor,"

When the shift ended, Edwin called a contact at the Burns Centre. He then returned to the locker room where he told Jack that Baby Anne was going to be OK. The consultant reckoned that the father's prompt action in cooling baby Anne under the standpipe combined with the air ambulance's rapid transportation to the point of definitive care, without delays at A&E, would almost certainly mean that no skin grafts would be required.

Jack set off home knowing that this had been one of those heart-warming days. He had been part of a team that had made a difference. Sometimes the human soul needs some assurance that one's existence on earth is for a purpose. There is a natural desire to leave a mark to show you were here, a small scratch on the world. Jack's knew that on that day his tiny scratch had been made and would always be there. The feeling he had inside was one he wanted to have over and over. It was uplifting to know he could cope, he would be alright, he thought, and once again thanked his lucky stars for Edwin's cool, calm professionalism.

11.30 – 'Diggers Rest' Car Park, Woodbury Salterton

Chief Superintendent Norris sat expectantly in his car waiting for Neil Jenkins to appear. His mobile rang, and he checked the ID on the screen. It was the boss.

"Hello, Norrie?"

"Yes sir, Norrie speaking,"

"Norrie it's Merrick,"

"Yes sir. ",

"Where are you?"

"I'm waiting for Jenkins,"

"I just got the word; he's been shot. Up on the Moor, last night,"

"Whhaaat? I don't believe it. What happened?

"I only have a preliminary report, but a motorist found him lying next to his car up at Rundlestone, shot through the head with a small-bore weapon, probably a .22,"

"Do you think he was deliberately taken out by somebody?"

"Well they found a couple of drunken louts lamping for rabbits with a .22 and brought them in, but they swear they were never closer than a mile to where they found Jenkins,"

"That will need looking into; it might turn out to be rather convenient. Who's in charge of the investigation?"

"Detective Super Nat Williams,"

"Do we know which side of the fence he's on?"

"Nat's one of the good guys, and I think you will find he's staying clear of any rough stuff, he retires at the end of the year,"

"Norrie, I want you to take a look over Nat's shoulder and see if we are in for any nasty surprises when they go through Jenkins' things. I think you know what I'm talking about,"

"Okay sir, I'll get on it. I have to go back to HQ and find out how much progress Nat has made to date,"

"Can we meet at the end of the day and catch up Norrie? Probably best for you to brief me personally,"

"Certainly can sir, where do you suggest?"

"Do you know our place, Norrie? Out at Hayne, just east of Tiverton,"

"No sir, but I'm sure I can find it,"

"We're at the end of Hayne Lane.

"Okay sir, I'll see you later,"

18.30 – Tamar House, Hayne, Tiverton, Devon

Norrie's Lexus crunched down the gravel driveway towards Tamar House. It was once a beautiful Georgian mansion, an aristocratic farmhouse that declared to all that came upon its beauty that the owner was rich and powerful. These days it had faded somewhat, but the gorgeous gardens and freshly repaired stonework were testaments to the vigour of new ownership - and new money. One might say 'new power' and in a way that would also be true.

The Chief Constable had heard Norrie's car and was waiting at the front door. "Come in Norrie, can I get you a cup of tea or would you prefer something a little stronger?"

"Tea would be fine, thank you, sir,"

"Come through to the drawing room,"

"Fiona dear, can we have some tea for our guest?"

"On the way Merri," The disembodied voice of the Chief Constable's wife came from the back of the house and Norris guessed that the kitchen was in that direction.

"Have a seat Norrie," said Merrick, pointing to a comfy looking armchair,

"What news?"

"Nothing good I'm afraid sir. It appears that Internal Affairs have had their eye on Jenkins for a long time and the minute they heard about his murder they were up to Rundlestone at the rush. They have taken over the investigation and quarantined all the evidence,"

"Oh dear, that muddies the waters, somewhat doesn't it?"

"Worse to come I'm afraid sir. Nat showed me the initial SOCO report generated after they photographed and documented the scene. The report shows that in the glove compartment of Jenkins' car there were two CDs in plastic containers. One was labelled Chief Superintendent Graham Donahue, and the other was labelled ACC Merrick Winstanley,"

"Good God. Why did he have one with my name on it do you think?"

"Tell me, sir, have you made the acquaintance of Jenkins before?" There was a long silence. Merrick felt the need for something a little stronger than tea. He went to the sideboard where a collection of decanters sat glittering in cut crystal splendour. Selecting the one containing his favourite Cognac he poured a good measure in a similarly splendid balloon. Fiona appeared with a tray and placed it on the table in front of Norris. Sensing the tension in the room she looked at Merrick, but there was no eye contact. She left and closed the drawing-room door behind her leaving an atmosphere so intense it seemed crass for either of the two to break the silence. Eventually, Merrick took a gulp of the amber fluid and peered into the empty glass.

"It was a moment of madness, stupid. Fancy celebrating your promotion by getting drunk and crashing your car on the way home from the party. I should have smelled a rat. It was Donahue who organised the celebrations for me," He paused to shake his head and then laughed at his own stupidity.

"I had driven up from Surrey for the party and was going to get a taxi, but Donahue said there was no need; I would be okay. Nobody hurt you understand just a very badly dented reputation. That was thanks to our Sergeant Jenkins of course. It was he who found my car in a ditch and me out of my skull behind the wheel. I gave him fifty pounds to drive me to my hotel and take care of the car.

"I guess Donahue and Jenkins already knew each other by that time because it does seem to have been a remarkable coincidence that Jenkins should turn up like that, out of the blue at two in the morning on a country lane in the middle of nowhere. Now it all makes sense. I should have known that chickens would come home to roost one day. I could fight it I suppose. Maybe apologise and try and brush it aside as an uncharacteristic one-off slip,"

Norrie could tell that his boss was fishing for an opinion.

"If the contents of the CDs are what we believe them to be then I'm afraid I can see only two ways out. The quick, but dignified exit on health grounds or the dreaded exposé on the front page of the News of the World," Merrick poured another measure of brandy, took a sniff and then drank it down in one.

"I had hoped I would get a bit longer in the chair, but there you are. If those CDs incriminate me, then I daresay Donahue and I will both be history very soon," Norrie could see redness and a definite moistening appearing around Merrick's eyes.

"Why do you think Jenkins was carrying my CD along with the one he made for Donahue?" Norrie shrugged his shoulders. "Well, we'll probably never know now, will we?" Norris made no attempt to reply. He could not imagine anything appropriate at that moment. "Well, Norrie, shall we catch up with things next week? I'll show you out,"

Norrie's drive home was just a blur, he was deep in thought. There was a real mess to sort out now. He had to ensure that the protagonists in this attempted 'coup' got their just deserts. Fortunately, he had some powerful friends in London who would ensure that things moved swiftly in the right direction.

Sunday, 18th June, 07.00 – Lower Spargo Cottage

Jack was up early. He needed time to think and contemplate recent events. His motorbike needed checking, and the extent of the damage to the petrol tank established. Fortunately, the damage was confined to the holes in the tank and these he quickly repaired with a two-part resin based filler he kept in his toolbox,

Happy that the bike was now fully serviceable again he returned to the kitchen where he found Pam preparing breakfast. She was unusually subdued and pensive.

"I checking the news online this morning, doing my bit and finding out how to find stuff on the internet,"

"Oh yes, anything interesting?"

"Just a line or two in the Western Morning News about a certain DS

Jenkins, shot dead on Dartmoor by rabbit hunters it seems," She stopped what she was doing and gave him the look, the steely-eyed, 'don't you dare bullshit me,' look. He sat down at the kitchen table gathering his thoughts. Should it be the whole truth or just enough to keep her happy? Remembering past occasions when bullshitting just made her angry he settled for an unexpurgated version of the evening's events at Rundlestone.

"Shit Jack, this is turning nasty, it's not a game of hide and seek anymore. The bastard nearly killed you,"

"It gets worse. Because I saw the whole thing, I am a critical witness if they ever catch who did it,"

"We know who did it; you have the e-mail sent to Jenkins,"

"No, I have had sight of an e-mail sent to Jenkins, an illegal sight obtained by illegal means,"

"But won't you have to report what you saw. The police are telling everyone that it was an accident. That rabbit hunters shot him by accident,"

"That won't stand up, and I think they know it. There is something going on here, and it involves people pretty high up the tree,"

"But you're in the clear; you had nothing to do with it,"

"I don't know sweetheart, If I pipe up now, then I could be in the shit big time. I don't like the idea of sticking my neck out just at the moment. All the other stuff will then come out, me following the Range Rover, the accident, the baby getting killed. The police know nothing about all that,"

"But you haven't committed a crime, have you? You'll be in the clear,"

"It's not that simple, I have committed a crime. They could have me for 'perverting the course of justice,' and that can carry a life sentence,"

"Jeepers, all this crap just because we want to help solve a murder,"

"Three murders, as a matter of fact,"

"Three?"

"Desmond Duffy, The baby and now Jenkins,"

"Who do you think is behind them, is it one man or a gang?"

"The Range Rover was registered to Western Hydro. A guy called Sir William Chaloner is the CEO, and I'm willing to bet that it was him driving it. You don't show off with fancy number plates and let the hired help get the kudos, do you?

"What do you want to eat, shall I do some scramblies?"

"No thanks, I think I'll just take a bowl of cereal and a cup of tea and go and do some work online,"

"Which reminds me, while you were at work yesterday I did have time to do a bit of Googling,"

"How did you get on?"

"Difficult to say," replied Pam, "I have done as you asked and searched for information about both Desmond Duffy and Sir William Chaloner. I haven't read it all, but I have printed it out. This is the file on Duffy, and this is the file on Chaloner," she took the two files from the dresser and handed them over.

"Crikey," said Jack, "so much!"

"Yes," said Pam, "at one stage I had to pop into town and get another ink cartridge,"

"And you haven't read it?"

"Not all," said Pam, "skimmed it here and there but as you can see, there is a lot of bio stuff that seems to be repeated in different places,"

"OK," said Jack, "I'll work through it bit by bit when I get a chance. I'm sure that somewhere there is a link between those two and when we find the link we will find the solution to this mystery,"

"So, we're still carrying on with this crazy thing?"

"Not if you don't want to,"

"Are you in the clear? Could this come back and bite us in the bum?"

"It might. I had a thought when I was working on the bike, the bloke driving the Range Rover managed to get behind me at one stage in our little tete-a-tete and if was smart enough to clock my registration."

"Oh shit, he will know who you – I mean we, are,"

"Makes you think,"

"Bloody right it does,"

"We, my darling, are between a rock and a hard place,"

"What can we do, we can't bury our heads in the sand and expect it to go away,"

"Believe me; this is not going away,"

"Then we must deal with it. You're a policeman, a bloody good policeman. You'll find a way,"

"I was a policeman,"

"Don't give me that old tosh. If you had genuinely stopped being a policeman, we wouldn't be in this mess,"

"Mmm, so now it's down to me to get us out of it I suppose,"

"Bloody right there, but I'm here to do my bit, as always,"

"What about the kids?"

"Well, Nat is thousands of miles away, so we don't have to worry about him,"

"And Josh?"

"I'll put on my thinking cap. In the meantime, Mum and Dad are coming for Sunday lunch,"

"What's on the menu?"

"The usual, you know my parents, if it's not a roast of some kind it doesn't count as Sunday lunch. Today it will be beef,"

"OK, well look, I'll take your files and go through them and see what else is on the net that might help us along,"

He picked up the files and went to his office. He sat for hours studying the stack of papers, occasionally going on-line to check a fact, a figure or a date. He just could not find the link between the names Desmond Duffy and William Chaloner.

At one point Pam announced that they had run out of milk and asked Jack to pop up to Perranwell Stores and get some more. Without more ado, he set off to walk the half a mile to the shop. Having bought a couple of pints of semi-skimmed milk and checked the Sunday papers, he sauntered back home feeling relaxed and calm inside for the first time in a while. Later, while sipping a cup of tea at the kitchen table, he studied the front page and suddenly stopped and stared at the paper in disbelief. There, at the foot of the page, was a small box containing a story with the title,

WIDOW ESCAPES AS HOUSE BURNS

The newly widowed Mrs Patricia Jenkins, the wife of Cornish Police Sergeant Neil Jenkins who recently died in a shooting accident on Dartmoor, was lucky to escape with her children last night as their house in Newquay burned to the ground in a fierce blaze. Police suspect arson.

His mind was racing, trying to make sense of these events. Murder, attempted murder and now arson and maybe with the intention of wiping out Neil's family. He showed Pamela the story in the paper. The tension returned, their conversations became clipped and tinged with angst.

Lunch with the in-laws was a subdued affair and sensing an atmosphere between Jack and Pam, Larry and Ann decided not to stop for tea.

22.30, Lower Spargo Cottage, Perranarworthal

Jack was upstairs in the office, and Pam was in the kitchen when there was a knock at the door. Late on a Sunday evening was an unusual time for strangers to be calling, so Pam went to the door and asked who was there. A weak and trembling voice said,

"Patricia Jenkins,"

"One moment," said Pam, "I'll open the door,"

Removing the bolt on the front door, she opened it to see a woman in her forties, with short dark hair and smudged mascara.

"Is your husband in?" she asked.

"Yes," said Pam. "Come in; I'll fetch him," She showed the woman into the lounge and went to fetch Jack. When he entered the room, he found Neil's wife sitting on the sofa, staring at the floor. "Hello Patricia," said Jack, "what can I do to help?" Jack realised that the misery this woman was suffering would be hard to comprehend.

"Inspector Mawgan, err... Mister Mawgan... Jack. He told me to give you this. If anything happened, if he met an untimely end, that's how he put it. If he met an untimely end, then I was to give you this. He gave it to me the day he died and told me to keep it safe," She handed Jack one of the new USB memory stick devices with a key taped to it.

"It was lucky it was in my handbag. They did it, didn't they? The people he was involved with. They killed him, didn't they? It wasn't an accident like they said, was it?"

"I don't know," Jack lied, "but probably, yes,"

"I had it with me you see. They must have guessed he had kept a file. Tried to burn us out, nearly had the kids and me too. But we were awake. Little Justin had a bad cough, and I was up taking care of him. Otherwise, we would all have gone up in flames. Anyway, I had time to grab my bag, and that's about all. He liked you Mr Mawgan, trusted you. He said they knew you were looking into the murder up at Withiel. You would know what to do. That accident with the little girl devastated him. Of course, you'd never know. Detective Sergeant 'hard-as-nails' Jenkins was too tough to cry, to get help. He found his help in a bottle, now look. He's dead, and we're homeless,"

Jack leant forward and took the stick and the key. Pamela was trying to take it all in. Trying to make sense of it all.

"What is this?" he said, examining the memory stick, and the key taped to it, more carefully.

"I'm not sure, but the key is for a safe deposit box at the NatWest Bank in Newquay. I've no idea what's in it," said Patricia, her voice now a little stronger, "but it was important to Neil that you got that thing and the key, so there, it's safely delivered, as he wanted," She made to get up and go, and Pam said.

"Mrs Jenkins, can we do anything to help, would you like a cup of tea?

"Very kind, Mrs Mawgan but I'd better get off now. The children are with my sister, and I promised I wouldn't be long as I've had to borrow her car,"

"Patricia, thank you, we're always here if you need help," said Jack. With that, she made her way to the front door and out into a chill and blustery night.

Jack and Pam sat down at the kitchen table and pondered the plight of Patricia Jenkins. "What was it that she gave you?" asked Pam.

"It's one of those new memory devices that you plug into a USB socket. It's got much more capacity than a disc and more portable too. I guess we had better find out exactly what this is all about," He got up from the table and went upstairs to the office and sat down in front of the computer, Pam followed and sat beside him. He peeled away the tape holding the key and the USB stick together and placed the stick in the socket of his computer.

There was only one file, a video. The screen suddenly changed to show a blank wall, amateurishly lit by a single naked light bulb. The camera wobbled as if being adjusted by an unseen hand then Neil appeared and took his seat in front of the wall. The overhead light cast shadows on his face that made it impossible to see his eyes clearly. It had an unnerving effect on Jack, now poised for the dramatic delivery of an astonishing story.

"Hello, Jack. If you are watching this then it means that I am no longer in this world. I told Patricia that there were a few bad things happening and I had fallen in with some dangerous people.

"I know it's hard to believe Jack, but I was a decent copper once. Unfortunately, you know only too well that now I'm just one of those dastardly 'bent' coppers you go on about.

"I can't remember exactly where it all started to go wrong, but you know what it's like in The Job. We live and work in the twilight where we see the best and the worst of people. It's a shitty unforgiving world; we have to be perfect while we see our masters breaking every rule in the book with greed and envy crossing our path on a daily basis. It's hard to resist once you've tasted the profits of being an evil bastard like them. Yes, Jack, I'm under no illusions, I know what I am; I have tasted the forbidden fruits and then became addicted to them.

"Even in the Force, there are senior officers that are at it. It pissed me off a treat I can tell you. I suppose it all began so gradually, you know, a little bit of 'nonsense' here, a bit of 'how's your father' there. Before I knew it, I was raking it in, and up to my neck in so much crap you wouldn't believe it. I've been lucky though. I must have used up my nine lives by now, so I'm not so optimistic that this one will pan out OK.

"I'm sorry that you decided to leave after that bit of bother over the cash-box. It wasn't my idea. Someone higher up the food chain wanted you taken down a peg or two. It seemed you were hogging the good PR and putting the North Devon boys too much in the shade. It was never meant to get so serious, but there you are. Herbie lost it after you made him look a right plonker up at Penvale Farm. He gave me the envelope to put in your locker, but he didn't reckon on you having some friends in management, and they guessed what was going on and promised me a free ride if I dobbed-in Herbie. Shame about your suspension but then you always did have a short fuse and no love of the press. Once you let Internal Affairs get their teeth into something juicy they're like hyenas on heat.

"It took that accident last year for me to realise just how bad things had become. I managed to get away with it because I could pull strings, some pretty high-up strings at that. I suppose the rot began to set in when I was at HQ in Exeter on the Road Policing Unit.

"It was my luck that I should stop a variety of influential people for drunk driving, speeding and carrying drugs, including some of our senior officers. Fancy that, one of our own sniffing coke and smoking pot. What is the world coming to? Of course, I let them off but not without a small contribution to my 'career development fund' as you might say.

"On one occasion, I stopped a bigwig businessman in the public toilets doing what queers do when they get horny… dirty bastards. That was my big mistake really because that bloody tail gunner lives with a maniac Frenchman, a hard-nut who filmed me taking a bit of cash from his partner so then he had the goods on me. Stitched me up good and proper. I should have been more careful. A bit late now though. He threatened me and told me that he would 'make me disappear' if I didn't do what I was told.

"Anyway, I made notes about all that in my diary. You will have some fun going through those diaries but do us a favour, keep the private stuff private eh. The videos of people I nicked are now on a bunch of CDs. You won't believe what's on them. You won't know whether to laugh or cry.

"You probably thought that I didn't spot you following me the other day, but I clocked the bike and later confirmed it was you. Couldn't work out why at first but I guess you would love to see me take a fall, given the accident and all. Then there was the note from Chaloner that ended up at Desmond Duffy's place by mistake. I thought I'd got away with pinching it, but when Sidney asked me about it, I wondered how on earth he could know. Then I remember seeing you on the CCTV tape, checking out that piece of paper in Duffy's hand. Trust you to ask Sidney about it. He's got a mind like a sieve these days and losing it good and proper. In my opinion he should retire. That would have been your next job Jack, but maybe somebody else had his eye on it.

"Once a copper always a copper I suppose! Just as well that Sidney is a trusting soul, he still hasn't clocked the fact that the letter mentioned in the witness statements was missing. He's hooked on the Glasgow Mafia being at the root of it, but I know it's got something to do with the helicopter crash last year. There was bad blood between Chaloner and Duffy over that. The word on the street is that Duffy had something on Chaloner, so he was able to keep the helicopter contract despite the crash.

"Sidney is another example for you, Jack. No meritocracy in The Job eh! A cesspool of 'who you know', which club you belong to or, as in my case, what dirt you can dish on anyone standing in the way of promotion. Watch out Jack I'm in with some seriously vicious 'bad-guys', and if they get me, then they may come after you too so take care and take care of the stuff in my safe deposit box. Get my diaries, check out the videos and sort out that bloke Chaloner and his very nasty bed-mate but be careful; those guys are not pussycats.

"By the way, the bank will ask for a PIN; it's '1966'. You enter the PIN into a keypad to get into the vault then the bank teller will remove the box from the rack using his key and leave you to open the box with yours. This whole crappy mess is the last thing I wanted for Pat and the kids. I want them kept out of it and I don't want you splashing this video all over the TV so if I have done my homework right and the bloke who sold me this memory stick thing has done his job right you won't be able to watch it again. Bye Jack, good luck. I'm sorry. So, sorry it ended this way,"

There was a fizzing sound from the memory stick and a smoke trail rose from it as Jack tried to pull it from his computer. "Ouch. That's hot," he said, dropping the still-smoking device on the floor. When it was cool enough, he put it back in the USB slot, but the computer would not recognise its presence. Whatever trick Neil had pulled it had certainly worked. He must somehow have devised a way of using the five-volt USB supply to fry the flash memory.

Pam put her hand on Jack's knee; he turned to see her holding a hand to her mouth.

"This is crazy. This," pointing at the blank screen, "is the kind of thing that happens in the movies not here in Cornwall," She hugged him close. "What do you want to do?" she said at last. He thought long and hard.

"I could hand the key over to the police and step back and let them get on with it,"

"Don't you dare, those bastards have it in for you, and they'll skin you alive. I wouldn't trust them one single inch,"

"It could get nasty. Maybe we should let sleeping dogs lie and walk away. Pretend it never happened,"

"Bit late for that my darling," she said, these people seem to play for keeps. You rolled this rock over, and now we have to face up the monster that' crawled out from under it,"

"There's something else that bugs me,"

"What's that?"

"I gave my word to my boss that I would not behave like a policeman while I was with the Ambulance Service,"

"That's a bit rich; I hope you had your fingers crossed. You've got 'policeman' running through you like a piece of Brighton Rock," Jack had to smile at that.

"Tea?" she asked sensing a moment for contemplation.

"Ideal," he replied, "What I mean is that I would prefer it if we could keep this under the radar, you know, keep it to ourselves,"

"You mean you want to carry on your campaign to stitch these bastards up and put them away,"

"Yeh, something like that,"

"Got any ideas as to how we might do that?"

"We've got a possible way out if there's enough in Neil's bank box to help me to clear my name. We'll have to take a look,"

"I hate to say this, but it might be a good idea if Josh and I found a safer place for a while. I can tell you are getting into tricky territory,"

"Maybe you're right the bastards that dished it out at my disciplinary are still there, and the rest of the management are likely to be looking after their own skin. I'm just as likely to end up a convenient scapegoat,"

"Okay, but we can't just sit here and wait for developments. If they manage to find you, then they find us too,"

"No, I guess you're right. But I suppose you could stay with your mum and dad,"

"I don't think so love, they wouldn't appreciate us barging in and I not sure I want them facing any risk either,"

"So where?" he said with a degree of exasperation.

"Funnily enough I was chatting with Mum today, and she told me that Auntie May's old cottage in Helford might be available. Her long summer let was cancelled last week, but the customers have prepaid a large non-returnable deposit, so she's not under pressure to re-advertise. We could move there for a while, off the radar screen. What do you think?

"Not sure but I suppose it could be our 'Plan B',"

"In which case shall I see what I can organise?

"Good idea,"

"What about Jenkins and his safe deposit box?"

"I'll go to the bank in the morning and see what's in it. If the information is enough to guarantee to put the bad guys behind bars, then I will send it to the Police anonymously and let them get on with it. If, however, the indications are that I may not be able to trust my ex-colleagues with the truth about my involvement then we will have to find another way forward, and I may need help. Remember, Neil said in the video that he had evidence of misbehaviour, maybe even crimes, committed by senior officers. I need to feel comfortable about breaking cover,"

CHAPTER 12

Monday, 19th June, 09.30 – NatWest Bank, Newquay

JACK HANDED THE KEY to the clerk; she checked the number and then guided Jack to the rear of the bank and a keypad beside the vault door. She entered her access code and Jack's key number and invited Jack to enter his PIN. The door clicked open. What looked like a regular wooden door turned out to be a heavy metal vault door. Opening it required some effort from the slightly built young clerk.

The vault was a garage-sized room with racks of secure boxes of various sizes, each equipped with two keys. He noted the small size of the boxes at the top and the very large boxes at the bottom and wondered what assortment of valuables was secreted within.

The clerk put her key into G29 and turned it 180 degrees, removed the briefcase-size box from the rack and placed it on a table. She left the room allowing Jack to inspect the box in private. He put his key into the other lock and turned it, lifted the lid and peered inside. It contained a plastic supermarket bag stuffed with hardback diaries and a collection of CDs in plastic cases. He sat down, emptied the contents out onto the table then counted the books and CDs.

There were fifteen annual diaries of assorted sizes and another well-worn book with index tabs.

Arranging the diaries in year order, he found they went back to 1985. Some were page-a-day versions, and others used a format that provided two pages for each week. He picked a random example and thumbed through the pages. Neil, for all his faults, was an assiduous diary writer and his entries were regular and sometimes so detailed that they filled the allotted space on the page and spilt over to the next day. His handwriting was, for the most part, neat and tidy but Jack found the entries for the current year contained passages that were not so easy to read and clearly written when he was less than sober.

He made himself comfortable and started to plough through the first diary in the pile. Halfway through this first year, 1985, he realised that there was so much information in Neil's records of his personal and professional life that it would take many hours to take it all in. He picked up the last in the series, the year 2000.

After reading through the pages covering the last few months, he decided he had seen enough, closed the book and placed it back at the bottom of the pile. He sat there, still and silent and deep in thought. He considered what he had just read. "Hell Neil," he thought, "what on earth did you get yourself into?"

He turned to the slightly battered indexed book and found it contained names listed alphabetically in the tabbed sections. Beside each name were dates and some had references to what looked like the material on the CDs.

Realising the importance of all this evidence he wondered if it would be safe to take it home. Paranoia gripped him, and he thought about Lower Spargo Cottage being attacked by Chaloner's henchman.

He put everything back in the plastic bag except the latest diary, put the bag back in the box and pushed the button marked 'ring for assistance'.

Back into the bank foyer, he asked the Customer Service Clerk if there was a copier he could use. Fifteen minutes later Jack stapled together twelve pages of photocopies. These focussed on the notes Neil had made in the last few months of his life. He folded them to fit in an envelope and put it in his jacket pocket. Returning to the vault room he replaced the diary back in the safe deposit box with the others.

Making his way to the Post Office, he felt the eyes of the world were on him. There he bought one small and one large Jiffy Bag and placed the key inside the smaller, then carefully slid it inside the larger. He addressed it to himself, care of his brother Denny in Birmingham and posted it in the box outside. He sent Denny a text message asking him to expect a package and to keep it safe.

Armed with the copies, he set off for home and the chance to read them through thoroughly. His paranoia was now getting to ridiculous levels, and he went twice around the roundabouts encountered on the way home. As far as he could tell, nobody followed him.

Pam was at work, so he sat on the sofa going through Neil's notes. They recorded everything Neil felt was important on that particular day. Sometimes it was personal, and sometimes it was work-related. Whenever Jack encountered what Neil referred to as 'another opportunity', Neil would record the victim's name and address, and his 'crime'. Alongside would be a sum of money that at first glance appeared to be a bribe, and although this was never referred to in the text as such, it is hard to conclude anything else. The CD reference may have been a video recording associated with the 'opportunity', but Jack would need to check that out. Right now, there were more important things to worry about. The crucial thing was that Neil had kept making notes in his diary right up to the night before he died. He must have stopped off at the bank before heading to Dartmoor for that final fatal rendezvous. Jack turned to the page recording the events back in April:

Saturday 15 Apr – We had a call-out today to an incident up at Tremayne House on the Boskenna Farm Estate, turned out to be a shooting. Somebody had done us all a favour and topped the governor up there, Desmond Duffy. I'm just about to go in the front gate of his place when that shite Chaloner calls on the mobile and starts ordering me around again. One day I'll do for him and that Girl Guide Frenchman of his. He's in a right flap about a lost letter and tells me to find it when I get to Duffy's place. I tell him I'm already at Duffy's place and all he says is 'funny old thing'. Something weird going on here! Found the letter he was after beside the body so maybe it's important. Maybe I can screw Chaloner on this then he will owe me big time.

Sunday 16 Apr – Gave Chaloner the news, he wants the letter back. He'll be in touch when the fuss has died down. I asked him how grateful he was going to be and the bastard just ignored me.

Mon 17 Apr – Thank god I remembered the CCTV. Wrote up the logs on the DD case. Erased the critical part, so nothing going to come back.

Jack pondered these revelations then he opened his filing cabinet and put the photocopied notes in the 'Electricity Bills' folder. Anyone who came looking wouldn't think to look there.

Pam popped home for lunch, and they sat down for a pow-wow.

"So, what's the verdict?"

"Not what we had hoped for I'm afraid, no knockout blows. I'm not sure there is enough to guarantee a conviction and these people have shown they're capable of almost anything. The stakes must be pretty high for them to do what they have done so as I see it we have to do three things in addition to keeping us all safe,"

"And what are they?"

"First we have to understand the significance of the note Neil stole at the murder scene. Second, we have to understand more about the business activities of both Duffy and Chaloner, and lastly, we have to find out more about this mysterious partner of Chaloner's that seems to be behind his dirty work,"

"Okay mastermind how are you going to sort that little lot?"

"I've been thinking about that, and I have some ideas about the note I want to run past you, but in the meantime, I reckon we need some help, and I think I know someone who might just fit the bill,"

"Who might that be? One of your policeman friends I bet,"

"No actually, he not a copper or even an ex-copper,"

"Well any help we can get would be welcome right now,"

"Did you ever meet Hugh Martin?"

"Maybe, name rings a distant bell,"

"He was on my Computer Science course at uni. He graduated with a first and was picked up by IAC, the big accountancy firm. He's head of IT in Bristol now, a big wheel. He's been giving me a few tips on the side as it were but I'm going up to Bristol tomorrow morning to ask him to get more involved. He can help us to understand the Challoner-Duffy relationship. He understands all that 'balance-sheet' stuff and with any luck will be able to give us the background to their relationship,"

"OK, so what about this note?"

"We have taken it as read that the note was from Chaloner to Duffy and tried to understand it in that context, but why on earth would a magnate like Sir William Chaloner want to blackmail an oik like Desmond Duffy? What if it was the other way around and Duffy sent the note to Chaloner? I only saw half the letter remember. The top part had been torn off. Supposing Duffy sent Chaloner a blackmail note and Chaloner tore off the incriminating part of the letter and then sent the note back to Duffy with that curious stamp on it as a sort of defiant gesture. After all, if Duffy was trying to blackmail Chaloner then he was promptly removed from the scene and therefore not a problem,"

"Very plausible, but why would a presumably intelligent man send a blackmail letter back to its author?"

"Who knows, arrogance, defiance?"

"Stupidity?"

"mmm… food for thought.

"By the way, I spoke to Auntie May this morning, and she will let us have the place free of charge, but if someone comes along who wants to rent it for the summer, then she may have to talk to her agent about an appropriate rent,"

"Okay, so 'Plan A' lives,"

"Aren't you least bit nervous about being the focus of some rather evil people, I know I am,"

"You don't look it,"

"No, well that's my 'stiff upper lip when the chips are down' look.

"Your sense of humour appears to be intact,"

"Well, I'm not going to be much use if I run around the house wringing my wrists and bursting into tears,"

"Even if that's how you feel?"

"Shit Jack, how did we get into this mess,"

"It's what comes of being married to an ambulance man,"

"You mean married to an ambulance man who can't stop being a policeman,"

"If you like. It's my civic duty,"

"Bollocks, it's your pride,"

"Alright, but let's not fall out, what's done is done, and it was with the best of motives in mind," The debate ran out steam at that point.

"Cup of coffee?" asked Pam, trying to fill the silence with something positive.

"Please,"

When it arrived, the conversation turned to the subject of Josh.

"Do you think we should send him away until we have sorted this," asked Pam.

"Won't that upset his schooling,"

"Of course, but what else can we do? We can't just leave him exposed to whatever comes our way,"

"I would rather we wait, and when the time is right, we'll start Plan A and move the three of us to Helford and keep a low profile,"

"When will the time be 'right'?" Jack's reply was to shrug his shoulders.

"I guess we will just know,"

"Let's hope that day never comes," She checked her watch, "I had better get back," Jack put his arms around her and gave her a hug.

"Don't worry; we'll get through this," Pam tried a smile and went back to Devoran Surgery feeling conflicted about supporting Jack. Part of her just wanted to run a mile, but she was going to tough it out instead.

CHAPTER 13

Tuesday, 20th June, 09.00 – IAC Head Office Bristol

JACK ARRIVED AT THE smart new offices of the International Accountancy Company in the centre of Bristol. The uniformed doorman directed him to a reception desk where he completed the necessary formalities, collected an ID badge, and then took the lift to Hugh Martin's office suite on the top floor.

The lift hissed to a gentle stop, and the doors parted to reveal a smart young lady wearing a dark blue trouser suit with a small yellow rosebud in her buttonhole.

"Hello Mr Mawgan," they shook hands, "my name is Monique, I'm Mr Martin's PA," There was the hint of an accent, and Jack was guessing French.

"Please come this way," Jack followed her towards a plate glass partition, the thick woollen carpet soaking up his every step leaving him with the feeling that he was walking on air.

A figure he recognised but carrying more weight than he remembered stood up behind his desk and came to greet him. They exchanged a firm handshake and a broad smile. Jack couldn't help noticing a slight limp, and a scar on Hugh's cheek that he was sure wasn't there when they were at university together.

"Hello Hugh," said Jack. "Kind of you to see me at such short notice,"

"Not at all Jack, it's good to see old friends again," Jack looked around him and took in the sight of Hugh's spacious penthouse offices and was suitably impressed. As one of the 'Big Five' accountancy firms with global coverage, he guessed their fees were able to justify this lavish presentation.

"Have a seat," Jack accepted the offer of a plush leather chair that was designed to make the occupant feel special. If you were the one paying those fees then you probably needed to feel special, Jack thought as he took in the impressive surroundings and the spectacular view over the heart of Bristol.

"Did you find the tips I gave you any help?" asked Hugh,

"Certainly did," said Jack, "very useful indeed,"

"So, what brings you to my door? I guess it's likely to be to do with your earlier requests,"

"You're right, but let me start by saying that you know from what I told you a couple of weeks ago that I am no longer a serving police officer. For reasons that will become apparent I have found myself involved in what was one and is now three murders," he touched the scar on his forehead, "nearly four. This whole thing could get a little dangerous Hugh, so if you don't want to get involved, then I will understand completely,"

"Crikey Jack, now you have got my attention and my curiosity. Do go on,"

"There are two company principals involved. I have identified that they were in a stand-off. I think one was trying to blackmail the other, but I don't understand their business connections and need someone who knows the business world to peer into their relationship and tell me why they are at loggerheads. One of them is now dead, murdered," Hugh stroked his chin in silent contemplation for a moment and then replied.

"Well, that doesn't sound too onerous. A simple business profiling would help and a lot of that we can do on-line. What's the timescale?"

"Yesterday, the sooner we understand what's going on the sooner can make a plan to wrap it up,"

"OK," said Hugh "I'll do what I can but if work intervenes it will have to go on the back-burner and be 'as-and-when' if that's alright?"

"Perfect," replied Jack, happy to have a recruit to the cause.

"Right, well give me the details and let's crack-on,"

"This is a venture not without risks Hugh, are you sure you want to be involved. You already seem to have been in the wars since we climbed mountains together," Hugh smiled.

"You notice my gammy leg, and yes, I was indeed in the wars. An IED got the better of me during Desert Storm,"

"Since when were you in the military?" said Jack astonished at this revelation.

"In a way, it's all your fault, you persuaded me to join the mountaineering club at uni, and when the Army went looking for reservists, I guess they thought that people who were daft enough to climb mountains would make ideal soldiers,"

"So, you were in the TA?"

"The SAS Reserves,"

"Christ, no wonder you didn't turn a hair when I laid this lot on you," Hugh chuckled.

"A lot of water under the bridge since our youth my old friend,"

"I can't wait to hear about it,"

"One day, we'll share a few beers, and I'll tell you all my salty stories,"

"Absolutely,"

"In the meantime, there is something you should know,"

"Go on,"

"I guess you are aware that there is a file with your name on it in the archives of Whitehall because of your Balkan adventure," Jack was suddenly tight-lipped.

"It's okay, my connections in MoD are pretty senior these days, so I've kept them in the picture about your run in with these two dodgy characters. You know how it works, it's a bloody Jungle out there, and every bit of intel is vital. The folk in Five are particularly interested in keeping the intel on Chaloner coming. He's got a history, but he is connected, politically and financially to some very senior people in Government,"

"Are you on their payroll Hugh, a closet spook?" Hugh laughed.

"I don't need their money Jack, but I do get some help in return when I run into the odd, let's say, a roadblock. I deal with many HNWI's and get to know a lot of 'private' stuff,"

"Sorry, HNWI?"

"High Net Worth Individuals,"

"You must also have the opportunity when it comes to hacking the odd database,"

"Let's move on before I incriminate myself. What can you give me as background?"

Jack gave Hugh copies of the files Pam had collated and explained the story so far. When Jack was happy that Hugh had briefed Hugh adequately, he explained that he had to be on his way. He had a night shift to deal with when he got back to Cornwall.

"One more thing before you go,"

"What's that?"

"I couldn't help noticing that your colleague on the Balkan adventure was Daniel Barclay,"

"Yes, that's right,"

"Daniel and I have worked together in recent years, unofficially you understand. He works in Exeter these days, runs what is ostensibly a Private Investigation Agency,"

"Ostensibly?"

"It is a bona fide PI business, but he does a little work for Five on the side. They like what he did in Serbia; he's a natural apparently,"

"Oh, really, what did they say about me?"

"They like you too, but you were married, Daniel is still on the market,"

"That's a revelation; he would shag anything that stood still long enough when I knew him,"

"No comment, all I can say is that he wasn't going steady when I last saw him. You need to get together with Daniel. He's your man to put together a profile on your targets. He does a first-class job, and he has the right kind of inside track if you get my drift. I'll give you his number. Call him and organise a meet and explain that you've been to see me and tell him what you need. I'm sure he'll be a great help,"

Lower Spargo Cottage, Perranarworthal

Jack arrived back home tired but buoyed by the prospect of sharing the workload with someone with some very useful skills. Pam made a pot of tea, and they sat at the kitchen table facing each other.

"So, this Hugh will help you with the investigation?" asked Pam, eager to find out how the morning went.

"Yes, he will try to use their in-house software and their analytical records to get to the bottom of this Chaloner-Duffy feud,"

"And this investigator chap?"

"Can't get hold of him at the moment. He's not answering his mobile and hasn't responded to my messages,"

"Let's hope he's not away on holiday," Jack didn't answer but was thinking the same thing. After supper, Jack helped Josh with his homework. It would soon be time for the end of term exams, and he was struggling with his maths and physics. He could not wish for parents more willing and able to help and cajole him along.

Just after eight o'clock, the phone rang, and Jack took the call.

"Jack?"

"Dan?"

"Yea, what can I do for you Jack, long time no hear?"

"Dan, I've been to see Hugh Martin in Bristol. He gave me your number and said you could help me with a little problem. I think we need to meet so we can talk face to face. What are you up to tomorrow?"

"Flexible," he replied.

"OK, well look I'm on night shift tonight, and I can come up to Exeter after I've had a bit of a kip when I get in from work. Say about three p.m.?"

"That will work. Do you want to meet me in my office or somewhere else?" Daniel was obviously aware that some clients don't want to be seen going into the offices of a Private Investigator.

"How about we meet at Exeter Services?"

"OK. Three p.m. Exeter Services, what car do you drive?"

"Silver S-Type Jag,"

"Silver S-Type, OK, see you tomorrow, bye,"

"Bye,"

"Who was that?" Pam heard the call and was earwigging Jack's conversation.

"That was Dan Barclay; we're meeting at three p.m. tomorrow,"

"Can I come too?"

"What about work?"

"Douglas was looking for a swap, he wanted Thursday off and asked me if I could do Thursday instead of tomorrow,"

"Okay, if I get in on time in the morning and can get six or seven hours sleep then we can set off about one o'clock, and I'll eat lunch on the way if you drive,"

"I'll make you some sandwiches and organise Mrs Mitchell, so we don't have to flap about Josh,"

"It's a plan then,"

23.00 – Bodmin Bypass

The frontal system moved into the West Country in the late evening cloaking the high ground in fog and raining the kind of summer rain that somehow seems to be twice as wet as regular rain. It made driving conditions hazardous and cranked up the possibility of someone having an accident.

As the rain eased off the fog thickened turning the unlit stretches of road into a nightmare for the few drivers daring to venture out.

Not long into their night shift Jack and Edwin received the inevitable call and were about to arrive at the scene of what was described as a 'multiple vehicle RTC' – 'Road Traffic Collision'. The night was to prove long and hard as the driver of a Ford Transit van containing an unknown number of young people returning from a pop-concert had lost control of the vehicle in the thick fog, hit and rolled over the barrier and were struck by three separate cars and a lorry as the pile-up intensified. It was pitch black and raining, and a thick fog had brought the visibility down to twenty-five metres.

The van had been torn apart by the series of impacts with oncoming traffic, and the occupants scattered over the carriageway. Some, number unknown, had been thrown into the hedgerows. The call went out for support units from all three emergency services, and when CornAmb 72 arrived, the chaos was unbelievable. The Police were trying desperately to understand the scale of the accident and the Fire and Rescue crews couldn't see where best to park their tenders in the thick fog. As Edwin and Jack began locating and checking the casualties, it became apparent that this was a bad one. Maybe once in five years, the emergency services get something this bad, but the weather was making it exceptionally difficult to locate the victims, let alone extricate and treat them.

A second ambulance crew arrived from Wadebridge, and a third was en route from Camelford. Edwin tried to estimate where the centre of the impact area was and concluded from the debris that they were close to it. The wreckage appeared to surround them.

"Jack, try to find as many casualties as you can in that section there," Edwin indicated the area ahead of their parked ambulance, "and I'll take this area," pointing behind them. "If you find someone, try to note their location and make a check of their vitals. Until more help arrives, we can only work out who needs attention the most, it's going to be a quick and dirty triage, here, take the walkie-talkie, and I'll check in with you using the vehicle radio in five minutes," Jack nodded, took the radio and set off, flashlight in hand to find his first casualty.

A fireman appeared out of the fog in a half trot.

"There are three in the remains of the van over here, we think one is dead and the other two look to be a bit of a mess, one is trapped by the legs, got his feet tangled up with the pedals," Jack approached the wreck with trepidation. The horrors that lay within were going to test his skills but would also take their toll on his inner strengths. The fallout from the worst incidents would come later in dark, quiet and lonely moments when the horror of it all would return to give you the shakes and stop you sleeping at night.

Jack recalled the first post mortem he had had to witness as a young policeman. The images of that gory experience were in complete contrast to what was supposed to be the simple and unremarkable process of dissection of the human body. His mind overcame the horror of that day, the sight of organs being removed, the smell of intestinal gases, but he wasn't able to sleep properly for three days as he fought to erase those images, burnt so deeply on his subconscious.

The situation was just as the fireman described. The girl was lying in amongst the cushions and blankets but was grey and had no pulse. The male driver was unconscious and had multiple injuries. His pulse was weak and slow; he was lying at an angle, but his airway was clear, and he was breathing steadily. The mangled remains of his lower legs were wrapped up in the twisted metal that was once the pedals. The third casualty was half buried by the blankets and cushions and was just regaining consciousness. The radio crackled.

"What have you got?"

"Three in the remains of a van which is on its side about fifty metres in front of our vehicle. One female has no pulse, one male trapped by the ankles and lower legs, multiple injuries but breathing OK, another female just regained consciousness and at first glance minor injuries,"

"Just double check that last one. I've had them bleed out on me before now. If they are wearing dark clothing, you can't always see the blood. I'm sending the Wadebridge crew over to you, and I'll get the Fire Chief to send you an extrication team,"

"OK, what about you?"

"I've got two purples in the ditch and two unconscious casualties in a car on its roof also in the ditch,"

The night was to continue in that vein for over an hour until the police had combed the area and they had located what they believe were all the casualties. Searching the hedgerows would continue as soon as reinforcements arrived. The road was closed not long after Jack and Edwin's arrival, which is just as well for they had already had one vehicle screech to a halt in amongst the carnage. Darkness and fog gave the whole scene an eerie feeling and destroyed the ability to judge distances and locations. On one occasion Jack tried to go back to the ambulance to fetch equipment but found he had set off in completely the wrong direction. In short, it was hell and severely tested everyone involved.

By dawn, they had carried four stretcher patients and two walking wounded in two runs back to Treliske. The Wadebridge crew had taken two to Plymouth Derriford, and the Camelford crew was on the way back to the scene where the Police were hoping to search for more casualties in the ditches and nearby hedgerows.

Altogether there were five deceased patients awaiting certification by the local doctor. The protocol in the world of the emergency services was that a patient isn't 'dead', officially, until a doctor has pronounced 'life extinct'. Ambulance personnel can make that judgement in the case of a catastrophic injury such as massive head trauma or if the patient's ECG has been flat-lined for at least fifteen minutes with no history of CPR. To avoid prolonged and pointless attempts at resuscitation they use twenty minutes as the maximum period for CPR. An exception is made for drowning victims and children.

Once declared 'deceased' then the triage process naturally put 'corpses' at the bottom of the priority list. The ambulance service didn't usually carry those that had been certified deceased for they then became the responsibility of the coroner's department.

Back at HQ, Jack and Edwin cleaned and restocked their vehicle in silence, both stunned by the night's events and both trying to deal with the traumas they had witnessed at very close quarters. Jack went home to bed and was fast asleep within minutes of his head hitting the pillow.

CHAPTER 14

Wednesday, 21st June,
15.00 – Exeter Motorway Services

PAMELA PULLED INTO A space at the lower end of the car park. As they stepped from the car, another drew up close by and a balding man in his forties got out of the driver's door and walked confidently over to meet them. He was muscular but without the bulk of a body builder.

"Hello Dan, let me introduce my wife, Pamela,"

"Hello Pamela, Daniel Barclay, a pleasure to meet you," There was just a hint of Bristolian in his otherwise 'middle England' accent that somehow contradicted his urbane and conservative appearance. He was wearing grey slacks and a tan coloured lightweight leather bomber jacket over an open-necked polo shirt. 'Dapper' might be one way to sum him up. They shook hands, and Jack joined in with a grip firm enough to match Dan's own.

Like many men who have served together in a disciplined service, sometimes in difficult circumstances, there was a bond that remained even though they had not met for many years. Such was the case with Daniel who, for Jack, was the best undercover policeman he had ever met. He was courageous, intelligent, fit as a marine and accomplished. If Jack were ever in a tight spot, then Dan would be his first choice as a partner.

They were both awarded the George Medal for their part in a very scary operation in the Balkans during which both received gunshot wounds. Jack got off quite lightly, but Dan was in the hospital for quite a while. One day, when it was safe to talk about it, and the operation declassified they would be able to wear their medals in public, but for the time being, they would have to remain unsung heroes.

"Where would you like to talk Jack, it's very public here?"

"Let's jump in my car, and I'll fill you in on the details," Pamela returned to the driver's seat while the two men sat in the comfort of the Jag's rear seat.

Jack explained the situation. Pam hung on every word as gradually the whole story came out.

"I need information about this chap Chaloner and his sidekick. I've scribbled a few notes, and this is what I know about them. I hope you can fill me in on the missing details," Jack handed Daniel an A4 page.

"When do you need it?"

"As soon as possible," replied Jack.

"Okay, well," Dan paused and checked his watch, "in that case I have to get cracking so if you will excuse me I'll take my leave and start on this right away. I have a surveillance job coming up, and I'll be tied up for a while so let's see what we can get on these two bad boys,"

He got out of the car and shook Jack's hand, waved his farewell to Pam and left in his anonymous-looking grey hatchback.

Later that evening Jack tried to get some sleep but tossed and turned. His subconscious was struggling with the nightmare of the Bodmin bypass, and the prospect of another scene of carnage in another place on another day. Was he cut out for this kind of work? Only time would tell.

A few days later Jack was busy loading the dishwasher when the phone rang. "Hi Jack," it was Daniel Barclay.

"I've just sent a dossier by motorcycle courier. He'll be with you in about one and a half hours. You're up against quite an interesting pair. These are not the run-of-the-mill villains that you and I are used to, watch your step. If you need to talk, then you will find details of my movements in the dossier,"

"Thanks, Dan. Please send the account to the cottage, and I'll settle up,"

"Don't worry about that, this one's for old time's sake,"

Jack was relieved to know that soon he would have some news about two of the most interesting characters in the story so far. He wondered how Hugh Martin was doing with his business analysis. News from him could make the picture a little clearer.

Just before eleven o'clock, the courier arrived, and Jack took delivery of a parcel containing a plastic folder with a dozen or so A4 pages of information. He sat down at the kitchen table and started to wade through the detail.

Daniel's file recorded the Chaloner family biography and a family tree going back to the turn of the century. His narrative gave a profile of Sir William's military career – official version, followed by the unofficial appendix that filled in the gaps. The official record had it that The Honourable William Arthur Chaloner, as he was then, served with courage and distinction in the British Army's third most senior Regimental Corps, The Royal Armoured Corps.

The unofficial record showed that the rather less honourable William Chaloner had also served with distinction in amongst the rent boys of Soho, the Orient and the Middle East. He escaped a dishonourable discharge thanks only to his connections. They were powerful enough, it seems, to have his entire Squadron removed from Aden before the withdrawal in 1967. The departure of his regimental detachment brought forward without obvious explanation although the inclusion of this detail was clearly down to something Chaloner had either done or hadn't done.

The mystery of that period is still talked about in those circles where ex-Eton 'chums' gossip about one another. Still, it seems his connections won in the end.

After leaving the military in 1970, Chaloner became Director of Overseas Projects for Western Hydro. This was a position he owed entirely to his old chum and school-mate Yousef Ali Aziz, a Lebanese Arab whose father owned the part of central London that the Duke of Westminster didn't get. The father left his entire estate to his astute and bi-sexual only-son. The next ten years saw Chaloner indulging himself in a life of hedonism while based variously in Hong Kong, Djakarta and Bangkok.

He managed to stay out of the newspapers but not out of sight of a discrete surveillance programme run by the security services who had reason to think his peripheral activities were borderline criminal and his local friends and acquaintances were a little too close to the drug barons of South East Asia and Central America.

In 1981, he was taken to the Lausanne Sanatorium in Switzerland. It was officially a 'holiday' to recover from 'stress'. Actually, he was suffering from a combination of substance abuse and HIV and took two years to recover to something like normal health and then promptly decamped to a lovely seaside villa owned by another school-chum, Herbert Frimly, to convalesce. The Frimly family were big in Investment Banking. Word on the street was that they were known in the trade by their nickname, 'The Magic Chinese Laundry', on account of their ability to take in bent money, wash it, dry it, iron it and place it where it can be used but can't necessarily be seen. It was while in residence at Villa De Veronique on Cap Esterel that Chaloner read about a Foreign Legionnaire who had been unceremoniously dismissed from the regiment for being gay. This was despite apparently having a record of heroic action while serving in Chad and Niger.

Chaloner was on the lookout for a gofer, so he tracked him down and offered him a job. The salary was ten times what the Legion paid him so needless to say he snapped it up. Our informants are a little short of information about this chap. He is estimated to be 20 years junior to Chaloner.

Since 1984 this ex-Legionnaire, who goes by the name of Gerard de Beaumont has been promoted to various positions within his personal Empire. By the time Chaloner returned to the UK in 1992 as CEO of Western Hydro, de Beaumont had become his man Friday, Mr Fix-It and live-in lover all rolled into one.

De Beaumont's record in the Legion indicates that he has a brutal streak and thinks nothing of using extreme violence to solve his problems. The Legion discovered he was gay after he was found buggering one of the many young teenagers who make a few Francs selling themselves on the streets of Africa.

Unfortunately for him, he was found by one young lad's mother who promptly stuck a large knife in him. That put him in a hospital in Nouakchott.

His unit was in Mauritania at the time and involved in some dodgy operations in the Trarza Desert on behalf of the French government. There is reason to believe that he uses a 'nom-de-guerre', which is common in the Legion. His background is mixed race, intelligent, officer material. About the only thing we know for sure is that he speaks Vietnamese as well as French and English.

Chaloner took over an estate in Devon after the death of his uncle, Lord Melkin, who never married and always favoured his nephew to be his heir.

The estate workers are tight-lipped and have been threatened with dismissal if they are caught gossiping. Some wag has christened de Beaumont

'Action Man' and the diminutive Chaloner 'Fraction Man'. I hope the humour isn't lost on you!

I had the nod that the incident in Aden is worth a detailed look but unfortunately my man can't get near the file just yet. It's got what's called a 'trip-wire' on it. It is ostensibly 'available', but my man has been tipped-off about the 'trip-wire' and won't go near it unless and until he gets an authorisation from someone higher up the tree. Fishing expeditions are rather frowned on in London so if anyone draws that file out of the library without some top-cover certain people will be notified, and the withdrawer would shortly afterwards be found in a dark room being asked awkward questions by anonymous men who will ensure his career takes a different trajectory, a bad one.

Of course, a Section Head would be immune from such attention and my man thinks he can persuade his S.H. to assist in return for being 'in' on your caper. Let me know if you want to deal.

You may be on the right track with the Range Rover issue as we have found out that the car now resides at the back of a 40 foot ISO container along with a piece of farm machinery and is due to be collected from the back of the stables on Tuesday morning. It's booked on the Maersk Victoria from Southampton to Lagos.

There was a hand-written note from Daniel scribbled at the bottom of the page; I still have a way into those 'masters of the dark arts' that you and I knew so well many years ago courtesy of a few favours I did for them over the years. They want you to know that they are hoping to get approval to get on the case and urge you to keep as low a profile as possible. They don't want you or your family to be caught up in any action they may have to take to bring this matter to a conclusion.

Dan's note had Jack thinking hard about the implications of his plans to deal with the situation. He figured that keeping a low profile was a good idea and set about planning his next move. He wasn't going to sit back and wait for Dan's colleagues to make their minds up about dealing with Chaloner. He trusted Dan but spooks he knew from experience, always have their own agenda and you could never trust that what they tell you is the truth.

Flipping through the rest of papers, he caught sight of a list of Chaloner's sporting achievements as a young man. He was the Royal Armoured Corps Cresta Run Champion in 1963 and '64, Combined Services Biathlon

Champion in 1965, Small-Bore Rifle Champion for the Army in 1965. That could be significant. Could Sir William be the shooter? Jack thought back to the night of Neil's murder. He recalled hearing the assailant disappearing on a trail-type motorbike and somehow doubted that a man of nearly sixty would be able to handle a bike like that over trackless moorland. The dossier made compelling reading, and when he had completed a quick read through, he sat quietly contemplating its contents.

One of the items on a list of intelligence reports was of particular interest. The container with Chaloner's Range Rover was about to disappear. He needed to contact Daniel straight away, if the container was due to be collected on Tuesday then he needed to find a way to capture it. There should be good forensics at least proving it was the vehicle involved in that accident.

Jack found Daniel's contact details on the last page. There was a series of dates and times and telephone numbers. Surely he couldn't have gone far?

Dan was, at that moment, involved with a little project up country. A project that was potentially quite dangerous. There were times when the Police, the Special Branch or the Security Services needed the services of skilled and capable operatives that were, as they would put it, 'independents'. Sometimes they were locksmiths or safebreakers, sometimes expert burglars and occasionally, very occasionally, they were killers. People who were prepared to carry out extra-judicial executions when no alternative solutions were available.

They had the ability to ensure that when they took on a 'black job' and the order was, 'no witnesses', then there would be no witnesses.

Dan was busy indulging in his speciality, placing bugs, trackers and other electronic devices into the homes, offices, cars, whorehouses and playthings of the criminal fraternity. He was dressed as a baggage handler and was securing a listening device complete with transmitter and recording system into the underside of the seat in the cabin of an executive helicopter parked for the weekend at Bristol Airport. It belonged to a gentleman from Russia who was the lucky owner of a bucket full of dirty money that came with motley collection of unsavoury associates. Dan's mobile number was on 'airport' mode and would be for another hour or so.

Lower Spargo Cottage, Perranarworthal

"Hello Jack, I got your message, what can I do for you?"

"Dan, sorry to bother you like this but having read your report I think we need to do something about Chaloner's Range Rover. It could be crucial evidence,"

"I'm scheduled to be away on a job for at least the weekend, maybe a few days more. I can't do much until the middle of next week,"

"But you say the container is scheduled for collection on Tuesday,"

"In that case, you will have to get your skates on and put a tracker on it before it goes,"

"A tracker? But we know it's going to Southampton. If it goes on the boat, then tracker or no tracker it will be gone,"

"Don't worry about that Jack. All you have to do is put a tracker on it. I have a contact in the docks at Southampton, and she will swap the papers for your container for an inbound one and swap the serial numbers so that your container goes somewhere in the UK. It's the kind of thing we regularly do when we suspect a container is full of contraband. The problem is we can't be picky about which container is swapped for yours so we can't guarantee to know when or where it will be delivered. That's where the tracker comes in. Sometimes the container is parked for days on the docks, and sometimes it goes out straight away. Once the tracker indicates that it is moving, we can intercept it in a quiet place and do the necessary,"

"Well that may be how you would deal with it but we, sorry, I, am not equipped to do any of that stuff,"

"Don't tell me that the Jack Mawgan I know can't do that stuff. You and I used to work together remember. I know what you are capable of and this will be a cake-walk,"

"Where the hell do I get a tracker from before Tuesday morning?"

"You call Angela, my secretary. You have her number on the contacts page. She will give you a lot of lip about being called on her day off, but she will let you have the stuff you need first thing on Monday. Just ask for Tracker 'A', and she will hand you a smart looking carry case. That particular box has a tracker with a magnetic base and built-in power supply. To save power put the slide switch on 'Motion'. The unit will then sit armed and ready until the container starts to move. Once it's on it will stay on, and the batteries are good for a month. The best place to put it is underneath, in-between the cross braces but not too close to the container attachment points,"

"Won't they see it there?"

"Containers are usually handled by crane units from above. Anything out of the ordinary on the roof would be picked up straight away. We learned the hard way. Don't forget we need the container serial number. You can send it to my mobile as a text message,"

"Okay Dan, I'll give it my best shot,"

"I'll be 'indisposed' for maybe a week, but you have my contact details during that period. Good Luck. Must go,"

"Thanks, Dan, bye for now,"

CHAPTER 15

Monday, 26th June, 18.00 – Exeter

JACK ARRIVED AT DAN's office just as Angela was about to leave. She handed over the briefcase with the tracker unit and bid him goodbye. Her social skills it seemed did not extend to small talk, but Jack could easily understand that working for Dan meant that it was not wise to say too much to strangers.

He couldn't help wondering what sort of background a woman would require to support Dan in his varied and 'interesting' work. She was certainly attractive, seemed to be efficient and was apparently young and fit. Maybe her first career had been in the armed forces. Yes, he thought, a definite possibility.

Back at the car, he inspected the contents of the black fibreglass briefcase. Its interior was padded with foam and contained two boxes. One painted a charming shade of 'rust' brown was about the size of two packs of cigarettes taped together. There was a slide-switch on one edge annotated 'ON', 'OFF' and 'MOTION'. The other was a black metal box the size of a very thick paperback book. Beside it was two aerials mounted on sucker-cups together with a power lead and car adapter that would fit the cigar lighter socket. A bundle of wires proved to be the connections between the black box and the aerials, which were, according to the booklet, to be mounted on the roof of the car used for tracking. The black box had a series of light indicators for 'POWER', 'RECEIVER HI' and 'RECEIVER LO'. A gauge like indicator, with a central needle, was annotated 'LEFT' and 'RIGHT'. A button and LED were labelled 'TEST'.

The booklet explained how to use the device to locate the tracker's transmitter when it was mounted on the target. That would have to come later. That night was all about making sure that there was a target to track. Confident that he had a general idea, he visited the toilets in the service area and changed from his jeans, T-shirt, and Timberlands into a black tracksuit, black lightweight roll-neck and black trainers.

Returning to the Jag, he set off to wait for the sun to set and cloak his secret activities in darkness. He found a convenient spot overlooking Exeter airport and amused himself doing the Sudoku in the daily paper and eating the sandwiches that Pam had begrudgingly made him. She was cross when he told her she couldn't come too. Someone had to look after Josh and with Mrs Mitchell away at her sister's; she had no one to fall back on.

Pam's acceptance of the plan to plant a tracker on the container at Cadhay Manor without a long-drawn-out argument took Jack by surprise but then he had made it sound like it was no more complicated than scrumping apples. Needless to say, in reality, it wasn't going to be anything like scrumping apples.

By eleven o'clock he was ready for the off and headed for Ottery St Mary. He had done his homework, and the Ordnance Survey Map he bought at Exeter Services had shown him the way to gain access without having to negotiate the main driveway. There was a back entrance to the farmyard and outbuildings via Cadhay Lane. He had performed a dry run earlier in the day and spotted a small garage at Fairton, a hamlet four hundred yards from the entrance to the lane and the garage had an array of cars parked on its forecourt. One more car in the line would not attract any attention. He would leave the car there and go in on foot. Arriving in Fairton just before midnight he locked the car and checked his equipment. He was using a small black rucksack, the kind used by cyclists and bikers. Inside were a flashlight, the tracker unit, his wallet and mobile, switched to 'silent' mode just in case somebody called him at an inopportune moment.

He also had a cunning disguise if he was compromised. This consisted of a high-vis tabard and some reflective ankle straps. If he needed to, he would become an innocent midnight jogger who got lost in the darkened lanes. He backed the car onto the end of a line of three cars that were all sporting sales information on their windscreens.

Closing the door as quietly as he could, he set off at a fast walk and soon came upon the entrance to Cadhay Lane. Turning right, he was pleased to note that all was quiet and peaceful in that part of the Devon countryside. The breeze in the tall trees created a low-frequency hum, but at ground level, it was eerily windless. He ducked instinctively as a barn owl on a hunting mission flashed by a few feet overhead, its sights set on an unseen prey.

He suddenly felt vulnerable, paused, took a deep breath and continued on his way. It had been many years since his spell with the undercover team, but it seemed that the skills he had acquired then had not been forgotten and the adrenalin was beginning to lubricate his mind in that very positive way that enhances each and every one of the senses. Soon he came to the farmyard. He paused to get his bearings. The container was supposed to be behind the stable building he had seen on his first visit.

The moon was in the last quarter, but the scattered clouds occasionally turned the scene black. He waited for a cloud to move away from the moon and when he could see his pathway was clear, headed for the back of the stables. There stood the container, dark and monolithic, sitting on the semi-trailer, all ready to go. In the darkness, it seemed bigger than he remembered, but it was another trick of the night.

Crawling beneath the trailer, he removed the flashlight from his rucksack and inspected the underside of the container, looking for a good spot to place the tracker. Selecting a suitable position wasn't easy as the trailer chassis hid much of it but midway between the support frames, he found a good spot that was easy to access. He took the rust-coloured box and placed it carefully on the metal surface. It snapped into place with a loud bang as the strong magnet grabbed the cold steel. The noise sounded like the Forth Road Bridge falling, but in reality, it was inaudible to anyone more than a few yards away. He struggled to make out the container serial number. A shaft of moonlight helped as he selected the sound recording function on his mobile phone and whispered 'BFT-U-956221-4' into the handset.

Relieved at the completion of Phase One he now had to get out and back home without being discovered. He was about to backtrack his route to his own car when he heard another approaching down the driveway. The hum of a powerful car heralded the arrival of a large BMW. The crunching of fat tyres on the gravel broke the silence of the night as it drew to a halt in front of the stables. There was the sound of voices. The doors of the car shut in turn... clunk... clunk.

"Well I don't care about it being difficult," said a cultured voice with an upper-class twang.

"Frimly says whoever they are they have hacked our systems and collected enough 'Project Cayman' related data to nail our backsides to the wall. The other members of the syndicate are bleating their hearts out about our lack of security. They want whoever is behind it to be dealt with, firmly dealt with,"

"I thought you said it was their security that failed?"

"I did, and it was, but it seems that those with the power in this sad nation of ours, have selective memories as well as nervous dispositions," The second man had an accent, a foreign accent, maybe French.

"They have traced the leak to Bristol; our accountants apparently are involved. They will have a name for us sometime tomorrow,"

The click of the boot lid closing was followed by the sound of feet retreating on the gravel driveway. The crunching noise faded into silence. Jack returned to the lane, then ran rather than jogged back down to Fairton.

By four a.m. he was back in bed and trying to tell a disinterested and dozy Pam that he would need to contact Hugh Martin as soon as possible, he may have some vital information. He set the alarm for six and tried to get a couple of hours' sleep.

Tuesday 27th June, 06.00 – Oak Tree Cottage, The Close, Kingston Seymour

Jack called Hugh as soon as he clambered from the sanctuary of his nice warm bed. "Hugh, I've come across some information that may be of interest,"

"What kind of information?"

"It's about something called 'Project Cayman' and somebody called 'Frimly'. There was a prolonged silence before Jack asked, "Are you still there Hugh?"

"Yes, I'm here. I'm sorry Jack... I did wonder. I was doing some homework on your two protagonists and came across a rich seam of data about the movement of funds in and out of the UK, Switzerland and especially the Cayman Islands. I've uncovered fraudulent declarations, forged documents and hidden assets and some were in unexpected places. Some of the activities involved my own company, so I had access to a lot of records. Perhaps more important I had the analysis of those records produced by our own people. That was very revealing,"

"Revealing?"

"Somebody in my organisation is covering up for those involved in what looks like a scam on an industrial scale,"

"What do you mean?"

"It's complicated, but the same assets appear on multiple balance sheets, but I have run a trace of some of those assets, and they are all mortgaged, sometimes more than once. Some of them don't even appear to exist. Many of these 'ghost' assets are either mortgaged or leased back to the original owners,"

"So, it's a big deal?"

"Huge. The cash raised disappears and never makes it to the right accounts. As long as these people keep creating new companies or continue to asset-strip any new acquisitions, there is always enough cash to pay the bills. But it's a house of cards Jack. It could collapse at any moment, and the terrifying thing is you won't believe some of the names I have linked to these goings-on,"

"Hell Hugh, you've rolled over a rock with a real bunch of nasties underneath,"

"I finished that report you asked for. I need to get it and the supporting files down to you so what chance Marjory and I can come down to Cornwall and stay with you for a day or so. We could do with a break. I need to go over the details with you face-to-face because, believe me, I have only scratched the surface,"

"That's fine with us; I'll ask Pam to get the spare room ready, when are you planning to set off?"

"Hope to be heading your way within the hour. Oh, hell, no I won't. I've lent my Land Cruiser to Simon, my neighbour. He's just bought a new boat and wants to take it down to Dartmouth ready for the coming weekend. Don't worry; we have a veritable fleet of cars in our family, so we'll sort something out and will be with you just after lunch,"

"Right, you'll need to know how to find us,"

Jack gave Hugh instructions on how to get to Lower Spargo Cottage and wished him a safe journey.

"Who was that?" asked Pam, appearing through the office door. She was in her dressing gown, bleary-eyed and in need of some coffee. Jack sat her down and gave her the update and asked if it would be okay for Hugh and Marjory Martin to stay a couple of days.

"I'm off to Truro this morning, I've got a hair appointment and some shopping to do so you'll have to get the spare room ready,"

"Alright, if they are down in time there will be four of us for lunch,"

"That's okay, I planned on making a quiche anyway, so there will be enough for four.

10.00 – Cadhay Manor

Sir William was enduring one of those annoying days when nothing seemed to go according to plan.

"Thank you, Francis, yes, I've got that, Oak Tree Cottage, The Close, Kingston Seymour, Somerset. Yes, a Toyota Land Cruiser, Triumph TR6 and Nissan Micra. Yes, I've got the registrations. What about the motorbike I gave you last Wednesday? What do you mean it came back as a milk truck registered to a company in Newton Abbot? Damn! Well, can you try some permutations I must have made a mistake with one of the characters, but for God's sake we are looking for a motorbike, not a bloody milk lorry? Yes, Francis of course I understand, but we are all in this together, so we have to do whatever is necessary. Yes, I know it's risky for your man in the Met. But please do your best will you, there's a dear. Fine, I'll call again tomorrow. Goodbye,"

Sir William put the phone back in the cradle with a thump. He was not happy. "Gerry, are you there?"

"Yes, right 'ere. The container has gone, here are the papers," Gerard came into Sir William's study and placed the documents on the massive oak desk.

"Frimly says that they have tracked down the person responsible for the security breach. We must deal with him. Do you want to do it, or shall I?"

"No, it's okay, I'll do it. I told you, I'll do all the tidying up if you look after the admin,"

"Right, here you go, Mr Martin's details. Now take care of him. Make sure there are no loose ends,"

"Of course, leave it to me,"

12.15 – Kingston Seymour

Gerard arrived in the village and parked in a quiet lane a quarter of a mile from the target. He approached the Jeep from behind, opened the passenger door and eased in beside the driver.

"Have you seen the house?" he asked.

"I took a walk around first thing," replied Andy with an accent that gave away his North American origins. He was an old associate from the Legion and one of the few that Gerard knew well enough to trust. Andy wasn't his real name of course. During his life of crime in the sleazy parts of New York, he made too many enemies for his own good so like many in his position he sought refuge and anonymity in the brotherhood that is the French Foreign Legion. When he was discharged from the Legion, his only skill set comprised of killing people and knowing how to steal cars. He learned how to kill people not on the streets of his native Bronx but in the hell-hole called the Sahel. There was not much call for the stealing of cars in the desert, but those skills proved to be very handy when he came to the UK. He settled in the St Pauls district of Bristol under his assumed name, Andrew McDonald. He figured the people he was trying to avoid back home would never think to look for him in that quiet corner of England.

These days he was known in the underworld as an 'odd job man', Only, in this case, Andy knew very little about setting up a Black and Decker hammer drill. His contribution to the day was to be Gerard's eyes and ears and to drive him around when required. He stole the Jeep the previous week only now it was sitting on cloned plates and would be a safe ride for a week or two yet.

"His Land Cruiser is in the driveway, but there's nowhere to park to get a clear view, so I'm waiting here. There's only one way in and out, so he'll have to pass us if he leaves,"

"What's with this guy anyway?"

"Oh, we just need to have a chat,"

"Well, I'm pretty sure he's at home if that's all you need,"

"No, we'll wait. It's going to be a very serious chat. Better we wait until it's dark. Tell me about the house,"

This occasion wasn't the first time that Andy has delivered Gerry to someone's home or business for one of his 'chats', but there had never been any 'come-back' to concern him. He figured he was maybe a kind of debt-collector and Gerry worked for an anonymous Mr Big. He paid well and always gave him fifty percent up front.

"Large single story residence looks like a great big garden. There's a paddock at the rear of the property, and they've got a conservatory on the back too. The place is surrounded by a tall privet hedge so no fear of being spotted once you're inside the gate,"

"Alarm?"

"Alarm box on the gable end,"

"We'll wait until dark unless they make a move before, then you can follow them. Let's hope they stay 'ome and make my life nice and simple,"

13.00 – Lower Spargo Cottage, Perranarworthal

Hugh drove into the driveway at Lower Spargo, and Jack went out to greet his houseguest.

"Hello, Hugh, welcome. How was the drive down?"

"Excellent, thanks, Jack, the old girl purred all the way down without a hiccup,"

"Is this the old TR you had at uni?" Jack asked, suitably impressed by the smart looking old classic.

"Certainly is but it's had a bit of work done on it since those days plus a complete paint job I had done professionally a couple of years ago,"

"Very smart. Don't worry about unpacking; you can do that later, let's have a bite of lunch. Pam said she's going to make one of her quiches with a bit of salad and we can even dine al fresco now that it's brightened up,"

"Sounds good, does your wife work nearby then?"

"Yes, but today is one of her days off, and she's decided to have her hair done and indulge in a bit of retail therapy in Truro. She works part time at the surgery just down the road in the next village, Devoran, about five minutes on a good day. At that moment, Pam arrived and parked her car outside the cottage. She came up the pathway laden with shopping bags and wearing that smile that made her look so beautiful and reminded Jack every time he saw it just how lucky he was.

She announced that she had changed her mind about the quiche and did not feel like wasting time indoors cooking. It had turned out so bright and sunny that she had stopped at the baker's and bought some pasties so it would be pasty and salad for lunch.

"Pam, let me introduce Hugh Martin,"

"Hello, Doctor Mawgan, pleased to meet you,"

"Pleased to meet you, Hugh. You're not veggie are you?" asked Pam.

"No, certified carnivore although my wife would probably say 'omnivore' as I am renowned for eating anything that's put in front of me,"

"Where's Marjory?"

"She'll be down this evening. She does voluntary work at the local hospice, not the kind of thing she can walk away from at short notice, unfortunately,"

"Not a problem, sit yourself down, and I'll get some lunch organised,"

The meal was full of chitchat about university days and the 'joys' of raising kids. They amused themselves going over the difference between raising boys and raising girls. Hugh had two teenage girls; one had just left Southampton with a first in Marine Sciences and was down in the Falkland Islands doing some work with a research group looking at the Penguin population. She was hoping to get a PhD course but had had no luck so far. The younger one was doing Politics and Philosophy at St Andrew's and was staying with a friend in France. Her father was a politician based in Marseille, and the intention was for it to be a 'working holiday' as an intern at his party HQ. Hugh made a joke about the very idea that a summer in the south of France could be described as 'work'.

The seemingly pleasant and relaxed luncheon was only marred by an underlying tension that all three knew existed in the wake of Jack's eavesdropping the previous night. Pam set about clearing away the remains of lunch and packing the dishwasher. Jack returned to the table in the rear garden where he found Hugh checking his mobile. He looked up at the sound of Jack approaching. "You don't get to be head of IT without the CEO having you on a piece of string, in this case, a piece of electronic string. No peace for the wicked,"

"Trouble?" asked Jack.

"Afraid so. Just as well I'm out of circulation," he put his phone away, "and just as well you can ignore a text message,"

"You got to go back?"

"Not for a day or so. When this has all blown over. The Frimly family are a powerful lot. They are stirring things at work,"

"They're rich I suppose?"

"And how,"

"And with money usually comes power,"

"This lot seem to wield an inordinate amount of power in the backrooms of City firms, the banks and the Treasury. I'm afraid I went and stuck my nose into some of their very smelly business. Not only are they so rich that no one can say how rich but they also have a reputation for making other rich people even richer. The problem is that not all the rich people are good people, so there are a few that are very keen to stay in the shadows. Then I come along and sniff out some of their dirty little secrets. Half the problem is that these Frimlys were so good that anyone in the 'know' was grabbing every penny they could and passing it to them to work their magic,"

"And our protagonists were involved?"

"From what I have tracked down so far I can say that both Chaloner and Duffy participated in the Frimly's schemes, but I have yet to figure out the details. For sure Chaloner has, wherever possible, been systematically turning everything in his entire corporation into cash and then giving it to the Frimlys who do deals according to how long you want to leave the money in their pot. The dividends are paid out into secret accounts in tax havens around the globe. The mixture of clean cash obtained by foul means and dirty cash from every shade of villainy is having a corrosive effect on city trading. I can only surmise that somebody high up in the Treasury has decided to interpret the money laundering rules in a new and 'innovative' way.

There seems to have been a collective decision to simply ignore the rules and consequently there is cash coming and going at breakneck speed," Hugh paused to take a sip from his glass of water.

"Coffee?" said Pam, looking around the table. There were nods of assent, and she disappeared back into the kitchen.

"There is so much cash disappearing under the counter that it's beginning to distort the markets. You know what disturbs me most?"

"No, what?"

"I found out that The Treasury, in other words, the Chancellor, appointed Frimly to the board of the FSA last year, that's the Financial Services Authority. They are the regulators of everything to do with the world of finance,"

"So the fox is guarding the hen house?"

"You could say that," Hugh smiled to himself at the amusing metaphor. His expression returned to a tight-lipped sadness in the grim realisation that his world, the world of banking, investments, and insurance had descended into a cesspit of corruption.

"The other side of that coin is that Chaloner has spent years stripping out every asset that Western Hydro owns but he hasn't done it openly otherwise his shareholders would have had a fit. He's surreptitiously sold a building here and there and then leased it back from a company that he already owns. Of course, he doesn't mind paying top whack for the lease, because he's benefitting on both sides of the deal as the corporate business picks up the tab,"

"And I guess he puts that money to good use with the Frimlys and gets a nice return from them?"

"Not only that but there's the bonus that the profit will disappear into his personal wealth where neither his auditors nor the taxman can find it because it will be wrapped up in a trust fund. As long as he doesn't want to touch it for five or ten years, then all is well. He gets healthy interim dividend payments to pay the bills but a big whack when the deal matures," Pam returned to catch the tail end of the conversation. Coffee was served in silence.

"From what I can make out though, something blew up between Chaloner and Duffy that upset the applecart. Suddenly they both needed more liquidity - cash - than they had available. Such was their greed that they had committed every penny they could lay their hands on. I'm trying to get to the bottom of it. Have you got a high-speed Internet connection?"

"Of course," Jack smiled, "you know me, gadget-man as always, I've got a BT ADSL connection. Probably not as fast as you have in Bristol but good enough for my use and a million times better than a 'dial-up',"

"Plug this Flank Speed box into your outlet with the green lead then plug your own lead into the back of it. Don't know if you've been following the latest developments but we've been experimenting with a new wireless access system in recent months and it's bloody marvellous,"

"How does that work then, and what does 'Flank Speed' mean?"

"'Flank Speed' is the name of the pre-production unit but in future, it's going to be called 'Wi-Fi'. If you have a receiver in your laptop then you can access the Internet from anywhere within range of that 'router' box, that thing there," He pointed to the box he had just handed to Jack.

"Wow, that's cool. Where can I get one?"

"You may be able to get one online, but so far only Apple has integrated the system into their laptops. Others will not be far behind I guess,"

"Right, well let's get you settled in the guest room then you can set up your laptop on the dining table, I assume that you did bring the laptop?"

"You bet. "They headed for Hugh's lovely old TR, which he had rebuilt himself over many years. Once he had unpacked, Hugh connected his Wi-Fi device to Jack's Internet system, and they adjourned to the dining room where Hugh set up his laptop and portable printer. Jack watched, enthralled, as Hugh quickly set about making his hacking techniques look amateurish. He was a master of his art.

"I got to where I am today by helping my CEO and his fellow board members stay out of trouble. I was once in a helicopter with a colleague returning to London Heliport from a meeting at Leeds Castle. As we approached Tower Bridge the pilot took great pleasure in announcing that we were now flying over the City of London, the famous Square Mile where 'there were more crooks than in all the jails in the Britain'. I don't know what had prompted that astute observation but let me tell you, he was absolutely right. The City of London is a vital organ in the world of finance, but just like a well-stocked larder it attracts the vermin, only these rats wear pin-stripe suits and don't have tails,"

"So how do you stay above all that when you are sitting at the heart of it all?"

"We have a great deal of difficulty staying out of trouble, so we run a huge team of analysts who are constantly checking the reports filed by corporations all over the world. I have some very clever lads and lasses working for me in our little Bristol hideaway, especially the group I recruited recently in Hong Kong and Chennai, in India. We provide auditing services for many corporations large and small, and when we sign-off on their accounts we usually have to turn a blind eye to a variety of issues and hope they don't come and bite us in the backside. If we know what those issues are then our team of experts run an analysis on the risks, we are exposed to. Then we go into the sign-off with our eyes open. That way we only get our backside bitten when something unexpected turns up. God forbid that should ever happen because if it did then my team would have failed and my bonus would be history. Maybe I would be history!"

"Hell, Hugh, I knew there was an element of corruption in the business world but I had no idea it was so bad,"

"I started to look into the Chaloner businesses, and their attempts to hide what they were up to were pretty amateurish. There were compromising e-mails everywhere and their attempts to hide assets and disguise the flow of cash were so pathetic that I began to wonder how they could do it and get away with it. When I looked closely at the press archives and searched with particular key personnel names I found some curious, unexplained deaths and then came across this piece in the Straits Times, a Singapore daily newspaper," Hugh took an A4 page from his briefcase and handed it to Jack who began reading.

"Lieu Weiping, Finance Director of Singapore Power and Light Corporation, was found dead at the foot of the stairs in his condominium in Marina Bay. Police say he died of a broken neck; they are treating the death as suspicious having found another threatening note with the chop 'OR GLORY'. In a rare admission, the Chief of Police said he was puzzled. Similar notes have accompanied three deaths in the last three years. Singapore Police were apparently cooperating with colleagues in Malaysia and Thailand as the murders are connected to foreign drug gangs,"

Jack sat open-mouthed, "Hugh, when Desmond Duffy was shot, Edwin and I were the first on the scene, and I found a note with a stamp on it, a rubber stamp, we thought it said 'FOR GLORY', but maybe it really said 'OR GLORY'.

"Then we have a connection with Chaloner,"

"We would have if I still had the note, but that's long gone I'm afraid,"

"I can show you information on maybe a dozen deaths connected with illegal commercial activity in Thailand, Singapore, Malaysia, Vietnam, Hong Kong, Australia, Philippines, and India. In fact, there is hardly a place in the developing world where Chaloner has not been selling or mortgaging assets such as buildings, land, plant, machinery and vehicles. The man is a rogue Jack, a bloody rogue and it seems that the only reason he has survived thus far is courtesy of a murderous policy of removing people who get in his way,"

"You know Hugh, I started this business with the intention of proving that a man I detested was bent. Along the way, a man in a Range Rover murdered a young baby. When I tried to get to the bottom of it all, I had to watch while an ex-colleague was murdered up on Dartmoor. I then became a target and that, believe me, focuses your attention. I need to get enough evidence on Chaloner and his sidekick to guarantee a conviction, and they need to go away for a very long time, nothing less will do, or I may be looking over my shoulder for the rest of my life. Now, can we connect Chaloner to Duffy?"

"My strategy, in the beginning, was simply to accumulate data and when I found something interesting to follow it to the end or until the trail ran cold. I did that with some ease for Chaloner because they were pretty inept at covering their tracks. Duffy was a lot more aware and pretty much kept his 'off-balance-sheet' activities to a minimum,"

"Meaning?" interrupted Jack.

"That money appears and disappears with no apparent traceable source or destination. I can tell you this much. There is a Scottish connection in all this. Haven't worked it out yet but I can tell by the counter receipts that an awful lot of Scottish banknotes are finding their way into the wash, rinse and dry process and there are too many for them to originate south of the border,"

"Duffy has strong connections with Glasgow going back a while. Has Chaloner got anything up in that part of the world?"

"No, at least nothing outside his grouse shooting with the Frimlys. He's essentially a 'developing world' man, but he has some very powerful connections high up in political circles in this country and particularly within the left of centre parties. You probably know that he's gay and the right wing ladies and gentleman steer clear of him in public. However, when you look at their finances you can see large sums of their money moving hither and thither under Chaloner's guidance,"

"But these tax havens are supposed to be water-tight, top secret and impossible to see inside. How on earth do you get all this information?"

"Please Jack, don't be so naive. This is a world where money talks, where everything has a price and everything is for sale. Some disaffected employees of Swiss Banks are infamous for having sold data on their customer's accounts to the authorities in other countries. Banking staff and lawyers who find themselves compromised in some way shape or form are the prime sources. We have ways of finding a pathway to their door and of facilitating the flow of data. That's all I can say on that particular subject I'm afraid, any more detail and I would have to shoot you," he joked.

They chuckled together, but then the seriousness of their situation descended upon them like a cold, wet blanket and the conversation faltered. Pam arrived with a tray of tea and biscuits and joined the discussion. Hugh was only too familiar with the old City maxim that those who talked didn't know and those who knew didn't talk. He knew all right, but his life at the office depended on not talking too much. He grew to understand the system and to hate its unfairness, but it's the rich and powerful that write the rules. It's not surprising that in a world that is apparently unable or unwilling to change, the rich countries will get richer and poor countries will stay poor. The elite in the poor countries, after all, are also the rich and powerful and they look after their own.

Hugh would help Jack as much as he could, but he too had to try his best to keep a low profile. He was under the impression that the financial world thought of him as a neutral 'worker-bee' so he was troubled that by simply delving a little too far into the Frimly's activities he had incurred such a negative reaction.

"You may be surprised to learn that one other significant source of information is e-mails. You wouldn't believe what people say to one another both in private e-mails and in business e-mails. They make the fundamental mistake of believing that nobody else will read them. Some think they are clever and try to send messages covertly,"

'How do you send an e-mail covertly for goodness sake?"

"They use puerile attempts at secret codes or try to hide the text another way,"

"How the hell can you hide text? Surely if you can't see it you can't read it?" observed Pam.

"They will write messages on a white background then change the font to white. To the uninitiated, it looks like a blank page but with two clicks of a mouse button all is revealed. They write messages then insert an image file on top. Delete the image, and there is the message. They write in foreign languages and particularly the languages of the Far East, which can be challenging, but a well-resourced office like ours has access to people that can easily deal with that kind of thing.

One thing I'm sure of and that is if we are poking our noses into that source of information then you can be sure that government agencies are doing the same,"

"If that's the case they don't seem to be doing much about it," added Jack.

"Yes, it begs the question why aren't these people being thrown in jail and there you have the enigma that underpins the whole stinking mess. The people who could throw them in jail don't because the argument goes that they are needed by a system that in effect would be bankrupt and unworkable without a black economy running in the background. It's the black and tacky 'grease' that keeps the wheels of the global economy going and as long as one country is trying to steal a march on every other country it will be tolerated,"

"Do you really believe that?" asked Pam.

"Every intelligence agency in the world uses the black banking system. They couldn't function without it. Another aspect of our troubled world is that some countries very close to us are actually the worst at trying to undermine our success. It's a brutal and unforgiving world out there, and Chaloner and Duffy are just minor players.

"People like me have to be very careful. I am, after all, piggy in the middle. Neither the good guys nor the bad guys like people who spy on their activities, and then know what they know," There was a pause while Jack took all that in.

"Hugh, I had no idea, I thought 'Head of IT' was a dull and boring desk job. It sounds to me that you're a more qualified detective than I ever was and you've been taking bigger risks than we normally do,"

"Dull and boring it is not Jack, but I have to admit that while there are times when I've had to worry about being unceremoniously removed from my post, this is the first time I have faced the possibility of physical harm. As far as I know that is,"

"What does your wife make of it all?"

"Marjory has been a brick. I think she must pretend it's all make believe. Maybe she thinks that if she shows her concern then I won't be able to do my job properly, but I have known her long enough to see through all of that bravado.

"The front door banged and in walked Josh. Jack marvelled at how the pristine, freshly pressed and polished young twelve-year-old who threw his satchel over his shoulder and marched out of the front gate in the morning would return looking like he spent the day wrestling cats in the hedges and ditches of Cornwall.

"Hi Dad, hi Mum. Can I have a glass of milk?" he said, poking his head into the dining room doorway.

"Sure, the fresh milk is on the bottom shelf," said Pam.

"This is Hugh Martin," said Jack, "come and say hello. He's an old friend from our university days," To his surprise Josh marched smartly up to Hugh and proffered his right hand,

"How do you do Mr Martin?" Hugh was quick enough to shake his hand and make the whole thing look totally normal.

"Very well, thank you," Josh was about to go when Hugh said, "Do you play computer games, Josh?" His eyes lit up and

"Of course, Mr Martin,"

"Have you heard of 'Octi' and 'Alpha Blitz'?"

"You bet, they're the tops,"

"Well here is a copy of each that you are welcome to," Hugh reached into his bag and brought out a couple of CDs.

"Wow, thanks, Mr Martin. Dad, can I use your PC?

"OK, but when Mum calls you for dinner you come straight away and take the CDs that Hugh gave you with you when you have finished,"

"Okay Dad," and he disappeared like a rat up a drainpipe.

"The salesmen at the software companies always send me free samples. I think they have missed the fact that my lot have flown the nest," said Hugh.

Jack smiled at how much Josh had come on at the new school. It was turning out to have been a good move. He exchanged smiles with Pam.

Later that evening, with the supper things cleared away and Josh busy with homework, Jack, Pam and Hugh returned to the dining room and once more gathered around Hugh's impromptu workstation.

"Things have been moving too quickly for me to be able to assimilate the big-picture so let's try to piece together the trail so far. At least, as far as we all understand it," said Jack setting the agenda for the evening's discussion.

"For me this all began with a note that I found in the hand of a dead man. Now, where does that note fit into this conundrum?"

"What exactly did it say?" asked Hugh.

"Hang on a minute," Jack went up to the office and came back with his replica.

"This is it as far as I can remember," he put the copy on the table in front of Hugh and Pam peered over their shoulders to take it all in.

"Well, ostensibly this is a note from Sir William Chaloner to Desmond Duffy. We know that Duffy brought the envelope containing the note home with him the night before but did not open it until breakfast the following day. The envelope apparently had no address on it, just his name, so it must have been delivered by hand, probably to Duffy's offices at Dragon Helicopters where he had been working that week," proffered Jack. "A pound to a pinch of salt that Chaloner didn't expect Duffy to take the letter home with him unopened. A letter left at the scene of a murder was sure to have been tested in every which way. I did at one stage speculate that maybe Chaloner had licked the envelope and handed the police his DNA. Maybe that was not such a ridiculous stab in the dark?"

"Yes, that sounds quite plausible," said Pam, "but it would have been a huge added risk as he had to use Neil Jenkins to take care of the note and envelope,"

"Indeed," said Hugh, "and Neil would have put two and two together and guessed that there was a link between them and the shooting,"

"Apart from which," said Jack, "there were some pretty serious risks if Jenkins didn't come up with the goods or got caught tampering with evidence,"

"Maybe it's time to get Neil's diary and see what we can make of his entries. I've already had a look at the relevant days in April, and there doesn't seem to be any answers to the question 'why'?"

Jack went to the office and returned with the sheaf of photocopies of Neil's diary extract. He handed them to Hugh who immediately began examining the details closely.

"Jack, we need a calendar so that we can mark off the significant events that we know about then we can put what we know together with Neil's diary and try to see where the connections might be," Pam volunteered one of the many drug company calendars that arrive on a GP's desk in the period before the new year.

While Hugh and Jack set about creating a timeline, Pam sat studying the replica note that Jack has drawn. After a while she said, "You know if you were to look at this note for the first time without the benefit of Jack's explanation it looks more like a note from Duffy to Chaloner rather than the other way around,"

"Do what dear?"

"This note, it's crude and unsophisticated. It's not in character. After all, Chaloner is a member of the upper classes,"

Jack stopped for a moment and thought about what Pam had just said. He picked up the note and looked long and hard.

"OK, supposing it was Duffy trying to blackmail Chaloner. Why? I've searched the files online for connections between Desmond Duffy and William Chaloner and got nothing,"

"Ah," said Hugh, "did this Duffy chap have a spouse or other adult family member?"

"Yes, a wife, Margaret Duffy," Hugh clicked away on his keyboard, and within a minute he said, "got it, Mrs Margaret Duffy is the Chairman and Managing Director of Dragon Helicopters, and they have a contract with Western Hydro, Sir William Chaloner is the CEO of Western Hydro. I bet that's your link. What a fool I've been. When you asked me to investigate Challenger and Duffy I did just that. Didn't occur to me to check the wife,"

"Mrs Duffy is the MD? That's barmy. She couldn't manage a box of Rice Crispies let alone a helicopter company,"

"Jack, if this guy Duffy has the kind of police record you've indicated then the UK Civil Aviation Authority would never grant him an operating licence in a month of Sundays. Instead, he does what a lot of businessmen do when the pathway to success is blocked by officialdom, they put their wife in the hot seat and then run the company as if she never existed,"

Hugh continued to rifle through an assortment of online material.

"Look, there are a dozen references here to the announcement of the two-year power-line inspection contract. Some press releases issued by Dragon Helicopters, plus a press release by the outgoing contractor Celtic Copters. There are news items galore about an accident, a fatal accident, involving one of Duffy's machines, a Bell Jet Ranger helicopter, registration G-DESD on August thirteenth last year. There's also a bunch of articles about the accident investigators looking into the maintenance of the helicopter, how about that for a good reason for them falling out?"

"We could be on the right path but who the hell shoots the principal of a sub-contractor just because he kills off an insignificant employee. This guy Chaloner doesn't seem the kind of guy to care a damn about a mere functionary," said Jack.

"Then what's this all about?" asked Pam.

"The note says SILENCE IS GOLDEN equals money and then asks for five more 'somethings'. At first, I thought it must be money but you know I reckon that is five more years, another contract worth five more years,"

"Hang on a minute," said Pam "why on earth would Duffy feel he was entitled to another five-year contract if he had just killed one of Chaloner's workers?"

"If what you suggest is indeed the case," said Hugh, "then the implication is that the accident was down to something Western Hydro did,"

"Or didn't do," chipped in Jack. Pam picked up the note,

"We must not forget that according to what you told me when you first showed me this replica it was written on the bottom half of the page, with the top half of the note missing, torn off. What was on the top half of the page?"

Hugh was deep in thought, "Supposing the top half of the note was the incriminating evidence and Chaloner tore it off before returning the note with this melodramatic stamp on it?" He said. "That would mirror the track record he has had for nearly forty years. Using that bloody stamp as a signature on what, in effect, are personalised death warrants for some poor unfortunates.

"To what end?" asked Pam.

"It was probably meant to be a snub. A 'stuff you'," said Jack, "a not very clever 'stuff you', but then again he has a reputation for being an arrogant bastard,"

After a pause Pam said, "Jack, didn't Neil Jenkins mention that these two were arguing about the helicopter accident in his video,"

"Yes. I think you're right. It's a pity I can't remember exactly what he said,"

"Nor can I. This chap Chaloner would be an excellent subject for a psychoanalyst. Look, here is a picture of the cap badge of his old regiment. It's a deaths head with cross-bones and the motto 'OR GLORY'. It fascinates me that he should take the regimental motto and use it for signing death warrants, but he doesn't use the entire device. He takes the most striking part, the skull and crossbones and leaves it off his rubber stamp. He then uses the words 'OR GLORY' to convey 'death'. Why didn't he simply choose the word 'DEATH' or use the skull and crossbones?"

Jack had also been trying to peer into the mind of this madman. "My guess is that he had a suppressed inner self that wanted to make his mark on the world and that using the words from the logo in the way he did it conveys upon him a kind of glory in taking somebody's life without ever having to confront his victim in person. He never kills; he commissions others to do it for him. He gets a kick out of letting the world know that in his eyes he is glorious and that the chosen victims are dead," The other two looked at each other in mock amazement at Jack's attempts at psychoanalysis.

Hugh joined in the spirit of the moment and came up with an interesting suggestion. "It's as if he craves anonymity for the device chosen is enigmatic, to say the least. At the same time, as Jack says, he somehow needs recognition and in his own mind what he is doing by eradicating his victims is bathing himself in glory,"

"Enough amateur psychology for one day," announced Pam, "as I said earlier this weirdo would be a classic study for those more expert than us,"

The trio sat in contemplation for few minutes chewing over the bits and pieces of this jigsaw.

"More trawling the web I guess," said Hugh, and he settled down to see what he could find about the situation between Duffy and Chaloner.

"I'll start by tracking down all their e-mail accounts and taking a look at their correspondence. As I said, people are dreadful at letting their guard down when they write to each other,"

Jack and Pam worked on the timeline, and Hugh combed the net and collected relevant e-mails. He had designed his own software that could search for e-mails using keywords and suck copies with those words onto his laptop via the 'diverter' expertise that he had shared with Jack. Josh had been fast asleep for a couple of hours when Pam eventually gave up, and Jack soon followed leaving Hugh still beavering away.

Jack was on early shift in the morning. He would be up at five a.m. and out the door by five-thirty.

22.00 – Kingston Seymour

Andy was tired and edgy after nearly ten hours of watching the well-off inhabitants of the neighbourhood go about their business. Most households were elderly retired couples enjoying life in one of Somerset's more affluent districts.

Gerry had sat dozing in the front passenger seat but was now preparing himself for his meeting with the target, Mr Hugh Martin, Mr Nosey Parker Martin. The interior of the Jeep was a muddle of cardboard coffee cups and empty sandwich packets.

Nerves were already stretched when the sound of a labouring diesel engine dragged them from their semi-comatose state. Hugh's friend Simon Pegg had collected Hugh's Land Cruiser and hooked up his boat for what he hoped would be a quiet and hassle-free overnight trip to the coast. This was Andy's first glimpse of the boat, so he was confused by what he could see coming out of The Close.

"Is that our Land Cruiser?"

"Maybe," replied a stunned Andy, checking his notes for the registration, "shit, yes, that's it,"

"And the boat?"

"There was no boat Gerry. There was no bloody boat,"

"We 'ave to follow, he may not be coming 'ome tonight and we 'ave to account for 'im before morning or I will be in trouble with the boss. Let's go, go go,"

The pair followed and argued about this unexpected development.

Andy was slightly troubled by Gerry's throwaway line. What did he mean by 'account for him'?

The Land Cruiser turned onto the M5 at junction twenty and headed south. Andy had an idea, "Sedgemoor services is just up the road, if I pull alongside just before the services entrance, you wave like hell at him and point to the boat. He should pull into the services to find out what's wrong. You can stop him and have a chat at the service centre,"

"Gerry seemed distracted but nodded agreement,"

"As long as he parks somewhere suitable I'll deal with him when we stop. Looks like he's alone,"

"What about his wife?"

"He is the primary target, forget the woman," More disturbing language from Gerry, 'target', surely not, not here?

Meanwhile, in the Land Cruiser, seemingly oblivious to the fact that two men were following him Simon was planning his first sailing weekend with the new boat. As he headed south along the M5 he suddenly became aware of a car alongside him, and the passenger was waving frantically and pointing to the boat.

"Hell," thought Simon, "what's wrong? Have I forgotten to secure something?" The rig was handling okay, but there was obviously something amiss. He looked up to see the sign for Sedgemoor Motorway Services and indicated his intention to turn off.

Gerry took out his Glock semi-automatic pistol and screwed a silencer into the muzzle before pulling the slide back and releasing it with a loud click. He checked the safety was 'on' and carefully put it back into his shoulder holster. Andy turned a shade of white and cursed under his breath.

Finding a parking spot with a boat trailer in tow wasn't easy, but he saw a space between two large articulated lorries in the bay reserved for trucks. He set the handbrake and jumped out, by which time the kind fellow travellers who had indicated the source of the problem were joining him at the rear of the boat. They were peering at the supports and checking the tension of the ropes he had used to secure the mast.

Gerry nodded to Andy, "this is perfect," Perfect, what was he saying?

"Hi," said Andy, as Simon approached with a concerned look on his face.

"Something 'as failed down 'ere," said Gerry, pointing at the axle. A puzzled Simon bent down on one knee and peered under the trailer. Gerry had a quick check to make sure that no one else was around, slipped his pistol from under his bomber jacket and placed the silencer on the back of Simon's head and pulled the trigger twice in quick succession. The noise was insignificant amongst the cacophony of air brakes and diesel engines kicking into life.

Simon slumped to the floor. An ever-expanding pool of dark red blood spread towards the nearby drain.

"Jesus fucking Christ Gerry, you didn't tell me you were going to top the poor bastard. I thought you just wanted to talk to him.

"I did,"

"That was a fucking short conversation,"

"Shut the fuck up and give me some 'elp ."

Without another word the two looked around for any sign that their activities were being observed. The trucks blocked the CCTV cameras on the front of the truck driver's café. The two nearby trucks both had their curtains drawn indicating their occupants were probably sleeping. Gerry nodded at the boat. Andy nodded back. They picked up Simon's lifeless body and with blood still draining from the ghastly head wound they pitched him into the cockpit of the Shrimper, out of sight. A few moments later they pulled out of the service area and headed back to Kingston Seymour to collect Gerard's car. Gerry took out his mobile and made the call.

"It's done,"

"Any... repercussions?"

"Very neat and tidy. I'm on the way back, one hour, some small things to do,"

"Small things?'

"We'll have to pick up my car get rid of the car we used in the job,"

"Make sure you leave nothing behind,"

"Don't tell me 'ow to do my job!"

"Calm down Gerry, I'll see you later,"

CHAPTER 16

Wednesday, 28th June, 11.10 – Cadhay Manor

At Cadhay Manor the day began like any other until the story about the murder of the man at Sedgemoor Services hit the news media. It was Sir William's habit, on days that were spent relaxing at home, to take elevenses in the orangery. He would listen to the music on the radio, but the 11 o'clock news rudely interrupted his meditations. The bulletin carried a headline about the success of researchers working on the Human Genome Project. However, the story about poor Simon Pegg, of Kingston Seymour was of more immediate interest. It caused Sir William to drop his digestive biscuit into his cup of Earl Grey in shock.

A teacher called Simon Pegg was apparently assassinated, a bullet to the head, at Sedgemoor Services, dumped, in his boat and left out at Dunkeswell Airfield. Police were looking for a motive and asked anyone who saw anything untoward last night at Sedgemoor Services on the Southbound Carriageway of the M5 to get in touch. They wished to interview Mr Pegg's neighbour, Mr Hugh Martin, who had disappeared from his home and had not arrived at his workplace that morning. There was a suspicion that the boat was to be used for smuggling as fingerprints belonging to a known drug dealer were found in the abandoned car. Police refused to give any further details citing 'on-going enquiries'.

Sir William set off in high dudgeon barely able to control his anger. He found Gerard cleaning his guns in the scullery and gave him the bad news. He was not a happy man.

"You killed the wrong bloody man you fool, idiot!" Gerard was taken aback and sought to defend their unfortunate mistake.

"For 'eavens sake, 'ow was I to know 'e wasn't the right guy. You gave me the registration, and we found the car parked at the address you told me about. We did not see a boat but when 'e appeared 'e was towing a fucking boat so we followed 'im and I did the job, personally,"

"Gerry this is a serious cock-up, you'll have to find the right guy now and deal with him soonest. Get on to it. If that man shares what he knows with the wrong people we are finished, do you understand, finished,"

"We will be sure next time,"

"Bloody right you will, if we carry on like this we'll have a trail of bodies leading to Cadhay that a blind man can follow. Why did you take the car and the boat? The Police are saying they found them abandoned up at Dunkeswell with this chap's body inside the boat. You need to remember about these forensic people. We don't want you connected to a murder now, do we?"

"I've told you before, don't tell me 'ow to do my job. So we got the wrong man, so we will find the right man and then make him pay. If you must know we left the car, and the boat in the truck park at Sedgemoor Services. We didn't even take the car keys, and I can assure you there's absolutely no chance of the police connecting us to the car and boat. Even the cameras were blind in our parking spot,"

"The cameras may not have caught you doing the deed, but they will have you coming and going, you can be sure of that,"

"So what, the tinted glass means that they 'ave no faces and my man 'as torched the vehicle so no forensics,"

"Well it's irrelevant now, you had better get on with things," Sir William stormed back into his office and began to deal with some difficult telephone calls.

12.15 – Trebah Gardens Restaurant, Trebah, Feock, Cornwall

Edwin and Jack were called to the quiet village of Mawnan Smith not far from the port town of Falmouth. This part of the Cornish coast is well known for a collection of sub-tropical gardens that were established by wealthy merchants in the days of sail when Falmouth was the first port of call for many ships returning from the Americas and the Orient.

The staff at Trebah Gardens Restaurant had called for an ambulance after an elderly lady had suffered an asthma attack.

"CornAmb Control this is CornAmb 72,"

"72 go ahead,"

"Roger Control, the patient is female, eighty-two years old, asthma attack. Inhaler located, patient now stable, no transport required. We are going to take our meal-break here if you are okay with that, over,"

"Roger 72, you're stood down at Trebah,"

"Cappuccino Edwin?" asked Jack.

"Ah, a cup of tea today if I may Jack,"

"Come on Edwin, live dangerously, their cappuccinos are great here, best for miles,"

"I'm sure you're right, but today I'll be happy with my tea thanks," The Courtyard restaurant at Trebah was pretty full, so they found a bench seat outside. It was an unexpected luxury to take a meal at a catering establishment instead of on the hoof.

They had each chosen a slice of cake from the delicious selection on display. Jack was a carrot cake man and Edwin a coffee and walnut. By some curious Cornish logic, Edwin had figured that a coffee cake was the best accompaniment to a nice cup of tea. At that moment, Jack's mobile rang.

The opening bars of the Rolling Stones' 'Brown Sugar' signalled an incoming call on Jack's mobile phone," He pulled it from a breast pocket.

"Hello Jack, it's Hugh,"

"Hi, Hugh. What gives?"

"Bad news, very bad news. It's my neighbour, Simon, Simon Pegg,"

"What about him?"

"He's dead Jack, murdered. They found him last night with a bullet in the back of his head,"

"Hang on, who is this guy, what is he to you?"

"Jack, Simon is the chap I lent my car to, the chap with the boat. It's all over the morning news and on the radio,"

"What happened? What's the story?"

"They found him near the old Dunkeswell Airfield, in the back of his boat. It looks like they really are after me Jack, I was a bit sceptical before, but we know for sure. Poor old Simon, dammit, why didn't I think about what I was doing?"

"Hugh, you don't know for sure that it tracks back to you. It could have been a simple theft. Handguns are two a penny these days, and it could be down to a drugged-up nutcase," Jack knew that as he said the words, he was indulging in wishful thinking. The first blow had been struck. No doubt there would be more to come.

"That's kind of what the police are telling the media. At least they say it was probably related to the theft of the car and boat and has a drug connection. They found the fingerprints of a known druggie in the car. Apparently, they had an anonymous tip off that the car and boat had been abandoned up at the Airfield with a dead body in it,"

"I see," said Jack trying to make sense of this worrying news.

"If this is connected to your business and I'm a target then it won't be long before you are too,"

"How do you work that out?"

"Jack, if they murdered Simon then they must have thought it was me in the Land Cruiser. That means they know where I live and know what I drive, but presumably, they don't know what I look like. If they traced me through the registration details, then they must have access to some privileged information,"

"That would be a logical conclusion," said Jack.

"Well here's another logical conclusion, when they realise their mistake they will then go looking for any other vehicle I own which means my TR6 which is sitting in plain view in front of your cottage,"

"OK, listen, if you go into the garage, you will find a tarpaulin at the back, on the shelf above the chest freezer. It should be big enough to throw over your car.

"Let's hope you're wrong and this is all some horrible mistake. I'll have to go now Hugh, work beckons. Hope to be home around two-thirty,"

"Okay, if you need to contact me use your house phone. I've switched my mobile off because the police are looking for me and right now I don't want to be found. The bad guys have clearly got someone on the inside so if the cops can find me the likelihood is that they can too,"

'Understood, speak later, bye,"

"Jack felt a cold shiver come over him at the realisation that with this turn of events he needed to think and plan ahead before those events overtook them. If they found out who he was, then they will be knocking on the door very soon. He must look for ways to put his family beyond the reach of these evil crooks. Maybe Pam's 'plan B' was the answer.

He saw a man talking to Edwin and could tell it was business. He snapped back into work mode. Apparently, a bee had stung a worker in the shop. The supervisor saw the ambulance and thought he would mention it. He was sure the young girl was okay and didn't really want to trouble the crew but could they check her over, just to be sure. She was resting at the back of the shop. Edwin disappeared with what turned out to be the Shop Manager and came back at the rush a couple of minutes later. "Jack, get me the resuscitation pack, O2, BP Monitor and defib, we're at the back of the shop, she's gone into anaphylactic shock, and she's not 'resting', she's bloody well dying, off you go,"

Jack returned loaded down with kit and found the group surrounding a young girl lying on the floor. Edwin was giving mouth to mouth but asked Jack to take over.

"She's going down quickly," He said, taking hold of the resuscitation pack and locating the small capsule containing the drug Adrenalin. He took a syringe and carefully drew one milligram from the capsule then delivered the dose intramuscularly to the upper thigh muscle using an extra-long needle. The effect was almost instantaneous, and the girl began to breathe spontaneously.

"BP and Pulse Oximeter, O2 reading please Jack," Edwin rigged the oxygen bottle and placed the mask over the girl's face, passing the elastic support around the back of her head. "What's her name?" Edwin turned to the manager, "Jeanette," he replied, "Jeanette Pearce,"

"Hello, Jeanette, can you hear me?" No response. "Jack, bring the gurney, tell Control we will be at A&E in twenty minutes with a twenty-five-year-old female, GCS four, anaphylactic shock, one milligram of adrenaline administered,"

Trying to remember everything Edwin asked him to do he went to the ambulance, returning shortly afterwards with the gurney. When he got back, Edwin had managed to get a line into her arm.

"She's almost completely shut down," said Edwin, "they will want to administer fluids as soon as we get to casualty," With well-practiced ease, Jeanette Pearce was placed on the gurney secured with the safety straps and loaded into the ambulance and was soon roaring off to Treliske Hospital A&E.

"Good job today Jack," mused Edwin, as they tidied up their vehicle at the end of the shift. "That lass was a goner if we had not been right there at the time. It was her lucky day. Funny how these things go," Jack was in a pensive mood and nodded in agreement. He shook himself back into reality, bid Edwin goodbye and set off for home where another problem awaited his attention.

The murder of Hugh's neighbour was a significant turn of events. If Hugh was right about the villains having his vehicle details, then somebody had access to the Police National Computer. That would mean that the bad guys had another bent cop on the payroll apart from Neil Jenkins. A more disturbing possibility would be that they were being aided and abetted by elements within the 'establishment' that believe that Hugh's activities were rocking their boat. He knew that sometimes governments have to resort to some nasty tactics, maybe the rot went a lot higher up the tree than he first thought.

When Jack arrived home, he found Pam and Hugh at the computer in the dining room. Hugh's wife, Marjory, had arrived and was busy making them a cup of tea.

"Shouldn't you be back at work by now?" he asked Pam, happy to see her but concerned that she had forgotten the time.

"No surgery this afternoon – admin staff training. We're getting a new computer-based prescription system apparently; her voice was cold and flat. The atmosphere was tense. They had been awaiting his arrival.

Jack was still in his motorcycle leathers so excused himself while he went upstairs to change. When he finally arrived downstairs, there was a conspiratorial air in the room. It was evident that Pam had been elected spokesperson. He sat down at the head of the table and waited for her to begin.

"Jack the situation is getting serious, very, very serious. So far we have been on the fringes of three murders. You two seem to have disturbed a hornet's nest. If what Hugh has told me is an accurate reflection of the situation, then we're all likely to be targets of these maniacs,"

"I can't deny it," Jack replied, "but there is no need to change our plans,"

"What plans?" she shot back at him.

"We move out, lay low,"

"Then what?"

"Hugh and I will turn the Internet upside down until we get enough on Chaloner to put him away,"

"You asked Hugh to go poking around in Chaloner's and Duffy's affairs before and look where it got us. You have managed to find nothing more than a bucket full of shit. If you excuse my French,"

"She's right Jack; it's time to call your ex-colleagues and get them onside,"

Marjory arrived with a tray and poured them each a cup of tea. Jack sat back in his chair, his lips were thin and stretched and his expression was grim. His temper was on the verge of exploding. The worry and fatigue generated by the previous weeks and months were beginning to take their toll. He began with a measured tone, trying to hold himself back.

"What the fucking hell do I tell them? That I interfered with evidence at a murder scene. Failed to notify the investigating officer as soon as I became aware that the note held by the dead man was missing. That I was complicit in the fatal accident in which a young baby died because I was arguably 'chasing' the car involved. That I was shot at while observing a murder on Dartmoor then failed to notify the police that I was a witness. Can't you can see that I can't go and tell my so called 'ex-colleagues' about what has happened. If they get their hands on me, then I'll be truly fucked. They will rub their hands with glee throw me in a cell and chuck away the key," By the time he finished, he had found himself yelling at them.

The others were clearly taken aback. His pent-up anger at the unfairness of it all, the lingering hurt of his ignominious demotion to Detective Sergeant, the fear generated by being shot at and the stress of trying to appear in control were all but pushing him over the edge.

"Don't you get it? Don't you bloody well understand?" he continued, "the police are not going to treat me as a friend anymore. The minute they get a sniff that something big is going on and that powerful people are implicated they will be terrified of it getting out of control. They will close ranks and hide behind their procedures and protocols while I languish in Truro nick. You can't do what I did and expect a nod and a wink. I don't have the kind of leverage that Neil Jenkins apparently enjoyed. In fact, I may turn out to be a convenient scapegoat. There are some very senior officers connected with Neil's nefarious activities, and they may have every reason to bury me, so I have no guarantee that I will be treated fairly. I can't break cover until we are sure who the good guys are so we can get some 'top-cover'. We need some hard evidence and people we can trust to deal with it effectively. My family, career, my reputation. Not to mention our way of life, they are all at stake here,"

"Jack, darling, don't you think you're a just a tiny bit paranoid?"

"No, I bloody well don't,"

The yelling didn't faze Pam one iota, and she turned him by the arm to face her and gave as good as she got.

"What about our lives?" yelled Pam, stabbing the words at him like a knife.

"Hang on folks," said Hugh, "I have a dog in this fight too so listen up. I can delve into the private affairs of people like Chaloner because the security services encourage me to do so. Don't forget that I am officially still on the books of HQ Squadron, 21 Regiment SAS Reserves,"

"I'm sorry," said Pam, what does that mean?"

"It means that since I was mobilised and sent to Kuwait, I have continued in Her Majesty's service but with a different sort of hat on. More of an invisible, part-time hat I suppose," Pam's expression revealed her lack of understanding of what was being said. Jack took up the narrative.

"Hugh served in Iraq during 'Desert Storm, Gulf War One, when Saddam invaded Kuwait, and we kicked him out,"

"Well, I didn't do much of the kicking, but I was what they now call a 'cyber warrior', working at HQ and acting as liaison with our Special Forces,"

"What does an accountant do in a war zone?" she asked.

"It's not my accounting skills they need but my ability to gather electronic intelligence. If you overrun a front-line position or in my case, one behind enemy lines, then you need to collect all you can from their computer systems, plans, maps and codes before the enemy realises that we have them. It's very valuable stuff,"

"Is that where you got your gammy leg," asked Pam.

"Yes, we were dropped into the desert behind a field HQ. The boys took out the defenders, and my interpreter and I were able to retrieve a lot of material before we got the hell out of there. Unfortunately, one of the Iraqi officers was not as dead as he should have been and set off a hand grenade. I was lucky; my interpreter wasn't, he was killed,"

"You still work for the Army?" Pam asked, intrigued by this revelation.

"In a way,"

"In a way? What does that mean?"

"It means that my contacts in the Security Services occasionally need to use my expertise to better understand what is going on in certain, let's call them, dark corners, of our governmental administration and their relationship with similar parts of the commercial world,"

"So, if we cut out the bullshit you're a spy!"

"I think 'spook' is the preferred epithet these days but my official response is that I am unable to confirm or deny such an assertion,"

"But what's your unofficial response?"

"Yes, I make my skills available to the Secret Intelligence Services in any way they think I can help. Which, since Jack first contacted me has been to get a handle on what Chaloner and his associates are up to,"

"What are they up to?" Jack chimed in.

"No good, is the short answer. They have fingers in many pies, but the big one is the one that the Frimlys are involved with,"

"If you are thick with the Security Service why can't we just hand them the problem and walk away? Why should we just sit here like a bunch of mugs?" Hugh and Jack exchanged glances before Hugh replied.

"There are some big fish involved, really big fish. They won't move on Chaloner or any of the others until they have cast iron evidence. They are working on it, but they are short of resources and need anything we can contribute. In the meantime, they expect us to show a stiff upper lip and do our best to stay out of the firing line. The room fell silent. Eventually, Pam filled the vacuum.

"I'm going to pour myself a G & T, anyone else?"

"Thanks," said Hugh.

"Whisky please love,"

They sat around the table quietly thinking and taking an occasional sip from their generously filled crystal glasses.

"Look, Hugh, it's clear that they somehow discovered that you were looking into their affairs. How could that be? With all the 'diverters' and multiple VPNs, how could they get to you?"

"I've been racking my brains ever since you told me that Chaloner knew my name. I can only suggest, and I hate to say this, that Chaloner's people must have someone on the inside in my company. Plus, to get the kind of information they obviously have then he or she would need to be senior to me, a board member maybe. I did most of my snooping on my system at home, but I did use my work computer and various other office computers located in other departments.

"Remember, I designed these systems, their antivirus software and their firewalls, and I set out the way my team were to configure them. I knew, or at least I thought I knew how to work within them without setting off any alarms. There are companies run by Chaloner and audited by IAC. Somehow, someone has been able to authorise a trip-wire on those accounts. To trace it back to me the 'mole' must have details of my log-on. I have to change that log-on every week and place a copy in my safe. There has to be a way for my successor to access my files if I get run over by a bus so that the vital data in my personal files can be located if required,"

"So, you are saying that somebody took a copy of your log-on from the safe and was able to monitor the files you chose to access and track that activity back to you," asked Jack.

"That's always a possibility. The combination is notified to our head of security in a sealed envelope and kept in his safe,"

"Doesn't sound very 'leak-proof' to me," said Pam, "who checks the checkers?"

"Yes, well, now you mention it I guess it sounds a bit simplistic. There is another possibility, and that is the dreaded bug,"

"What, a listening device?"

'No, a different kind of bug. This is a bug that fits in between the keyboard and the computer and transmits every keystroke to a receiver that then records them. When played back it shows every key you pressed. You wouldn't have to be an expert to work out my log-on,"

"Don't you have the place swept for bugs?"

"Of course. But when you stop and think about it that's not much good if those doing the sweeping are the ones who put the bug there in the first place,"

"Did you know about all of this Marjory?" Pam asked.

"Most of it but what worries me is that Hugh must have been under surveillance for quite a while,"

"I had no idea. I was completely unaware that I had drawn attention to myself,"

"Your digging around must have upset someone,"

"The most worrying thing is that they outsmarted me and that hurts,"

"What a mess," said Pam.

"I'm afraid it gets worse," said Jack. They all rounded on him as he psyched himself up to deliver some more bad news. With both cheeks puffed out and clearly marshalling his thoughts he began.

"You remember I told you that when I was following the Range Rover from the Tank Museum, the driver pulled that 'fast-one' and went twice around the roundabout at Salisbury," Pam and Hugh exchanged glances.

"Yes," said Pam, "what about it?"

"The Range Rover came up behind me. I was so shocked, I suppose, but it didn't occur to me until last night," The three exchanged looks.

"What didn't occur to you?" said Pam at last.

"He probably clocked the registration of the bike,"

"Hell!" said Hugh.

"My God!" said Pam, "they'll know who we are by now,"

"But look, that was the bad news. The seriously bad news would have been the heavy mob turning up here the following morning. The good news is that they didn't turn up. That can only mean that they did not clock my registration after all,"

"Either way we cannot be complacent," Said Hugh

"All they have is a link to Neil Jenkins and a man on a black motorcycle," said Jack, "they don't even know that you and I are working together,"

"I can't imagine that they are not trying to find you," said Marjory, "they will need to know who their adversaries are. You could be from the police or even the security services, but I doubt they would be expecting a lone civilian to be working on his own behalf,"

"I'm for taking the advice your lot gave us and bugger off out of here," said Pam, "all we have to do is remove ourselves from the scene and let them get on with it. Then, when they have them all behind bars we can get on with our lives," Jack and Hugh looked at each other, both thinking the same thing. Jack spoke first.

"The trouble is that they would have done that by now if they had the evidence they needed. Reading between the lines, I think they are still in the learning phase," Hugh then puts some meat on the bone in support of Jack's theory.

"They have yet to gather sufficient evidence against those in high office, and until they do so they, themselves, are in peril,"

"You make it sound like a game of chess," said Pam.

"With respect, it's a bit more serious than that, but I do think your instinct to remove yourselves... ourselves from the field of battle is the correct one,"

"So, we head for the Helford and lie low in Auntie May's cottage," said Pam.

"Sounds like a plan," Jack added.

"I'll make a call to the agent and start packing," she replied.

Pam and Marjory left the room. Hugh came close to Jack and in low tones said, "There is something I haven't told you," Jack raised an eyebrow.

"Go on," he replied.

"We are the 'hare' for the team working on this case," It took a moment for Jack to work out what Hugh was saying.

"You mean that they, your MI5 boys, won't step in and stop the bad guys from finding us?"

"They cannot, not until they have the evidence they need,"

"For Christ sake... you had better not tell Pam; she'll go nuts. And by the way, there are five of us involved. Don't forget young Josh,"

"Look, there is no need for us to sit idly by. I have turned up a lot of good stuff on Chaloner, but we may be able to tie him into the Duffy murder and then we'll be in business,"

"So, keep looking for a trail,"

"Exactly,"

"Does Rose Cottage have internet access?"

"I believe so; the original summer tenants paid for a line to be put in specially for their use,"

"OK, well, we will indeed be in business. Just where is this place, Helford Village?"

"Helford Village is about forty-five minutes from here by road, about half that if you take the ferry," offered Pam as she and Marjory returned.

"Car Ferry?"

"Unfortunately not, it's just a small boat that operates on demand,"

"What about Josh's school? We need a plan," said Jack.

"I'll call Dr Harvey," said Pam, "The Head of School, I'll explain that we have arranged for Josh to attend a series of private maths classes being run this summer by a famous IT Manager from a firm of top city accountants. I'll promise he will be back for the end-of-term exams," Jack gave a chuckle,

"It might work I suppose," he said.

"As long as he is with us he'll be safe because we will make sure he stays safe, won't we?" asked Pam. "I couldn't bear to send him away; I would worry myself to death.

"We'll do our best, for sure,"

"That will have to do then,"

"Damnation, said Hugh, staring at his cell phone,"

"What's up?" asked Pam.

"I can't use this now, in fact, I can't even turn it on,"

"Why not?"

"Because the system will detect my signal as soon as I switch on they will triangulate and know exactly where I am. Time to go 'off-grid',"

"Off-grid?" asked Pam, "explain,"

"No mobile phones to be used unless they are untraceable pay-as-you-go throw-aways, no credit cards, no ATM cash withdrawals. In fact, no interaction with anything that may record your presence and then store that information,"

"Sounds a bit excessive," said Pam, I need to stay in touch with people, my kids, my parents, you guys,"

"Don't worry. I'll sort it," Hugh assured them.

"What isn't sorted is my job," she said.

"Can you find a locum?" asked Marjory.

"That's down to my Practice Manager, but I'm sure I can sweet talk her. I tell her my beloved is taking an unscheduled holiday,"

"Will she wear that?"

"Needs must I reckon. She'll have to. I don't see we have much choice,"

"I've got a similar problem," said Hugh, "but all I can do is keep off the radar and hope I have a job to go back to work. What about you Jack?"

"I'll put in for a couple of weeks' compassionate leave after my assessment on Friday. If I make it to my assessment that is. If I don't make it, then I may not have a job when this lot is all over,"

"Looks like I'm the only one with no complications. Oh, the joys of being a housewife," said Marjory.

"Where exactly is Helford anyway?" asked Hugh.

"I'll take you there tomorrow," said Pam, "I'm taking a day off and need to stop by my folks and say 'hi'. We could take a run down to Helford and show you Rose Cottage. By the way, what shall I tell my mum and dad?"

"Is that absolutely necessary?" said Jack, with a pained expression, "the less other people know, the harder it will be to find us,"

Pam wasn't happy with that. She needed to share her situation with somebody, and her mum had always been there for her.

"I'm going to stop by their place and tell them not to worry if they don't hear from us for a while," Jack knew when he was beaten.

"OK, but just remember you two, we cannot, I repeat, we cannot be complacent. Pay attention to who is following you and keep a look out for anything unusual," he said, with his stern tone making the point that he was serious.

"May I make a suggestion Jack?"

"Yes Hugh, go ahead,"

"When we go 'off grid' on Friday we will need communications. I suggest I go to the local phone shop and buy some cheap pay-as-you-go handsets that we can use for the next week or so. We will need five plus one spare,"

"OK," said Jack, "good idea,"

"Oh, not another new phone and I've only just learned how to use the one I have," said Pam,"

"Don't worry these will be very simple handsets. I'm sure you will manage,"

"Thanks. I think we owe you an apology you wouldn't be in this mess if we hadn't asked you to poke around in the affairs of some very nasty people,"

"As far as I can tell you just accelerated the pace of something that was already bubbling away. In fact, you may have handed the boys in London exactly what they need,"

"That's all very well, but I don't believe we should sit around and hope that your boys in London will save our backsides and this will all go away," said Jack. "I'll believe that when we know exactly why the Chaloner-Duffy nonsense was going on, we will be able to work out how and why Duffy was assassinated and who did it.

"The web is the best way I can think of to reconcile that issue; it will need some painstaking work, but the information is there for us to find. You already have a vast amount of data but from what you say you need time to analyse it all. As you are the financial man, I suggest you carry on with the process of tracking down where the money comes from and where it goes. I will set about trying to understand how these people are connected and why such a diverse group ended up at each other's throats.

Josh kept a lone vigil by the TV and was for once allowed to have supper on a tray on his lap. He was excited about bunking off school and was itching to learn anything he could from Hugh, his newly found computer hero.

By bedtime, Jack's efforts had produced a possible link to explain the antipathy between Chaloner and Duffy. He called them together for some cocoa and a chat. He revealed that he had been trawling through the e-mails at Western Hydro.

"It's simple," he said, "but time-consuming. The first one I tried produced hundreds of hits from many different employees but one exchange between Chaloner's secretary and one of the receptionists was of particular interest.

"It describes the row that Chaloner and Duffy had the day before the Duffy shooting. After the row, the subject of which is unknown at this point, Duffy left. He returned later that day, but Chaloner refused to see him, so he apparently left again and then returned with an envelope. He gave the letter to the receptionist who passed it to Chaloner's secretary. It was her custom to open all company mail unless marked 'personal' so she opened it. Inside was a photocopy of a letter written by Sir William but written on the bottom was a curious message that she did not understand but mentioned the words 'Silence is Golden'.

"I think we have found the top half of the note, the missing portion. Well, at least we have an idea that it was a letter from Duffy to Chaloner but what it was about is still a mystery. Still, at least now I can narrow my search a bit,"

"That's good news," said Hugh, "but I'm not happy that we should hang around just waiting to become a target. I'm getting nervous. I think we should move now and just disappear,"

"Define 'now'," said Jack.

"Tomorrow, or at least as soon as possible. We need to get 'off grid' as soon as we can,"

"I agree," said Pam, "sitting around here is just making me more and more nervous. To hell with our jobs and Josh's schooling let's get away or get some protection of some kind," Jack could see from their expressions that they were looking to him for leadership. He sat thinking for a moment. He went to the cocktail cabinet and poured a glass of whisky and sipped it without offering a drink to any of the others. They sat watching his every move aware that he was working up an answer to their concerns and were patient in their anticipation of a safe and workable way forward.

"OK, we move, but we can't bale out without making preparations. We need to set up Rose Cottage, pack up the essentials from here and take care of Josh and Marjory. I'll call in sick before we go to bed and you will have to do the same in the morning, Pam,"

"No that won't be necessary, I've already arranged a day off remember,"

"OK, that makes it easy. It looks like I'll have to give my Ambulance Technician's assessment a miss,"

"That won't make you very popular with Edwin,"

"Let's just see how things go. Remember they may not be aware of the connection between Hugh and me yet. They have been chasing the guy who hacked their computer system on the one hand and the chap who followed their Range Rover on the other. That could be to our advantage. We have the big picture whereas they don't,"

"Maybe," said Hugh, "but if they ever got to realise that we were cooperating you can be sure they would make determined effort to kill two birds with one stone,"

Pam became upset at his poor choice of words, and Jack had to put his arm around her and reassure her.

"Look, folks, if we stay ahead of the game, we will be fine. If we don't, then we go straight to the Police and to be sure we stay ahead of Chaloner's men I'm going to bring in some reinforcements,"

"Reinforcements?" said Pam, "who?"

"I'll give Dan Barclay a call and get him down here to help. If we turn Rose Cottage into a safe house and protect it effectively, then we will have the time to work out how to bring this thing to a satisfactory conclusion. Running to the cops may sound like a good way out, but if all it does is put us in greater danger from those vested interests that we have upset so badly then, in the long run, we will be a lot worse off. Once we are in the hands of the authorities, it will be easier for the bad guys to ensure that we are silenced for good. If we are to get out of this cleanly, then we have to use our brains but be prepared to use muscle if we have to,"

Jack called the Control Centre at Ambulance HQ and reported in sick with a tummy bug. He told the duty controller he hoped to be fit by Friday.

With plenty to contemplate they wearily adjourned to bed.

CHAPTER 17

Thursday 29th June – Cadhay Manor, Ottery St Mary, Devon

SIR WILLIAM WAS UP bright and early feeling cheerful about the world after a good night's sleep. He took his breakfast in the dining room, taking his seat at the head of a long highly polished mahogany table with just one place setting.

The silverware glinted in the morning sunlight as the butler delivered his eggs benedict. Gerard wasn't a breakfast person, and a large cup of black coffee and a croissant or 'pain chocolate' taken in the scullery in front of the TV was his usual start to the day.

With breakfast over it was time to deal with the affairs of state, the affairs of the 'Chaloner' state at least. In his hands lay the future of more than ten thousand overseas employees and two thousand in the UK. He had accumulated a vast fortune and was wedded to the process of accumulating more. At a dinner party, he had once asked his guest, 'Albert, do you know how much money is enough?' The puzzled and disinterested guest had no idea, but to hoots of his own laughter Sir William replied, 'just a little bit more.'

His mobile rang, and he answered immediately. "Hello Francis, have you had any luck old chap, only I'm rather keen to track this fellow down… yes I know, it's very perplexing, he's appeared out of nowhere, and his only connection that we are aware of is through Detective Sergeant Jenkins… okay Francis well, keep trying. I can't believe that I got any more than just one digit of his number plate wrong... righto, Francis good-bye for now... alright dear... and to you," Gerard appeared carrying the daily newspaper.

"Any joy?" he said.

"Unfortunately not, we are going to have to get some more help Gerry, and we need to be smarter. I have been nurturing a suspicion that our mystery man might be one of Detective Sergeant Jenkins' colleagues but possibly from Internal Affairs. If he has been as careless as I know he can be then they may well have been watching him. Stupid man,"

"Alors... what do you want to do? I am just one man; I cannot search the west country alone, and I know 'ow you hate to involve others,"

"I think we will just have to bite the bullet, Gerry. We can use some 'odd-job boys' that one of my old chums has recommended. They can help to make enquiries and sniff around the bazaars and delights of the area where Jenkins lived and worked. In particular, we must try to find anyone who is prepared to discuss his contribution to the Devon and Cornwall Constabulary. I need a complete picture,"

"Are you sure about these people your friend 'as recommended. Can they be trusted?"

"Look, here is a profile on each of them. I asked for serious players only and received this fax an hour ago," He handed Gerry a sheaf of papers held together with a bulldog clip.

Lower Spargo Cottage, Perranarworthal

Jack and Pam had taken a load of bedding and a suitcase full of clothes to Rose Cottage to check all was ready for their occupation. It wasn't. The decision to move in straightaway had backfired. The agent said that he had been told to release the keys on Friday and refused to hand them over without explicit permission from Auntie May. It was a frustrating morning and Jack wasted much of the day in a fruitless attempt to contact Auntie May and get ahead of the game. It turned out she had just left for her sister's and wouldn't be back for another week. They would have to spend one more night at Lower Spargo and try again on Friday morning. They left Jack's Jaguar in the Helford Village car park and returned in Pam's Clio.

Hugh missed his trip to Mullion and Helford in favour of a bus ride into Truro where he had found what he needed in the way of cell phones and arranged some cash for the week ahead. He knew there was a risk of being traced if he went to a bank so after a brief search he found Probus Pawnbrokers in Chapel Street. Here he did a deal for £1,000 on his Rolex watch.

When he came back at midday, Pam had finished her packing and managed a final shop at the Asda Supermarket in Penryn. Hugh issued the mobiles and explained that he had loaded the numbers and details of their owners into the memory of each so it would be possible for everyone in the group to contact each other. From that moment on, Hugh emphasised, they were to switch off their existing phones. Jack would make sure that Josh received his new phone and would remove the old one.

With nothing to be done until the next day, Jack should have taken out his Training Notes and swotted for the assessment he was supposed to attend in the morning. There were, however, other priorities and he settled down with Hugh to analyse the progress he had made with their on-line investigations.

"I think I have a handle on the cash inflow north of the border," he announced with a proud smile.

"The bad guys have obviously got a tame manager at Clydesdale Bank HQ. There are three branches of the Clydesdale in Glasgow plus the HQ, which also functions as a branch. Large volumes of cash are paid in through these four branches and are then moved on to accounts abroad. Any one of these accounts should, by rights, have been flagged up as suspicious given the amounts flowing through them. Somebody is manipulating the computer records so that it only displays one stream of funds under the name D. Jones.

"Now, this means that they must also have a tame auditor. Unfortunately, or maybe fortunately, IAC, my company provides their auditors, so I have poked my nose into the personal accounts belonging to our staff in Scotland. Of course, any accountant worth his or her salt would not be stupid enough to pay money from a back-hander into their own account, so the usual trick is to pay it into the account of a trusted member of the family. Tracking the relatives of all the IAC employees in Scotland would take forever, so I started by looking at the Glasgow office and guess what? Hillary McKay, Senior Auditor at our West George Street office, has a brother in Newcastle and for a car park attendant, Mr William Morris has a very healthy bank balance. I reckon we have nailed it, at least as far as that part is concerned,"

"Wow," said Jack in admiration.

"Now hold on to your seat because what I have to tell you will blow you away. The funds that leave Scotland end up in accounts controlled by Desmond Duffy, and if you are looking for a connection, then I'll give you two. Hilary McKay, the senior auditor remember, is Desmond's cousin and Deirdre McKay, Hilary's daughter, is married to Davy Gordon. I believe he's a bit of a wheel in the underworld up there,"

"Hang on a minute, I know that name," said Jack, fumbling through a pile of papers on the table. "I'm looking for Detective Inspector Sidney Patterson's notes following his visit to Glasgow at the end of April… here we are, the number one villain in the Glasgow area is a Davy Gordon,"

"Well this chap Gordon is using Desmond to launder his stash," said Hugh.

"But look here," said Jack, pointing to Sidney's notes, "Sidney clearly says that it was Bernie Gordon, Davy Gordon's father that ordered Duffy out of Glasgow on pain of death,"

"All is not what it seems," said Hugh enigmatically, "I bet it was a setup, I mean, who leaves the Glasgow underworld under that sort of cloud without a pair of crutches?"

"Quite," replied Jack after a pause and scratching his head. "But that means that all this time Desmond was linked to the Glasgow Mafia,"

"Didn't you tell me that Desmond took a copy of the Glasgow Herald on a regular basis?

"Yes, it was delivered a day late, but he always read it religiously according to Sidney's interview with his wife, Margaret,"

"Ask yourself why a guy like Des would read a day-old local paper that relates to a city five hundred miles away?"

"Don't be so disparaging of our Scots neighbours. The Herald is a 'tour de force' north of the border. I would say it's quite natural for Des to have a fond regard for his old home town,"

"That's as maybe, but I am willing to bet that the only part that Desmond read in detail was the 'Personals',"

"What are you on about?"

"How do you think Des and Davy Gordon communicated, bearing in mind that they had gone to so much trouble to make people believe they weren't on speaking terms? Particularly when the police are concerned,"

"Are you saying that Des received his instructions from the Gordons in the newspaper?"

"Exactly, and he probably sent back messages in the same way although now we are in the age of e-mail they may well have found out how to use modern communications to replace their covert but somewhat antiquated means in the newspaper. We will need to dig into that question sooner rather than later. If they are using e-mail, then we stand to learn a lot from what they say,"

"You will need to show me that newspaper trick. Then I'll believe you,"

"Sending messages hidden in the personal columns is as old as the hills and probably saw its most famous manifestation during the Second World War when the BBC sent instructions to the French Resistance using coded personal messages,"

"OK, so Des was told what to do and when to do it and presumably these messages related to monies flowing in and out of the accounts that Des managed on behalf of the Gordons," said Jack.

"Quite probably. They wouldn't want the funds to hang around too long so the timing would be an issue. They almost certainly ran a variety of accounts and would direct the funds to them as they thought best. I'm guessing that being a family-run 'firm', each family member would have an account and would receive a payment according to their status and performance. The bulk funds would be received by Des and apportioned in accordance with instructions sent by the head man or maybe his finance manager or even a lawyer,"

"What happens to it then and how do they get their money back?"

"You see, generally when you have dirty money you swap it for the clean stuff and pay for the privilege. You pass a million through the 'Laundromat' and get back five hundred thousand. That's a significant loss, but clean stuff is spendable and more importantly, untraceable. That's probably the way things were until Mr Frimly appeared on the scene,"

"What's so special about this guy Frimly? Does he own his own printing press churning out dollar bills or pound notes or what?"

"No, ostensibly the bank they run is legit. What they do better than any other is disguise the ownership of the funds they take in, the funds they manage and invest. To better understand the scale of what goes on in the real world of commerce and banking you need to be aware that more than half the world's trade, at least on paper, passes through what we recognise as tax havens but don't misunderstand. The biggest tax havens are not tropical islands or European principalities but are in fact New York and London,"

"London?" queried Jack, "How can that be? We don't have banking secrecy laws like they have in Switzerland,"

"No.," said Hugh, "we have the 'trust fund' system and the City of London instead,"

"How do they work then?"

"The trust fund system goes back centuries to the days when the landed aristocracy would go off to the Crusades and leave their wealth in the hands of a trusted steward in case they didn't come back. The crucial thing about a trust fund is that ownership of that wealth is transferred and the arrangement can remain one that is between the 'steward' and the 'principle'. These days the steward is your lawyer, and he just follows the Deed of Trust that instructs him on how the wealth is to be managed. The existence and details of a trust are subject to lawyer-client privilege so of course, they remain secret.

"There is usually a clause in the Deed that explains that 'investments' are to be guided by the hand of a 'responsible person'. You can guess who that will be,"

"The guy who set it up?"

"Correct, and you can assume there is provision made for the death of the principle and the transmission of wealth to his beneficiaries. You cannot tax wealthy people if they apparently have no wealth. One day, when we have more time, I'll tell you the story of the Vestey brothers who, in a way, started this whole trust fund method of tax avoidance back in the 1920s.

"We could surmise that Chaloner introduced Duffy to the Trust system and he, in turn, converted the Gordons who, presumably were delighted to be getting a net profit while also hiding the identity of the owners of these new investments,"

"But surely the Inland Revenue can monitor these trusts and tax them accordingly?"

"Sorry to disappoint you Jack but for the most part, the Revenue doesn't even know these trusts exist let alone who controls the funds. For those with cash that originated as the product of some criminal activity this is a boon, for their money is treated like any other and they not only get back the face value, they get a hefty profit on top,"

"And how does the City of London fit into the picture?"

"You may have noticed when in London that the police in the city wear cap bands with a red and white check pattern rather than the black and white of all other UK police forces. That is because they police a different kind of territory from any other part of UK. The City has its own corporate government system and is protected by charters and structures going as far back as the Roman era. The finances of this nation were always controlled from that part of London, and they have written their own rules ever since. Non-democratic it may be, but no single corporate body has as much power and influence as The City Fathers,"

"That can't be so. What about Parliament?"

"Yes, Parliament rules but a charter going back to William and Mary protects them from any attempt at regulation by others. They even have a representative in the House of Commons. He sits at the opposite end of the chamber from the speaker in a cubicle built especially for him. He is the historical link between the monarchy and parliament and is the formal representative of the Corporation of London. He has been keeping an eye on things ever since the days of Henry VIII who taxed the nobility and incurred their wrath as a result,"

"Wow, a state within a state. Where do Chaloner and Duffy fit in this picture?"

"Chaloner is delivering funds to Frimlys that originate not only from his own coffers but Duffy's too,"

"How come?"

"I'll make an educated guess,"

"Go on then," said Jack anxious to hear more.

"I believe that Desmond has been at this laundering lark for a while, but when he met up with Chaloner, he stopped doing it the old-fashioned way,"

"What old-fashioned way?"

"As I said earlier, selling dirty money for 50% of its face value. Then, I reckon, Chaloner introduced Duffy to the Frimly's Trust system,"

"Why on earth would he do that, they don't exactly move in the same circles do they?"

"My guess is that Chaloner was taking a cut from Duffy's share, so the more he could push through Frimlys, the more he earned from the turnover. Ten percent of ten million pounds is one million pounds. Certainly, this not to be sniffed at and as we are beginning to realise, Sir William is beginning to run out of things to sell to keep him in the manner to which he has become accustomed. It won't be long before he has to start drawing on his secret stash that in theory is lodged in a bank in the Caymans but, in reality, is sitting in a bank here in the City of London in the hands of an obscure trust fund,"

"Where does all this profit come from?"

"Well 'profit' in the heady world of complex tax avoidance schemes can mean different things to different people. The objective is to persuade one particular group, The Revenue, that the 'profit' is notional and doesn't really exist. That, of course, is relevant to our discussion if we are talking about legal means of minimising tax. My investigation revealed that Frimlys have their major base in the Caymans. Investors decide how much money they wish to shelter and then pay Frimlys about seven per cent of that sum in cash. The balance was a theoretical loan and would be used to buy the right to a dividend issued by a separate offshore company.

"Complex tax law allows a company to receive the right to a dividend tax-free. The same company can claim the cost of buying the dividend as a 'deductible' expense. Frimlys thereby allowed investors to send money on a path that creates a tax loss without actually losing any money. In essence, you take the dirty money, clean it up, invest it, make a sizeable profit, pay virtually no tax, reinvest, make even more profit, and so on and so on. A real financial multiplier,"

"It would be great if you could get the details of those involved at the top,"

"It's a deal, but later, there's work to do. I have a list of personalities and top names already, actors, musicians, sportsmen, people with loads of money to 'invest'. I think I can grow that list a lot more and believe me, from what I can see already the names are going to add up to a stunning list of the crème de la crème of British society,"

"Okay," said Jack, "I've had enough reading e-mails at Western Hydro. Time to tackle those from Dragon Helicopters,"

After supper, the adults lingered around the kitchen table, and Josh went off to get on top of the pile of homework he had been given as part of the quid-pro-quo with his form master for his pending 'absence'. Hugh and Jack shared their progress with Pam and Marjory. The scale of wrongdoing bewildered Pam who had never before had to consider in such detail the ways and means of the rich and powerful.

"So where will all this money be going," she asked Hugh.

"Right now, I am tracking some investment funds used to clean up the dirty money. It takes the usual route through shell companies, companies that only exist as a name and a plaque on the wall of nameless firms of lawyers all over the world. The route can seem endless, but finally, you get to the 'big pond'. This, it appears, is where the funds reside until they find an investment programme that will keep the profits flowing. Legitimate funds that can be used as venture capital for everything from building hospitals and schools in government sponsored programmes to city centre skyscrapers, developing new aircraft, building ships, the list is endless,"

"What do you mean, about hospitals being built with this money?" said Pam, her composure disturbed at the prospect of the NHS being sullied by dirty money.

"Quite simple," said Hugh. "The government decide they want something they can't afford so they get it on HP – the never-never, the money comes from those investors we talked about. They not only pay the costs of the building but the deal also includes everything you can imagine for that hospital to function for say, twenty years. Of course, the NHS provide the medical staff and the bills are paid in instalments but the up-front costs are met by investors, and the profits they are making would be described by economists as 'super-normal'. It other words it's a very good deal to be in on,"

"My goodness, is it happening a lot?"

"It's been going on for years," it was Marjory's turn to chip in. "The Labour Government signed up to it not long after Tony Blair was elected but it was first used by John Major's Government, and they got the idea from Australia. Don't forget the basic concept of private finance for government projects has been around since the Middle Ages. Right now, the jury is out as to whether the current plans are 'good' or 'bad' but such activities represent fertile ground for those officials and ministers who have an eye for the fast buck on the side,"

"Excuse me asking, Marjory," said Pam, but how come you know about so much this subject? I sense there is more to your history than just being a wife and mother,"

"You're right, before I married this reprobate I studied economics and law at Durham. I spent a few years as a company lawyer with a large corporation but then used my qualifications to sneak into the teaching world at a private school teaching economics,"

"You're a dark horse," Pam said admiringly.

"She's darker horse than you think," Hugh added, "She used her holidays to terrify the pants off us part time soldiers,"

"What, Marjory was in the TA?"

"Not just the TA, the Intelligence Corps! She was their lead interrogator on the escape and evasion courses,"

"Don't tell me; you two met in a trench on Salisbury Plain,"

"Not quite," said Marjory, "when I first clapped eyes on Hugh he had a hood over his head and was covered from top to toe in cow shit,"

"Bloody Hell," said Jack.

"It was," said Hugh. I had decided to hide in a pile of manure, but the smell was awful, and there were creatures crawling around in it. I couldn't keep still, and the buggers spotted me,"

"So you won't be trying that trick again?"

"A long time ago, mate. I do things differently now. These days I do my very best to stay out of the guano,"

"Not always successfully, as our present situation would testify," Marjory said, delivering a playful scowl.

"Anyway," said Pam, these so-called back-handers you were on about,"

"Kickbacks," said Hugh, "if I give you the contract you pay me a 'commission'. Or, it works the other way around. I come to you, a government minister, and suggest that it would be in the national interest for Ludlow to have a state of the art new hospital, school or college. You are a little sceptical, so I pass a brown envelope across the table and say, 'this is our detailed proposal, read it carefully'. You then find, to your utter amazement that some very crispy banknotes are nestling inside. They would be the sweetener of course. You can't put the kind of money we are talking about in an envelope. You would need a small suitcase. The real payoff has to be a trifle more covert and handled very carefully.

"Then.... funnily enough at the next cabinet meeting there is a proposal to build a new college at Ludlow to replace the old polytechnic which is no longer 'fit for purpose'. There you have it. Everyone wins, the public benefit from the new facility, the builders profit from the project, and the wheels of government are lubricated for another year,"

Pam looked deflated. "I live in Great Britain," she said after a pause, "it shouldn't be like this. We are honest people. How can we put up with this going on?"

"Honest people? If you find a politician who became rich by being a politician, then you are staring corruption in the face. Britain, remember, is not even in the top ten when it comes to honesty in business and politics and I haven't even touched on the subject of 'soft corruption'," said Hugh.

"Soft corruption?" said Pam, "what's that?"

"Simple, if I want to disguise the transfer of a bribe then I simply find another way of delivering payment. For example, you work for a company that sells military hardware, and I am the minister responsible for signing off the dealt to buy equipment worth tens of millions, or the civil servant who makes the recommendation to buy. I cannot be seen to receive a 'commission', so I let it be known that the school fees at my son's private school are due for payment – twenty-five thousand pounds a year at Eton – and miraculously an anonymous donor pays the bill.

"Then, when he goes to university, the company that has the contract for your logistical support provides the apartment he lives in - free of charge. The weekly groceries are delivered gratis, courtesy of the company that has the cleaning contract at your HQ. They call it 'oiling the wheels of commerce'. I call it soft corruption,"

"It's always been like that Pam," said Jack, "there have always been 'white-collar' crooks at every level in society. You won't believe this, but while searching the Internet for information about Chaloner, I found that there was a William Chaloner in the late seventeenth century who was executed at Tyburn after an unsuccessful career as a counterfeiter and fraudster,"

"But don't we have the policeman trained to catch them at it?"

"The police have been working hard to counteract these modern-day crooks by creating special Organised Crime Squads. Unfortunately, their political masters have felt uncomfortable getting too close to this kind of 'baddy', they are powerful people and a few would not baulk at donating a pair of concrete boots if you got too close to them. Look at us, we are nibbling away at the outer edges of this black empire, and we are now running scared. It's not just a case of detecting the crime; we have to find a way out of this. Preferably one that leaves us able to pick up our lives where we left off before all this crap descended on us,"

"Amen to that," said Pam

"So, come on Hugh, this 'big pond'. Where is it?"

"'Big Pond' is where it's been for many hundreds of years. I'm sure you recognise Switzerland, Lichtenstein, Monaco and The Vatican, the usual suspects. But did you realise that City of London controls some of the worst offenders? The City sits at the hub of a network that includes Jersey, Guernsey, Sark, The Isle of Man, Gibraltar, the British Virgin Islands and the Cayman Islands to name just a handful. Wall Street has its equivalent network that includes Panama, the US Virgin Islands and home-based states such as Delaware and Florida. The biggest tax havens on this earth are run by the UK and the US. A fact of life that is glossed over every single day,"

"That can't be so Hugh," said Pam, "surely the government would crack down on them if they were under British jurisdiction?"

"Smoke and mirrors Pam, smoke and mirrors. These tax havens would not exist if they did not support the general thrust of government policy,"

"Which is?"

"To soak up as much of the world's global capital as possible even if along with the legitimate comes the illegal. It's all the same when it comes to wealth. If you can hide the ownership of wealth, then you can accept it no matter where it came from. Why do you think we have such a healthy overseas aid budget? I'll tell you why. Because it comes straight back to us, either as trade, or illegitimate deposits in our banks. Don't forget that the tax haven banks in British protectorates or territories are effectively our banks,"

"But that means that we are sitting at the heart of government sponsored criminality,"

"No laws have been broken, so you can't call it 'criminality'. Evil deceptions, cunning duality, maybe, but remember that every developed nation is 'at it' and we have to keep up or lose out. It's been getting worse. The difference today is that we live in the age of computers. When the digital age came along, it brought powerful checking and monitoring systems with it. Mind you, it didn't take long for those who needed ways around them to discover new opportunities.

"Their new tools include the VPNs, Virtual Private Networks. These are electronic 'tunnels' through the Internet. VPNs are legit and legal and used by almost every major corporation to maintain the integrity of their global IT system. You can buy one yourself if you want. Go to somewhere in the world where the government monitors every phone line, and you can use a VPN on the Internet and be invisible.

"You can even choose to 'surface' anywhere in the world, so when you log on to your e-mail account, the server thinks you are in New York or Aukland, New Zealand, all clever stuff, but quite routine. Where things have smartened up is in the use of some software that will create multiple VPN networks and then flip between them while sending messages. This is virtually impossible to crack and is giving the various law enforcement agencies around the world a serious headache.

"That's the stuff I sent to Jack. He can work unmolested on the Internet and appear to be operating almost anywhere. Where did you set up your terminal Jack?"

"Er, Argentina," replied a dozing Jack.

"Just don't tell anyone where you got that little gem of a trick,"

With the supper things cleared away and Josh packing for his 'trip', the Mawgans and the Martins gathered around the dining table to discuss their plans.

"Jack?" said Marjory, "what do you see as the likely turn of events? Have we done everything we can to be ready?"

"I guess there are best case and worse case scenarios," he replied after giving the matter some thought.

"Give us the worst case," said Hugh.

"That would be where the bad guys work out who I am and therefore where I live. In the short term that would put them at our door and we are then at risk. I don't think they are likely to want a conversation and from what I saw at the Boskenna Farm Estate when they killed Desmond Duffy, on Dartmoor when they killed Neil Jenkins and at Sedgemoor when they killed Hugh's friend and neighbour they are very ruthless. The intelligence we have gathered about Chaloner's past indicates that this sort of murder was a routine part of his version of 'doing business',"

"We must not forget that they have been able to get away with their activities for years, decades and that is because they have people in high places in their pocket and in my experience, they can close ranks faster than you can imagine. When it comes to escaping responsibility for any misadventure then, trust me, government departments and agencies are past masters. They run the system, and they have the power. Our total focus over the next week or so has to be on finding an Achilles Heel and using that to put these people away good and proper. I feel in my gut that there is a way and I am sure we can find it,"

"So," said Marjory, "what will happen when they arrive at the gates of Lower Spargo Cottage?"

"I guess they won't be aware that we have moved out and they will think we are at home and will attempt to take me out. They probably don't realise who Hugh is but if they do, then he is a marked man too,"

"So, what about the rest of us?" asked Marjory.

"I wish we could keep everyone else out of it, but there is always the possibility that they would attempt to get to us through family, so we have to circle the waggons and bring everyone in the firing line into the protected area. Hence Rose Cottage,"

"So will they break in here and look for us or look for clues as to where we have gone?" asked Pam.

"It wouldn't surprise me," said Jack.

"Maybe we should leave a few clues of our own?" suggested Hugh.

"I like the way you are thinking," replied Jack, "we can work on that idea, but we must also be sure that we don't leave anything behind that will help them,"

"You've got an alarm system I can see," said Hugh.

"Yes, but it's not working, unfortunately. Bloody thing keeps going off for no reason. We don't use it now,"

"Still the alarm box on the gable end is a bit of a deterrent," observed Hugh.

"My assessment at HQ is supposed to be tomorrow, but I'll have to give that a miss and hope I can catch up later," said Jack, "I guess Pam and I can take a load over to Helford in the morning. What about you Hugh what are your plans for tomorrow? Have you got anything you need to do before we go? We need to have you and Marjory over at Helford sometime during the afternoon,"

"Marjory and I are planning to sort out some domestic matters, then have a bit of a walk and have a bite of lunch down at your local pub. We have been set on the back foot by all of this as you can imagine and we have a lot of things to try and sort out. I'm a little nervous about hanging on around here but if we can spend a couple of hours down at the Norway Inn writing e-mails and working out how to deal with our domestic situation and then get to grips with my problems at work. We will come back here to the cottage then pack the last of our stuff into the Micra. I'll leave the TR6 here in the garage out of sight. Marjory's pretty tired after the drive down, so we are not planning too much else for the morning if that's okay with you?"

"OK, fine, are you happy about navigating to Helford Village?"

"Why don't you leave the Micra and your bike at the car park in Helford Passage," suggested Pam, "I drove the long way around via Gweek yesterday, and it's at least thirty minutes longer,"

"Good idea but we would need to use the ferry to get across to the village,"

"True but don't forget we will have our own boat and it gives us options with vehicles on either side of the estuary,"

"OK, but I'll need to show Hugh how to get there so maybe I'll take my bike to Helford Passage in the morning then come back and join Hugh and Marjory for lunch at the Norway. I can then lead them down to Helford Passage. Do you know what time the ferry runs?"

"Yes, I checked yesterday, nine a.m. until nine p.m. at this time of year,"

"Anyway, let's get things ready for our trip. I'll take my laptop, Pam's laptop and of course Hugh has his. I'll pack-up all the files we have generated so far, but I don't think I'll need my PC. I reckon we can get by with the laptops once I have loaded the software,"

Cadhay Manor, Ottery St Mary, Devon

"Thank you, Francis, what can I say? I'm very grateful. I'm sure that we can find our man now. Many thanks for all your efforts...yes I'll be at the Regimental Dinner as usual. See you there. Bye bye for now,"

"You 'ave it?" asked Gerard.

"Well, a shortlist but I think we can rule out this Vespa scooter from

Manchester, this Honda from Ludlow and this Ducati from London. Our man is, therefore… a John Robert Mawgan who is the proud owner of a black Triumph Thunderbird and hails from some unpronounceable village in the Wild West, otherwise known as Cornwall. Damn you Mr Mawgan, you are making my life very difficult, but we will soon deal with you!" He handed a list of names and addresses to Gerard and pointed to Jack's details.

"I will take Andy with me. If we use the gas, we can make it look like a burglary,"

"No cock-ups Gerry, please, no cock-ups. We've got more important things to attend to rather than running around in circles chasing troublesome people on motorbikes. I will have my friend at the Home Office run a profile on this chap Mawgan and let you know if anything of import shows up,"

CHAPTER 18

Friday, 30th June, 07.00 – Lower Spargo Cottage, Perranarworthal

THE FAMILIES CONGREGATED OVER an early breakfast and discussed the subject of hiding their presence in the quiet village of Helford. Jack came up with a solution and asked Pam to stop in Penryn on the way to Helford and visit the 'Motor City' shop on Commercial Road and buy one large and two small car-covers plus a motorbike cover if they had one.

With the Clio loaded Pam and Jack were about to leave for Helford when the phone rang.

"Hello, Jack?"

"Edwin… good morning, how are you?"

"Where are you Jack, they are waiting for you in the Training Office?" Jack checked his watch; it was eight forty.

"I'm not going to make it Edwin, I'm down with the lurgy, D and V, you know. At least that's the story I need you to circulate, but the reality is more complicated,"

"Fuck you, Jack, listen don't muck me about. Do you want to do this bloody job or not? I didn't give you the benefit of my labours for you to flush them down the bloody toilet. I don't care about all that nonsense you're involved with. This assessment is essential so if you ever want to work with me again get your sorry arse up here now. If you don't, you won't have a chance in hell of getting an Advanced Skills course before you die of old age,"

"It's very difficult Edwin." His voice tailed off as he realised that

189

Edwin had given him so much over the last six months and by missing this assessment he would be letting him down badly.

"Okay, Edwin I'll be there as soon as I can," He quickly explained to Pam and the others what was happening climbed on his motorbike and went roaring off in the direction of Truro.

Pam was furious at this unnecessary diversion and stormed out to her car giving the back door a good slamming on the way. Hugh and Marjory looked at each other and shrugged their shoulders.

"I think the pressure's getting to them," said Marjory.

"I think you're right," said Hugh.

Parking in Helford was difficult, and parking out of sight near impossible, as Auntie May kept her late husband's old car in the only garage, even though she didn't drive anymore. Jack had no idea what sort of car it was, but it was obviously very special to her. It was a standing joke in Pam's family that every year it would be serviced and the MOT and insurance were kept up to date. He guessed that it was by way of a consolation and that while that car turned a wheel Uncle Ron would still be with her in spirit.

A brief diversion to Cury Cross allowed Pam to see her mum and she explained that they would be out of town at a secret location.

"You mean Rose Cottage," her mum said, "but don't worry dear, I'll keep your little secret if that's what you want. What's that all about then? Auntie May thought you were having a holiday break,"

"I'll tell you all about it when we get back, but you won't be able to contact me on my old mobile, I've got a new one. I'll write the number down on the memo pad on the fridge door, and you can always get me if you need me,"

"You'll be lucky dear. Auntie May always said the one thing the visitors regularly complained about was that there was no mobile phone signal at the cottage. But I'm sure that won't worry you. You deserve a holiday. It's been a challenging year for Jack, I can tell, so the break will do you both good,"

Pam was furious that Jack had forgotten to tell Auntie May to keep their visit to Rose Cottage a secret nor had he checked the mobile situation. She must remember to scold him for the oversight.

Jack arrived at HQ in a fluster and took his place with two other candidates who had joined on the same day as him and served their probation in North Cornwall. Together they went through the written exam, and then after a coffee break, each, in turn, was given an oral examination. They were required to demonstrate CPR techniques on a 'Resusci-Anne' manikin and explain the protocols for a variety of injuries. When all was completed to the satisfaction of the Training Officer, they waited for the interview with the Big Boss, the Chief Ambulance Officer.

When Jack walked into Ken's office, he was shaken by the hand and congratulated on passing his Probationer's Assessment, then invited to take a seat. Ken picked up a piece of paper and inspected the content.

"Good marks all round, Jack. Then again, I wouldn't have expected any less with your background," Ken paused, gathering his thoughts. "Jack, you've the makings of an excellent Ambulance Technician and a good team member, but you have to realise that a lot of your colleagues were less than pleased at the prospect of an ex-policeman joining their ranks. They don't want to feel they are being watched or judged and they don't want to fear you running to your old chums with tittle-tattle. You will need to prove to them that you are part of this team, not still a policeman at heart,"

"Thank you, sir," said Jack, showing due deference to his boss, "I hope I can repay your trust in me by living up to the best traditions of the Ambulance Service,"

"Jack, your leave request has been granted. Your driving course begins in Bodmin in two weeks on Monday 17th July. Twelve-hour shifts commence at seven o'clock this Monday morning, and from that day my position as Chief Officer will become redundant. Roger Hill, the Devon Chief Officer, will be in charge of the newly merged Devon, Cornwall and Somerset Ambulance Service Trusts, under the title of the South West Ambulance Service NHS Foundation Trust," Jack struggled to take it all in, but the Chief just ignored his rather blank expression and held out his hand. Jack grasped it firmly only to discover that Ken did not let go. Their eyes met.

"I believe I will have cause to remember this day Jack Mawgan, don't give me cause to regret it," Jack didn't know what to say but nodded, and Ken's released his grip. Jack adjourned to the locker room and changed back into his motorcycling gear and was about to leave when his new mobile rang. It was Hugh. "Jack, are you there?" said Hugh in hushed tones.

"Yes Hugh, what's up?"

"They're here Jack; I'm sure they're here,"

"Hang on Hugh, who is where?"

"It's them, the people who are after us. We went to the pub as planned, but Marjory had left her handbag back at the house, so we walked back to the cottage and there they were,"

"Where exactly?" said Jack

"There is a black Jeep with darkened windows parked about one hundred yards downhill from your gates and as we walked past we could see at least two suspicious looking men sitting in the front. I told Marjory to keep going, and we walked into Perranwell and decided to call you straight away. What should we do?" Jack had to stop and think for a moment and weigh up the possibilities.

"Go back over Cove Hill. I'll meet you in the layby on the main road near the pub. As you pass them, see if you can tell how many people are inside. I'll be with you as soon as possible,"

With that, Jack returned to his bike and set off with his heart in his mouth at the prospect of confronting the people that probably had their minds set on his demise.

He found Hugh and Marjory waiting nervously beside the layby.

"Are you and Marjory OK?"

"Yes, yes, we're fine,"

"Can you show me where they are?" Hugh led the way to the corner of Cove Hill and, trying not to be too obvious, indicated the Black Jeep Cherokee with darkened windows. Jack studied the scene. About fifty yards away, on the right-hand side of the road, there was a builder's pick-up facing down the hill towards them. Behind it, facing up the hill was the black Jeep. It was strategically placed to observe the entrance gates to Lower Spargo. The hairs on the back of Jack's neck stood up, and he shuddered involuntarily. The very sight of that black and menacing shape made him think that Hugh was right. They were here, they had found them, at least they had found the house. Jack was determined that he and his family would stay out of reach of these monsters. He returned to the main road, out of sight of the men sitting in the Jeep.

"Hugh, we are going to have to abandon the house for the time being. Best we get back to your car and get you both over to Rose Cottage as soon as possible,"

"Only one problem with that idea Jack, Marjory left her handbag in the house. She keeps her mobile in her bag, and all our cash is there too along with credit cards and driving licence,"

"Oh bugger!" said Jack, "that's a blow," he stood, deep in thought, then peered around the corner again.

"When you went past the Jeep did you notice if it had a tow hitch?" Hugh thought about it, and Marjory said, "I'm pretty sure it had one. Don't all those Jeeps have one?"

"Not all but the probability that it has is fifty-fifty. Look you two, I think there is a way to get the handbag and not get caught. If I can dash into the house, I can get the bag and be back on the bike in less than a minute, but I just need to be sure that those guys in the Jeep will be busy in that minute. Here's my plan,"

As soon as Hugh and Marjory had been briefed on their part, Jack returned to his bike, removed the first aid pouch from the side box and took out the Tuff-Cut paramedic's scissors. He removed the rucksack he was wearing on his back then, much to Hugh and Marjory's amazement, set about cutting off its webbing straps from the backpack with his scissors. When he had finished, he had two one-metre long nylon webbing straps. Car seat belts were made of the same material as the shoulder straps on the rucksack and they, he knew from his Police training, had a breaking strain of about five tonnes. He didn't know if the Berghaus backpack webbing would be that strong, but he had an idea that they would keep the Jeep busy for one vital minute. Tying the two lengths of webbing together, he created a loop.

"The builder's pickup has a winch on the front, so I am betting on it having a tow hitch too. If I slip this over the two tow hitches, it may just hold them up for a minute while I nip in and out. If you two can handle a walk past and create a diversion I can get in behind the pickup without being spotted. When I've fixed their little game, I'll jump on the bike, ride up to the gates, leave the bike on the prop-stand, dash inside, collect your bag and hopefully make my escape before they can react. I'll catch up with you later.

Plan A is to meet in the pub within the hour. If they take off after me, then I will do my best to get away. I reckon motorbike versus Jeep is a no-contest, but you never know,"

He shepherded Hugh and Marjory to the corner of Perran Road and Cove Hill, "Are we ready?" Hugh and Marjory nodded, and they set off along the pavement, walking close together. Jack crouched behind them, and as soon as they drew level with the front of the pickup, he dropped down behind it and crawled underneath. The high ground clearance of the pick-up made crawling to the rear quick and easy. His luck was in, and both vehicles were equipped with tow hitches and with a flick of the wrist he put his loop of nylon webbing over them and quickly shuffled down to the front of the pick-up.

Hugh and Marjory had started a ferocious row right on cue just ahead of the Jeep, and Jack made it back to the end of the road, around the corner and out of sight. He peered around the corner to see if there was any reaction to his hasty retreat. The stage-managed argument between Hugh and Marjory had successfully prevented him being observed for there was no apparent movement in the Jeep.

Helmet on and bike running, he set off up the hill and stopped at the cottage gate. He heard the starter whir on the Jeep and hurried inside. He grabbed Marjory's bag from the hallstand and on impulse grabbed the spare crash helmet that was kept on the rack below. Back out in twenty seconds, he was on the bike and away and immediately heard the Jeep engine note change to a roar.

A passer-by would have been amazed to see a Jeep Cherokee, tyres scrabbling for grip, towing a white builder's pickup up Cove Hill. After a few moments, the driver of the Jeep realised something was amiss and stopped. He jumped out and went back to see why the pick-up truck had apparently mated with his Jeep. Swearing like a trooper he cursed his luck and tried to remove the webbing loop but it was drawn too tightly between the hitches, he could not move it. He returned to the driver's seat but was confronted by the owner of the pickup who had stormed out of a nearby cottage and was remonstrating with the man who was apparently trying to steal it.

When the matter was finally resolved and the two vehicles separated, the Jeep driver, obviously infuriated by this embarrassing trick, kicked at the driver's door in frustration before taking his seat and roaring off, leaving the pick-up truck in the middle of Cove Hill with its puzzled owner scratching his head. Jack, by this time, had disappeared and a pursuit was hopeless.

The reunion took place at the Norway Inn. The tale of the love affair between the Jeep and the pick-up truck was told with a certain amount of relish, but the atmosphere was subdued as they realised that their situation had taken a step in the wrong direction and their previous comfortable state of anonymity had now been now blown apart.

After lunch, Jack led Hugh and Marjory through the narrow country lanes to the car park at Helford Passage. They crossed over to Helford Village on the ferry and found their way to Rose Cottage. Jack had no sooner walked in the front door with the news that he had passed his assessment than Pam greeted him with a wigging. She scolded him for not telling Auntie May to keep their little arrangement quiet. He was suitably embarrassed by the knowledge that Auntie May had been chatting with his mother-in-law and worried about what that meant regarding overall security for them. He decided it was not a big deal so long as Pam's folks didn't blab all over the village but it was unsettling to know that the circle of people now involved in their plight was growing.

Pam passed on the news that a regular complaint at Rose cottage was a lack of mobile phone signal. Hugh and Jack looked at each other as if to say 'whoops'.

"Nothing much we can do about that," said Jack, "We have the internet connection, but Auntie May wouldn't allow a regular phone because it's too difficult to settle the bill with the short-term tenants. Let's see how it goes anyway,"

Hugh was busy checking out the Internet connection and wasn't too impressed with what he found.

"We won't be able to use the VPN for much of the day, as the peak traffic on the Internet is horrendous in this part of the world. Hopeless bandwidth. Normal Internet browsing won't be too bad, but my stuff needs a much better line. "With the immediate issues sorted it was time to get the kitchen into gear and get some supper on the go.

The atmosphere on their first evening together at Rose Cottage was less than wonderful. The incoming evening tide of the Helford River Estuary seemed to be bringing with it an undercurrent of gloom and foreboding.

14.30 – Cove Hill, Perranarworthal

"When are you going to tell the boss?" asked Andy.

"Not yet," replied Gerry, in a clipped voice that conveyed his displeasure at being so comprehensively embarrassed.

"I am still trying to work out 'ow they knew we were 'ere. It is very disturbing. It means we are not dealing with idiots and for that stunt with the fucking webbing strap I will make them suffer... bastards,"

"So, what's the plan?"

"We keep an eye on their 'ouse and hope they return, but somehow I think that is not going to 'appen. Everything we see tells me they knew that we were coming in which case they will have set up 'ome somewhere else. So... we will wait until dark and then we will take a look inside and see if they have left any clues about their new location. I hope we find something otherwise we are in the shit... big-time.

21.30 – Cove Hill, Perranarworthal

Gerard and Andy were pinning their hopes on digging up some useful information about the Mawgan family. They may have taken flight from Lower Spargo, but chances were they had not gone far. The events earlier that day indicated that they had left home in a hurry. Maybe there were some clues to their whereabouts to be found.

"OK, let's go," said Gerard, and he and Andy left the Jeep carrying a bag of equipment. Andy used a jemmy to force the side door to the cottage, which seemed to be the most vulnerable. A quick check of the house revealed that there was nobody at home. Gerard and Andy scoured the house for any sign of a clue as to where their targets were hiding, leaving a trail of disruption behind them.

Gerard checked the garage and found Hugh's TR6 under a tarpaulin. He checked his briefing notes for John Mawgan and realised it wasn't listed. He took a note of the registration. A blue Triumph TR6 was ringing bells in the back of his head. They were about to give up when Andy spotted a Post-It note stuck to the side of the fridge. On it was scrawled,

COTTAGE RENTALS LIMITED
HANSY COTTAGE – 01736-35377

Friday 30th June (2 weeks)

"This could be interesting," said Andy, "look, it's dated today,"
"Yes, this is good! Let's go,"

21.40 – Rose Cottage, Helford Village

By sunset the two families were settling into their new accommodation, and the atmosphere had lightened sufficiently for a sense of normality to descend on this quiet corner of a remote Cornish village. Josh was in his element and eager to explore. Pam thought that as 'host' she should take charge in the kitchen. Marjory was easy-going and was keen to support Pam in any way she could. Jack had tried to call Daniel Barclay several times on the journey down to Helford, but he was obviously busy and unable to return his calls. His PA wasn't able to help and told Jack to try again tomorrow.

Predictably the men were busy getting their computers up and running and testing out the Internet connection. Hugh had left a webcam in the office at Lower Spargo hooked up to Jack's PC. It wasn't long before it saw some action.

"Look, he's just entered the office," said Jack,

"Can you see his face?" said Hugh.

"No, he's using a flashlight, wait, yes look, a clear view," They were both peering at Hugh's laptop and watching the output from the camera.

"I'm recording this so we can print that image. We will then have a record of what one of our adversaries looks like. There is noise in the background… conversation. There must be at least two of them," said Hugh, "such a pity I didn't have more time. I could have put a couple more cameras into the system,"

"I wonder if they will see the note and take the bait?" said Jack. "Let's hope so, we need time to do our homework, and we can't do that if we are running scared,"

"I wonder how many 'Hansy Cottages' there are in Cornwall?" said Pam as she and Marjory arrived with a tray of tea and toast.

"Quite a few I can imagine given that Hansy was the name of a famous shipwreck down on The Lizard," said Jack.

"I hope the occupants of the Hansy Cottage you chose are out when they call," said Pam.

"Ah! I hadn't really stopped to consider that but I think we may be able to put a spoke in their wheel. Are you sure these phones are untraceable Hugh?" asked Jack, holding up his new mobile.

"Why, have you got a signal?" Jack checked the display on his phone.

"Hell no, I forgot about that,"

"I did a walkabout while you were unpacking and you can get a signal if you walk up Orchard Lane about fifty yards or walk around to the village car park where we left the cars,"

"OK, back in a while," With that Jack stepped outside the front door of the cottage into the night airs drifting in from Falmouth Bay. The smell of drying seaweed and ozone lifted his spirits and he strode off in search of a mobile phone signal.

He returned fifteen minutes later and told the others that the Devon and Cornwall Police had just received intelligence, from an unknown source of course, that two armed and dangerous drug dealers in a black Jeep Cherokee with a Bristol registration will be holding a meeting at Hansy Cottage, Church Lane, Madron, near Penzance this weekend,"

"Is that the address you put on the note?" asked Pam.

"No I just left a phone number, but for someone who can locate me through the DVLA, translating a phone number into an address will be easy. They could be outside the door by morning,"

CHAPTER 19

Saturday, 1ˢᵗ July, 09.25 – Church Road, Madron

THE TWO DETECTIVES FROM the West Penwith Drugs Squad sat in their unmarked Mondeo and took stock of the situation. They had been observing Hansy Cottage since seven o'clock, just one hour after they attended a task force briefing at Camborne Police Station. They had noted with a certain amount of relief that a black Jeep Cherokee arrived in Church Road not long after they had parked up. Since then they had observed no sign of activity from what they believed were two men in the target vehicle. The tinted windows made it difficult to see exactly how many were on board.

The Armed Response Team was out of sight in an anonymous white transit van at the other end of Church Road. A long and tedious observation task, stuck in a vehicle wearing personal body armour, was an uncomfortable prospect, so the arrival of the Jeep Cherokee lightened their spirits. It promised a speedy resolution to what their briefing told them was likely to be a low-level drugs stop. The involvement of the Armed Response Team and the use of the uncomfortable bulletproof vests were, in their opinion, an overkill born of an obsession by their Chief Inspector who saw Machine Gun Kelly behind every tree. The anonymous report received the previous day mentioned that the criminals were 'armed and dangerous'. That probably meant they had a flick knife and a baseball bat, but The Chief Inspector figured they were due a training run for the armed response unit, so they were sent without much expectation of anything more than a punch-up.

The Mondeo crew checked that everyone was in position and ready for action.

"Target in position on the eastern side of Church Road facing North, Go Go Go,"

The silence of that Saturday morning was suddenly broken by the roar of a diesel engine. The noise caused the occupants of the Jeep to jump with alarm. These were experienced combatants whose skills were honed in some of Africa's least hospitable places. They reacted automatically to the sniff of a threat to their safety. Within seconds Gerry was out of the Jeep and assessing the situation in a low crouch, pistol in hand Andy started the Jeep and scanned the area for threats,

From one direction, a white van was hurtling towards them. Whatever it contained it wasn't going to be Christmas presents. From the other direction, two men in plain clothes and wearing what looked like flak jackets were running at them with guns drawn. They were yelling something unintelligible and one, alarmed at the sight of Gerry's pistol, panicked and fired a round that went harmlessly above their heads. Suddenly all hell let loose.

Being shot at was Gerry's least favourite pastime. He skilfully dropped the two approaching men in a flash using a double-tap, BANG-BANG... BANG BANG. Was this a hit from a local gang or was it the law? There was no obvious sign until with a squeal of breaks the armoured Transit van pulled up just short of the action. The driver caught sight of the wounded men lying in the road and yelled a warning to his colleagues. Gerry emptied the rest of the magazine into the front of the van. The hail of bullets seemed to have no effect as they bounced off the armoured windscreen and ricocheted off the steel bodywork.

"Come on, let's get out of here," yelled Andy. Gerry did exactly that and with wheels scrabbling for grip and the engine screaming Andy took off through the narrow village streets and out into the wilds of West Penwith before the armed response team could fire a shot.

The wounded were a convenient distraction that served Gerry and Andy well. Preoccupation with the two fallen detectives meant that a few vital minutes were gained before the police were able to set off in pursuit in the detective's Mondeo.

Policemen from the van treated the wounded. The officer in charge was calling frantically on his personal radio for ambulances and more support.

The ambulances duly arrived and the casualties shipped off to the hospital. Soon the village was swarming with police and SOCOs.

The final count was two policemen with gunshot wounds, one seriously. The police had their equipment to thank for the fact that neither was killed, although it may still be touch and go for one detective who had received a nasty wound to the neck.

The unfortunate family from Rotherham who had rented Hansy Cottage had a very difficult day. They were not too pleased to find that they had become suspects in a drug bust. The Police issued a Press Release at midday.

DEVON AND CORNWALL CONSTABULARY PRESS RELEASE

Following an anonymous tip-off, two armed men were confronted in a village in West Penwith in connection with firearms and drugs offences. During this incident, shots were fired, and as a result, two officers received bullet wounds. One officer is in a serious but stable condition at Treliske hospital. He will undergo further surgery this evening. The second officer is recovering at home after receiving treatment for a wound to his left arm.

A burnt-out black Jeep Cherokee vehicle believed to be connected to the incident was found between Poole and Camborne, two hours later. If the public has any information relating to this incident they are requested to contact Camborne police station or Crime Stoppers on 0800-555111.

12.30 – Rose Cottage, Helford Village

The news about events in Madron came as an unpleasant surprise. Jack's little game had not gone according to plan.

"Hell," he said,

"What is it?" asked Hugh.

"I just caught the news on the radio. Our little game out at Madron played out well, but the police missed them. There was a shootout, two policemen wounded.

"In that case, Monsieur Nasty Bastard Frenchman I heard at Cadhay Manor is still out there.

"At least they have the cops on their tail now. That will cramp their style a bit… maybe.

"'Maybe' is right. I was hoping that our little trick would take them out of the game. It just means we can't relax after all," said Jack, obviously disappointed.

"Maybe… that's not a bad thing," replied Hugh.

"Lunch is ready," came a cry from below and Jack and Hugh left the makeshift office in the fourth bedroom and took in the delicate aroma of grilled sausages and frying chips.

They all responded to the call to lunch and sat at the long oak table in the dining room that had been Uncle Ron's pride and joy. He was a carpenter and shipwright, and much of the village's furniture had been produced in his workshop, which had now become the annexe to Rose Cottage.

Lunch over, it was time for another chat.

"We need some ground rules folks. If we are to stay safe, then we must take care not to let our guard slip. If we have taken enough care making this move, then no one will be aware of where we are except Auntie May, her agents in Falmouth and Pam's parents. We are for the time being safe and can, to a certain extent, relax. Having said that, we need to be aware of strangers,"

"The place is full of visitors Jack, they're all strangers," said Hugh.

"True, but visitors are easy to identify. They are either running around with kids in tow and laden with buckets and spades or elderly retired folk. The people we are worried about are likely to be younger and dressed like townies, not dressed for leisure. I think you will know them if you see them,"

"What about Josh?" asked Pam, "should we keep him in?" Jack thought for a moment.

"If we set the car park as one limit, and the ferry station as the other we can let him roam free within that area. I'll have a chat with him and brief him about being watchful. He'll lap up the idea of being a detective. He's already spoken to me about the boat that comes with the house and seems to know where it is. He's itching to go fishing, and I promised him that we would try our best to fit in a trip out to the bay and catch a few mackerel,"

"Don't expect me to come with you," said Pam.

"What's up?" asked Marjory, "Don't you fish? I thought every Cornish man and woman went fishing,"

"Pam gets sea sick if the bath is too deep,"

"Very funny, I've seen you go a bit green on the Scillonian when we went over to the Scillies last year,"

"Hell, the Scillonian! Even Nelson would be sea sick on that flat bottomed vomitorium,"

"Look, Josh is here, why don't you have your chat," said Pam.

"Good idea," said Jack.

Jack found Josh outside the cottage rearranging the concrete garden gnomes that stood guard along the front pathway.

"Josh, come here son, it's time to explain to you why we are all here in Helford," The two perched together on the doorstep, and Jack began. "This trip to Helford is not a holiday. There are some bad people out there and they are looking for us. We are going to hide away here for a week or so until they go away," he explained.

"You mean you haven't paid the bills?" said Josh, to the Jack's amusement, "only Biffo Bedford, my mate at school when we were in year six, he said they had some bad people come around. They were sheriffs I think. They took Biffo's TV because they forgot to pay the council tax, then he left the school 'cos his dad didn't pay the School Fees,"

"I think that would be the bailiffs rather than the sheriffs," Jack explained. "No, it's nothing like that. These people want to harm us, so we need to stay in the village and be wary of strangers,"

"Does that mean we can't go out on the boat?" said Josh, looking rather downcast, 'you did promise we could go fishing,"

"I'm sure we can find some time to catch a few mackerel but not today," said Jack.

"Okay," replied Josh with a degree of sullen resignation.

"If you go off and explore the village you can give us all a report on what you find, but you don't go past the car park where we left the cars or," Jack turned and pointed in the opposite direction, "past the ferry station at the end of that track. Got it?"

"Got it, Dad. Can I take your binoculars?"

"OK, but take care of them, they are not toys,"

"All right, see you later," and with that Josh departed, on a mission.

Peace and quiet descended, and Marjory served coffee.

"Don't you worry Pamela, he's a good sensible lad, he'll be fine," Pam's smiled at the attempt at reassurance, but the smile was tense and uncertain.

Hugh left his laptop for a moment and went over to Jack who was busy working on his computer.

"So how are you getting on, has Dragon Helicopters got something to tell us?" he asked,

"There is a picture emerging, and from what I have been able to piece together there have been some naughty goings on at Dragon, and Mr Duffy is at the heart of it,"

"Does that surprise us?" asked Hugh, "given his track record,"

"I guess not but listen up, Duffy started the rot by buying spare parts for his helicopter on the Internet auction site in the US called 'eBay',"

"Is that a problem?" asked Pam, "I hear you can get just about anything on eBay, what's wrong with buying spare parts online?"

"It's the provenance," said Hugh, "aircraft parts are controlled and have to come from authorised suppliers,"

"How do you know about that?" asked Jack, intrigued to discover another area of expertise in Hugh's library of skills.

"I used to be on the auditing staff at British Aerospace at Filton. I know all about the production of spare parts, if not their re-sale. I also know that any part they produced was accompanied by a large label called a 'Form One' that contained details of its manufacture, you know, part number, serial number, batch number, dates, stamps, signatures, all very formal. It's one reason why spare parts for aircraft are so expensive. I've seen a part that we bought in from a maker of car parts, and it was to all intents and purposes identical to its automotive equivalent but cost one hundred times the price,"

"How come?" asked Jack.

"The parts looked identical, but the manufacturing process for an aircraft part had to include an inspection of the item at every stage of manufacture and quality control of every item at every stage of assembly. All that checking is expensive,"

"You mean every nut and bolt is inspected?" asked Pam.

"That sort of mass produced component is made in batches then sampled on a regular basis, one in fifty or something like that. Depends on how critical the component is,"

"How critical would a tail rotor blade be?" asked Jack.

"Very, I would guess," replied Hugh.

"Well, Mr Duffy apparently bought a tail rotor blade on eBay from a supplier in the USA. The offer included all the necessary paperwork and Desmond paid five thousand dollars for it, which was twenty-five percent of the list price of a second-hand, overhauled and certified example,"

"Sounds like a deal," said Hugh. "Yes, but when it arrived everything was present except for the serial number. According to the e-mails I have read so far, there should have been a serial number engraved on a data plate fitted to the root of the blade, but an engineer by the name of... Jack consulted his notes... Peter Kellie, I guess he was the guy in charge of maintenance at Dragon, refused to accept it. He apparently told Desmond that he believed the engraving had been 'polished' away. He and Desmond had a huge row about it. He threatened to resign, and Duffy threatened to sack him,"

"Then what happened?" asked Pam.

"I can't say for sure because there are no more e-mails exchanged between them so one way or another I guess they parted company,"

"Does the story end there?" asked Hugh.

"Not entirely. There are e-mails between Duffy and another helicopter company in Exeter. Duffy was trying to arrange for engineering cover for an 'annual check' on the helicopter that was on-contract to Western Hydro,"

"Was that the machine involved in the accident last year?" asked Hugh.

"Certainly was. Now there appears to be a three-way fight between Western Hydro and Dragon who are claiming bad maintenance and between Dragon and the firm in Exeter who are being blamed by Duffy for not doing the annual check properly,"

"I guess that this tail rotor blade has figured somewhere in the dialogue," said Pam.

"Most definitely, the Preliminary Report, issued by the Air Accident Investigation Branch in January, points to a failure in the tail rotor area as the likely primary cause. They are carrying out on-going tests on the relevant components according to a summary sent to Desmond back in April,"

"If the engineer working for Des refused to fit the tail rotor blade how did he manage to persuade the company from Exeter to fit it?"

"I don't know. I haven't been able to piece that together yet. One possible clue is an exchange Duffy had with a small company in Bristol that makes data plates and placards. If he purchased a new data plate for his otherwise anonymous tail rotor blade, then he would have been able to fool the engineer who did the inspection,"

"That sounds a bit suspicious, but he would have had to generate paperwork to cover his tracks. Every major component needs a log card that records its history and those are all inspected during the annual check,"

"Well, somehow he must have managed it,"

"I suppose that if Mr Duffy wasn't already history, he would certainly be history by the time the courts have finished with him. How about you, how are the financial investigations going?"

"Complicated would be the first word I would use and moreover that isn't the most important thing I want to talk about,"

"Go on,"

"It's all very well reading other people's mail but what I would need to do is take charge of some of the computer systems involved and make one or two things happen,"

"How do you propose to do that?" asked Pam

"He will get me to do his dirty work again," said Marjory, and all eyes turned to hear the fascinating story behind that little comment.

"If he's planning to get into someone's computer system then he will put one of those naughty bits of software hackers use to take control of corporate intranets on three or four floppy discs with a fancy and enticing label on it. Then he will get an innocent looking me to wander around the HQ building leaving these attractive looking discs here and there. Sooner or later some idiot will pick one up, and finding their curiosity irrepressible, put it into their PC to see what's on it. There's usually an amusing little slide show that plays long enough for the software on the disc to download into the system,"

Pam and Jack exchanged looks, amazed that these two should have had such an intriguing past.

"You have done this before then?" asked Pam.

"Once or twice," replied Hugh. "It's all part of my job, the part that's not detailed in any 'Job Description'. It is a battleground out there Jack, dog eat dog. The baddies try their best to avoid being found out, and we have to keep up with them. If we don't know the risks we are exposed to, then we cannot do the necessary risk-management. Knowledge is power, Jack and knowledge that others believe is secret is real power,"

"So, what are you suggesting we do?"

"Just as we have done in the past. I'll get Marjory to visit Western Hydro as a potential employee or some other valid excuse, and she will get to see enough of the building to leave some discs around. Then we do the same over at Dragon Helicopters and sit back and wait,"

"Wait, what do you wait for?" asked Pam.

"An e-mail telling us the good news," said Hugh.

"What?" said Pam.

"A little trick I added to the software. Once it has successfully loaded on the host computer, it writes me an e-mail to tell me. Not to my regular address you understand but to one of the addresses that cannot be traced back to me,"

"What does it say?" asked Pam.

"It says 'arrived home safely'," said Hugh.

"Suitably enigmatic," said Marjory.

"So, when do we set this up," asked Pam.

"I thought we could maybe do it on Monday. I have a pack of discs that will do the job nicely all labelled, "Company Newsletter,". Half a dozen will be about the right number for a first pass. I can set them up tomorrow and Marjory can do the necessary,"

"But don't you need an appointment to get into the offices?" asked Pam.

"Not essential," said Marjory,

"If time is critical, then I can usually talk my way into the HR department but if that doesn't work we then have to forge an invite from a manager that gets us in the building,"

"What happens when you arrive at the manager's door?" said a curious Jack.

"I just play it by ear, but my days in the University Drama Society do come in handy,"

"Remarkable," said Jack, "what a pair you two turned out to be, full of surprises. Let's work on doing that on Monday then,"

"Meanwhile, back to the salt mines and endless e-mails,"

"Me too," said Hugh, "I'm hot on the trail of a particular government official at the MoD who has been taking back-handers from a major defence contractor and shoving his ill-gotten gains into the Frimly 'multiplier',"

16.30 – Cadhay Manor, Ottery St Mary, Devon

Back at Cadhay Gerard was delivering the bad news. "This is another bloody disaster Gerry, are you sure they cannot be traced back to you, us?

"Don't worry, I torched the car. They 'ave nothing,"

"So, Mr Mawgan is a smart kiddie, well, Mr Smarty-Pants we will have to deal with you once and for all,"

"It will be my pleasure to do exactly that,"

"If you want to repay Mr Mawgan back for your heartache Gerry then you had better get out there and find him. There is a complete profile on him and his family on my desk. Read, digest and bloody-well get rid of him,"

"This car was found in Mawgan's garage. It's not on the list, but it rings a bell," he handed him a note and Chaloner went to his desk and checked a few pages of computer printouts.

"Gerry that car belongs to our Mr Martin, the gentleman from Bristol, he who would be our nemesis," Chaloner was quietly seething beneath the calm, stiff-upper-lip exterior.

"It would seem that Mawgan and Martin are now working together. Find them and dispose of them. Please, Gerry,"

20.15 – Rose Cottage, Helford Village

Helford Village offers its inhabitants some wonderful advantages compared with those unfortunates who live in the big cities. These include the joy of taking fish, crab and lobster, fresh from the boats as they arrive back from a day at sea. Today's offering was mackerel, cod and whiting from Robbie Mitchel on 'The Falmouth Flyer' and crab and lobster from Danny Milburn on 'The Gladys'. The other pleasures include a village pub, The Shipwrights, named after Uncle Ron's workshop and across in Helford Passage, the Ferryboat Inn. It could be idyllic but for the current worries and concerns that stopped Jack and Pam from relaxing and enjoying their time in those beautiful surroundings. They talked about what they would do when they retired, and Helford would be an attractive place to live - if they could ever afford a property there. They argued over which part of Helford would be the best, the Village or the Passage.

The after-dinner conversation turned to an analysis of the day's progress.

"I think I may have found something interesting," said Pam.

"What's that then?"

"Look, here is an article in the Yemen Post. It's an English Language newspaper that's been around since we pulled out of Aden in the nineteen sixties. It's about a series of assassinations that took place under British Rule but were never reported at the time. The article says that each one was discovered with a note pinned to the chest of the victim but only one note was ever seen in public and it was reported as being a revenge note, written in Arabic but signed with the words 'OR GLORY'.

"The deaths were blamed on the 17th/21st Lancers by the Yemenis but again nothing was ever said in public, and nothing ever came to light while we were in charge there. The motto of the British cavalry regiment accused of the killings was 'OR GLORY'. As it happened the regiment was serving in Aden at the time but, according to the newspaper, was suddenly withdrawn a good six months before the British started pulling out. I was wondering how I could find out where Sir William Chaloner was serving when he was in the Army? Do we know what regiment he was in?"

"How on earth did you find that little titbit?" asked Jack, "this could tie Chaloner directly to specific crimes and may even be enough to build a case against him,"

"I just decided to use the Google search engine and typed in 'OR GLORY' and got millions of hits and I've been ploughing through them all day. I was just about to give up and try something else,"

"Pretty sure from what I remember of my early enquiries that Chaloner was in the Cavalry but what you need is his Who's Who entry," suggested Jack, "have you tried Who's Who online?"

"No, but if you hang on a tick, I'll pop up and see if they are available on the Internet," Pam returned half an hour later. "Had to take out a subscription but I got a printout of his details," she said, brandishing a sheet of paper. Jack and Hugh exchanged looks.

"How did you pay?" asked Hugh.

"Oh goodness," said Pam, "I clean forgot, with my credit card,"

"Which one?"

"American Express," said Pam blushing at the thought of letting them all down.

"I reckon we have two days before they know our IP address and can work out where we are. That assumes that they have the wherewithal to access that level of data. I would have to say that we would have to be up against some serious players if they can get inside the banking system like that,"

"Hang on," said Jack, "your Amex Card is the one you have had since university, isn't it?"

"Yes," she replied. "What name does it have on it?"

"Yes, of course, Doctor Pamela Walters,"

"How come?" asked Hugh,

"Unmarried women who earn the right to the title 'Doctor' have certificates that show their name at the time of the award so for that reason tend to keep their maiden name for work-related activities after marriage and fortunately I have done exactly that," Pam explained.

"What address is it registered to?" asked Hugh,

"Lower Spargo," said Pam.

"Well, if they perform a search on Pamela Mawgan then we are in the clear, and that's almost certainly what they will do. An address search is not the norm. Let's try and be a little more careful in the future, shall we? Now show us what you found out in Who's Who," Pam looked at the piece of paper.

"It's the usual bullshit, and we had most of it already, he served with the British Army in the 17th/21stLancers in Germany, Hong Kong, Aden, and Borneo. So, we had him in the right place but was he there at the right time?"

"I know a man who can find out," said Jack, and picking up his new mobile he disappeared up to Orchard Lane and dialled the number for Daniel Barclay.

"Hi Dan, it's Jack Mawgan,"

"Hello Jack, I guess it all went well with your container exploit? When can I get the box of tricks back? At some stage, we will have to go find the bloody thing, and without the receiver and antenna we are stuffed,"

"Sorry Dan, it's not that I forgot, but we have stirred up a hornet's nest, and we had to bail out of Lower Spargo. You were right we are up against some nasty people. At the moment, we are managing to stay one step ahead, but I won't pretend that we couldn't do with your help down here,"

"Sounds serious, are you sure you know what you are getting into?"

"We are already in it mate, up to our necks. There's no going back now. I'm working with a chap from Bristol,"

"Yes, I know, Hugh Martin,"

"How the hell did you know that?"

"Hugh and I work for the same team in London. When I put together the profile on Chaloner, they asked me to keep them informed, and they let me know that Hugh was also involved,"

"We need your help again, but it's probably your connections we need as well as physical help,"

"Shoot," said Daniel.

"A while back you said that if push came to shove, we could take a look at Chaloner's classified file. We need to understand some details about his service record back in the sixties. Your contacts in Whitehall will be interested to know that we have come across a possible link between at least one murder here in the UK and a series of murders in Aden,"

"What sort of link?"

"A curious imprint from a rubber stamp appeared on a document found at the scene of the murder of Desmond Duffy. It matches the description of one mentioned in a story we found in the on-line archives of an old Yemeni newspaper. We believe it tracks back to Chaloner, but we need confirmation. There are other reports of murders in the Far East but only a very loose association with Chaloner,"

"So where is this document now, the one with the imprint on it?"

"I regret that we have lost track of it and in all probability, it has been destroyed by Chaloner,"

"Who told you about this document?"

"The only people I know for sure saw the note I am referring to are Desmond Duffy, Neil Jenkins and me. I am the only one still alive,"

"Okay Jack, I know what you are talking about. I suppose you want this yesterday?"

"Absolutely, we are trying to put together a strategy that will extricate us from our dilemma but to do that we need all the information we can muster on Chaloner and his cronies,"

"Okay, I'll get on it as soon as I can, but I can't get down right away. As soon as I have things under control up here, I'll call and sort out a rendezvous,"

"Thanks, Dan and please log this number, it's the only way you will get me as I can't use my old mobile at the moment. If you can't get through, leave a message; the signal is a bit 'iffy' here,"

"OK, will do, bye for now,"

Jack returned to the cottage and gave the news to the others, "Dan will have something for us as soon as he is able and will join us as soon as he is free,"

"I think I made a little progress today, but there are times when it's like trying to see through a fog," said Hugh, "and trying to understand what is going on is bloody difficult. As far as I can tell the Gordons were feeding funds into Duffy's accounts at the rate of fifty to a hundred thousand pounds a week. It looks like he was allowed to keep about ten thousand a month, presumably to cover his expenses and pay his salary. He passed the rest on together with his contribution to Chaloner. Chaloner then passed it to the Frimlys along with his own contribution.

"Altogether Chaloner was making monthly transfers to the primary receiving accounts at CayBank, the Cayman Islands branch of Frimly Overseas Investment Banking Limited or 'FOIBL' as it is known in banking circles. This amounted to an average of a million pounds each month. Every six months FOIBL were sending out statements professing to show the value of the assets purchased on their behalf and would make dividend payments at the same time, but of course, these would always be sent to Chaloner as he kept his sources under wraps. I guess that Duffy, in turn, kept his sources quiet too.

"There was an exchange of confidential letters between Western Hydro and Throgmorton, Willis & Day, their London lawyers, following the fatal helicopter accident last year. In those letters, dated January this year, the lawyers told Western Hydro to make a fifteen-million-pound provision on the balance sheet for the current financial year in anticipation of a compensation settlement for the dead employee's family and other related expenses. Now here is the interesting bit. I found another letter, sent back in April, the lawyers were worried and were asking for the provision to be increased to fifty million pounds to take account of the possibility that they may have to pay exemplary damages,"

"So what happened between January and April?" asked Jack.

"That is a very good question; there is more to this story than we first thought,"

"Go on,"

"The Trades Union representing the Western Hydro workers who fly with the helicopters wrote to the CEO on January the eighth this year informing him that a whistle-blower at Dragon Helicopters had accused their management of falsifying maintenance records and using unauthorised spare parts,"

"That must have stirred things nicely,"

"They demanded that Chaloner replaced Dragon with another operator,"

"Could he have done that, contractually I mean?"

"Almost certainly,"

"So why did Chaloner persevere with a lame duck? Do you think that he wanted to maintain good relations with Duffy? Or did Duffy have a hold over Chaloner?"

"You mean this business of Chaloner refusing to supply the safety equipment for his guys,"

"Yes. I'll print off some of the e-mails I have turned up, and you can give me your opinion," Jack went to the 'office' and returned ten minutes later. He placed the e-mails on the table one by one.

"This one was sent in March 1998 from Western to Dragon at the start of the Power Line Inspection Contract,"

March 2nd, 1998

Dear Mrs Duffy

Many thanks for your letter dated February 23rd outlining your requirements with regard to equipment for the helicopter and personnel involved with the inspection of the region's overhead power distribution system. I draw your attention

Geoff Newman

to para 14.3 of our contract document in which the details of our obligations in this respect are detailed. There will be no extension of these provisions, and any additional equipment will be the responsibility of Dragon Helicopters.

Sincerely

H.W. Warburton
Contract Management Department

"The letter referred to is this one:

February 23rd 1998

Dear Mr Warburton

Ref: Contract 1123-98

In preparation for the commencement of the above contract, we wish to draw to your attention the recommendations of the Helicopter Consultancy and Advisory Service. As our independent safety experts, they recommend that all the occupants of helicopters involved in aerial work should wear appropriate protective clothing. We are happy to arrange for the acquisition and maintenance of the equipment thus ensuring commonality with that supplied to our pilots. The current provisions are:

1. Flying Helmet – Alpha (Helicopter Type), with clear and tinted visors and fitted with correct microphone and earphones suitable for the Bell 206 series helicopter (single jack-plug type). Provision – One unit for sole use for each rostered crewmember plus two spares.
2. Flight Suit – Fireproof material. Provision – Two units.
3. Flight Boots – Leather or composite boots with a composite sole, ankle length. Provision- One pair for winter use (incorporating suitable insulation) and one pair for summer use.
4. Thermal underclothing. Provision – Two sets for winter use.
5. Flight Gloves, Cape Leather, fire-resistant. Provision – one pair.

If you wish to acquire this equipment directly from the suppliers, please verify *with the Chief Pilot that the specification of the equipment you intend to purchase is fit for purpose. We look forward to receiving your instructions in due course.*

Yours sincerely

Margaret Duffy
Managing Director

"So here we have the beginnings of a dispute, right at the start of the contract," said Hugh, "and here is the Dragon response," Hugh placed another printout on the table. It read:

March 9th 1998

Dear Mr Warburton

Ref: Contract 1123-98

We are in receipt of your letter referring to Western Hydro's refusal to make appropriate equipment provisions for their employees. The responsibility for the provision of Personal Protective Equipment (PPE) is the employer's, and details of the standards and quantities issued are included in your Health and Safety Manual in line with current regulations. I draw your attention to the Western Hydro HSE Manual delivered to us as part of the tender process.

I believe the relevant section is Part 2, paragraph B, which states, 'All employees will be issued with appropriate PPE according to the industry standard for the task undertaken.' We can of course act as intermediaries in the acquisition of the equipment detailed previously, but a management fee will be charged in addition to the equipment costs, which we estimate to be £7,000 non-recurring and an estimated £1,000 per annum recurring costs based on six individual Western Hydro employees. Our fee will be a one-off charge of £1,000.

Please advise your intentions.

Yours sincerely

Margaret Duffy,
Managing Director

Geoff Newman

'Then there is a cracker of a mail from the top man,"

2nd April 1999

Dear Mrs Duffy

> *My company is paying a great deal of money to Dragon Helicopters for a service, please get on with providing that service and leave the safety of our employees to us. We have no intention of providing the ridiculous and unnecessary inventory of expensive equipment you have specified. I fly in helicopters on a regular basis and have never felt it necessary to indulge in such extravagance, and the wearing of a crash helmet in a helicopter seems to me to be nothing short of barmy. We are planning to inspect power lines not going to war.*
>   *Please stop this stupidity now.*

Yours sincerely

Sir William Chaloner CBE

Chief Executive Officer
Western Hydro plc.

"Wow, wouldn't that have created some waves after that chap was killed in the accident? Didn't you say he died of a head injury," said Pam.

"Certainly would," said Marjory, "I would guess that if Western Hydro's lawyers saw that last e-mail, they would have a blue fit. The victim's family could be in line for exemplary damages because of the tone and content of that letter,"

Seeing the surprise on the faces of Pam and Jack, Hugh said,

"Don't forget that Marjory's first degree was in Law, Durham Law School,"

"Corporate Law was so dull. I found teaching a lot more fulfilling," added Marjory.

"So, what do you make of this little lot?" asked Jack, pointing to the collection of e-mails spread out on the table.

"I would say that given the contents of this letter Sir William has put his company in an extremely difficult position. Putting aside any claims the family of the deceased employees make for general and exemplary damages he may well have opened the door to criminal charges relating to Corporate Manslaughter. Such a case would be a difficult one to win but even so it could lead to a massive fine on the Company plus a possible custodial sentence for the key player, Sir William Chaloner,"

"Bloody Hell that's an eye-opener," said Jack.

"The other thing worthy of note, ladies and gentlemen, is that the financial situation of both companies, Western and Dragon, is not good. Neither company could withstand the kind of losses that a court case could inflict on them. Their real liquidity is extremely low; despite what the public record indicates they are highly leveraged which means their liabilities are extremely high. Their strategy of turning everything they could into cash and paying it into CayBank left them almost devoid of working capital. Any bad news will draw the attention of the financial community who would look very closely at the detail surrounding the many lease-backs on their books. Many have been conveniently disguised or omitted from the public record. A sniff of anything untoward would be a threat to the stability of Western Hydro would decimate their share-price. You can be sure that the press hounds would smell a story and would start to dig into Chaloner's activities like they have never done before,"

"We have to ask the question, why has none of this surfaced in the press before now?" asked Jack.

"I can only imagine that Chaloner has managed to suppress it," Hugh replied.

"Yes, but Duffy could easily have blown the whistle. Don't forget that he will have a copy of that e-mailed letter and if he ever published that he could crucify Chaloner. What a mess," said Jack,

"Duffy fits illegal parts to the helicopter. Helicopter crashes, killing Western's employee, Western have denied a helmet to their employee who dies of a head injury despite receiving professional advice to supply one and contrary to their own HSE Manual. Western stand in line for serious financial losses and Chaloner stands to face criminal charges. Dragon will almost certainly face charges from the Civil Aviation Authority if they prove that they ordered the fitting of an illegal part,"

"That's not all, Jack," said Hugh, "the cash flows that provide the returns for those who are putting money into the various investment vehicles are supposed to pay out every six months, but it looks like nothing was paid out last January. Previous payments have been made on the fifteenth of each of those months. Of course, they may have moved to different accounts, but I've been monitoring twenty-one accounts in Switzerland, Lichtenstein and Luxembourg plus nineteen accounts in the Cayman Islands, Panama and Andorra. The first lot are Chaloner's and the second Duffy's. There is something going on that is disrupting the flow of funds out of the Frimly's legitimate investment vehicles and then on to Chaloner,"

"I can't see any of that lot being happy about the money drying up. You said that they had committed every penny. It's not surprising that Duffy couldn't afford the twenty thousand dollars for a new tail rotor blade," observed Pam.

"What is more," said Hugh, "right at the end of the food-chain are some seriously nasty people who have been remarkably quiet on the subject. There has not been a single mention of the Gordons in anything I have read so far but what we have not yet done is focus on them. It may be useful to see if they have moved with the times and have indeed found a better way of communicating than the Glasgow Herald personal columns,"

"I remain sceptical about that Hugh," said Jack, "personal column indeed,"

"You wait; I'll prove it to you one day,"

"Well, tomorrow I'll get stuck into researching the Gordons and maybe we will find out. Right now, it's eleven fifteen and time for my bed,"

CHAPTER 20

Sunday, 2nd July, 09.00 – The Brookdale Hotel, Truro

THE BROOKDALE HOTEL LOOKS down upon the main avenue that brings traffic from the east into the heart of the City of Truro. The heat of the morning sun was turning its black tarmac, damp from a recent shower, into a curious river of steaming vapours.

Now and again the wisps were blown away by the sparse Sunday morning traffic. From one of the suites on the second-floor Gerard de Beaumont looked out on this peaceful setting.

The mirrored lenses of his designer sunglasses reflected the image of slate roofs and sycamore trees. The nineteenth-century gothic revival Cathedral with its unusual three-spire design stood prominently at the centre of one of England's smallest cities. Gerard's world was not so peaceful, however, for he had murder on his mind and was gathering a small team of the 'odd-job-boys' with the intention of tracking down the troublesome Mr Mawgan and his friend Mr Martin.

His team had beavered away hoping to find at least one of Neil Jenkins' colleagues prepared to discuss his time working with the local Police Force. Gerard was looking forward to finding out more about the man he so recently snuffed out in the wilds of Dartmoor. More importantly, he was hoping that one of Neil's contacts could shed some light on where Mr Mawgan might be hiding. He sat on the edge of the bed and studied the file on John Robert Mawgan, known to his friends as Jack. The picture that stared out from the file showed a determined face that clearly found the process of having his passport photograph taken irksome. He seemed to be an impatient man, but his strong jawline and sharp blue eyes gave Gerard the impression that below the surface and impatient exterior lay a calculating brain, a worthy adversary. His mother now lives in the US, father deceased. Wife Pamela a doctor and two kids, one at University and the other at home. Wife's parents live locally south of the naval helicopter base near Helston. They were likely candidates for a 'night-call'. The Mawgans may have gone into hiding, but Gerard knew that if you are going to tell anyone where you are going, then you would tell your mum. 'Cher Maman', he thought to himself. 'You will know; I feel it in my bones'. The phone burst into his thoughts with a rude and loud blast of its old-fashioned bell. "Hello?"

"Good afternoon Gerry, how are things?"

"Good, well, promising at least. A Sergeant Alex Sullivan is coming 'ere at one o'clock for the lunch. Andy met 'im last night in a bar and has offered him an excellent lunch at this four-star hotel if 'e is willing to meet with me and 'ave a chat about Jenkins. Apparently, they were good friends, so there's a chance 'e will give us something on Mawgan,"

"Sounds a bit of a long shot,"

"That's all we've got at the moment. I've put feelers out across the region, but I can't pretend that we don't need a break,"

"Maybe he's skipped the country,"

"I don't think so, but we are taking a close look at other family members,"

"Okay, well good luck, keep me informed,"

"Will do, speak later,"

He put the phone down just as there was a knock at the door. It was the three guys he was counting on to help him. One was an ex-Legionnaire, and the other two were ex-military men recommended by friends of Sir William. The first was Bernard Fermier, a retired Belgian soldier in his forties with excellent English. He had been working in Africa for a UK security company specialising in close protection, medium height, thin faced, wiry, dark hair, goatee beard and well-tanned.

The second was Douglas Morrisey, a short, stocky Scotsman, another member of that exclusive club of British ex-Legionnaires but one that Gerard had yet to meet.

The last was Jeff Barnes, ex-REME, a skilled mechanic with large, well-worn hands, tall and slim with a weathered face, small lips and large Gallic nose. He was dishonourably discharged from the British Army and joined that jolly band of slightly suspect ex-SAS people working in the twilight world called 'Security'.

Gerard told them to take their jackets off and make themselves comfortable then handed out a file of notes and mug shots of key players to each man. He spent half an hour giving them a detailed history of events so far, at least, as much detail as he believed wise.

"We 'ave to locate this guy John Mawgan as soon as possible. I want Bernard and Douglas to take the Ford and keep watch on the 'ouse at Cove Hill. If any of the family shows up, call me. Jeff, you and I 'ave a lunch date and then this evening we will visit the family of Mrs Mawgan. They live south of this town Helston," He pointed at a map of the area and indicated the location of Pam's parents.

The restaurant manager called Gerard's room to tell him his lunch guest had arrived. He and Barnes collected their jackets and went to find the restaurant and they were shown to a table by the window. An attractive woman in her thirties, wearing a smart blue suit, already occupied one of the seats. Turning to the waiter, he said, "There must be some mistake?"

"Gerard? I'm Alex Sullivan, Detective Constable Alex Sullivan,"

"Alex, how nice to meet you. I am Gerard de Beaumont, and this is my colleague Jeff Barnes,"

"How d'you do?" They shook hands.

"Alex, can I get you something to drink?"

"That's very kind, red wine please, Merlot if possible," Gerard's discomfort was obvious to the canny detective. He had not expected to be hosting a woman. She could read him like a book.

"A woman who knows exactly what she wants. I like that," Gerry was back-pedalling as fast as he could.

The waiter arrived with their drinks, and some menus and the trio made their lunch selection.

"Do you know who we are, Alex, and why we are here?" She knew that he was gay, funny how women can tune into that sort of thing. The slight inflexion in his voice, the subtle mannerisms, the gentle shake of the manicured hand. From the military bearing and body honed by regular workouts, he was every inch the man's man, as some would put it, but she knew a different version of that phrase applied to Monsieur De Beaumont.

. "I was told that some guys from Interpol were looking into Neil's death.

Do you mind if I see some ID? It wouldn't be appropriate to discuss Detective Sergeant Jenkins with someone outside law enforcement, would it?"

"Yes. Yes. All in due course. But we don't 'ave to talk business right away. Please let's enjoy our luncheon,"

Alex played along and let him lead the small talk. She was an experienced policewoman and a very astute observer of the human species. Her brief affair with Neil Jenkins was long forgotten, one of the 'mistakes' that seem to punctuate her life since her divorce five years ago. Nonetheless, Neil had been a good lover and a kind man for whom she still held some affection. His death had been a shock, and the minute the word had spread that someone was looking into his murder she had been keen to find out more. Neil had been as screwed-up as any copper trying to balance the demands of wife, kids and The Job and taking to the bottle had been the last straw.

By the time the coffee was served Alex had consumed two large glasses of wine and was holding her emotions inside with great difficulty. She thought that her host was an arrogant, devious apology for a man. As for his sidekick, she was struggling to work out what the hell he was doing there. He was coarse, and his table manners would not have been out of place in a truck driver's café. These two were like chalk and cheese and had no place dining at the same table. It was obviously a fix to deal with her 'interview'. What on earth could they want? The alcohol was threatening her judgement, and a flashpoint could erupt at any time.

"So, gentlemen, are we going to get down to business? Let's see some ID; then I show my gratitude for such a delicious meal by helping you with your enquiries,"

"I'm sure my colleague Andy explained that we were very sad to hear of Mr Jenkins demise."

"You mean Detective Sergeant Jenkins' demise, don't you? Please, let's respect a fine officer cruelly murdered in the course of his duties,"

"Murdered, surely not, the newspapers say he was shot by accident," Alex had to bite her tongue.

Jeff Barnes sat mystified; he didn't have a clue what they were talking about. He guessed he had received just enough information about the gig and nothing more. He tried to look interested but couldn't help but admire this good-looking woman and like most men in these encounters he couldn't help himself imagining his performance in bed with her. 'Just give me the chance' he thought, 'just give me a chance'. Her blouse was undone one button too far to be discrete but enough to make the most of her ample figure. He was aroused by the thought of fondling those lovely breasts. He wished to hell he knew what the two of them were on about.

"Accident? That's as maybe, but I am not convinced. Neil has dealt with some serious criminals in his time. My money is on Neil being taken out. ID gentlemen, do you have some official capacity as your friend Andy implied or are you just a poor excuse for journalists looking for some sensationalist crap to sell your papers?" The hackles on Gerard's neck rose at the unexpected harshness of Alex's words. 'This ungrateful bitch had better deliver, or we'll kick her arse' he was thinking. He too was trying not to lose it. Alex was their only lead, and he didn't want to waste it. He took a large brown envelope and placed it on the table in front of him. The flap was ostentatiously left ajar with the rosy glow of fifty-pound notes beckoning.

"Is that your ID?" Alex asked with a delicate touch of sarcasm, "I thought you guys were supposed to be part of Interpol?"

"We are not the official Interpol you understand; we are, you might say, the unofficial Interpol. I don't believe they pay people for information whereas we very definitely do,"

Alex peered at the envelope. What the hell was going on. She became morose at the thought of Neil's death. He didn't deserve to die, she thought, and then returned to the question asked

"I see," said Alex, who most definitely did not see.

She had been told that the people interested in finding out more about Neil were from abroad and would be able to make sure her efforts to help were properly recognised. She was now unnerved by the discovery that they were apparently nothing to do with law enforcement and were about to hand her what amounted to a bribe.

"Andy tells me that you and Detective Sergeant Jenkins 'ad a relationship at one time?"

"Did he? Well, he should mind his own business and not go telling tales to all and sundry,"

"Did you by any chance 'ave relations with a Jack Mawgan? Only we need to find 'im and thought you might 'elp us," Gerard's mastery of the English language didn't extend to subtlety. His comment was the last straw, and Alex exploded. She stood up suddenly, knocking the table and upending the half-filled coffee cups all over the crisp white table-cloth.

"What are you suggesting? That I shag my way around the local police station? You, arrogant, creepy little poof," She picked up her handbag and stormed off but only made it to the restaurant door before striding back to the table wearing a look like thunder. She picked up the envelope and looked an astonished Gerard in the eye, "Neil's widow can do with some cash, I tell her about your generosity,"

With that, she stormed off into the car park and set off home.

Gerard turned to Jeff Barnes, "Follow her, if she stops to make a phone call before she gets to her home, then I will bet my life she is calling Mr Mawgan. I want her mobile phone, and I don't care how you get it. If we can get his number, then we can get a trace on it.

"Right Boss, what about your money?"

"Keep it, your bonus," Barnes headed off to his hire car.

Alex lived in an apartment in the new complex at Falmouth Harbour. To get there, she had to drive past Devichoy's Wood, and it was here she stopped to make a call, turning off the A39 on to the Mylor Bridge Road. She reversed her Mazda sports car into the small parking area used by those who enjoyed walking in this popular ancient oak woodland. She was too preoccupied to notice the Mondeo that also turned off behind her. She removed her phone from her handbag and dialled Jack Mawgan's mobile. She thought he needed to know that a weird stranger was asking after him.

Jack didn't respond so she left a message. She took out a cigarette, wound down the window, lit it and tried to make sense of lunch with the mysterious Gerard De Beaumont. Barnes meanwhile had stopped a little further up the hill. He assessed the chances of approaching Alex from the verge and ruled that out, as she would have a clear view of his approach. Instead, he climbed the low wire fence and cut through the woods to approach the Mazda from the rear. He made his way to the driver's side.

Stealing the woman's cell phone was his stated mission but the horny Jeff Barnes could not resist the possibility of abducting this good-looking woman and enjoying a nice shag before he disposed of her. His first move should have been a decisive blow to render the target unconscious. But, just in time, Alex saw him in the wing mirror and had time to press the window button and grab her pepper spray. Contact with the top of the driver's window deflected Barnes' punch, and he just caught Alex a glancing blow. The window continued its upward journey trapping Barnes by one of his large hands. As Barnes struggled, Alex leapt from the passenger side and ran around to the other side of the car determined to disable him. She hit him with a dose of her pepper spray, but too late she saw the flash of a flailing blade. Barnes had a knife. The knife blade caught Alex on the elbow, and she yelled in pain and fell to the ground but the impact had removed the knife from Barnes' grip, and it landed at Alex's feet with a 'clump'.

Without hesitation, she aimed more pepper spray at Barnes who finally broke free from the Mazda's grip and clawed blindly in Alex's direction, but she was nimble and very very angry. With a skip to one side and a swift movement of her one good arm, she scooped up the knife and buried it in Barnes' neck. He slumped to the ground.

Alex was breathing heavily and sat down on the muddy woodland floor and stared at Barnes as he laid gurgling and choking on his own blood. He breathed his last and lay still, silent.

Some minutes later a dog walker arrived to take advantage of a woodland walk with her Labrador and tried to take in the scene. A woman in distress and the body of a man lying dead and bleeding with the handle of a wicked looking hunting knife sticking out of his neck. Alex was crying uncontrollably from the effects of pain, shock and relief.

The ambulance arrived followed not long after by a posse of police cars and support vehicles. The news hit the TV and radio in time for the evening bulletins. The newsreader told the story about the stranger who attacked a woman at Devichoy's Wood and got more than he bargained for.

Sitting watching the six o'clock news Gerard took the revelations badly but knew he had little time to deal with the likely fallout. He needed to re-organise the other crew, checkout of the hotel and make it down to The Lizard before nightfall. He was furious at yet another setback but chose not to enlighten his boss. Why couldn't he find people he could trust? Did he have to do every job personally?

15.00 – Rose Cottage, Helford Village

Jack called a post Sunday lunch conference but promised Josh that they would take advantage of the rising tide and try out the little motor boat that came with the cottage just as soon as they had finished reviewing the day's progress.

"First things first," said Jack, "do we have a plan for the delivery of Hugh's secret weapons tomorrow?"

"Yes, we do," said Marjory. "I will take the ferry across the river first thing in the morning, pick up my car and head up to Exeter,"

"No problem. You will need a map to find the Western Hydro HQ, so I'll print a route out for you before you go,"

"Okay so, Hugh, are your 'missiles' ready?"

"Yes, all done. The plan will be for Marjory to arrive in Exeter at lunchtime which is usually a period of comings and goings and attentions tend to wander, and guards tend to drop,"

"The first ferry is nine-thirty, so you should be on your way by ten and arriving Exeter at midday. If you leave by say, two o'clock you should be back here by four and miss the rush-hour,"

"Sounds good," said Marjory wearing a broad, conspiratorial smile. She was obviously enjoying the cut and thrust of the war against those who use computers and the Internet for nefarious purposes.

"What about the Gordons, Hugh. Did you have any luck finding any signs of modern communications?"

"Well I may have to eat humble pie over the communications between Des and the Gordons, but I wouldn't rule out the personal column tactic altogether, after all, electronic communications were nothing like they are today when Duffy first arrived in Cornwall back in the early '80s. I've been able to track back through various e-mails in Duffy's 'inbox' and locate a couple of addresses that I believe are those belonging to the Gordons. Nothing is ever signed, and the words 'David' or 'Davy' or 'Gordon' never appear anywhere, but regardless of that the e-mails are directed at the Dragon Empire and backtrack to a Glasgow ISP.

They use very simple security measures with no serious attempt to hide the origin. There is also a correlation between the origins of the Dragon e-mails you have found and the origins of some of the transfer mandates that are going in and out of accounts run by Duffy,"

"But how do they do this?" asked Pam. "How do they move all this money around without being found out? There are laws against money laundering, surely,"

"The one thing that some people who work with money develop is a tendency for greed and that can be all-consuming. If enough people in the finance game decide that the rules are inconvenient and can be ignored, then a kind of anarchy descends on the system. One of their favourite techniques is called 'wire-stripping'.

"Every time a Telegraphic Transfer or 'TT' is used to move money, called a 'wire' in the terminology of the banking world, those that are part of the 'dirty banking' community will remove various details from the transaction forms. They then substitute the digital equivalent of 'Mickey Mouse' or 'Donald Duck'. Hence 'wire-stripping'. So many TTs are sent every day that they can only be monitored by computers and they are programmed to reject 'irregularities' not 'regularities',"

"OK," said Jack, "let's get together later tonight and compare notes,"

The St Anthony boatyard was a thriving little enterprise in the middle of nowhere that offered a variety of services including the rental of small motor and sailing boats. One lucrative cooperative venture was to offer the use of a boat to those visitors that rented local cottages as part of a package. This was very popular, and Jack was thanking his lucky stars that by choosing Rose Cottage he and Josh would get some time together fishing from the little boat that came as part of their package.

There were no other takers for the boat trip; there was an unspoken consensus that the pair of them would do just fine by themselves.

Their boat was called CYGNET II and was on a drying mooring not far from the mobile jetty used by the ferry. A chat with the ferryman and the passing of a few pounds meant that their boat would be moved as soon as the incoming tide allowed, moored on their side of the river and made ready to go.

Stepping aboard, they set about inspecting their vessel. Jack read the laminated instructions that were firmly attached to a piece of A4 sized plywood. There was an air of excitement as they got things ready and Josh was jabbering away asking questions and commenting on this and that new discovery. Jack had some experience with boats and knew enough to be careful and respect the dangers of small boats in the hands of inexperienced sailors. He had carried out several enquiries into fatalities on the River Helford and had no intention of becoming one of those statistics, particularly with Josh aboard. He wanted to set a good example to his young son who was at an impressionable age and impatient to get on with their fishing trip. Each boat had its particular set-up as far as the engine controls were concerned, and Jack followed the instructions carefully and soon had the little single cylinder diesel engine puttering away. With the mooring lines free they set off for the river mouth in the hope of some fine mackerel fishing.

The hand lines left for them were simple fishing devices with a weight on the end of a line and a dozen coloured 'feather' lures attached at regular intervals a few feet above. When they arrived at what looked like a good spot the lines were deployed from both sides of the boat and the speed cut to a gentle pace. Josh was chatting all the while but his animated conversation tailed off into concentration as the prospect of catching real live fish took centre stage.

Soon the flickering silver darlings were tugging on his line and were safely delivered, splattering and flapping, in the bottom of the boat. Josh giggled with excitement and delight.

Harvesting food from the sea is such a basic human instinct, and they both enjoyed the experience enormously. Within the hour, they had more than a dozen good fish to add to their larder.

Heading home at the top of the tide, there was a magical sunset in prospect. They sat together in the stern sheets, each with a hand on the tiller. Jack's thoughts drifted into the realms of the dark reality that he faced on his return to Rose Cottage. The weight of responsibility for this growing circle of friends and family was taking its toll. He was abruptly dragged from his thoughts as Josh moved his hand from the wooden tiller and put it on his. He turned to look at his young son who stared back, not with the eyes of a young boy anymore but with the eyes of a young man. "Are you and Mum going to be okay Dad?" he said, getting straight to the point. His tone was serious and far more adult than Jack was prepared for.

"Sure, of course," he choked back, overcome and surprised by his own emotional reaction. His words were delivered almost instinctively as if challenged by the sudden realisation that he was no longer dealing with the ignorance of youth. The look on Josh's face was genuine concern, and he could tell that the question was more about their current situation rather than his relationship with Pam.

"Mum's been crying a lot lately. She doesn't realise that I have seen her crying, but she has. She's upset, and I don't know why. Have I done something to make her unhappy Dad?"

"Lord no, son," said Jack now worried that this whole wretched business was dragging the family into new and uncomfortable territory.

"My mate Johnny Hanson says that you were kicked out the cops. They all tease me about it. Now you are just a bloody ambulance man. Is that why Mum's so unhappy these days?" It was the first time Jack had ever heard Josh swear.

"Josh, listen. Listen to me carefully; I resigned from the police because I was no longer happy in my job. I had a bit of a problem, but that was resolved before I left,"

"They said you were caught thieving, but I didn't believe them,"

"I would never steal anything, and that was the conclusion the disciplinary hearing came to,"

"I knew that really,"

"I said some things I shouldn't have, and I was punished for that, but my career with the police was near its end anyway, and I needed a new challenge,"

"So, you're going to be a paramedic and save people's lives like they do on TV,"

"One day Josh, one day, I've got a lot to learn first,"

"These people you want to get away from, are they angry because you were chasing them?"

"In a way,"

"Why are you chasing them if you aren't a cop anymore?" Jack was looking ahead at the approaching quay and trying to plan their arrival. He turned to Josh and looked at his young and innocent face realising for the first time that his son had felt let down by the events of the last six months. His pride in his father had been shaken, and Jack had completely ignored the traumas that had overtaken Josh at school as a result.

"There's unfinished business I can't explain right now Josh, but we have to be careful. There are those people out there I told you about, bad people, who want to harm us and we have to find a way to put them in jail before they have a chance to do that,"

"I'll help dad, I'm not a kid anymore I'm twelve and a half, nearly, and I can help,"

"Yes, you can Josh. You can keep your eyes and ears open and make sure that you let us know about anything or anyone unusual. Hugh and I have a plan, and with any luck, we will be back to Lower Spargo and back to normal in a week or so,"

"Okay dad," he said, his face turning to a broad conspiratorial grin, "we'll look after Mum and the others. Trust Nathan to miss out on all the fun. He won't believe me when I tell him,"

"I think your brother has discovered girls and has other things on his mind these days," They both laughed at the prospect of brother and son, a 'would-be David Attenborough', putting a 'girlfriend' above chasing wildlife. They pulled alongside the quay and secured the little boat, tidied up the equipment and put the fishing gear away in the locker. They bagged up the fish and were about to set off back to the cottage when Josh came up to his dad and hugged him tightly. He was a foot shorter than Jack who tucked Josh under his chin and returned the hug. They looked at each other for a moment. Neither could find the right words, but the mutual love and affection were unmistakable.

They then set off for Rose Cottage with Josh standing a little taller and Jack feeling proud of his young son's developing character. They marched triumphantly into the kitchen holding their bag of mackerel high whereupon Pam told the both of them that they would have to dress and fillet their fish themselves.

They set about their task with more gusto than skill, but the result was good enough for amateurs.

Sunday was the day Pam would think of her folks so not long after Jack and Josh returned from their epic trip and while Marjory served them a late supper she quietly took herself off up Orchard Lane to get a signal on her mobile. Darkness was settling evenly on the little village as she made her way up the narrow lane. She called their house but no reply. She called their mobile numbers but again, no reply. Something in the back of her mind began to ring alarm bells, but she put it down to a kind of paranoia caused by recent events. She tried to convince herself that everything was okay as she walked back down the hill to the cottage.

21.30 – Seahawk Cottage, Cury Cross, The Lizard

Gerard's patience was wearing thin, and with no news from Jeff Barnes he worried that yet another part of his plan to track down Jack Mawgan had run into trouble. Barnes would not answer his mobile phone with every attempt to contact him going straight to his voicemail. Eventually, he gave up and recalled the team watching Lower Spargo to attend a rendezvous in the village of Cury Cross, south of Helston. They were told to recce the bungalow belonging to Pam's parents then meet Gerard in the car park of The Wheel Inn, just a few hundred yards from their target.

'Seahawk Cottage' was the home of the only close relatives known to be living in the area, and with any luck, there would be clues to Pam's whereabouts somewhere inside. When they arrived, they found Gerard sitting in his Range Rover, one that had been fitted with a rear-mounted custom rack for what looked like a serious off-road motorbike. They climbed into Gerard's car and delivered a verbal account of their tedious day at Cove Hill.

"I'm afraid Mr Barnes will not be joining us, and he is not answering my calls. We will have to manage without him. Bernard, you brought the gas kit with you, yes?" asked Gerard.

"Yes, but I couldn't get any more of the knock-out gas, we've got to use the other stuff. It's more likely to kill than disable but under the circumstances." He left the sentence unfinished, but Gerard nodded his understanding.

"Don't worry Gerry we have two gas masks to go with it,"

"Okay, so we can be assured of a quiet entry,"

"Why don't we just break in and capture these old folks, then torture them until they tell us what they know?" asked Bernard Fermier.

"We found out in Niger; you need to capture the kids first, then the parents will talk. It doesn't work so well the other way around,"

"We carried out a drive-by recce one hour ago," said Morrisey, "we know there are two of them and there are two cars on the driveway, so they are both at home, we will just give the gas more time to make sure, say an hour before we go in," Gerard was wearing a nervous expression. "Don't worry. We will be ready to finish them off if they are still alive,"

"Douglas,"

"Yes, sir,"

"Call me when you are inside the house then disappear back to your hotel in Truro, ventilate the place before you leave. I will search the house myself. Unfortunately, I have had to check out of that hotel, and now I will be at the Duchy Hotel in Falmouth. Wait in Truro for my instructions. If

231

you get started now, I will watch the road from here and call you if there are 'complications'," Gerard checked his watch, "ten o'clock, let's say that you are in by eleven-thirty and then you will be back in Truro by half past midnight. If you don't hear from me by eight o'clock tomorrow morning, then make your way to the Royal Duchy Hotel and get rooms there. I sense that our targets are close by,"

With that final exchange, the two left for the cottage in their rental car. When they arrived, they quietly collected their equipment together and approached the building. Walking slowly on the gravel driveway, the crunch, crunch, of their steps sounded loud enough to wake the whole neighbourhood but once on the concrete pathways they were able to move in silence. Each carried two heavy bags and knew exactly what to do. The wooden window frames were easy to deal with. A simple eleven-millimetre bit in a cordless drill and the job was done. A thirty-centimetre-long piece of ten-millimetre plastic pipe, then a rubber tube between the cylinder of gas and the pipe. The valve on the cylinder was opened, and the fatal mix safely dispatched into the room. Within half an hour each window had received the same treatment, and the job was essentially over. They waited for another half an hour then collected up the empty cylinders.

Removing a large jemmy from the equipment bag, Morrisey set about the back door, the one furthest from any other habitation and therefore least likely to create a problem with neighbours. The door turned out to be unlocked. A surprised Morrisey donned his gas mask and stepped into the utility room, eased himself past the washing machine and into the kitchen.

Fermier began to open the windows, and together they moved into the hallway. They were about to enter the bedrooms, and each man prepared himself for what lay beyond the doors ahead. Fermier held a baseball bat and Morrisey a carpenter's hammer.

CHAPTER 21

Monday, 3rd July, 07.00 – Rose Cottage, Helford Village

WHEN THE SUN RISES over the Helford Estuary the dawn chorus begins with the murmuring of the waders feeding on the mud banks then the occasional duck adds to the volume until the piping of the oystercatchers breaks into your consciousness. To be sure you are wide-awake the raucous crows, and the squawking herring gulls join in the cacophony.

"Morning Dad, can we have the fish for breakfast?" An overenthusiastic Josh stuck his head around the bedroom door and found a father slumbering and a concerned mother sitting on the edge of the bed. She had been up for an hour and had already been up to Orchard Lane twice and been unable to raise her parents. They should by rights have been at home at that time on a Monday morning.

"No problem Josh," said Jack, "we'll grill a couple just as soon as I get up," Josh disappeared to the kitchen to choose his breakfast from a plastic container in the fridge full of lovely mackerel fillets.

"Jack I've tried to contact Mum and Dad twice already this morning but there's still no reply, and I just know that something is wrong,"

"Right," said Jack. "As soon as we have had breakfast and have Marjory on her way we'll pop over to Cury Cross and check they are OK,"

"Thanks, Darling, I know you think I am silly, but I really do have a bad feeling. Something is terribly wrong; I can feel it in my bones,"

By nine-fifteen Marjory was ready to leave on her 'mission'. Hugh escorted her down to the quay, and across to Helford Passage. He took the cover from the Micra and checked it over for her. The car started the first time, and Marjory was soon disappearing up the hill towards Mawnan Smith.

Back at Rose Cottage Pam decided to run up to Orchard Lane and try to call her mum and dad one more time, but before she could make the call, she received the double 'bleep' that told her she had voicemail. She tapped the keys and dialled the messaging service then listened to the preamble. Her mother's voice then came on the line.

"Hello Darling, please call, something awful has happened," She couldn't help herself bursting into tears as she dialled her parents' home number, partly relieved that her mother was alright and partly terrified at what the 'awful' event may be as it obviously involved her father.

She listened as the number rang at the other end.

"Hello, Ann speaking,"

"Mum, thank God, what on earth has happened, is it, Dad?"

"Oh, your father is alright, silly fool, tripped on the extension lead when he was cutting the grass and cracked his head on the doorstep. Silly old bugger knocked himself out. Had to call the ambulance then the doctor in A&E insisted on keeping him in overnight. I tried to call and tell you all this, but nobody answered. I had to leave a message on each of your phones. I couldn't remember which numbers you were using so I just called your old number, Jack's old number and then the one you left on the note. None of you responded so I was getting quite worried about what on earth had happened to you all. You will insist on playing these silly games. No, you don't have to worry about your father. He isn't the problem, he's built like a tank, and sometimes I think a blow to the head is the least dangerous injury he could suffer,"

"Well, what is it then?"

"We've been burgled; the house was attacked!"

"What are you talking about?"

"Someone broke into the house last night, while we were out at the hospital,"

"What did they take?"

"That's the strange thing, nothing at all. The Police are here now inspecting the damage, but the only thing I know for sure is that they took the note with your number on it. I know it was there last night because I used it to call you when your dad knocked himself out. This morning I went to call you, and it had disappeared. If it hadn't been for the memory thing on my mobile phone, I wouldn't have been able to leave my message this morning,"

"What sort of damage did they do when they broke in, did they just vandalise the house or what?"

"The Police found holes drilled in every window frame and as you know dear I never lock the back door, so the damage is very slight but very confusing as the detective chap said the holes are consistent with them trying to gas us. The forensic chaps are busy doing tests as we speak,"

"Well I am relieved that things are under control please give my love to Dad and tell him I'll get over to see you both just as soon as I can. Lots of love, speak later, bye," Pam hurried back down to the cottage and gave the news to Jack as he was trying to grill the mackerel.

"They broke into Mum and Dad's last night and tried to gas them,"

"Hang on a minute, slow down, tell me what happened," Pam related the story of the break-in exactly as it had been told to her.

"How is your father now?"

"He's as well as can be expected I guess. Mum doesn't seem overly concerned. But what worries me is that it looks like they tried to kill my mum and dad," she burst into tears. Jack was mortified by the news, put his arms around Pam and hugged her tightly.

"They got into the house, but the only thing they took was the note I left Mum with my new mobile number," Jack stepped back and looked her in the eye, "Are you sure, is she sure?"

"Absolutely. Mum said that it was definitely on her pinboard last night as she had to use it to call me. Today it had disappeared," Jack sat down at the kitchen table. The breakfast was forgotten for a moment while he took in the news.

Josh appeared wanting his breakfast. Grilled fish was duly served together with toast, and jam and cups of tea. It was a breakfast without much conversation. Hugh suddenly came clattering in the kitchen door and announced that Marjory got away OK. Seeing the look on their face, he asked, "What's up, am I late for breakfast or something?" Jack explained the news. Pam was clearly upset by the turn of events, and Jack could sense the tension building between them once more.

"Hugh, we have to find a way to end this business, if what Pam says is true then they are getting too close to home, and now they have Pam's mobile phone number, so presumably they can pinpoint our position?"

"They will track us to Orchard Lane, but yes, I guess they will soon know we are hereabouts. We may have to give some consideration to leaving here and finding another bolt hole,"

"One other thing Hugh, Pam's folks left a message on my old mobile, and despite today's events, I think that it will be wise to continue to leave it switched off. That also means that I cannot access any messages on my phone unless there is another way? There could just be some important messages that I need to know about,"

"Of course there's another way Jack, you dial the designated answerphone for your service provider using a landline or another mobile phone, follow the prompts, enter your PIN and away you go,"

"I don't know my PIN; I have never used that system,"

"Ah! Like many others, so your voicemail messages can be heard by anyone who cares to listen because at this very moment it's protected by nothing more than the default PIN, 4321, 1234 or 0000. Do you have the number for your voicemail service?"

"Yes, it's in my contact list,"

"Right let's pop up to Orchard Lane and see if there are any messages of interest," Hugh and Jack walked up the Lane until Hugh had a signal, dialled Jack's call service and entered the default PIN. He cued up the messages and handed the handset to Jack.

"A message from someone called 'Alex'"

'Hi Jack, it's Alex again, I guess you didn't get my first message, so I'll try again. I'm in hospital following a brush with some people who showed an unhealthy interest in you. One of them attacked me, but I got him instead. We need to talk. Bye.'

The only other message was from Pam's mum:

'Jack, we've been burgled, but we're OK, call when you can, love Ann.'

"Hang on a minute," said Jack.
"What's up?"

"Some messages are missing; could someone have deleted them?"

"Of course, you have no effective PIN protection. Shall I set up a PIN for you?"

Jack thought about it for a moment then said, "No, let's leave things as they are, we may be able to use that to our advantage. I'm not sure how or why but at least we know that someone is monitoring my old mobile number and also interfering with my voicemail messages,"

They returned to the cottage and explained the news to Pam.

10.00 – The Royal Duchy Hotel, Falmouth

The Royal Duchy Hotel stands in Victorian splendour, staring proudly out on Falmouth Bay from its prime location on the seafront. When the days are glorious, and the tide is low, then there is no better place to 'take the air' but when the south-westerly gales are doing their worst the palm trees in the hotel gardens bend like the limbs of a bow and their long thin leaves thrash wildly in the salt-laden winds.

That day it wasn't quite 'glorious', but it was pleasant enough with a light breeze and long sunny spells. By decamping from Truro to Falmouth, Gerard had managed to avoid a difficult discussion with the police by the skin of his teeth and now sat expectantly awaiting news of Jack Mawgan's whereabouts. The mobile number he had found the previous night had been passed to Sir William's man inside the Home Office, and he was sure they would soon be homing in on these two troublesome men.

Eventually, the call from Sir William arrived. "Gerry, where the hell are you now?"

"The Royal Duchy 'otel in Falmouth,"

"Look, Gerry, we have to wrap this up, I had the Police knocking on my door at midnight last night looking for you. They need to question you about your apparent relationship to a Jeff Barnes, recently deceased, a former colleague of yours I believe?"

"Yes, yes but I can sort that out when I come back in a day or so. Do you have a location for our friend Mr Mawgan?"

"Yes, we have tracked him to a village called Helford not far from where you are now if my geography is correct,"

"Right, Helford, we'll get on it. I'll call with news as soon as I have it. Bye for now," Gerard shook his head in frustration and swore under his breath. He called Morrisey and Fermier who arrived at his room within minutes. They were ready for action and eager to please.

"We've got what we were looking for," he told them, "we know roughly where they are. They are in a small village called Helford. This is it, here on each side of this river," He was pointing at the one-inch Ordnance Survey Map spread out on the table.

"The north part is called Helford Passage and the South part Helford Village. It is a long way by road between them, but this map indicates a ferry across the river,"

"What kind of ferry, do we know? Does it run twenty-four seven?" asked Fermier.

"The information available indicates that it's a passenger ferry and it runs nine-thirty a.m. to nine-thirty p.m. at this time of year. Not ideal but maybe we can hire a boat if we need one. I'll look into that,"

"We will leave at eleven and take my Range Rover, and both rental cars, Douglas and I will head for the north side, Helford Passage, and Bernard you will go to the south side. According to the map, there is a public car park in Helford Passage. Douglas will leave his car there and begin a reconnaissance of the waterfront and the houses close by. Bernard, you will do the same on the Village side. We are searching for their hideaway so that we can make a plan of attack.

We will need to do our best to get in and out without causing a stir. The local police are based in this town here, Penryn. They can quickly cut off the main roads out of the area but luckily their helicopter is a long way away, up in Exeter so we should be able to get well clear before they can respond.

There are binoculars for each of you over there on the bed together with copies of more photos of Target One, Mawgan and Target Two, Martin.

"If we get lucky we can do the job tomorrow night and be away before the following morning. We have the gas, Douglas?"

"Plenty," said Morrisey.

"You both have weapons?"

"Sure, said Morrisey, patting his left breast where the shoulder holster held his pistol snugly under his left armpit. He turned to Fermier.

"SIG, 9mm," said Fermier, again signalling the presence of a shoulder holster.

"Now I know why you wear the jacket one size too big," said Morrisey smiling at his own joke.

"We only use these in emergencies, he held up his pistol. I have some friends in high places in this country, and they can make a lot of things go away, but if you use your weapon and get caught, then you are on your own. I expect to be back here tonight so you can leave your bags in your rooms. Let's go,"

12.30 – Rose Cottage, Helford Village

"Where did Josh go," asked Pam, "lunch is on the table,"

"Not sure, I'll give him a call," said Jack. Walking to the front door and stepping into the road he peered each way and could see no sign of his son who was having a whale of a time proving that he could get up to just as much mischief by himself as did with a bunch of mates.

"Josh," he yelled. No sign of human activity anywhere. He walked around to the side of the cottage where the large wooden garage housing Uncle Ron's old car stood. It was firmly padlocked, and Auntie May had the only key. Josh appeared from the undergrowth and announced that he had made a great discovery.

"Come on Josh; lunch is on the table. You can tell us all about it while we eat," The four of them sat quietly during the meal with the odd scrap of conversation punctuating the clink of knives and forks on porcelain plates.

"I found a car like the Queen's in Uncle Ron's garage," announced Josh.

"Really," said Pam in that tone that parents use when they are trying to sound interested in what their offspring has to say.

"Yes, really Mum. I found a way through the bushes to the end of the garage and right at the end there's a hole in the wall, and I could see it, one of those 'Roller' things,"

The grown-ups looked at each other wondering how to respond. Josh promised to show them after lunch so when the plates had been cleared, and coffee had been consumed, he led them around the back of the garage and showed them the little knot-hole that allowed a peek at what was hidden inside.

"Bloody Hell," said Jack.

"Jack, please, language!" scolded Pam.

"No, he's right, I can see the radiator of a Rolls Royce," They each took turns in peering at the amazing sight of an old Rolls Royce car, sitting in Uncle Ron's old wooden garage.

"But Auntie told me that she kept it taxed and insured and did the MOT every year," said a confused Jack.

"Maybe Auntie sees it as an Uncle Ron substitute. You know, as long as the car goes, Uncle Ron is always with her,"

"Yes, but Uncle Ron was a modest carpenter, how come he has a Roller?" asked Jack.

"What kind of bodywork does it have?" asked Hugh. "That may give us a clue," He touched the side of his nose as if conveying the fact that he knew the answer to that question and went to the side of the garage fighting his way through the brambles. Finding another knothole, he peered inside. "The light's not very good but I can just make out the rear of the bodywork, and as I suspected, it's a hearse,"

"A hearse," said Pam.

"Yes, a hearse,"

"But why a hearse? Uncle didn't collect old cars, let alone funeral cars,"

"Because," said Hugh, "he was the village carpenter, and in rural areas, the village carpenter is the undertaker, he makes the coffins. In fact, in more recent times the carpenter was also the joiner, cabinet-maker, wheelwright and in seaside, lakeside and riverside villages, the shipwright. He had the skills, equipment and workshop,"

"But being an undertaker means a lot more than just knocking up a coffin," said Jack. "What's complicated about washing and dressing a body and putting it in a box?"

"Okay, I'll give you that,"

Somewhat amused by their discovery the mood had lightened a little, and they headed back to the cottage but then Jack brought things down to earth.

"I'll check my messages," said Jack, "what about you Hugh?"

"Good idea, there may be something from Marjory,"

"Can you give Mum a call and find out how Dad is?"

"No go," said Hugh, "they may be monitoring all calls to your parent's phone and mobiles,"

"Damn, I need to know how Dad is,"

"We'll find a way, don't worry,"

The two men walked up Orchard Lane until they got a mobile signal. Jack had a message from Daniel. He returned the call. "Dan, it's me,"

"Hi Jack, can't talk for long so get this. You have the right guy in Chaloner, you will never get written proof, but I was allowed to see his file and an additional annexe that is classified Top Secret. He was the one behind a series of murders in Aden in the sixties. He was indeed the one using the 'OR GLORY' stamp. It was his trademark. His connections go to the top, and they kept him out of harm's way and kept the Military Police off his back. That's all I can say,"

"Thanks, Dan, that's what I needed to know. He must be an arrogant son of a bitch to do something so stupid as to leave his so-called trademark littered around every murder he is involved with,"

"Was that attack on the policewoman anything to do with the people you are busy trying to avoid?"

"What attack on a policewoman?"

"Alexandra something or other, I forget her surname, she was attacked not far from your place in Perranarworthal, but she got the better of her assailant who is now lying on a marble slab in the local morgue. The thing is the press have somehow got hold of the fact that the assailant was part of a group of men visiting Cornwall and one of that group was rumoured to be de Beaumont, Chaloner's live-in lover,"

"Actually, they are connected, Alex left me a message, on my old mobile, in fact, she left more than one message but the other side is reading my voicemail and deleted at least one message from her,"

"Hell Jack, you have some serious players lined up against you if they can do that,"

"It was down to my ignorance of the voicemail system; I didn't realise that I had to set up a PIN, so anyone out there could have been prying into my messages,"

"Either way you are up against some heavyweights. There are some other folks I want you to help me deal with, and that's the Gordon family in Glasgow,"

"How do you know about them?" said a surprised Jack.

"It's our job to know about the people involved with Chaloner and thanks to your efforts we now see the link. I want you and Hugh to find a way to get a message to them then I want you to send it as if it came from you. I'll send you the text by e-mail then if you need a hand give me a shout,"

"Okay, we will await your mail and get on it right away. Are you busy right now? I could do with some eyes and ears down here. This thing is coming to a head, and the bad guys are closing in on us, last night they tried to take out Pam's parents but we got lucky, and they didn't succeed,"

"Where are you?"

"We are in Helford Village, on the south side of the Helford River,"

"OK, I'll be down there tonight, do I stay with you?"

"Sure, there's a ferry to our side of the river, and we also have a little boat if you arrive outside the ferry hours,"

"OK, I'll be driving a dark blue BMW three series, what about comms?"

"Mobiles are a bit hit and miss I'm afraid, and it's a holiday let, so there's no land line,"

"I'll bring some walkie-talkies.

"Thanks, see you later, bye for now,"

Hugh was just finishing his call to Marjory, "Okay Darling, well done, see you in about two hours,"

"All right Hugh?"

"She's done it. On her way home,"

"Okay before we go back I need to find out about Larry, Pam's dad... any ideas?"

"We could try hacking the hospital computer system and getting what you need to know from their records,"

"Worth a try, let's go," They returned to the cottage and set about finding a way into the hospital systems in Truro. Within the hour they were reading the computer log in A&E. Hugh announced, "Mr Laurence Walters was discharged," he checked his watch, "one hour and forty-five minutes ago," Pam was relieved, but the growing tension was beginning to wear her down. The constant need to display a brave face and pretend that this was just a holiday was taking its toll. Jack could tell that Pam was in need of cheering up.

"The good news is that Dan is on his way, and, we will know how successful Marjory has been very soon,"

"I'll go over on the ferry and wait for her," said Hugh, "help her to put the cover back on the car," With that, he left for the quayside to call the ferry.

The little ferryboat normally sat parked against the floating jetty on the Helford Passage side of the river when not in use or tied up on a mooring line on the beach when the tide is out. On the village side of the river, there is a simple device for calling the ferryman. Hugh followed the instructions on the adjacent notice, and soon the ferryman was heading across the river to pick him up.

There are times when strangers stick out like sore thumbs. Holidaymakers wear clothes that sometimes defy fashion and despite the advice of their best friends will wear shorts or skimpy clothing when the acres of flesh should more often than not be under wraps. It's possible to put this down to a kind of declaration of intent, 'I am on holiday, and I don't care what the weather is or how I look, I will dress in my beachwear'.

In the villages around the coast of Cornwall members of that particular club were plentiful, along with the sailing and boating community who blend in with expensive Italian Polo shirts, windcheaters with designer labels and the ubiquitous 'deck-shoes'. It was therefore not surprising that the overdressed gentleman wearing a bomber jacket and making a poor attempt at looking nonchalant leaning against the sea wall stood out like a wart on the nose of the Mona Lisa. His searching gaze never stopped scanning the area. He was looking for something or someone. Hugh spotted him as he stepped off the ferry, paused to take in this curious figure then turned immediately to the right and walked off along the beach and then took the narrow road up towards the car park.

He had to intercept Marjory before she arrived in the village and managed to catch her by the junction near the top of the steep descent into Helford Passage. Marjory, startled by the sight of an exhausted husband staggering up the road pulled over and wound down her window.

"Hugh, what on earth are you doing?"

"They are here Marjory, I'm sure of it, down by the ferry," he gasped, "there is a suspicious looking character waiting outside the pub. We will have to go the long way around via Gweek," He climbed in beside her, and she turned around and set off to take the long way back to the Helston road and the narrow lanes through Gweek, Mawgan and Newtown St Martin.

Pam and Jack sat looking at the clock and worrying about where on earth Hugh and Marjory were. At five to five they finally walked in the door and blurted out the news that Hugh was pretty sure that there were strangers in Helford Passage who were not dressed for summer days on the beach.

"We thought that if they were in Helford Passage, they could be here in the Village, so we found a back way through the lanes and the footpaths we found on the OS map,"

"What did you do with the car?" asked Jack.

"We parked up at Kestle Barton and walked down. Sorry we took so long,"

"Sit down you two, I'll get you a cup of tea," said Pam.

Was this the moment they had feared? Had their hiding place been discovered? Maybe this was a false alarm but either way, they could not afford to be complacent. The dining table became the conference desk as they sorted through the piles of printouts accumulated so far and Hugh and Jack took turns at peering at each other's laptop.

By eight p.m. everyone was getting hungry, so Pam and Marjory set about cooking while Jack and Hugh prepared a plan to present after dinner. Chili con carne with rice and served on the kitchen table was as much as the cooks were able to offer under the circumstances. This simple fare was devoured in silence as thoughts were gathered and the reserves of nervous energy were replenished. Jack began the after-dinner conference.

"The news that there may be strangers across the river may mean that the net is closing in. They may even be watching us as I speak. Please, everyone, stay alert, and keep your eyes open for anything unusual,"

"So how do we end this Jack?" said Pam.

"That's the million-dollar question," said Hugh, "but we have some ideas. First, we have to hope and pray that Marjory's visit to Western Hydro was successful, we have to be inside their system to do what we need to do. Somewhere in there is a computer with all the necessary authorisations to tinker with their secret accounts. There has to be at least one server within the Western Hydro computer network used to manage the flow of funds into 'Project Cayman', if we can get control of that server then we can use it as a Trojan horse and get right into the Frimly systems. Once inside we can turn their nicely ordered system into a chaotic mess,"

"But how will that get these people off our backs? And what about a Plan B?" asked Pam.

"That part of the plan will take care of the support structure that protects Chaloner and his lieutenants because we will simultaneously ensure that certain information reaches the public domain. Hugh reckons that there will be an attempt to close ranks but if we spread the news far enough there will be nowhere for anyone to hide. You will see the press having a field day and some big names embarrassed by their association with what amounts to serious financial criminality,"

"But Jack, we are in a very precarious situation here, we don't have time to play fucking computer games, what's our Plan B for god's sake?" Jack was stunned; he had never heard Pam use such bad language. He struggled to find the right words to deal with a situation he thought might spin out of control.

"I won't let anything happen I promise. Plan B will be to evacuate Rose Cottage tomorrow night under cover of darkness. Hugh has enough cash to finance a trip up country, and we will just have to find a hotel in a quiet spot. As soon as we are safe, I'll try to find the best way of getting the police involved. I'm sure that Dan can help if I ask him. He has contacts in all the right places. If we are outside the Devon and Cornwall Constabulary area, then there is a chance we will get a fair hearing. I spoke with Dan earlier today, and he is coming down to help us. He will be an enormous asset. Our aim is to neutralise de Beaumont and any fellow travellers he may have with him,"

Pam was barely able to control her anger and wasn't convinced that Jack's intentions were anything more than just words. Jack took Hugh to one side, and they spent a few minutes discussing their next move. Jack disappeared to Orchard Lane and returned ten minutes later.

"Dan is here and will come over on the ferry as soon as he can. I'll have to go and meet him, back soon,"

Hugh checked his computer for any sign that one of the discs planted at Western Hydro had been plugged into their system, nothing yet.

Jack arrived with Dan, "Hi everybody, this is Dan Barclay. He's an old friend and former colleague," Dan did the rounds shaking hands. When he came to Hugh, there was a conspiratorial nod as two people who know each other pretended not to.

"Have you eaten Dan?" asked Pam, there's some chilli left if you are hungry,"

"Perfect, thanks,"

22.00 – The Royal Duchy Hotel, Falmouth

A smiling and confident Gerard addressed his two remaining co-conspirators in his opulent suite at The Royal Duchy.

"Gentlemen we may have had a fruitless and frustrating day, but we have some good news at last. I heard from the boss that we have an intercept on a message left on one of their mobiles. We know that our targets, wherever they are hiding in the delightful village of Helford, have ordered a taxi for one of them tomorrow morning at nine-forty-five. They plan to cross from Helford Village to Helford Passage as soon as the ferryman arrives.

It will be an early start in the morning. Douglas, you will take your car and park in the car park again," he pointed again to a sketch he had made of Helford Passage.

"You will then proceed on foot and wait here," indicating the road close to the ferry's mobile jetty. "When you see the taxi arrive you will take control of the vehicle and wait for the targets. You will proceed back to the car park and terminate the target and the taxi driver. There are no cameras but take care to minimise any fuss. Collect your car, return to London and I'll send the balance of your money to the normal address,"

He turned to Fermier, "Bernard I want you to take your car around to the other side of the river again and check out the situation in that part of the village. The car park you used as a base today sounds like a good spot for checking out the flow of people in and out of the village. Check as many cars as you can. We need to know exactly which house they are in and the cars may be the clue. Look out for the targets around eight thirty as they head for the ferry. Call me with the sitrep as soon as you see anything of interest. We understand that one of the targets will cross on the ferry. That will leave one other to dispose of.

"Yesterday we had communication problems with the mobile phone signals, but I have I found an ideal place to wait where the signal seems to be solid. It's in the car park at Glendurgen Gardens, here at the top of the hill. I will be coordinating activities from there. We know that Target One uses a motorbike so I have mine in readiness. This is not the kind of countryside where car versus bike works very well but if I have to chase him down, then I have the equipment to do it ready to go. The time now is twenty-two eighteen. Breakfast at six-thirty, we depart at seven. Good night gentlemen,"

The two men wandered off down to the bar to get a much-needed cold beer leaving Gerard to report his progress back to Sir William.

23.00 – Rose Cottage, Helford Village

"If they are somewhere nearby then we need to keep a lookout overnight just in case they try the gas trick again," Jack whispered to Hugh as they sat in their makeshift office. They were putting the finishing touches to their plan to destroy the financial resources of much of the country's elite and one or two criminal masterminds. He mused how they might actually be one and the same. The others had gone to bed having been reassured that with reinforcements in place all would now be well. Dan was sleeping and would take over sentry duties from Jack at 04.00.

Hugh was about to reply when a little window opened up on his screen.

"Jack! Jack, we're in. The game is on; someone has loaded one of the floppy discs and the e-mail has just arrived,"

"At this time of night, who the hell is working at this time of night?"

"No idea but he gets my vote whoever he is,"

"So what next?"

"I will now try to take control of the Cayman Project server and see what sort of connections it has with the rest of the Frimly network. With any luck Chaloner had authoring rights and automatic log-on but if not we'll have to use the password cracker and get in that way. It just takes more time. The programme I have written this evening will move their cash around as we discussed and by tomorrow night there will be four or five hundred wealthy individuals that are not quite as wealthy as they were this morning. How is your side of the plan coming on?"

"I have the press releases ready they will now go out on the web at nine a.m. tomorrow. I have narrowed down the Gordon's e-mail addresses to a couple of mails that, from the pattern and contents of their messaging, seem to come from the very top. The message that Dan sent me earlier I have transcribed into our e-mail and added a bit about their financial situation. It goes like this:

Dear Mr Gordon

By the time you receive this message the funds you have so carefully accumulated over the last twenty years will have been redistributed to more deserving members of society.

The man responsible for your demise is also the man who killed Desmond Duffy. His name is Sir William Chaloner, and he can be contacted at Cadhay Manor, Ottery St Mary, Devon.

As proof of his culpability in this matter, I attach a link that will connect you to a website on which are published the details of all your transactions with Desmond Duffy and his transactions, in turn, with Sir William Chaloner.

You will also find detailed company accounts that indicate that Sir William was using your funds for his own use.

Sincerely

A Well Wisher

"Wow, that will get their attention, what do you think they will do?"

"Do you know I haven't stopped to consider it, but it is probably not beyond the bounds of possibility that Sir William will need a pair of crutches if he can't reimburse their losses,"

"I think a pair of concrete boots and a wee trip down the Clyde will be more likely,"

"You could be right. How much longer will you be?"

"Quite a while Jack, you get some sleep, and I'll wake Dan at four o'clock then he can take a turn as the lookout,"

CHAPTER 22

- -

Tuesday, 4ᵗʰ July 04.00 – Operations Room, Devon & Cornwall Police HQ, Middlemoor, Exeter.

"IT'S DEFINITELY HIM SIR, we've run voice-analysis on the tape and compared it to the man who tipped us off about the Madron incident. They are identical,"

"Thank you, sergeant, well, we will have to take this second tip-off very seriously. I'll let ACC Operations know what's on the cards. We need to work out a plan,"

07.00 – Rose Cottage, Helford Village

"Jack, Jack, wake up," it was Pam; she had a cup of tea and an attempt at a reassuring smile. He knew that behind that smile was the underlying feeling that there wasn't much to smile about. "What do you want for breakfast?"

"Let's start with a cuppa then when I've got my head together I'll check out my appetite,"

OK, tea it is. Hugh's been brilliant apparently. Dan says he's come up with a bit of a brainwave and says he has set a time bomb under Chaloner's entire empire,"

"Great, that means he must have completed his master plan. If we can finish this whole thing without anyone knowing that we were up to our necks in it then it will be a very welcome miracle and if we get to punish those who would wish us harm so much the better. What we must do is make sure they go away for a very long time,"

"You will keep your promise, won't you? I don't think my nerves are up to much more of this,"

"One way or another we will finish this today. If not, then tonight we wait until dark then head for the hills and pass the buck to the authorities,"

Jack was reluctant to tell Pam that he was going to be the bait in a trap for Mr De Beaumont. She wouldn't understand and wouldn't let him go. If the police had responded and were lying in wait, then all would be well. If their plan worked, then the police would take care of Chaloner's foot soldiers while Hugh's plan would deal with Chaloner.

"What are you going to do today?"

"I'm going across to collect my bike and bring it around to Rose Cottage. If we are bailing out tonight, then I want to take my bike with me. It could come in handy. Hugh will come back with Dan and show him the layout here,"

"Are you taking the ferry?"

"Actually no, I'm going to take our little boat, it's still tied up at the jetty. The tide will be falling this morning, but I'll make it across okay,"

"What shall we do?"

"Wait here, keep your eyes open and stay calm. If things go well, we may even be out of here today,"

Pam's smile had disappeared. She had a feeling in her bones that Jack was up to something and he wasn't telling all he knew. At nine o'clock Jack went down to the jetty and boarded the little motorboat. He was dressed for the motorbike and carried his crash helmet. Heading away from the jetty, he steered the boat downriver. His intention was to land about 50 metres east of the ferry. He could see the ferryman opening up his little kiosk.

He turned towards the land and soon the keel was scraping the gravelly shore. Jumping into the shallow water, he dragged the boat up the beach and then took the painter up to one of the iron rings attached to the sea wall. Leaving the boat secure he looked around. All was quiet with just a few people ambling around the beachside road in front of the Ferryboat Inn. His heart was in his mouth as he set off to the car park where the Triumph sat anonymously under a grey plastic cover.

09.15 – Municipal Car Park, Helford Village

Bernard Fermier stood at the edge of the car park peering across at the activity on the other side of the river through his binoculars. He was providing a running commentary on his mobile to Gerard who was paying close attention as the situation unfolded just a few hundred yards away from his vantage point at the top of the hill. Bernard monitored two males as they left a cottage on the waterfront and made their way to the quayside. A small boat set off across the Helford River leaving a bow wave that rocked the fleet of small boats lying at anchor on this calm and peaceful morning.

"A boat has just pulled up on the foreshore, one male occupant. He's wearing leather clothing and carrying a crash helmet," He checked his briefing notes and looked at the mug shots. "I think we have Target One here. The ferryman looks like he's preparing the ferry for the nine-thirty service but no customers so far. I see Douglas approaching from the west, along the road. Here comes the taxi, it's a regular Mercedes car with 'A2B Taxis' in big letters on the side. It's turned the corner and approaching the ferry kiosk and... yes, it has stopped.

"Douglas is approaching the driver of the taxi. Damn, the driver is on the wrong side, I can't see, yes there is a weapon, hang on, hang on there are police, armed police. They are all over the place. Douglas is down. The police have him. Gerard, what shall we do?"

"Where is Target One?"

"He's walking towards the car park."

09.32 – Helford Passage

Josh decided to help by using his initiative and taking the rubbish down to the recycling bins in the village car park but the news he brought back headed off a scolding from his frantic mother.

"All their cars have got flat tyres, and there's a guy spying on us with binoculars from the car park," Daniel turned to Hugh who heard Josh's report.

"They're here," Dan went to his overnight bag and unzipped a side pocket. He removed a semi-automatic pistol and a couple of magazines. One contained hard-tipped penetration rounds and the other soft nosed rounds with low powder content designed for close quarter 'indoor' combat. He loaded the soft-nosed clip into the pistol and pulled back the slide to load the chamber. He checked the safety then he put it in the front of his waistband. The others stood mesmerised. Suddenly, shockingly they were faced with the reality of their situation. Pam's face drained visibly, but she tried to sound strong.

"What shall we do, we can't escape now?"

"Listen-up," said Dan, "We need to take the initiative. If they have identified this cottage as our refuge, then we can anticipate that they will shortly be coming in the front door mob-handed,"

"What do they want to do, kill us all?" asked Pam.

"Something like that," replied Hugh, although it's me they are after. I'm the one rocking their boat. Maybe I should leave and avoid the rest of you having to face these reprobates," Marjorie moved to his side and held his arm as if to prevent any such pointless gesture.

"A very honourable gesture I don't think, you idiot," she said, furious at what she considered to be a ridiculous suggestion, "the cars have been disabled, so unless you fancy a foot race up to Kestle Barton to fetch my Micra you had better stick with us," Hugh looked suitably chastised.

"Is that a real gun Mr Barclay," said Josh, "does it fire real bullets?

"Yes Josh, this is a real pistol, and it fires real bullets,"

09.45 – Municipal Car Park, Helford Village

"Target One is now in the car park and preparing to use his motorcycle,"

"Okay Bernard, I will take care of Target One. You must get to their house and deal with Target Two. Don't let him get away,"

Gerard went to the rear of his Range Rover, slid out the ramp on his custom bike carrier, flipped off the transit locks holding the Suzuki off-road bike safely in place and rolled it down to the ground. He heard Jack approaching the main road and then accelerate past the entrance to Glendurgen, on his way to Mawnan Smith. "Damn," he muttered, "I must be quick!"

He pushed the electric start button and roared off up the road without stopping to put on his helmet, gloves or Barbour Jacket. By the time Jack had eased his way through the congestion at Mawnan Smith Gerard was just a few hundred yards behind him.

Helford Village

Bernard may not have been in the first flush of youth, but he was fit and combat ready. Trotting down the slight hill from the car park he took the water splash shortcut across the stream and continued towards Rose Cottage along the waterside road. The smell of seaweed and the rank odour of the mud banks failed to divert his senses one iota as he focussed on sizing up the options for gaining entrance to Rose Cottage with the minimum of fuss.

Looking around for a sign of anyone watching and finding that all was quiet Bernard peered in through ground floor window. Marjory and Pam were in the kitchen and engaged in deep conversation. Hugh was hiding behind the firmly bolted kitchen door to protect the ladies as they set about the task of creating an air of normality.

Bernard took another look around, all clear, he tried the door front door handle and found it opened easily. With pistol poised he stepped inside. He walked towards the kitchen door but only made it one step when a voice behind him said,

"Stand still, put the weapon down," Bernard froze, his instinct was to make out he was complying with the demands made by the voice of authority behind him. Surely nobody would make such a demand without himself being armed. Or was this a clever bluff by someone pretending to be armed. Bernard had lived in the UK long enough to understand how the laws controlling weapons worked. Guns were almost unheard of unless you were dealing with criminals or the police. These were not criminals, and surely they could not be police. He was about to call Dan's bluff when Josh, came tumbling down the stairs and landed in a heap at Bernard's feet. Josh had been watching from the upper landing but in a rush to help Dan came a cropper on the top step and fell down the stairs.

Josh was Manna from Heaven to Bernard who seized him with his one free hand and held him up as a shield backing away from Dan. His blood ran cold as he saw Dan's weapon. This was no bluff.

"Now it's your turn, get on the floor push your weapon over here," To his undying credit, Dan didn't move a single muscle when he saw Pam emerge from the kitchen behind Bernard holding a monster frying pan above her head. Like any mother protecting her offspring, she was fired up, so much so that the wallop she delivered to the back of Bernard's head probably cracked his skull. He went down like a sack of potatoes and lay still.

Mawnan Smith to Gweek Road

Taking the Constantine road, Jack was oblivious to the fact that he was being followed until he got to Gweek where the sharp left turn up the hill to Garras allowed him to look at the road below. He caught sight of another bike and then recalled seeing it in his mirrors ever since he left Mawnan Smith. Alert to the fact that he was being tailed by someone on what looked like a dirt bike he ran through a short list of who this might be. He had a shrewd idea, and if he was right then, he was in mortal danger. He accelerated to try and put some distance between him and his pursuer. Around the narrow twisting lanes of The Lizard Peninsular, he had little advantage over a bike designed for cross country use, but he knew that not far away were roads where he could release the power of his T-Bird and show the trail bike a clean pair of heals. His tyres were struggling around the bends at Mawgan as he rode like a madman. De Beaumont managed to keep up for he was an accomplished rider and handled his off-road bike like a pro. If Jack could lead his pursuer on a high-speed chase towards the village of St Keverne, he knew that the infamous double bends at Zoar Farm would be impossible to take at speed on that sort of bike. Its high centre of gravity was designed to deliver ground clearance, not high-speed cornering.

Murder was not on his mind, but self-preservation was. With any luck, he would be able to force his pursuer to crash and take the guy out long enough to get the rest of the family safely away from Rose Cottage. He needed to lead the chasing rider past the turn-off to Helford and instead take the long fast road past the huge dishes at Goonhilly Earth Station. If he could tempt the chasing rider into thinking that he was able to catch him, then he could gradually increase speed and suck him into the trap.

Jack hurtled across the junction at Traboe his twin cylinder motor humming like a deranged bee and on towards the complex of wicked bends that marked Zoar Farm. As they reached the magic figure of 100 mph, Jack looked ahead to judge his braking point. At that moment, Gerard took the opportunity to take a shot at Jack. He was outpaced by Jack's T-Bird on these open roads. Now he was close it may be his last opportunity.

He reached inside his leather flight jacket and slipped the Glock from its shoulder holster. With his right hand, he cocked the weapon on his thigh. The rush of 100 mph wind was making his aim difficult, without goggles or visor, his eyes watered so much he could hardly see. He put his sights on the middle of Jack's back and was about to pull the trigger when the unthinkable happened.

Jack didn't see it, but he certainly heard the crash. There was a dreadful crunch of metal into metal. Looking over his shoulder, Jack could see that a tractor had pulled out of a field gate onto the road, and directly into the path of his would-be assassin.

Unable to stop, de Beaumont had smacked straight into the back of the tractor. Jack had enough experience to know that if the rider survived that impact, he would be very lucky indeed. He turned around and rode back to the scene. The tractor driver was wandering around in a daze when Jack arrived, removed his helmet and parked his bike.

"Are you OK?" Jack asked him.

"I'm OK," he said, "but I reckon I've done for that guy," Jack could see that the tractor driver was trembling with the first signs of shock. He had soiled himself, and despite his apparently calm exterior, he would be nursing the kind of turmoil that only someone who has caused a fatal accident can know.

Walking to the back of the tractor Jack could see that the mangled remains of the bike were a testament to a hell of an impact and there, wrapped face down around the wreckage was the twisted corpse of Gerard de Beaumont. Jack wanted to walk away. It was over. But a real Ambulance Technician would not do that. He knelt beside the body and took a pulse... nothing... no surprise.

He needed to know what the man that wanted him dead looked like and grasped his shoulder to roll him over. As he did so, he did not, of course, realise that de Beaumont was about to use his firearm when the tractor pulled out. The post-accident report would determine that there was no evidence of Gerard attempting to stop and this was attributed to his holding the pistol in his right hand at the moment the tractor appeared. The front brake is operated by the right hand, and you cannot brake and shoot at the same time. Of course, that would be established later but at that moment the semi-automatic pistol was cocked, and de Beaumont's finger was still wrapped around the trigger.

As Jack turned him over the gun went off. He crumpled to the ground, another victim of a crazy day.

Rose Cottage, Helford Village.

"That's accounted for one of them at least," said Hugh.

"Do you think there are more of them?" asked Marjory.

"Let's play safe and not rule it out. In which case, we need to get out of here. If the cars are disabled what vehicles do we have available?"

"Only the little Micra up at Kestle Barton, this guy slashed all the tyres on our cars," said Pam.

"Don't forget Jack will be here soon but we won't get far on one motorbike and the Micra. There are now six of us and one prisoner," Dan checked his watch and did a quick calculation.

"Jack should have been here by now. He told me he would be at the cottage in half an hour. He's twenty minutes late," A look of panic crossed Pam's face.

"There's the Roller, Dan," said Josh keen to help his mum who was looking decidedly worried and no longer totally in command of her emotions. She knew that something had gone wrong, something had happened to Jack.

"The what, Josh?"

"There's a Rolls Royce in the garage; we can use that,"

"Why didn't you say earlier, I thought all the cars were in the village car park?"

"Well the garage is locked, but it's only a small lock,"

"Show me," Bernard began to stir and within a few minutes was sitting up nursing a monster headache.

"I'll look after him," said Hugh, "you go and check out the car,"

Josh took him outside to the garage and showed him the lock. Dan looked around and found a cement garden gnome close to the front door. Trying its weight, he thought it would be heavy enough for what he had in mind. He stepped over to the padlock and gave it a severe blow with the gnome, which promptly broke in two. Another blow with what remained was enough, and the hasp, complete with padlock, was torn from the old wooden door.

Inspecting the interior of the garage they found the hearse in amazingly good order.

"Look they have even left the keys in the ignition. This will be perfect," said Daniel. "We can all get out in this, let's hope the battery isn't flat," Dan jumped in the driver's seat and turned the engine over. The battery was fine; on the second attempt, it burst into life and filled the garage with dreadful exhaust fumes.

They opened both garage doors, and the choking fumes gradually subsided. The open doors allowed them to see that the garage was more than just a place where Uncle Ron stored his hearse. Above them in the rafters were sample coffins.

Pam was alarmed at the prospect of leaving the village in a hearse but was assured that the old-fashioned Rolls had seats for three attendants just behind the driver and front seat passenger and the oak coffin they had brought down from the roof beams turned out to be a perfect way of delivering Bernard to the police.

The coffin chosen was designed for someone smaller that Bernard so it was a tight fit, but nobody was unduly concerned about Bernard's comfort. At two o'clock precisely an immaculate, if slightly dusty, 1954 Rolls Royce Silver Wraith Hearse, apparently carrying a driver and four attendants and one rather shabby sample coffin cruised slowly out of the village and up the hill towards Manaccan.

Nobody attempted to stop them and when the Rolls Royce was on the outskirts of Helston Dan drove the hearse into a layby and made a few calls to his contacts in London. Within thirty minutes a police van arrived, and the prisoner was delivered into the custody of two constables for transportation to Truro. The sight of a 'corpse' being transferred to a police van must have caused a degree of vexation amongst the passing motorists, but none stopped to enquire why this bizarre evolution was taking place in a layby.

There was no news of Jack, but Dan's enquiries with the local police revealed that there had been a serious motorcycle accident on The Lizard and the casualties were on their way to Treliske A&E. Dan passed this information to Pam but didn't tell her that the accident included at least one fatality.

Now relieved of their 'guest' and in the firm belief that the accident on the Lizard involved Jack they set off for Truro. Pam was dreading the worst and remained ashen and silent throughout the surreal journey by hearse to the hospital.

18.00 – A&E, Treliske Hospital, Truro

When Jack woke up in his hospital bed, he found Pam by his side. She was overcome with relief and fell upon him in a suffocating embrace. When he started to cough, she relented and released him so he could breathe normally. They had chatted for a few minutes before there were voices outside. It was Edwin.

"Do you mind if I come in?" he asked. Pam nodded.

"Do come in Edwin. I believe he wants to request some sick leave,"

"Jack Mawgan," said Edwin, "seems to me you are a bit of a liability at times. You attract accidents like a magnet,"

"What happened?" He said in a voice that was barely audible.

"You copped a ricochet on the forehead young man. What were you up to?"

"Nothing Edwin, just minding my own business and I come across this bike versus tractor incident,"

"Well, Jack, if that's what it was I'm a monkey's uncle,"

Edwin chatted with the Mawgans and then announced that he would have to go. Turning to Pam he said, "Remind him he has a driving course on the seventeenth and he had better be ready because I'll be running it,"

No sooner had Edwin closed the door than another uniformed figure entered. It was time to speak to the police and draft his statement.

CHAPTER 23

Saturday, August 26th – Cadhay Manor, Ottery St Mary, Devon

SIR WILLIAM WANTED TO bury Gerard on a hillside in Provence that had some special significance for them both, but with his passport confiscated that wasn't going to happen. Instead, he chose to bury him on a small knoll close to the woods on the south side of the Cadhay estate, with a view over the Devon countryside that this exiled Frenchman apparently grew to love.

On this, the day of the funeral, there were just a handful of guests prepared to pay their respects although the list of those anxious to speak to Sir William about their missing millions was growing by the day. Sir William had made more enemies in the weeks since Gerard's passing than he had made in all the years he was in business.

When the simple ceremony was complete, they drifted away leaving Sir William contemplating the events of the last few weeks alone. His empire had been destroyed, his wealth gone, lost in the ether. The British government was in turmoil; the British establishment had been rocked to the core.

Revelations of misdeeds, corruption and bribes left taxpayers reeling at the extent of their losses. The Internet was full of it. The website 'whistleblower.com' was threatening to disclose even worse news, and panic had set in with all those in authority living with a guilty conscience. Charities the world over had suddenly been the beneficiaries of huge anonymous donations and funds drained from overseas tax havens back into the real economy leaving bankers the victims of the complex systems they, themselves, had designed.

As the few guests drifted away, the peace and tranquillity of that part of Devon returned. Sir William bent and scooped up a handful of the freshly dug earth. He stepped forward and scattered the rust-coloured Devon soil onto the coffin of Gerard de Beaumont.

"Au revoir Gerry, see you in heaven," Sir William wasn't a religious man, and he wasn't stupid. He knew that if they met again, it in all probability, wouldn't be in heaven. Standing with his head bowed and hands clasped he contemplated his situation and was lost in his thoughts.

A single shot suddenly rang out from over a mile away. Those who claim to have heard it say it came from somewhere in the woods on Chinway Hill. It was the unmistakable bark of a sniper rifle, and the bullet was obviously fired by a very capable assassin. For a headshot to be successful at that range a very accurate assessment of the wind is required plus a great deal of skill and experience.

The now late Sir William Chaloner fell backwards and lay for a moment on the mound of earth beside the grave. Gravity then intervened as if in a final judgement and the corpse rolled into the open grave. Sir William Chaloner would no longer trouble the world with his murderous version of 'business as usual' and for once was beyond the helping hand of powerful friends.

At three o'clock that afternoon the newly promoted Assistant Chief Constable Norrie Norris sat in his Lexus and looked on from his vantage point on the A38 where it crossed the M5 Motorway on the Devon-Somerset border. Norrie had been an 'inside man' for MI5 ever since he joined the Police Force twenty-five years earlier. Sometimes even the watchers need to be watched.

As a 'sleeper' there was little to do other than observing and reporting back to London, but lately, things had been different. The job of, let's say 'adjusting the landscape' within the Devon and Cornwall Constabulary and removing Chaloner from the scene altogether had given him the opportunity to make a difference. That's all one can ask for in a career of public service, the opportunity to make a difference.

Eventually, a black Audi 4x4 followed by two black Audi A6 saloons were seen travelling north on the M5. They were unremarkable travellers, heading home, their part in this drama was over. Norrie turned to his passenger, and they exchanged a look of grim satisfaction. The Head of Section could now return to anonymity, and a desk somewhere in London and Norrie could get on with his life. Promotion meant more work, more challenges.

The dark clouds of criminality had been blown away leaving the West Country to enjoy a brief moment of righteous glory but the greed and corruption would no doubt return. The struggle for the supremacy of good over evil was not about one shining moment but about the relentless struggle by those we trust to do that job on our behalf.

EPILOGUE

Room 523, Home Office Building, London

IN AN ANONYMOUS ROOM in an anonymous corner of the Home Office, a small group gathered for a vital debriefing session on the results of a recent operation intended to remove some of the rot in the heart of government and to destroy some of its related tentacles in the more distant reaches of the land.

The chairman of the meeting was the Head of Section; he was an old MI5 hand. Accompanying him was a younger assistant who nervously shuffled papers and prepared to take notes. On the other side of the desk sat Dan Barclay in blazer and check shirt with a silk tie of modern design that was slightly out of keeping with his otherwise sober appearance.

The meeting was an important one for the top management in MI5 for they would need to answer some difficult questions raised by their Lords and Masters. The Deputy Head of MI5 sat in his office not far away, monitoring the progress of the meeting on his TV monitor, courtesy of a discretely placed camera mounted in a clock that was fixed to the wall behind the agents conducting the interview. With him was ACC Norrie Norris.

"I won't beat about the bush Dan," said the Head of Section, "the last few weeks have been a cathartic experience for everyone in and around government, and before we can move forward it's vital we ensure that we have all the information relating to the Chaloner case. As one of the main operatives assigned to the South-Western Region I, first of all, want to congratulate you on a job well done. Where is the weapon now?"

"There was no time to make arrangements with the quartermaster, so I put it a wooden box with some quick setting concrete then took it fishing with me in my boat later that day. I consigned it to the bottom of Lyme Bay,"

"Good man. Now, Dan, I see on your initial report that you have had a full debrief from Mawgan and Martin. I want you to give me the essence of that information now. The Prime Minister has asked me to brief him this evening, so we do not have time to wait for your detailed report,"

Dan duly delivered a blow by blow account of the 'Chaloner' case from the inside.

Back in the Deputy Head's office, it was time to compare notes. "Norrie, would you take issue with anything that Dan has said so far?"

"No sir, from my point of view we obviously had some tidying up to do after the murders of Duffy, Pegg, and Jenkins but with de Beaumont deceased those cases will officially remain unresolved although we won't be looking for anyone else in connection with those particular murders. The death of the young baby at Wilton as a result of Chaloner's driving will I'm afraid, also officially remain unresolved,"

"There's always the prospect of civil action by the victims' relatives. They should be able to claim damages against Chaloner's estate,"

"Yes, that's a possibility, but it's early days. As far as Chaloner's demise is concerned my people are, at least officially, at a loss. Dan's free and clear. No witnesses and no idea where the shot came from. As for the situation at HQ, let's just say that it took some doing, but we have managed to get rid of a wide range of troublesome dead-weights in one fell swoop, some by design and some by accident,"

"Well, Norrie, in summary, we could say that because that arrogant swine Chaloner would not spend a few bob on a safety hat for his man he was blackmailed by Duffy. Then, because he murdered Duffy, he brought Jack Mawgan into the picture. That led Jack to call his old friend Hugh Martin who just happened to be one of the best IT investigators in the country. Hugh then had the evidence to compromise the Frimly operation, so Chaloner needed to get rid of him and when he tried to do that his man De Beaumont became the main casualty. Then, in one final play, we were ordered to remove Chaloner before he could embarrass the great and the good in this wonderful land of ours,"

"Yes sir," said Norrie, "all for the price of a hat you might say," The Deputy Chief nodded, smiled at the irony and agreed, "For want of a nail the war was lost,"

"I beg your pardon sir?" said Norrie.

"Oh! Nothing, just an idle thought. Best you get off now Norrie you will have to sort out the Strathclyde boys. They won't be too amused over our little ruse to lure the Gordons down from their highland nest. Still, it muddied the waters quite nicely didn't it?" Norrie smiled.

"I don't think we have heard the last of that," He then gathered his things and left. He made his way to a little-used exit at the rear of the building and emerged into the daylight en route to Paddington Station and a first-class rail trip to Exeter St David's.

Meanwhile, a short distance away, the Head of Section collected his notes, checked his wristwatch, turned to his visitor and said, "must dash, have to see the PM, you know the way out don't you," With that, he left the room. Dan and the young assistant looked at each other with a degree of resignation. Dan set off for the back door and cab-ride to Waterloo Station to begin his journey back to the West Country. It was going to be a long winter, but at least the Spring-cleaning had been completed in time for a New Year full of hope and expectation.

With that little caper put to bed, it was time to get back to normal, and he had brochures and data sheets on the latest bugging devices to study on the way back home. Sometimes it didn't pay to try and work out who were the goodies and who were the baddies in British society. So long as the balance of probabilities had him working for the goodies and supporting people like Jack Mawgan he was happy to make a nice living as one of the nation's silent army of brave and fearless underground soldiers.

Jack Mawgan meanwhile recovered in time for his driving course with Edwin and continued his education in the challenging world of the Ambulance Technician. His ambition to qualify as Paramedic drove him on but now and then he would stumble on a situation that demanded his detective skills. The majority of these were simple punctuation marks along the way, but occasionally he would find himself involved in something that would draw him into conflict with the forces of evil and provide his chronicler with another fascinating tale to tell.

THE END

LIST OF PRINCIPAL CHARACTERS

Andy Swarbrick – A British ex-Legionnaire working for Gerard de Beaumont.

Ann Walters – Pamela's mother, a retired nurse.

Bernie 'The Hammer' Gordon – Desmond's protagonist and the man who kicked him out of Glasgow in 1980. Died of a stroke in 1992.

Dan Barclay – Old chum of Jack's from his early days in the police. He also won he George Medal during the undercover operation early in their careers. Now runs a Private investigation business and does some work on the side for the UK security services.

Davy Gordon – Son of Bernie and the man now run his criminal gang.

Desmond Duffy – Businessman, born in Glasgow, entrepreneur in Cornwall

Dr Pamela Mawgan – Jack's wife, Part time GP at Devoran Surgery.

Edwin O'Connor - Paramedic

Gerard de Beaumont – Ex French Foreign Legionnaire now the live-in lover of Sir William Chaloner.

Hugh Martin – Head of IT at International Accounting Company. (IAC).

Jack Mawgan – Ex Detective, now Ambulance Technician and would-be paramedic.

Josh Mawgan - Jack and Pam's youngest son. Born 1988, now age 12 and at private school in Truro.

Laurence 'Larry' Walters – Pamela's father, ex Fleet Air Arm pilot.

Margaret Duffy - Desmond's long suffering wife.

Mary – Housemaid for Desmond Duffy.

Montague Hardwick - Director General at the Treasury.

Nathan Mawgan – Jack and Pam's eldest son. Born 1982 now age 18. and studying Zoology at Bristol University and visiting Canada on a wildlife expedition.

Neil Jenkins – Detective Sergeant, works for DCI Sidney Patterson at Truro CID.

'Norrie' Norris – Chief Superintendent in Devon and Cornwall Police and 'sleeping' agent of MI5.

Patricia Jenkins – Neil Jenkins' wife.

Ronnie 'Magnum' Morrison – The hired gun working for the Gordon Gang.

Sidney Paterson – Detective Chief Inspector in charge of the Truro team of detectives.

Simon Pegg – Hugh Martin's neighbour who borrows Hugh's Land Cruiser.

Sir Herbert Grainger - Permanent Secretary for Defence

Sir Francis Dashwood - Permanent Secretary at the Home Office.

Sir Gordon Hunter - Permanent Secretary for Health

Sir William Chaloner – CEO of Western Hydro

Tony Bell – Police Federation Rep.

Trevor Grover - Director General at the Home Office

The Jack Mawgan Trilogy
Book 2
RENDER UNTO CAESAR

Synopsis

JACK MAWGAN IS ABOUT to fulfil his ambition to become a qualified paramedic when an incident involving a young Muslim found naked on a Cornish road in broad daylight draws him into the sinister world of 'Extraordinary Rendition'. This campaign was run by the US security services and involved their operatives in torture in their search for information about Al Qaeda's activities. Jack's involvement sets off a chain of events that leads him to the depths of the African interior in pursuit of a self-proclaimed jihadist fomenting rebellion and heavily involved in the drugs trade.

(This story is built around real places, real people and real events, but the plot and characters in the book are entirely fictional.)

The Jack Mawgan Trilogy
Book 3
THE MARK

TO SUGGEST THAT THOSE generous souls who put themselves forward as trustees of the many Air Ambulance Trusts around the country are uniformly evil is of course hyperbole. I am sure they are entirely without blemish but unfortunately if that were true it would not provide an interesting plot for my story so I beg them not to take my aspersions seriously.

That said we know from our newspapers that corruption is everywhere and our public services are particularly vulnerable to the few who break our bond of trust. Occasionally it is our elected politicians that let us down. Lord Acton, a prominent historian of the Victorian era, once said in a letter to Mary Gladstone (daughter of the Prime Minister, William Gladstone, and his confidante and advisor).

"I cannot accept your canon that we are to judge Pope and King unlike other men, with a favourable presumption that they did no wrong. If there is any presumption it is the other way against holders of power, increasing as the power increases. Historic responsibility has to make up for the want of legal responsibility. Power tends to corrupt and absolute power corrupts absolutely. Great men are almost always bad men, even when they exercise influence and not authority: still more when you add the tendency or the certainty of corruption by authority. There is no worse heresy than that the office sanctifies the holder of it."(Wikipedia)

Whether you agree with Lord Acton or not we must always be prepared to take our leaders to task when they overstep the mark.